**LATE
MARRIAGE
PRESS**

Praise for the writing of Pablo D'Stair

"The first thing that occurs to you when you pick up a volume of D'Stair is that it has no business being good. No credentials. None of the usual apparatus that tells you a book has appeared: publishers, agents, press releases. The industry didn't cough this one up. The second thing, once you start to turn the slippery pages, is: how the Hell can such good writing come from nowhere? Who the Hell is Pablo D'Stair, anyway? The final note, the one that makes D'Stair a little troubling, is that this writing is a voice inside your head. Nothing can prepare you for that ... Pablo D'Stair is defining the new writer. There is NO ONE else. As reckless as Kerouac's 120-foot trace paper, D'Stair's independence from all of us needs to be studied and celebrated ... This is revolution. Each word seems to want to wage war. Nothing is settled, nothing is as it should be - and we know as we read and it starts to sink in that this is how things are ... D'Stair's late realism needs to be included in any examination of the condition of the novel."
TONY BURGESS, award-winning author/screenwriter
(*Pontypool Changes Everything*, *Idaho Winter*, and *People Live Still in Cashtown Corners*)

"[The work] is written by someone who cares about language - you'd be surprised at the number of novels written by people who don't. It takes a lot of daring and ambition for a writer to tease out a book like this in such minute detail, and D'Stair is committed ... you stop yourself from skimming because you start thinking you might be missing something - [the work] is too well written to skim ... again and again you're drawn in ... you get used to the rhythm and follow it because the work is obsessive. We find ourselves in a languid kind of suspense, bracing ourselves..."
BRET EASTON ELLIS, author/screenwriter
(*American Psycho*, *Rules of Attraction*, and *Lunar Park*)

"I knew he could write, and I suspect he can do about eighty other things as well - if our minds are hamsters on wheels, then Pablo has more hamsters than any of us ... D'Stair doesn't just write like a house afire, he writes like the whole city's burning, and these words he's putting on the page are the thing that can save us all."
STEPHEN GRAHAM JONES, Bram Stoker Award-winning author
(*Mapping the Interior*, *Mongrels* and *All the Beautiful Sinners*)

"Over the years I've stopped being astonished at the multifarious things that Pablo D'Stair can do well. Let's just say it: whatever he puts his hand to he accomplishes and with a style and panache that is his alone ... Original. Idiosyncratic. Off-kilter. Strange. The slap-back dialog, the scenes as accurate as if directed by Fritz Lang. This is D'Stair's world. Welcome to it. I envy you if this is your first time in."
COREY MESLER, author/screenwriter
(*Memphis Movie* and *Camel's Bastard Son*)

"D'Stair is clearly a master. Like Jean Patrick Manchette reincarnated."
MATT PHILLIPS, author
(*The Bad Kind of Lucky* and *Three Kinds of Fool*)

THE GOLDBERG MUTILATIONS

a giallo

Pablo D'Stair

LATE
MARRIAGE
PRESS

Copyright © 2022 Pablo D'Stair

All rights reserved. No part of this book may be reproduced, stored in a retrieval system or transmitted in any form or by any means without the prior written permission of the publishers, except by a reviewer who may quote brief passages in a review to be printed in newspaper, magazine or journal.

THE GOLDBERG MUTILATIONS is a work of fiction. No actual person or event is described in the text. Any similarities to persons living or dead, or to events past or present, are purely coincidental.

First Edition
ISBN: 979-8-3483-5953-9

Published by Late Marriage Press

for Dr. Sarah D'Stair

THE GOLDBERG MUTILATIONS

THE GOLDBERG MUTILATIONS is a work of fiction. While allusions are made to aspects of Glenn Gould's life and work, liberties have been taken with chronology and specifics. The novel in no way seeks to present an historically accurate version of any person or event referenced.

I want to do what I want when I want to do it,
not be dictated to by audiences.
DARIO ARGENTO

I detest audiences ... I think they are a force of evil ...
At concerts I feel demeaned. Like a vaudevillian.
GLENN GOULD

THE PSYCHOLOGY OF IMPROVISATION

GLENN GOULD DREAMT OF BUTCHERY. Cold blood in Technicolor. Annihilation. Murder. Slumber, tonight, was the *Grand Guignol*.

The images dreamt were precise.

But fleeting.

Staccato.

His eyes, under spider-veined lids, writhed and shunted. As though hurriedly jotting notes across a music staff.

Correcting.

Second guessing.

Scribbling over.

Here was a woman. Young. A girl, in fact. Teenaged. Sat to a barrel. On the barrel, stenciled letters. LIVE BAIT – DO NOT REFRIGERATE.

The scene was a dock.

A gathered crowd.

An audience. Rapt.

The girl. Her jaw was chewing. Her lips puckered. She blew a bubble. Sugared. Pink.

A dreamt sensation of *Pop*.

With it a flash of olfactory nightmare. The pocket-change taste of burping up blood.

Here were hands.

Piano keys.

His hands, perhaps. Striking at keys.
Fingers skeletal. Hungry bird beaks.
No music where there should be Scarlatti.
Each key depressed groaned some other sound. Indistinct. Atonal. Warped. As though tinny, muffled television heard through the wall of the room next door.
The pink bubble's pop.
Thud of hatchet through skin and meat of a shoulder top.
Gasp of the girl's young mouth.
Opened wide in shock. Wider than the spherical stretch of the bubble. Contorted in throes of agony. Matching the shrinking squirm of the bubble's burst.
The sound of an arpeggio is overdubbed with gurgle.
With wheezing.
As thin pink blood slips round gnashing teeth.
White.
Pink.
Peppermint piano key ivory.
But were the hands his?
How could it be?
Is that not he, Glenn Gould, in the crowd?
Off to one side.
Watching the girl.
The bubblegum.
Pop.
Watching her pinch it with fingertips. As it slithers from between kissy lips. As she secures it behind her. Snugs it underneath rim of the barrel-top.
Are those not his eyes, meeting the eyes of whoever's hands it is striking the keys?
Now these hands. Conducting hatchet.
Prying it. Out from where it had dug, inches deep through creamy flesh of adolescent neckline.

The same hands?
Different?
Thin leather gloves grip a wooden handle.
Leather imperceptibly dotted with hemorrhage.
Scarf the same. Thicker spills of gore lost to its stitching.
Coat's tweed hides further spatter.
Tea-tinted eyeglasses adorned in droplets.
Dot dot dot.
These evidences floating in field of vision as though cataract blanks.
The hands must be Gould's.
He dreams the ache of tension in his wrist.
As the hatchet cleaves trachea to lodge in the vertebrae behind.
The dream flickers.
Blade descends toward young eye, horribly open.
The dream flickers.
A bubble of sugared pink.
Pop.
The dream flickers.
Soft patter like pebbles thrown in the lake as hatchet raises back overhead and blood arcs the ceiling.
Flicker.
Hatchet descends.
Flicker.
Girl's remaining eye, closed hard.
Flicker.
Veiny pink sugar.
Pop.
A pop which becomes the sight of a barrel crashing through the lake's surface. Sound of applause as bubbles scream upward from its descent. The letters spelling LIVE BAIT – DO NOT REFRIGERATE miniaturizing.
  As Glenn Gould watches.

Dropping hatchet in after them.
Hatchet which, in the dream, seems to grow.
To the size of the midnight lake's face.
Rippling. Black.
And silent.

Now Gould was uncertain.
Was he dreaming, still?
If so, the dream was from his present position. In bed. Laid stiff. Perspiring. Eyes shut. Wriggling.
Was he dreaming they were *open*?
Or was he dreaming *with* them open?
Were his open eyes darting about, he simply dreaming them centered?
Because in what he was uncertain was a dream, Gould was looking up. Steadily.
Into his own face.
That was he, on the bed.
Leaning overtop of him.
His face above his face.
Noses nearly touching.
Breath from his maybe dreamt mouth above pushing into his prone throat through his perhaps dreaming breath beneath.
A hand moved toward his face. Pad of its forefinger and thumb, held together, making contact with the thin of his shuttered eyelid.
Though he could see.
The blot of obstruction. The watery ink of it.
Could see the finger and thumb spreading apart. As though they'd opened one of the eyes he was watching from.
Left eye, first.
Then right.

The parting of the blurry fingertips revealing again his face looking at him.

Tongue pinched between its teeth, absently.

A slight twinge of grin to its lips.

Eyes squinted. As though concentrating intently on some minute detail of a painting. An amusement to the slight wrinkles from the effort.

His voice asks 'Are you still asleep, Glenn?'

He feels himself attempting to answer.

Or else dreams he feels himself attempting.

Or else feels himself asking 'Are you still asleep, Glenn?' without realizing the question is his.

There is the pressure of some utterance at the base of his throat.

Gravel.

Dry rattle.

Real.

But imagined.

Imagined.

But real.

Then a sensation like vertigo.

Hands at his back. Lifting him. So that he is sat upright. Head lolling off to one side. Skull a sack dangling his vision over his shoulder.

All images strangled.

As though his eyes were forcibly rolling back.

This sensation followed by that of a slick warmth to his cheeks.

Two palms gently steadying him.

Positioning head.

Upright. Forward.

Straightening his gaze across the oily blur of the room.

The gloom was difficult to make out specifics in. An anonymous murk. Dim light through cracks where curtains met or had tears in them.

But it seemed, from where he sat, he could see himself seated. At a small table. Not quite round. Oblong. Perhaps four paces distant from the foot of the bed his legs hung over the lip of.

Though, of course, if he saw him it wasn't *him*.

Someone, then.

Dressed in his likeness.

His caricature.

Arranging sheets of paper into the portable typewriter.

Steady, meticulous motions. Confident and accurate.

Despite the darkness.

Obviously unreal.

Surely a dream.

For presently Gould had tipped back onto the mattress. Top of his head shy of the soft of the pillow. A cool sensation of drool through the left crease of his lips. Eyes ceilingward.

But before him he yet saw himself at that table.

Someone like him.

Craned forward.

Squinting at whatever was the last thing written on the page set and pinned to the roller.

Before positioning fingers.

Striking down at keys steadily.

Tack. Tack. Tack.

Tack. Tack.

Tack.

Gould woke to the abrupt hack of a stabbing cough. The scraping scythe of a gasp choked down his throat, its membrane dry and prickly like baled hay.

As he wheezed into consciousness, his now fairly gagging body was bent. Doubled-over. Fetal.

Cramps of pain twisted his ribs.

As though a hand closed around him.

He a crisp paper.

Crumpled in disdain.

If seen from above, his body would resemble exactly the forlorn scrunch of a discarded draft.

For several minutes after drinking from the tap at the bathroom sink, Gould remained plopped at the lip of the bed.

Swallowing.

Clearing his throat.

Found it difficult to get his vision to focus.

To settle his gaze in any direction.

Absently rubbed his shoulder.

Wiped at the fronts of his teeth with the side of left index finger.

It took several moments more for it to dawn on him that the room, seeming twilit due to the drawn window dressing, betrayed a dim shade of daytime.

Only after he'd been staring at the typewriter on the oblong desk for an indeterminate length of time longer did it occur to him how the typewriter ought not be there.

He ought not be there.

Had no idea where or what room this was he'd awakened in.

A motel.

Obvious from the no nonsense arrangement of the clapboard furnishings. The suddenly over apparent clamor of roadway traffic, practically just outside the door.

Which motel?

Why had he taken the room?

When?

Gould's bleary survey of his surroundings showed no evidence of an extended stay. Other than the sweat soaked bedsheets, the typewriter, several discarded leaves of paper on the carpet to either side of the chair and table legs, there was zero sign a stay of any duration had been intended.

In fact, he didn't see any overnight bag.
This causing sufficient alarm to roust him standing.
Move him around.
A bit of a lurch to his motions.
Flails to his arms.
Slaps of his tremoring palms.
He leaned to the wall.
The tabletop.
Sink basin.
Soon settling to the perch of closed toilet bowl, catching his breath.
He never would've taken a room, even for one night, without his pills. Impossible. Therefore concluded that whichever luggage he'd arrived with would be in the car he'd driven.
Getting himself to such car would be his next obstacle.
The effort involved in such undertaking seemed far beyond him, at present.
Decided it best to break the adventure down.
First to the window.
Part the curtain.
Peek out front.
Make certain his car was there.
These tasks he would tackle just as soon as he had his sea legs beneath him.
His blood, presently, felt as though it were millipedes scrambling through him, subcutaneous.
A migraine was beginning its dismal, diagonal progress from the back bottom corner of his left eye toward the tight crease at the bridge of his nose.
As he braced against these afflictions, it puzzled him why he didn't also need to urinate.
Couldn't think of the last time he'd awakened without a sizzling necessity to void being present.

No car.

Or, more peculiarly Gould supposed, no ... *cars*.

Absolutely no vehicles of any kind parked outside the room.

Cheek to window glass, craned to see as far down the lot as could be managed.

Left.

Right.

Nothing.

Certainly not the car he'd been driving.

Though ... which car ... had that been?

Brief wave of giddiness passed over him as he attempted to focus on any memory of arriving at this motel.

Of leaving ... *where*?

Where had he been?

A sudden cough dislodged a coin of phlegm against the window glass. The perverse slap of it, its slug trail making slow descent down the pane, enough to wreck his concentration.

The curtain fell closed as he backpedaled, disgusted.

Swatted the wall switch. Arbitrary gesture. Had already tried the overhead lights once before. Discovered their addition made little difference so far as his ability to see.

Pupils completely dilated. He was certain.

Tinnitus had also begun.

Postnasal drip.

Possible bronchitis waiting in the wings.

There was a taste up his throat suggesting he'd regurgitated violently. Not long ago. Could almost feel the grainy texture of whichever food had been brought up but not yet fully washed back down.

Closed his eyes.

Steadying breaths.

Metronome.
Mustn't allow blood pressure to run riot.
Tried to slow his pulse by tapping his foot.
Evenly. Serenely.
To make those taps his heartbeat's pace.
Tap. Systole.
Tap. Diastole.
Tap.
Tap.
Tap.
There were bound to be cars out there. Further along the lot. Depending how occupied the establishment was, presently. Or was whenever he'd shown up.
One of those cars perhaps his.
Except this made matters all the more baffling.
If he'd parked a distance off, certainly he wouldn't have left whichever baggage in the vehicle.
His pills.
Blood pressure cuff.
Thermometer.
To suggest he'd have carried this typewriter in but no other luggage?
Sat working on whichever writing for however long?
To suppose he'd retired for the night without medicating?
'Preposterous' he muttered, unknowing he had.
Foot tap. Metronome. Blood pressure. Pulse.
Breathed out a long sigh.
Paused.
Took in a regular length breath.
Control. Control. Control.
Regardless: he'd been driving a rental.
This much a certainty.
Before coming here.

Could easily have hired another car, though.

Reached instinctively down to dig hands through pockets. Expecting his coat. Finding only pants to scour.

Touched finger to bare throat. Gripped fingers to bare flesh. Had expected his scarf.

It was a bridge too far to believe he'd shown up just like this.

But hadn't he made a circuit of this stingy little box?

Discovered nothing but the mangy clothes covering him?

Furiously tugged at the bedcovers, expecting his missing attire to be revealed. Could tell from where he stood there was no underneath to the bed. Box-spring unit fused to the floor. Mattress atop.

He intended to struggle the mattress to one side. See whether it covered anything.

But decided to check everywhere else first.

Exhaust all possibilities.

Before entertaining the notion he'd gone so far round the bend.

Why would he squirrel his clothing away?

Another fit of coughing. Horrendous.

Expectorated blindly.

Dull thump of phlegm to the carpet.

A moment later his bare foot squishing into the glob.

Rubbed his sole over another spot of carpet. Against the fabric over the side of the shin of his opposite leg.

Moved back to the sink.

Drinking directly from the tap.

Unable to slake his thirst.

―――――――

His coat, with scarf, was behind the closet door.

Overlooked previously as he'd not imagined a hook would be found there.

Not in the closet of a room like this.
Frankly, he didn't understand why there was such a hook.
In this room or any.
Why he'd used it.
How he had.
In order to utilize the thing, a person would either have to be stood inside the closed closet or else know it was there, beforehand. Give awkward reach around the inward swinging door to set the garment hung.
On the closet's interior bar, three paper-covered wire hangers jittered.
Swayed slightly.
Nonstop.
Perplexing.
Until he noticed a vent in back of them. Itself vibrating silently. Leaking lukewarmth. Obscured by the dark cut of shadow from the overhead shelf.
Which he patted hands to the flat top of. Ran palms along. Hoping to discover his hat.
But his hat remained no place.
As did his wool gloves.
Leather driving gloves.
Driving glasses.
Short lived, the relief over finding which garments he had.
Obviously he hadn't expected the magic of clarity to descend upon him at the sight of them … except … being honest with himself … he'd expected exactly that.
No clarity attained, his preoccupation became the hat.
Gloves.
Glasses.
Those. Those would lock his perceptions down.
Make the world coherent.
'Nonsense' he muttered, not knowing he had.

Grit his teeth, frustrated.

Needing to ground himself.

Winced on purpose, quite harshly. Hoping tears would draw. Lace down his cheeks.

Instead, he became cognizant of how dry his nose felt inside. Acutely aware of the scent of his nostrils. Tangy. Like after a nosebleed.

Nosebleed sometime the day previous.

A lingering aroma.

A residue.

His headache turned the whine of a cello string instead of the plunk of a dripping faucet. Eyes didn't even sting when he opened them. Gave Novocain stare at the fizzing dark of the peculiarly deep closet. Focus going from black to blur as he turned toward the bed.

Contents of the coat pockets were little help.

Wallet.

Driver's license.

He is who he thinks he is. According to laminated card, anyway.

So, some relief there.

A hotel key. Loose. Which he held up. Ran thumb-tip over the cut of. Hoping this gesture might stir recollection of exactly *which* hotel the key allowed him entry to.

Had a vague feeling of the place.

As well as a sensation that it was nearby.

Nearby.

It *felt* nearby.

Despite he didn't actually know where he was.

Not *exactly*.

Couldn't say where.

Name where.

But did feel he *knew* where.

The same as he knew the longer key on the keyring, also found in coat pocket, was to his car.

Knew what the car would *look* like.

That it was *brown*.

Recently *waxed*.

The image of this car cemented itself.

He'd driven it. *Yesterday*. No other car.

Yes. Absolutely.

In his most recent memories he'd been driving that brown car. Memories which would've been from events the day before.

Returning to his *hotel*.

To his hotel.

His hotel ... which he could *almost* recall the name of.

Returning from ... *from* ...

But that he couldn't *quite* pin down, either.

But *felt* it.

He did *feel* it.

Information wriggling its way to his forebrain.

At the very least, all signs indicated the car, his car, his brown car, should be parked outside.

If there were another car, he'd have another key.

But he didn't.

Knew what every other key on the ring was used for.

None of them with local purpose.

Because he knew he wasn't in the town where he resided.

No.

Away from home.

On business.

In town. For a purpose. Short time.

Some reason.

———————

Gould's bare foot pressed down onto one of the loose sheets scattered across the carpet. He could tell his big toe had punctured the cheap paper. How the tensing of his remaining toes, curling as though into a cold fist, had torn it further.

With foot held partway up, toenails still brushing contact with the paper's face, he experienced another wave of lightheadedness.

Felt depleted, utterly.

Slumped back to the bed lip.

Sat nodding.

Doing his best to gather himself. Get his bearings. Collect his thoughts.

Realized with a start, after some moments, how a string of drool was dangling several inches over his chin.

Slurped.

Wiped at his face.

Forced the butts of his palms in furious circles against the sensitive bulbs of his closed eyes.

Head bowed, bobbing, jaw slack, some further time passed.

When next he opened his eyes, they slowly came into semi-focus. Regarded the paper he'd trodden on.

Bent forward with hazy effort to retrieve it.

Then strained a bit in an attempt to fetch over a second sheet but, unable to get his fingertips all the way to it, simply sighed.

Seized up at the sound of footsteps outside the room.

Twisted to face the door. Effort earning him cramp in his ribs and a strain at his neck he was certain would result in half-a-week worth of stiffness.

Noticed the light through the holes in the curtain blocked then unblocked by someone's passage.

Blink.

Blink.

Blink.

The shuffle and thud of footfalls abruptly ending.

As though a figure loitered just beyond the latch-chain of the room's flimsy entrance.

Waited for anything further.

An incontrovertible happening to excuse his growing certainty of an interloper.

Someone out there.

Waiting for him.

If those steps had been innocuous, it meant whoever had been passing by pivoted on exactly that spot.

Behind the door.

Then proceeded straight ahead.

Down the curb.

Into the parking lot.

Why?

There were no vehicles parked there.

A companion had perhaps pulled up?

So why no *thump* of door closing?

No cackle of lulling engine?

What had been out across the lot, directly?

A fence?

Dumpsters?

Gould had peeked out the window ten minutes ago. Yet no sensible image of what he'd seen was retained. Indeed, the image of the world outside the motel room was so amorphous he almost grew hopeful his car might yet be waiting mere steps away, somehow carelessly overlooked.

Shook his face.

Still hadn't accounted for the halted passage of his exterior tormentor.

Stared at the doorknob.

Expecting it to be attempted.

The door to be opened.

Expecting ... no.
No.
He shook his head harder than before.
Wouldn't allow the thought to gain traction.
Why would he even *consider* such a thing, let alone *expect* it?
Where had such a notion come from?
After hardly a moment, the footsteps started up again.
Continued on.
Brief clicks of dark as the light was blocked at the punctures to the shabby curtain further along.
A man had stopped to light a cigarette.
Paused to think of a telephone number.
Patted pockets to be certain their wallet hadn't been left behind.
Noticed an attractive woman, so lingered at the perfect vantage to glimpse her a moment more.
Ordinary things.
Nothing to do with Glenn Gould.
Whoever it'd been had walked on.
Nothing to do with Glenn Gould.

To give his mind another task to focus on, hoping such would allow the whip-tight of his joints to relax, Gould examined the shabby leaf of paper he held.

Typewritten all down it was some portion of a dialogue.
Two participants.
One labeled *GG*.
The other *gg*.
Yes. This was an initial draft for an article he was working up. Self-interview. Interrogating himself concerning his thoughts and opinions on Beethoven.
Began reading from a random spot toward the top of the page, starting mid-statement.

gg: ... I simply suggest to you that there is perhaps something significant in the fact that all the works you've mentioned, by that very yardstick to which you've alluded, found him at the time of their composition in a state of, for want of a better word, flux.

GG: Every artist is in a state of flux or he wouldn't be an artist.

gg: Please, Mr. Gould, don't be tedious—in a state of flux, as I say, if not between the early and middle years, then between the middle and the late ones.

Puckish little venture, for the most part. But he was altogether serious about the piece. The method. The conflict.

At present, looking over the words served as a balm.

Gould remembered this.

Writing this.

Not here at the motel, *per se*.

But he did *remember*.

Or, better say, he recollected toying with the concept.

The notion for such an article.

From time-to-time.

Over the years.

... no ...

A squirm of disappointment, anxiety trickled into his brief moment's peace.

He now barely skimmed over the words on the page he held.

It was going too far to say he remembered actually *writing* them. Clacking the typewriter keys. Watching them materialize over paper blanks.

He *recognized* them.

The sentiments.

As his thoughts.

The words he would choose to express himself with in a serio-comedic endeavor.

Everything typed was something he *might* say.

Might have written.

Despite this, a glaze of unease crept over him.

No choice but to admit the bald fact: he didn't recall the actual effort of composition.

The more he dwelt on this detail, the more his disquiet deepened.

His gaze moving back to the room window.

The shut door.

To the thought which had intruded before chance had allowed him to pretend it'd been casually and forever dismissed.

He'd *expected* the doorknob to be tried.

Expected the door to be *opened*.

Expected someone to *enter*.

Expected whoever had *brought him here* to have returned.

Which meant some part of him knew he hadn't *arrived* at this motel.

But rather had been *transported*.

Against resistance.

Or some part of him, if not knowing this for certain, *believed it* at a subconscious enough level he'd instinctually reacted as though against a returning molester.

His still present tremble, the hiccough of his pulse, more than suggested he'd struggled against someone.

Recently.

On more than one occasion, judging by the intensity of his reaction over what he'd assumed was a coming trespass. The arrival of someone, something which would dismantle the absurd blip of childish calm he'd invented.

Arms sluggishly through coat sleeves.
 Coat-front buttoned firm.
 Protective fit of the tweed's weight pressed down on his shoulders.
 Scarf over shoulders, too. As yet not muffled round his throat.
 Gould made a final inspection of the motel room.
 Preparing to vacate.
 As hastily as he might manage.
 It'd struck home that he didn't know how long he was permitted to occupy the space. How soon until housekeeping might knock on the door, requiring him gone.
 He could verify.
 Request a late check-out.
 Pay another day's rent.
 Bed-stand.
 Telephone there.
 Zero would dial the Front Desk.
 Except: what the devil would possess him to remain in this room a moment longer?
 Closet clear.
 Bathroom.
 Bedsheets stripped and patted through.
 Pillowcases searched.
 Trashcans.
 Sills of the windows.
 The only thing present of his was the typewriter.
 The stacked papers beside it.
 Those strewn to the floor.
 Which he collected, paying little mind.
 Needing to gather himself, once again, Gould sat to the chair.
 Folded arms to the desktop.
 Put his head down upon them.

Promised himself he'd stand, would leave, after counting down sixty.
Lost count. Restarted.
Lost count.
Restarted.
Lost track how many times this glitch occurred.
But soon found himself sitting up straight, about to close the typewriter into its case.
One sheet was still set to the roller of the device.
Only some small amount of type showing on it.
He pinched the top, gave gentle tug to free it, thinking to add the paper to the collected pile which would then be zipped into the built-in pouch of the case's flexible top flap.
Got, however, no further than holding it in front of him.
Giving the words on it a glance.
Before he recoiled.
Slumped back.
Pulse quickening.
Chest going taut.
Throat constricting.
Hoped that once he turned his head back from where he'd averted his gaze, once he opened his eyes from how firm he'd clamped them shut, what he thought he'd seen written would be revealed for a phantasm.
Stress-based hallucination.
Vagrant fleck of a dream misfiring into his waking mind.
Smacked the paper flat to the table.
Trilled the fingers of his right hand on it then brought them together. Blade of his palm trembling as he covered the writing with thumb facing toward him.
Shifted the shield of his hand down along the page-front.
Cautious to reveal only one portion of the typed dialogue at-a-time.

Breath becoming audible. Harsh out his nose as he proceeded.

> GG: The difference between you and me is purely political. You see, we both play good piano, right? But I'm the proletarian of the keyboard and you're the bourgeois. You play for Art. And you enjoy it. I play for survival. That's not the same thing.

> gg: While I never would begrudge you your fatuous moment of mirth, Glenn, perhaps we could venture back toward the subject under consideration.

> GG: Of course. A thousand pardons. Though, before we do, I might make important addendum to my remark. I realize, despite our difference, there is a key similarity between you and I—downright fundamental, I might go so far as to say, and, indeed, of greater import than any aspect in which we aren't kindred.

> gg: And what—I ask out of only the vaguest curiosity, I assure you—might that similarity be?

> GG: You have killed. And you'll kill again.

Gould tore the paper in half. Stacked the halves. Tore those in half. Repeated this process until the stack was too thick to tear any further with his fingers. At which point he took each scrap. Tore it in half. Then each smaller scrap. Until he'd amassed a pile of shreds on the table in front of him.

Confetti.

Impossible to know any piece had been written on.

Even if a speck betrayed it'd been touched with ink, a letter or two still decipherable, there was no way to stitch the mess together again.

Make it cohesive.
Coherent.
Any sentence, any word perceptible.
But not enough.
No.
Gould set the bathroom sink running. Stopper in place.
Moved back to typewriter table.
Scooted the shreds, approximate handful at-a-time, to the edge, drifting them over into the scoop of his waiting palm.
Ferried these piles to the sink.
Took a moment to lessen the force of the water from the faucet before letting the near-scalding flow dribble over the paper.
Which he tightened his fist around.
Knuckles white.
Veins showing ropey up his forearm.
Leaned forward and grit teeth.
Fusing the wetted mash into a firm pellet.
After a few trips to-and-fro, he stopped the faucet running. Collected three of the six total pellets in each hand. Lowered these into the water filling the basin, the steam from which had clouded the mirror glass, obscuring his reflection.
Brought his palms together.
Squeezing.
Twisting.
Jaw aching from the strain of its clench.
Eyes bulging with fixation on the task.
Once a single, stiff mass of damp paper had been compacted, Gould removed the wrapper from the cake of soap he'd noticed on the shower shelf.
Wetted it.
Scent of false lime impregnating the wisps of loitering steam.
Ran the soap sloppily over the sodden fist of paper.
Afterward, he pulled length after length of toilet tissue free of

the roll. Wrapped the soapy mound of crushed paper inside. Dunked everything into the basin.

Wrapped further toilet tissue around.

Lacquered it with soap.

Dunked it.

Finally, he plopped the substantive blob he'd created onto the carpet at the foot of the sink.

Stood on it.

One shoe.

The other.

Stomping.

Stomping.

Until he was too exhausted to continue.

To hands and knees he went.

Checking the carpet around the desk for any stray trace of paper. Any flake which may've been overlooked.

Removed his shoes to be certain nothing stuck to the soles from his recent efforts.

Toddled on knees back over to the wad of paper and toilet tissue.

Kneaded it with the blunt bases of his palms.

Then with elbows.

Wanting it as flat as could be managed.

Before tearing it into three chunks.

One going into the plastic bag he'd pulled from the toilet trash.

Second into the bag from the wastebin he'd found near the room heater.

These two pieces going one down each coat pocket.

Final piece set to the desktop.

Waiting.

Clacked shut the latches of the case to the portable typewriter. Curled fingers around its handle. Let the weight of the object jostle his shoulder as his limp arm fell to his side.

This tug drew an audible pop from the joint.
The pop cuing back up the sharp whine of tinnitus.

The light and the cold, as he stepped through the door, were violent. Vindictive. It felt as though someone had splashed a cupful of spearmint flavored antiseptic wash directly into his eyes.

The brightness of the sun hung horrid. Unfiltered due to lack of cloud cover. The remains of the snow and ice didn't reflect it back skyward, at least.

No.

The snow and the ice were colored gulag grey, peppered with specs and splotches of cinnamon brown in patterns and density reminiscent of the uncleaned curve of a highway rest stop's toilet bowl.

He shrank back.

Unable to shield his face with his hands.

Left held typewriter case.

Right held the non-pocketed portion of paper tumor.

Leaned shoulder to the outside of the room's window. Then turned all the way to tilt his forehead against the glass.

The dim reflection of the area behind him afforded by the window allowed Gould to get some bearings, at least.

There was a dumpster almost directly across from his room door. Rather overflowing, at present. Which in some ways made it the ideal spot to rid himself of the cold bundle his fingers now shivered tight around.

But as a truck passed, he could make out that though the road pavement had a firm and audible crust of ice overtop, for the most part the lot was a wet and freezing expanse of exhaust-port blackened porridge.

Wanting to spare himself the torment of wading his way

through such slop, not to mention the maladies which would result, he settled on another plan.

Down the length of several rooms, Gould noticed the parking lot seemed properly populated.

Head down, made his way forward.

Stopped a short distance off from the nearest car.

Glanced around.

Needed to be as certain as possible no one had direct eyeline of him.

Glare of sun off parked van windows and overall frostbit haze to those of every other vehicle made this impossible to discern.

Feeling assured enough, however, he took a stride toward the car immediately in front on him.

Bent to a knee as though to retie his shoelace.

Quickly secreted the paper mound in the frigid, discolored slush behind the car's front tire.

Then stood, removing one of the bagged portions of paper from his coat pocket.

Figured it like this: had anybody watched him crouch and, while doing so, remarked how both his hands had been filled, he'd now give off the same appearance upon standing.

If whichever party were still playing voyeur, they'd think nothing of him.

Over cautious, perhaps.

But one can never be *too* over cautions.

Best to protect against any unwelcomed curiosity.

Not that it'd matter if anyone crept over to verify whatever they'd fantasized he'd concealed.

The ideal, simply, would be to have the object go uninspected.

Allow the grit and muck of the road-cover to further sully it.

The weight of the vehicle backing out flattening it into the ice-base.

A freeze overnight.

With luck, another wheel would pull in exactly overtop.
Stay parked on it for hours.
Yes. Gould understood this was ridiculous.
Told himself so, even as he considered it all.
Hurriedly staggering in the direction of the Motel Office.
Brow down.
Arms wrapped around himself.
Typewriter bumping one hip.
Knew all his attentions to that torn paper had been absurd.
Was embarrassed about even tearing it.
Almost blushed as the Office door got nearer with each shuffle of his lurch.
But for the moment, he could think of nothing sensible he might replace such considerations with.
Never one to dwell on the horrific, after all.
No.
Over the *horrific* he'd choose the *ludicrous*, ten-times-out-of-ten.

The man Gould took to be the Motel manager stood a distance back from the Check-In desk. Engaged in conversation with a rather gruff voice whose owner was obscured by a partition.
 Both individuals speaking German.
 In quite a jovially animated manner.
 Gould resigned himself to waiting things out.
 Drifted back a few steps.
 Was glancing from the percolating coffee pot wedged in the office corner to the television mounted toward the ceiling above it when 'Herr doctor, good morning!' was rather bellowed in his direction.
 'Was the room to your liking? Ah! Do not tell me! They have

disturbed you. I told the housekeepers: the doctor has requested *privacy*—good money for *privacy*!'

During this address, the man clapped, then drummed, then clapped again his meaty hands to the countertop. With the final clap sticking himself on a tear to the laminate which covered papers displaying room rates and advertisements for local restaurants.

Sucked at the miniscule puncture.

A disproportionate slurp accompanying the ministration.

Though taken aback by every aspect of this, Gould moved toward the counter.

Casually.

Set down his typewriter.

Rested hands on top of it.

The manager noting this with seeming alarm.

'Not *leaving* us, doctor? If you were *disturbed*, I will speak to housekeeping, again.'

Gould lifted palms.

Peaceably.

Wrists still rested on case.

'Not at all. The room and amenities were …' he disguised a pause as a cough into bent elbow '… exactly as should be advertised. As for the staff, let me set your mind at ease. They've performed all duties with the very pink of courteousness. Allowed my morning ablutions and meditativeness to go quite unperturbed. I thank you.'

The manger nodded along with Gould's report, visibly relieved.

'I merely have an *errand* to run' Gould continued. 'A liaison with an *associate*' he invented, feeling it best to have a story. 'To discuss some *matters*' he added, tapping the typewriter with his knuckles.

The manger laughed 'Of course, of course, herr doctor!' rolling his hands as though to assure Gould he'd not meant to pry, would never ever.

Leaning in, only slightly, to affect an air of conspiracy, Gould glanced left. Right. Then said 'My present problem is entirely self-based.'

'*Problem*, doctor?'

'Admittedly, my mind is elsewhere. You see, though I've scoured the chilly lot and fairly wracked my meager brains raw, I cannot seem to locate my car. At a loss, I wondered if perhaps …'

But noticing the manger's expression had turned befuddled, Gould trailed off.

Raised his brow in question.

Punctuated by widening his eyes.

'Yes?'

The manager didn't want to embarrass the good doctor but '… if I may *remind* you, you arrived by taxicar.'

'*Taxicar*?'

Late the night before. Oh the manager well recalled it. How he'd been asleep in his chair. Which 'again, I promise' wasn't something he tended to do.

Gould tried to recall this.

Could hear the squish of his swallow as though his throat began in his ear.

'If you were *asleep* … I hope you'll pardon my *asking* …' he tested, not wanting to betray his deepening confusion '… how do you *know* I arrived by taxicar?'

The manager squinted.

As though trying to sort out the game.

Then, apparently satisfied of their friendship, guffawed expansively.

Reminded Gould how he'd had the taxicar's driver blare the horn. When the bell on the desk hadn't roused him.

'You were quite drunk, doctor!' he laughed.

As did the voice from behind the partition.

'It's nothing to worry about. But you were quite drunk. It's little wonder you don't remember.'

The manager rolled his eyes a bit, smiling at Gould who'd briefly glanced over from where he broodingly paced. Explained into the telephone the exact same thing, for the third time.

It would've been the night before.

Shy of midnight.

This shouldn't be complicated.

'Yes yes—a hat and glasses and gloves.'

'Perhaps a bag' Gould chimed in, lifting his chin a tap, then returning his nose to the fingertips of his palms pressed together as though in private prayer.

Certainly they might inspect every taxi which had been on duty, the manager sighed. But what he was, now for the fourth time, suggesting was that only *one* taxi had arrived.

Last night.

To this motel.

The patron, his guest, had only been in that *specific* taxi.

'Yes yes—a *hat* and *glasses* and *gloves*.'

'Perhaps a *bag*' Gould again interjected, a touch more pointedly.

But the manager had turned his back.

Obviously closing out the conversation.

'Very well ... yes, yes ... thank you.'

Phone hung to cradle, the manager shrugged with lips twisted.

'They will *look*. The driver who arrives will report.'

'You might've mentioned the possibility of a *bag*.'

Swatting at the air with a playful 'Bah' the manager explained a bag went without saying.

'If they find a bag, doctor, why would they ignore it?'
Again swatted the air.
Surely Gould had to agree?
'They are *professionals*. Would not leave a bag unremarked. After going to the trouble of offering to search every vehicle, even. They will cover all bases, doctor. You *hat* and your *glasses* and *gloves*.'
'And ... *bag* ...' Gould might've added dryly.
Were the circumstances not what the circumstances were.
In the normal run of life, absurdities culled from the mundane would be welcomed.
But in this present circumstance?
While he wished such trivialities might so much as distract him, they instead drove home the off-kilter of his nightmare. This funhouse glass morning. This untenable situation he increasingly hoped might resolve itself *deus ex machina*.
Was it something which could ever truly be considered *resolved*?
Say his life marched forward, from this moment on, exactly as it might've had whatever transpired the previous night never done—say there not once arose occasion he'd need revisit this mystery he'd awakened to, this horror show he was yet enduring—wouldn't every day spent knowing this day meant *nothing* be a nightmare, in *itself*?
To discover it some non-repeating aberrant ... wasn't that more unbearable than whatever explanation might be revealed?
He let out a breath, trying to keep from shuddering.
Let it be to some purpose.
Whatever it was.
Poured himself some of the freshly brewed coffee.
Positioning his body so the actions of selecting cup, filling it, returning pot to burner would conceal his also slipping one of the bagged hunks of paper from pocket to wastebin.

An action illustrative of his point.
What a thing to be doing!
In aid of what?
Behaving as though in the grips of *delirium*.
Systematically disposing of ... but why was the word *evidence* the first which sprung to mind?
Good God, why was he concerned over the chance someone might see him disposing of this rubbish?
Why presume the manager would inspect his refuse, the moment opportunity presented itself?
Even if, through some science or alchemy, the content of what had been written on the page were reconstructed ... *so what*?
Gould wanted to tell himself he wasn't thinking these thoughts.
But knew he most certainly was.
Not only thinking them.
Acting on them.
Fervently.
Knew failure to do anything less terrified him.
To his core.

The taxicar. Roundish. Compact. Dirty burgundy. Lettering on it white. Greyish. From years in this weather. Private company logo. Distinct.
Gould didn't recognize it.
At all.
Had never once seen such a taxi.
Let alone been passenger in one.
He could swear it.
But the driver recognized Gould.
Popped out of the taxi to meet him as he exited the Office.
Opened the vehicle's rear door.
Seemed delighted even as he imparted the bad news.

'No hat and stuff, doc. *Trust* me, though. You were my last fare. Nobody *touched* the ride until I clocked in this morning. As you see: spic and span. Clean it nightly. Clean it first thing. No hat. No *nothin'*.'

Gould didn't suppose there'd been any bag, then?

Driver shook his head 'Naw ...' pointed to Gould's typewriter '... looks like you hung on to that, alright.'

Gould glanced down.

Blinked.

The syntax of the previous statement taking a moment to hit home.

'This is my *typewriter*. I meant a *bag*. Travel bag. *Duffle*.'

'No no, yeah.'

The driver read him. Loud and clear.

What he was saying was how the *'typewriter* or *whatever it was'* Gould currently held was all Gould had had on him.

Last night.

Driver had figured it was a doctor's bag.

'So you ... presumed I was a *doctor*? *Because* of the ... bag?'

Driver let out a big barking laugh as he rounded to let himself into the cab.

'You *told* me you were a *doctor*, doc. *Assumed* about the bag because of *that*.'

The sensation to press, to interrogate was intense.

But as he closed himself inside the taxi, got settled, Gould thought it best to let things lay.

Take these statements in.

Let them marinate.

See if he could jog some memory of his own.

Why come off unhinged?

No need to start scrambling, at this point.

He was finally getting somewhere.

Getting *out*.

'Where we headin', doc?'

Gould didn't respond.

Until the question was repeated.

Until the driver had turned in his seat to ask 'You forget something *else*?'

Gould apologized. Went ahead with pretending he was, indeed, doing a thorough mental checklist.

Really, it was dawning on him how he didn't have a destination to give.

Knew where he *wanted* to go.

Again had a sensation it was quite *nearby*.

But no specifics.

'Just take me back to the hotel' he said.

'You mean the *diner*?'

The driver was addressing Gould by way of the rearview mirror, now.

Gould addressed the driver's reflection, likewise.

'*Diner*?'

'This is the *hotel*. You mean take you back to the *diner*?'

'This is a *motel*.'

Well anyway, that's what the driver had meant.

'Hotel … Motel …'

Point was, the only two places the driver knew which had anything to with '*you*, doctor' were '*here* and the *diner*.'

A crawl of nausea mingled with Gould's worsening headache. A headache, he could tell, which would develop into an earache, any moment.

He was unable to speak.

Throat constricting.

Salty.

Sour.

Knew if he tried to get any word out tears would well in his eyes. He'd hyperventilate.

So as not to make a scene, held up a finger. As though requesting silence. Put finger to forehead. Gazing downward. Intently. As though on the verge of some important remembrance.

Acted like he needed to consult something in his wallet.

Dug it from coat pocket.

Flapped it open.

Stared.

Nodding.

Nodding.

Finally had himself together exactly enough to say 'Yes. To the diner, then.'

Sank into the taxi's rear corner.

Closed his eyes.

The inertia of the vehicle backing up, halting, moving forward stirred despair akin to seasickness.

Some facts of the matter:

The manager recognized him.

The driver recognized him.

Both had conducted entire, specifics-laden conversations.

With him.

Just today.

In the past half-hour.

His face on display.

Voice to take in.

Neither had batted an eye.

He'd interacted with these two people before, then.

Last night.

Absolutely.

Both of them, this morning, had called him *doctor*.

Seemingly at his *insistence*.

These things were inescapably true, every one.
Gould took steadying breaths.
In.
Out.
Twenty seconds apiece.
Lips O-puckered.
Equilibrium returning. Physically, at least.
The driver had the radio tuned to a News program.
Sensationalism.
… body of a young woman walled into some room of a private house, unlived in for years … corpse uncovered by a woman who claimed to've been led to it by psychic vision …
Gould breathed in. Out.
In. Out.
Twenty seconds.
Twenty seconds.
Tried to picture this diner he was being driven to.
Situate himself inside it.
Booth?
Counter?
Image after image after image of diner after diner after diner came to mind.
But all were affixed to distinct memories.
Times. Places.
Nothing felt as recent as *yesterday*.
Nevertheless, the idea of the diner calmed him.
The driver lightly honked at somebody. As though over his shoulder said to Gould 'Sorry about that, doc. This idiot. No way to drive. You just relax, though. We'll getcha there.' Lightly honked, again. 'Christ Jesus, just understand that's your lane, partner!'
Yesterday.
Gould remembered returning to his hotel.

In the afternoon.
In his brown car.
Coming from the studio.
The motel manager had said *shy of midnight* was when he'd arrived.
Checked in to the motel he'd just now vacated.
Claimed he'd arrived in the very taxicar he now rode in.
Returning to the diner.
The diner where this exact driver claimed to have picked him up.
From the radio poured more lurid details.
... psychic woman's husband had been suspected, incarcerated, then freed ... due to information culled from her visions ... images confirmed as facts, irrefutably ... sordid double-lives of prominent members of whichever community had been uncovered ... a detective eventually suspected of the ghastly crimes ...
Not even ... *six* hours Gould couldn't account for?
Less than six.
Finished in the studio four o'clock.
To the hotel.
Say he'd been there until five.
Left ... left ... for *whichever* reason.
Arrived to the diner by ... *eleven*?
Ate a meal.
Been driven to the motel.
Arrived shy of midnight.
Five hours.
Some of which were accounted for by transit.
Hotel-to-wherever.
Wherever-to-diner.
Four hours?
Four-and-a-half?
The radio explained the psychic woman had eventually been

walled into the very same room from her vision ... by her husband who was the culprit of the original crime ... another freshly dead body she'd seen vision of also her husband's victim ... killed hours before he'd attacked her ...

'You *listening* to this, doc?'

Gould's breathing had become more natural.

The motion of the taxi less abrasive.

Even lulling.

Four hours.

Didn't seem much worth fretting over.

Except ... *drunk*?

When would Gould have been *drinking*?

Why ... would Gould have been drinking?

'Maybe you left your hat and stuff at the diner, doc. That's what I'll betcha.'

... the psychic woman would've died if not for a friend leading police to the estate ... nick of time ...

'*Stuff of nightmares*' the radio said.

Nightmares ...

Gould watched a hatchet rise.

Cleave a young girl's eyeball.

Dot dot dot of blood spatter strike against the glasses he wore as it did.

Opened his eyes with a sharp breath as the taxi took a turn. Abrupt up-down of it cresting a speedbump jostling him.

'Sorry about that, doc.'

Realized he'd been asleep.

Voice from the radio now discussing a horse race.

As the taxicar coasted to a stop.

And the driver said 'We're here.'

Gould would've been more relieved had not the words *exactly where you left it* been included in his first thought upon spotting the car.

His car.

His brown car.

Freshly waxed.

There it was. Parked the furthest space over. Bumper encroaching into the sidewalk outlining the diner front.

He'd no recollection of parking it.

This diner?

Other than looking how all diners did, it was no place he'd ever laid eyes on.

What he saw across the lot struck him the same.

Generic flavor of such views, but equally brand new.

Those words *exactly where you left it* unfooted him. Just when he'd hoped to feel stabilized.

It was a grim sensation.

Like being convinced a costume he wore was his genuine self. Accepting a false narrative rather than returning to reality.

Impossible to shake. The feeling of *imposture*.

Impossible, also, to ignore how he was welcomingly accepting what he suspected to be false.

Wasn't doing so no different than giving up on the truth?

He shook this query off.

Could fuss over such esoteric trivia later.

For now, he unlocked the car. Motions fluid. Natural.

A thousand times familiar.

The tone of the light. Fragrance of the closed space.

Nothing about the vehicle's interior was foreign.

Passenger seat floor. Rear seats.

No bags of any kind to be found.

Opened the trunk.

Nothing there.

A fresh churn of nausea rattled though him. Hands tensed to claws against the chill of the vehicle's roof.

Viced his eyes shut.

When they opened, it was in the direction of a public telephone.

What the devil was he doing with himself?

How had his first thought upon waking to this insane situation not been to call …

… to call … *whom*?

Call … and then explain *what*?

That he was in the parking lot of some random diner?

Didn't know where he was properly staying?

Had spent the night at a no-tell motel for reasons unknown?

All morning behaved like a criminal due to the discovery of some bizarre writing he'd spent perverse energies destroying?

Writing he'd no memory of the composition of?

Took a seat behind the wheel.

But already had settled his keys back to coat pocket.

He was being led like a show-pony back through his missing hours. Simple as that.

Breadcrumb trail.

Left by … himself?

Left by … whoever had abducted him?

Was he ready to accept as actuality that he'd been *abducted*?

Ready to accept, then, that he must yet be under *watch*?

That his life was proceeding at some third party's dictate?

Did it matter?

How long had he gone without his pills, by now?

How long could he go on without them?

Returning to this diner or having been *led to it* was all the same.

Obviously he was meant to go inside.

Yes.

Meant to.

Certainly he didn't *want to.*

Wanted anything but.
Yet was utterly terrified what would happen if he didn't.
Chuckled.
As though with foreknowledge.
In this establishment he'd be recognized.
Have returned to him his hat and his glasses and gloves.
But no bag.
There never would've been any bag.
All of his belongings, his pills, would be at his actual hotel.
A hotel he was being *manipulated* back to.
A hotel which was being made to no longer feel *his*.
Inside this diner he'd come to learn which hotel that was.
These circumstances making such knowledge a further assault.

As instructed by the sign encountered upon entry, Gould seated himself. Corner booth.

Noted with a sigh of gratitude how the establishment didn't have its overhead lights activated.

Despite this grace, however, the bleat of sunlight had worsened considerably since first he'd ventured from motel room.

The abundant chrome fixtures littering the environment, sheen to the tabletops, various glass confection cases, and mirrors lacerated his already overburdened senses with daggers of redirected noonday glare.

Adjusted the blinds of his booth and the unoccupied booth in front of him to allow for as much peace as possible.

The establishment was bustling and Gould had protectively cupped palms over his face, so wasn't certain if the 'He doesn't need a *menu*, I got him' chirped through the clatter was in reference to him.

An accurate statement, if so.

A waitress approached.

Slowing as she did.

Giving Gould a wave and an overdramatic squint.

Immediately after his tentative wave back, she sucked on her lower lip and made several wide, kittenish strides, pointing fingers of left then right hand at him as though pop-guns brandished in child's play.

'It's … *scrambled* eggs … *bottled* water … and … *ketchup*!'

She clapped as though entirely certain of herself, covering the remaining distance to the booth at a quick hopscotch.

Unable to help himself, Gould smiled sincerely.

Joined in with the second round of applause she gave herself.

'See? I *told* you I'd remember!' the waitress stuck out her tongue after exclaiming.

An instant later, however, was blushing. Bashfully saying she supposed it wasn't exactly a trick to launch a *career* off of.

'It'd only been last night, after all. But a deal's still a deal, *right*?'

Not wanting to break the lighthearted spell of this moment, Gould opted to concur.

'A deal is most certainly a deal. Very aptly named for that exact reason.'

The waitress laughed far more than necessary at the quip. Gingerly bumped the table edge with one knee as though only a smidgen too much a stranger to give Gould's shin a flirty tap of her toe.

'I did *my* part … so let's hear it.'

'*Hear it*?' Gould echoed.

Puffing out one cheek, pressing down on it with two fingers like popping a bubble, the waitress then moved hand to petulant hip. Called him a fourflusher.

'Why'd you stop playing the piano?'

The question was so unexpected, Gould stammered and blinked

repeatedly. Eventually managed to defensively bumble out 'I most certainly haven't *stopped playing* the piano.'

She gave cartoonish frown. Crossed her arms.

'You know what I *mean* ...' she bullied with a wink '... don't be a wise-guy.'

'You know who I am?' he asked at a rush, holding hands up both apologetically and as though held at gunpoint.

Well, she hadn't had any *real* idea what it *meant* when he'd told her, last night. But after he'd gone, she'd told her mom about the conversation and 'Boy oh boy isn't she sure a great big fan of yours. So you'd *better* tell me. Because I told her you'd tell me. She'll think I'm holding out.'

Gould was about to reply, in a manner which might both dodge his yet having no idea what was happening and also give valuable context to his missing hours, when the waitress turned and addressed some remarks across the dining floor to staff members stationed at the cashier counter.

'I'll be right back' she pouted.

Adding how, by the way, he'd forgotten some things when he'd left.

She'd bring them over with his order.

'But you'd better get it together by then or I'll never bring you extra ketchup, again.'

Careful not to let on he was pumping for information, Gould conducted his tidbit interviews in such a manner that recap of last night's conversation naturally mingled with their in-the-moment rapport.

Each time the waitress happened by, he gathered another puzzle piece.

Quite the heart-to-heart they'd had, to hear her tell it.

Diner quiet that time of night.

Had become real fine pals.

The elaborateness to the details she chattered out was considerable.

All news to him.

All doing nothing to ring any bells.

It'd been he, it seemed, who'd mentioned being a pianist. On flimsy pretext. He 'didn't exactly just bring it up' but things 'got around to it' only 'somehow.'

He'd not given his name until she'd asked.

His honest name.

Glenn Gould.

The girl under no impression he was a doctor of any kind.

As to letting drop how he'd retired from the concert stage, that was on account of she'd asked if he was famous.

This business of having his meal preference down to memory?

Of his owing her explanation for his withdrawal from the limelight?

Stakes which'd been introduced 'just kinda because.'

She'd bragged how she'd know him next time he was in.

Have his food brought without his needing to order.

Claimed to be an ace in that arena.

If she pulled it off, he'd promised to confide in her all his secret reasons for 'abandoning the Big Top.'

If she forgot, however, his eggs would be on her.

What interested Gould most was to discover he hadn't seemed the teensiest bit drunk.

Not to her.

Though admittedly she'd 'been around very *few* drunks.'

He'd seemed, she shrugged, like he was now.

'Pretty normal.'

Into the bargain, Gould was able to deduce he'd spent an hour on premises.

If not more.

Waitress laughing at the recollection of how sheepish he'd been.

Apologizing twice for loitering.

'Fearing the bum's rush.'

Also of importance: the fact she'd no idea a taxicar had been summoned.

Certainly he'd not asked any company number off her.

Or any staff member.

So far as she was concerned, he'd simply made it a point to tell her what a treat it was having met.

Paid.

Then left.

Maybe half-hour before her shift ended.

'Midnight or thereabouts.'

So ... suppose he'd arrived to this diner between ten and ten-thirty. In that case, if his *honest hotel* was at least as far from the diner as was the *motel*, which seemed likely, and supposing, though unlikely, he'd left the hotel *immediately* after arriving from the studio, there would've been half-hour travel time to wherever he'd *initially* gone. Supposing wherever such place was was nearby this diner.

Which was his working theory.

For now.

Made things gibe, neatly.

He'd left the diner approximately eleven-thirty.

Likely called for the taxi from the payphone in front.

Company chosen at random from the directory.

Taxi probably took five, ten minutes to arrive.

Getting him to the motel by midnight, no sweat.

A four-to-five hour interval, at most, was, indeed, all that could be missing from his life.

That and a reason he'd taken such obvious pains to impress himself on this young waitress.

And a reason he'd gone to so specific a motel, half-hour drive from so specific a diner, when there must've been several nearer and he'd a room in a hotel, besides.

And a reason the taxicar driver and motel manager said he'd called himself *doctor*.

And a reason the motel manager had thought him *quite drunk*.

And a reason he was anxious to keep playing dot-to-dot with his life …

… while also trying to convince himself there was no point prying any further into his own affairs.

There he was.

Reflected in the toilet mirror.

Flat cap. Coat. Scarf.

Tinted driving glasses, leather driving gloves.

Himself.

Glenn Gould.

Add in the effects of the aspirin, ibuprofen, bismuth the waitress had brought and he even *felt* like Glenn Gould.

Himself.

Somewhat, at any rate.

Enough.

Amazing how ingesting an honest meal and some over-the-counter curatives centered him.

To be assured a few moments full privacy, he closed himself into one of the stalls.

Didn't undo any of his clothing.

No urge or need to void.

Sat only briefly, the bowl being set awkwardly low.

Just stood.

Leaned to the wall.

Hands down his pockets.

Attempting to let his mind go blank.

Which is when the name of the hotel he was keeping a room at occurred to him.

Exactly as simple as that.

Exactly as preposterous.

As unnerving.

But undeniable.

Yes. That was where he was staying.

The name. The room number.

Nothing more dawned on him.

Not the establishment's location relative to the diner.

Not when or why he'd left it.

Simply the name.

Room number.

Jointing seamlessly into the memories he'd never seemed absent of.

The building's façade.

Interior lobby.

The layout of his suite.

His initial disquiet at this information popping back into place so suddenly after such energy spent fretting over its absence passed after a moment.

It made sense, this recollection.

Made sense it coming to him now.

Psychologically it fit, neatly.

He'd awakened under stress.

Been feverish.

Preoccupied with immediate oddity after immediate oddity.

Now, with so many superficial mysteries at least partway resolved, his mind could return to typical function.

Never had it been logical to presume so surgically precise a memory as the exact name of a hotel could've been excised from him.

Panic—sheer, personal panic had tunnel-visioned his concentrations.

A survival instinct.

Response to a *trauma*.

Or ... perhaps to the application of a *drug*.

Yes. That summed well enough.

A period of time surrounding the *administration of* and the *waking from* an anesthetic, for example, could conceivably leave memory blanks equivalent to the period of time still missing from his ledgers.

'No ...' he muttered to himself, realizing how tense he'd become, cinder stiff in his lean to the tile of the restroom wall '... you're not saying that's what *happened*, Glenn. Merely citing example. An *analogous* circumstance.'

Nodded.

Nodded.

Absolutely he wasn't suggesting he'd literally been *anesthetized*. In such condition, he couldn't very well have driven from his hotel to this diner. Arranged transport from this diner to that motel. Couldn't have taken *any* of the steps necessary to have awakened as he had.

Nevermind how he couldn't have engaged in whichever activity *during* the vagrant timestamp.

In any activity at all.

Three separate, wholly unconnected persons had now given accounts covering many of his whereabouts and behaviors.

Once he returned to his hotel, he'd no doubt learn precisely which hour he'd vacated it.

Once able to medicate, clean up, return to his usual patterns, it'd be only a matter of time until all which remained presently unaccounted for would be recollected.

Perhaps he'd suffered a shock.

Physical.

Emotional.
Taken a spill.
Received a piece of distressing news.
Now that he recalled where he'd come from, all manner of perfectly ordinary explanations for his experiences today occurred to him.
Every one of them making perfect sense.
Down to having left his room without his pills.
His working on some Beethoven article, out of the clear blue sky.
Even his typing bizarre remarks into it.
Obviously just before passing out.
Waking in such distress.
Something had *happened*.
Something of acute impact but perhaps only of trifling consequence, big picture.
Gould was prepared to leave it at that.
Something. Had happened.
Nothing more.

His waitress insisted on giving him a hug. In thanks. For keeping his word. Parceling her such juicy insider gossip to curry favor with her mother. She'd put his secrets to good use, she assured him, at the same time promising his secrets were safe with her.
Overjoyed he'd be out the door immediately afterward, Gould allowed the physical contact.
Thanked the waitress, in kind, for keeping an eye on the belongings he'd so absentmindedly left behind.
Vowed he'd return.
Habitually.
After all, none could deny her service was an impeccable cut above.

Forgave himself these falsehoods as the cold of the afternoon struck his face.

Having learned the diner was located a full hour's drive from his hotel had further brightened his mood.

Less and less time left gouged from his existence.

Perhaps there'd been no instigating factor for his hotel departure.

It was his penchant, after all, to take a casual drive. Well into the evening. Often aimless. Listening to the radio. Enjoying the company of his own considerations.

Could be he'd not departed his hotel until nine o'clock.

For exactly such habitual jaunt.

May've been he'd done nothing but roam roads, at random, in the direction of this diner.

Such timeline accounted for everything.

Except, perhaps, choosing to stay at that motel.

Though going with his theory of some insult to his faculties, it wasn't beyond reason to posit whichever insult had transpired only after his *exiting* the diner.

Or shortly before.

With such central tenet in mind, stabilizing scenarios were plentiful.

He may've taken ill.

Not wanted to drive.

In so decrepit a state called for a taxi.

Wound up at the motel.

Being the worse for wear might've come off as drunkenness to the sleepy motel manager.

Truth be told, Gould could easily picture himself insisting he was a doctor to fend off strangers' offers to take him to hospital or else to have a physician summoned. Medical concerns aside, it was the sort of ruse he'd employed for privacy, unprompted, several times before.

Certainly it was feasible that all he'd desired was to pass out.
Recuperate.
In a state of sudden physiological distress he hadn't behaved coherently.
Yes.
Such idea even accounted for the peculiar lapses in memory. As with anesthesia, such an acute onset malady had expunged the details leading up to it.
As he inserted key and the vehicle's engine turned over, Gould chuckled.
Then froze.
Jaw tensed.
Skin going clammy.
Because of a phrase.
A phrase which ruined everything.
He gripped the wheel. Glanced at the rearview. Certain he'd find someone reflected in the seat over his shoulder.
Another Gould.
Who'd been the originator of the intrusive words.
Words which he now muttered aloud.
Staring at the reflection of him staring.
This reflection reflected in the tinted glasses his reflection wore.
'It's not as though you were *fleeing* anything, Glenn ...'
Except, no.
No.
This wasn't the full phrase.
He shut his eyes.
Grit teeth.
Whispered the interrogative end.
'... *was it*?'
A strangulation of moments experienced since waking flooded his mind.

Coughing into consciousness.
Rummaging sheets.
Peering through windows.
Turning out pockets.
Tensing at knocks to the door.
Tearing papers.
Stomping.
Stomping.
Stomping.
Moments from before waking joined this barrage.
Dreamt moments.
Hatchet.
Lake water.
Bubblegum.
Barrel.
Eyeball.
Each accompanied by the sound of a typewriter key.
Images of himself striking these keys spliced between each clack.
Letters in gargantuan type, superimposed, transparent, overtop.
You. Have. Killed.
A vice of pressure sizzled between his eyes and his arms began to judder from how fiercely he gripped the wheel as he whispered '... *and you will kill again.*'
Body going limp.
Slumping back in the seat.
Head lilting sideways.
Striking the window.
Jaw slack.
Issuing from it a limp strand of viscous saliva.

Gloved hands on steering wheel.
 Calm.
 Still in the parking lot of the diner.
 Car's engine lulling.
 Gould found himself sat proper upright.
 Exactly where and how he'd been ... minutes ... an hour ... thirty seconds before?
 Fleeing.
 That word.
 It dragged on him.
 Fleeing.
 A key which slipped perfectly to the lock of his mislaid memories.
 But one he refused to turn.
 Undeniably, his every action since coming to this morning had been infused with an air of desiring escape.
 He'd remarked as much to himself.
 Several times.
 No point denying it.
 Panic.
 Panic had ruled the day.
 Unrelenting.
 A mindset downright criminal had underscored all of his activities. Especially the most outlandish.
 Fleeing.
 Yes. At a rush. Without his pills.
 Fleeing his hotel.
 But had he been seeking to wrest himself from some horror, why had he been equally insistent about returning to that same hotel?
 Why not just have ... *kept fleeing* it?
 Especially were he postulating he'd perpetrated said horror.
 Which he all too obviously was.

Perpetrated.

The word so gleefully joined with *Fleeing*.

Almost as though no other could.

Except, he insisted silently, the word *Witnessed* would serve just as well.

'I might've *witnessed* something…' he spoke to his reflection, holding its gaze until he'd made it reply to him ' … yes, you might have.'

Did he actually *want* to know?

Want to return to a life wherein he'd be confronted with a circumstance terrible enough it'd jolted him to this degree?

Return, utterly uniformed of what he may be in for?

Whether he'd *done* something or merely *seen* something done, was he so eager to willfully traipse back to its aftermath, blind?

What was he proposing, otherwise?

Vanishing?

As much as he, in theoretical terms, would never deny a frequent desire for such, he was hardly the sort of person capable of a prolonged and irrevocable prestidigitation.

Were he being honest.

Though perhaps he'd no desire to be honest.

Not that he'd trust himself, in this moment, to honestly address his feelings on honesty.

Being honest, in fact, the only path forward he felt appropriate was to treat himself as though under the authority of *immunoresponse*.

Put the car in drive.

Foot to pedal.

Drift out of the lot.

See where the vehicle was unconsciously directed.

If he fled, he fled.

Returned, he returned.

Wouldn't choose either.

As he was certain he'd not chosen whatever had led him here.
To this moment.
Of not choosing.
Gould clicked on the radio.
Rotated the knob absently.
Left it on the sound of a disc-jockey's voice as he checked mirrors. Reversed.

... chickadees, here's the one you've been asking for and it's dedicated to Paul from Doris, to Marianne from a secret admirer, and to all the men in the special detention detail out at the ...

Tension melted from his shoulders as he waited behind two other cars to merge onto the main road.

... Institute from Big Bertha and the gals of the H.M.S. Vagabond riding at anchor ...

The road offering left.
Offering right.
Traffic thick both ways.
Gould uncertain which was better for toward hotel, which for away.

... a cozy quarter mile beyond the national limit ...

Didn't care to know.

... Pet Clark with that question we've all been asking ...

Would soon find out.

... 'I walk alone and wonder Who Am I?'

GLENN GOULD ENTERED THE HOTEL as though ill belonging. At best. Felt closer to intruder, entire.
The hotel, it seemed, was how his mind still framed the matter. *The*. Not quite yet *his*.
Accompanying him through the carousel doors was the tingle of a numb ache along his left-side ribs. More prominent, however, was his imperative need for Reserpine. Fully confident the quarter-filled bottle set among the dozen or so others arranged along his bathroom counter would assuage his blood's imbalance.
Head down, one hand stuffed into pocket, other gripping limply the handle of portable typewriter, he made his way across the spacious lobby.
In his mind he was, as though the rosary, thumbing through the full list of medications he'd need to gulp down posthaste when the approach of a hotel ambassador interrupted.
An expression of apologetic concern.
Warning of the considerable police presence which would be discovered in the corridor immediately outside his suite.
'A murder ... they believe, a murder ...' the hotel ambassador eventually put a somewhat non-committal point on.
'*Murder*? Well, not a bad one, let's hope' Gould replied absently, tense from what he felt certain would be a touch to his arm.
Perhaps an insinuating grip.

One of those gestures made as though intimacy was appropriate.

Close-in. Conspiratorial.

The popularly designated and so unavoidable way to impart details of whichever scandal.

He'd seen this particular man behave such.

With other guests.

'And a detect-tet-ive ...' the hotel ambassador began to go on, the stammered word dribbling into two timid throat clearings.

Gould, relieved he'd not been physically accosted, widened his eyes when nothing further was verbalized after several seconds of dead air.

Made a slow trilling of two fingers from the flap of the limp wrist of his free hand to indicate *Please go on*. This gesture ornament to the now more notably impatient cadence of his prompting 'A *detective*? Yes ... to pair with the *murder*, I suppose?'

As the hotel ambassador sorted his way through a further hem-haw, Gould caught the eye of the young man working the registration counter.

Clearly going to be detained from the toilet some few moments longer, decided he ought just as well collect whichever bundle of correspondence had amassed in his absence.

The detective would want to have words with Mister Gould, certainly.

With all guests of the hotel, in a way.

But with Mister Gould.

Quite *particularly*.

As Mister Gould's suite was directly across from the room where the murder transpired.

'And ...'

Eyes flitting up beneath furrowed brow from his half-hearted whisking through the fronts of various envelopes, Gould fairly lullabied '... *And* ..?'

But the hotel ambassador seemed quite abruptly to have forgotten all about any *And*.

His portly face in mute daze.

Tinge of guilt.

As though having uttered an exact word it'd been cautioned under hazard to keep unsaid.

'There are ... simply ... a *detect-tet-ive*. A murder ... they believe, a *murder* ...'

Then some official verbiage of regret for the obvious inconvenience to a figure not only of Gould's standing but of such nuanced, tender sensibilities. Yes. Mister Gould should let management know anything they might do to allay whichever discomforts might arise.

'You play the harpsicord, I'm told' were the first words spoken to Gould by a rather fashionably dressed woman in the corridor leading to his suite.

He'd been approaching with dubious expression. A bit jolted by the sudden words, the familiarity of their tone.

Wet his lips, meekly pointing at himself while saying 'I'm Glenn Gould. You're the ... *detective* ..?'

'*Detective-inspector* ...' the woman corrected with a chummy laugh, then added '... *Dziurzynski*' with a wink as punctuation. 'I know it's a tough one to *remember*, but you'll get the hang of it.'

The woman then pinched the pencil she'd just pointed at Gould in her teeth. These showing almost hyper-realistically white against the object's chewed-shabby red length.

Extended that now empty hand, taking Gould's unprepared palm in a quick clasp.

Gould winced.

Retracting arm as though stung or like having touched fingers in a dollop of something unpleasant.

Blushed as he became cognizant of the impression this had likely elicited.

Demurred that he could, and did on occasion, perform tunes on the harpsicord.

'But bad as it may've gone in at least several of those instances, it has *never* resulted in murder police outside my door.'

Pencil retrieved from mouth, Dziurzynski jotted a few words on the paper of a yellow leather pad.

This pad then tucked to breast pocket of her butterscotch blouse.

Explained she had 'a daughter who's looney for the harpsicord. Married some mutt because of it. Or so the story goes. We're estranged. For unrelated, nonspecific reasons. My updates come secondhand.'

Gould was about to venture comment when Dziurzynski continued.

'You're a far prettier man than I'd imagined. When I arrived and they told me it was your record playing, I surmised you'd not be altogether pretty. Would instead have that robust, meaty physique I tend to associate with pianists. As it is, you present a *strikingly* pretty man. I hope you don't object to my pointing this out.'

'Not at all …' Gould purred as he offered a quarter-bow gesture, an approximation he felt befitting to rapport while remaining respectful of the nearby homicide '… I've often remarked so, myself. Therefore it's bracingly pleasant to have a chance to consider it and not feel immodest. Allow me to earnestly reciprocate that you are a notably handsome woman.'

He made peck gesture with his nose, drifting briefly to tip-toes, meant to express he was keen to continue into his own suite.

'Do you honestly play harpsicord, though? I made that up for effect, this very minute. I'm forever up to such tricks. Thinking it'd either unfoot you or else be funny in a *non-sequitur* way ... but you *do* play?'

Gould nodded.

Now in a politely suffering manner.

Clasping hands behind himself.

Glancing over his shoulder a beat.

Then met Dziurzynski's smile. Business-like.

'I'm told there's been a murder? It wasn't *me*, I hope.'

'I'd hoped the opposite' Dziurzynski sniffed. Pencil pinched gingerly between forefinger and thumb-tip while she scratched the underside of her chin with a pinky.

'Hoped ... I'd been the *victim*?'

'The *perpetrator*. Little things like that, Mister Gould, can make my job much easier.'

Feeling on his guard, now, Gould put forth a graver air. Suggested in a direct and unambiguous way how perhaps they ought not be joking about this affair.

'Certainly not within earshot, so to speak, of the *infelix victima*.'

'Were you joking?'

Dziurzynski plucked leather pad from breast pocket.

Jotted what seemed a single word or else an underline.

Gould nodded.

'So you did hope ... the victim ... was *you*?'

Her pencil hovered atop pad.

Gould held his expression. Nonplussed.

'I'm still joking, it seems' Dziurzynski sniffed with an aw-shucks tilt of her head. Then transcribed herself as she furthered '*You've ... caught ... me.*'

Flapping pad shut, afterward.

This time slipping it to right-hand pant pocket.

'If *jokes* were *murder* and *you* a *police-lady*, Mister Gould—well, your career'd be off to a cracking good start.'

Members of police squad and Medical Examiner's office. Occupied in various postures throughout the corridor.

Gould made a count.

Three, four, five, six.

Strained to listen through their bustle as he and the detective-inspector moved toward his suite.

Wanted an idea what was happening.

Past the open door of the victim's room.

Only enough indecipherable commotion to surmise at least as many people were inside it as were out.

From various quacks of wordmash and pop-splash of flash-bulbs he'd also guess several of the parties he couldn't see were journalists.

Entering his suite, finally, Gould left the bundle of correspondence in a lump atop the typewriter which he'd set hurriedly on the table toward the corner window.

Then made an overly erudite *excuse-me* to Dziurzynski.

Hastily closed himself into the washroom.

Reserpine swallowed.

Thorazine for good measure.

Librax for the irritable bowel.

And about this situation with his left-side ribs?

Three tablets of *Fiorinal*.

Plus the generic ibuprofen.

The latter little more than a *placebo*.

But so sweetly packaged. The pills two-by-two.

He'd warmed to the establishment's eagerness to provide them.

To presage his requesting.

The pea-pod duos prominently displayed beside his shaving kit each day.

Delightful enough he'd quipped to more than one of the women making up the room how they ought perhaps be left on his pillowcase in *lieu* of mint chocolates.

There was only so long he could comfortably be absent from the detective-inspector, of course.

The immediately soporific quality bred by the snug semi-echo of the closed room was something to be fought against.

No. He wasn't at all pleased with this Dziurzynski loitering about. Unattended.

Little matter to him what she'd be doing out there.

But whatever it was, he was within his rights to wish she wouldn't.

Not to mention, were he actually using the toilet to void, she may be able to overhear his exertions. Even without being the nosey kind she obviously was in order to have attained her rank.

In such scenario, she might come away with certain impressions of his physical health and overall mental character. Prejudices she'd neither verbalize nor, if she happened to make so bold, he'd feel obliged, in her company, to defend.

Aldomet.

A fine idea, right now.

Prophylactically.

His blood felt particularly untrustworthy.

'Positively low-down' he chuckled.

Touched three fingers to forehead after bottle-top popped and pills were gulleted.

The steam from the faucet was a comfort.

But a false one.

One which need be short lived.

Enough noise it'd cover his untucking shirt.

His raising its fabric for a look at this left side of his, proper.

Depressed the toilet flush for good measure.

Probably best, though of little consequence, for the detective-inspector to hear him reshuffling his clothes to presentable fit only after a ruckus verifying what he'd implied he was in need of the facilities for had been brought off. In this way giving an impression he was as commonplace as the next man behind closed doors.

Bruising.

Long, wide.

A lick from armpit almost to hip.

Not uncommonly dark or of coloration alarming for contusions … but still …

Enough reason to consult a doctor.

At this precise moment, however, such attentions seemed inadvisable. Certainly not to be requested with a tang of especial imperative.

He'd lived this long, after all.

Yes.

Tucking his shirt sharply and verifying his fly was closed, he had to admit how he'd, thus far, survived.

Could no doubt endure another five minutes of formalities without keeling over.

'Picking up from your Latin …' Dziurzynski began, turning her attentions from typing a last few letters onto a sheet of paper pinned to the roller of Gould's now opened typewriter '… I think it best I summarize the *corpus delecti*. Unless …' she suddenly seemed to sparkle, a schoolgirl flirtatiousness '… you'd like to *tour* the site yourself?'

Gould blanched.

Would prefer to be spared that.

'If such option is on tap.'

Dziurzynski assured him the victim's remains had been 'wagoned off ages ago. It'd be, for all intents and purposes, no different than poking through an amateur theatre troupe's moderately artful rendition of a crime scene.'

'Detective Inspector ... forgive me. I need rest. *Je ne suis vraiment pas dans mon assiette*. Perhaps the briefest summation possible. With a polite preamble of what it's got to do with me. I trust you are proposing I have some, I'd imagine *peripheral*, stake in these goings on? Or does every guest of the hotel get the floor show, complimentary?'

Almost stumbling overtop the punctuation of Gould's question, her tone of voice so abruptly changed in timbre it seemed studio spliced from an alternate take, Dziurzynski said '*Preamble* ... Yes ... Your *record* was playing. In the *room*. Where the *cadaver* was arranged.'

She then slouched in the chair exaggeratedly, giving unblinking regard to Gould's increasingly wary and, just then, marginally insectoid posture.

'*My* record?'

'*The Goldberg Variations*.'

Gould huffed once. Down his nose. Higher pitched than he'd have liked.

'I thought you might've meant a disc of vinyl which *belonged* to me.'

Dziurzynski sat up. Clapped affably. Pointed at Gould with the hands still together.

'That would've been an even *niftier* clue.'

This glibness prompted Gould to temperamentally inquire 'How exactly does a record I *performed on* but the copy of which *doesn't* belong to me become synonymous with *clue*? At least so far as my being sought out for consult? I daresay the seedy results of many a scuffle gone wrong among the denizens of Dive Bar, Nebraska might be stumbled upon to the jukebox strains of some swamp rock trio. I take it, with you on the case, such minstrels would find themselves deputized and pressed for insights?'

Oh, the detective-inspector liked his wit well. Was honor bound to say so.

'But this situation has going for it that—well! Dead woman, for starters ... *Goldberg Variations* on the turntable ... the very man tickling the ivories in the room next door ... record at least *resembles* a clue.'

Gould bristled.

Explained he was in town for business nothing remotely to do with music.

Added how the fact that the guest leasing the room adjacent happened to be a fan who'd brought a record along from home seemed, to him, irrelevant.

'There is no guest in the room adjacent.'

Gould could over-distinctly hear the soft pop of his dried lips as they parted.

Cleared his throat.

Scratched at his right eyebrow.

Closed his eyes.

Then, in this rather melodramatic posture, said 'Detective-inspector, I'm more than happy to jot the wholly unremarkable extent of my recent itinerary down for you before we part ways. Though I've little doubt it won't be difficult for you to sleuth.'

'Oh my goodness, Mister Gould. I already know all that stuff. They teach us about cobbling together such things even in the remedial courses.'

Dziurzynski stood.

Gently returned the chair to its place beneath the desk.

Gave its backrest a pat as if it were a puppy.

Hand to handle of suite door, Dziurzynski halted. Spun on her heels.

'You don't travel with copies of your own records?'

Took coy steps his direction.

Squinting as though catching him out.

'Hock them after the show sort of thing?'

Gould had been about to examine the paper the detective-inspector had typed on. Turned casually. Clasped one hand in the other. Stance of formal address.

'I've certainly been known to carry my own records. To hotel rooms. Though not for resale purposes. This trip, I hasten to add, there'd be no *show* to *hock* anything in the wake of. I'd not even have a record player except the suite came equipped.'

'*This* suite? The suite adjacent didn't come equipped with a record player. How'd that record player *get* there, I wonder.'

'Not being the occupant of the suite adjacent, I have little insight to offer.'

'There was *no occupant* to the suite adjacent. Had you forgotten that?'

'I'd neither forgotten nor recalled. Being *reminded*, I concede. Without protest or provocation. There was neither occupant nor record player in the adjacent suite.'

'But there *was* a record player. Or had you forgotten?'

Gould took a seat at the typewriter desk.

Lifted the bundle of correspondence he'd set down, previous.

Moving top letter of stack to bottom.

Again.

Again.

First without looking.

Then paying only superficial attention.

His focus snapping back to Dziurzynski when, with kind of a sigh, she explained 'The murdered woman was a housekeeper. The two of you had met.'

'*Met*?'
Gould held eye contact.
Felt his cheeks flush.
Averted eyes back to letter fronts.
'As far as such things go, yes' Dziurzynski continued.
A grey envelope was revealed at the top of the stack.
Typewritten return address with the name

>Dr. Herbert Von Hochmeister

'She wasn't *fond* of you, this housekeeper. Or better let's say: you'd left an impression on her.'
Gould mumbled as he struggled to break a medicine-head fixation on the envelope. '*Impression* ..?'
'According to various staff. Thought you were quite the *spook*. Always gloved and scarved. Flat-cap. Greatcoat and glasses. Said it was like encountering the Invisible Man.'
'… *Invisible Man*?'
'As like in the novel. H.G. Wells … *Invisible Man* … all *disguised* …'
Gould noticed Dziurzynski's vocal pace had slowed.
'… exaggerated winter apparel …'
Realized she was paying him curious attention.
'… bandages …'
Shifted grey envelope to bottom of the stack.
'… pasteboard nose …'
'She was literate, then?' Gould abruptly interjected.
Dziurzynski blinked.
'*Literate*?'
'At least so far as Wells would qualify one to such honorific?'
'The victim … could *read*, yes. Played the *viola*, as well.'
Gould stood.
Performed gestures suggesting he was absorbing these personal details.

Made a point to exude the air of a man moved to philosophic consideration.

'... It's regrettable. The *effect* I have on people. While not *oblivious* to it ... and certainly not *responsible* ... I nonetheless bear a ... a ... I can't think of any word, I apologize ... You say it was next door ...?'

'Adjacent' Dziurzynski nodded. Expression having morphed to raw puzzlement during Gould's little monologue.

'Across the hall, hadn't we agreed? Wouldn't *adjacent* suggest ... *adjoined*?'

'Did you ... want to *see* the room, Mister Gould?'

He patted himself up and down. Seemed alarmed to find he wasn't dressed precisely as the detective-inspector had only just been describing.

Dziurzynski, picking up on this discomfiture, asked if he needed a moment.

At his vague motion of assent she gave a playful bow. Snapped her fingers. Mentioning there 'was something I wanted to *show* you over there, too. This'll save me the bother of bringing it in.'

The heavy coat tethered Gould. As soon as he'd recloaked, he felt more present. Actual.

Had left it draped over the shower bar.

Hardly recalled having done so.

Didn't matter, now.

Popped bottle. Pill to palm.

Trifluoperazine.

Swallowed.

Scarf in a fold on the toilet tank. Now snug in place round his throat.

Bottle. Pop.

Septra.

Washed down.
Expected his hat to be curled in coat pocket.
But no.
Gloves, though. Driving gloves.
Not the gloves he wanted.
Where was his *hat*?
Bottle. Pop.
Aldomet ... but had he taken that already?
Didn't much see how it mattered.
Swallowed.
Hat still nowhere to be found.
Even looked in the waste-bin.
Checked his reflection.
Resolved not to panic.
After all, his driving glasses weren't here, either.
Knew they'd been left in the car.
Probably his hat along with them.
Pop.
Valium.
Swallow.
... Pop ...
... *Valium* ...
... Swallow ...

Actually, the flat-cap was just there. Desk. Beside the typewriter. Noted it before he'd stepped fully from bathroom.

Spotted the fingerless knit gloves he was after, as well. Across the room. One on the arm, other on seat cushion of the comfortable armchair by bookshelf and reading lamp.

Fitting hat to head, he'd just about taken first step toward retrieving them when his gaze was drawn to the typewriter.

The detective-inspector ... she'd typed something.
He'd never verified what.
Moved around desk.

Hands to pockets.
Gave a casual lean forward.
Squinted.

    Bwahahahaha

Gould was certain he was reading this wrong. That a word in foreign language had been printed. His mind not recognizing it. Shunting to some nonsense approximation.

But no.

That was what Dziurzynski had typed.

He could feel the curl of a snarl developing on his lips. The tight from a nostril flaring.

Yanked page from the roller.

Exactly the same moment as the telephone rang.

Got himself composed.

By third ring, had set the offensive sheet down primly to the desktop. Patted it straight.

By fifth had crossed carpet to take up the receiver.

'Hello, this is Glenn Gould.'

The line was silent.

Kept silent through two further prompts of 'Hello?'

Though he was able to ascertain someone's presence on the line.

Breathing.

A smeck of lips.

'Are you able to hear me?'

But other than the faint scratch of static there came no response.

'I do apologize, but if you're hearing me, I'm not getting anything over the line.'

Static ... or else the unspeaking party letting out a prolonged, low volume hiss.

As he glanced to the cradle, thinking to end the call, a raspy whisper stabbed in 'Why have you returned to the hotel? Are the police there with you?'

Too shocked to be shocked, Gould took a swallow.

'Police ..? A detective ... *Dziurzynski* is—'

'Tell her nothing, Mister Gould' the whisper hissed curtly.

Was about to stammer a polite beg-pardon, but the whisper continued, jostling, snake-sip punctures to the sentences.

'Say nothing to Dziurzynski. Absolutely nothing. Don't be a fool.'

Then a tangle of gruff, crumbling dissonance in his ear.

So jagged he tensed away from receiver.

Silence when he cautiously moved his ear back.

Only then any details of what'd been said during the call hitting him.

Receiver to cradle, he tottered to the desk chair.

Rubbed at his ear.

Worked finger inside.

As though he might dislodge the intrusive conversation, physically.

The only result of his effort a cackle like faucet full blast.

Gush of white noise splashing over remembered whispers in a voice he couldn't pin down.

As Gould opened the suite to exit, he discovered Dziurzynski with hand poised to knock. Back of fist toward him so as to strike with top knuckles. Cigarette pinned between index finger and third.

This she ducked behind her as Gould instinctively fanned the air in front of his face.

Backpedaled.

Suite door slamming shut.

Positioning scarf over his mouth, Gould cautiously re-entered the corridor.

Dziurzynski several paces to one side. Finishing a drag. Cigarette whisked behind back, again. Exhaling with head turned almost entirely around.

After inhaling another lungful, she addressed Gould cordially 'I was about to play search party. Never meant to startle.'

Gould kept to the doorway. Scarf protectively arranged. Through it, he muffled, somewhat curtly, how he couldn't have been alone but five minutes. Had told her he'd be along, presently.

Dziurzynski knew that, of course.

'However, one can never be *too* cautious.'

Explained, from still ten paces off, how 'On an early case of mine, *unbelievable* as it'll sound, a man, not so different from you, told me he needed to step back into a hotel room. To fetch an umbrella. How much you wanna bet the next thing I knew he'd been *suffocated*? In his bathtub. Not *drown*, mind you. Rather *asphyxiated* with a length of thick plastic wound round his head. Ghastly business. Meantime? Neither of us had any inkling of even the possibility of an intruder. Good God, Mister Gould, we'd only just enjoyed an entire meal from Room Service together. When I found the body, get this: windows were locked. All of them. From *inside*. Killer must've slipped out while I was discovering the corpse. You'd agree that's bound to make me *antsy*, going forward.'

Now indicating with a hand gesture she'd taken his scarf to heart, Dziurzynski milked a final puff from cigarette then snapped at another officer to come fetch it.

Slowly closed the distance toward Gould.

Asked amiably 'You don't enjoy an *occasional* cigarette? Wouldn't it look neat? Paired with piano playing?'

Yet through his muffler, Gould explained he nursed 'as hearty a fear of cancer of the lung as you do of people being in their rooms alone for a moment.' Lowering scarf, halfway, he furthered 'Does flagrant paranoia *aid* you in your duties? Or do you find such pathology an *encumbrance*?'

Frankly, it was a thorn in her side. First to admit it.

'Little quirks, though. We all have them. Take yourself, eh? I imagine for every cigarette you *don't* smoke, there is, so to speak, a cigarette you *do*.'

Gould allowed his scarf to fall naturally. But retained as much distance from Dziurzynski as decorum allowed.

'If I might inquire, before our tour: what is the *atmosphere* ..?' he pecked nose in direction of the victim's suite.

Not to worry on that front.

No smoking.

Dziurzynski's strict policy.

How come? Gould might wonder.

'One time, there'd been a cigarette. Stubbed to the floor of a crime scene. Figured it was a lucky break. But a local constable explained the thing'd been his. Apologized. But too late. The entire case, I couldn't get over what an *amazing* clue that cigarette butt would've been. Got so fixated on it that any theory of the crime which failed to explain its presence I'd dismiss out-of-hand. To this day, a murderer walks free.'

Gould stared.

Offered no reply.

Unmoving. Unblinking.

Finally, Dziurzynski rolled her eyes. Gave a paly jab to the air in front of her as though chucking Gould's jaw.

'Obviously you know to ignore the *majority* of what I say, by now. Night to day, I'm to be not the least little bit trusted.'

'The girl had been arranged in that green chair.'

No longer a girl. By then.

But Dziurzynski always preferred to say it that way, first.

Calling it *corpse* straight out of the gate seemed *indecorous*.

'Calling her *it*, just as much, I admit. Makes things easier, as the years press on, however. Such shortcuts through the atrocities.'

The chair had been moved from near the window.

Positioned at the foot of the bed.

Facing into the room, proper.

Oriented in the direction of the spot where the slaying had actually occurred. Clear on the other side of the suite.

The intensity of blood-spatter proved this.

Gould could see for himself.

'There, for example? Multiple concentrations. The more pronounced spot likely from when the already wounded body had been held in place. Wriggled against the wall. See how it resembles brushstrokes? Swish swish. From her struggle.'

The higher, smaller swishes meant the face had been specifically forced into the plaster. Those downward rivulets of blood more noticeable than cousin rivulets leaking from the larger stains produced by the gored torso.

'Also there's saliva you can't exactly see. Teeth discovered on the carpet. Represented by those numbered pins.'

The thinner splotch would've been from the nose.

When it splintered.

'See the blunt sprtiz? As though she'd sneezed with her mouth uncovered? From initial impact. Hair tugged back. The second, pudgier clot, as you might guess, is from the same shattered nose being mashed to place.'

Point being, the victim would likely have been vital when whichever blow was struck to cause the spray of blood along the carpet there.

And there.
And those dots on the window.

'This business on the ceiling was likely on account of the hatchet dislodging from flesh or bone. Wielded overhead. Brought down. *Plonk.*'

Dziurzynski would guess that *plonk* had buried the instrument into back of the skull.

Killer expending a lot of energy getting it undug.

'Why the overhead blood seems so *higgldy-piggeldy.*'

Also why driblets had spattered way over in that direction, all by themselves.

'Here's what else: this same blood-spatter proved the record player had been arranged only *after* the butchery.'

Not a squirt of blood on it.

Nor on the record.

Which Dziurzynski referred to as *your record.*

Pointing at Gould when she did.

'But I've strayed from my point ... the corpse had been positioned in this green chair. When discovered ...'

Positioning it, thus, gave suggestion the massacred body was serenely absorbing the music. Its legs crossed. Causal. Fingers of hands laced. Laced hands rested on knee. Head tilted back. Almost as though moved to some personal speculation.

'If not for the fact the face had been very noticeably cleaved in half...' Dziurzynski explained '... I'd have thought *Aww ... she's listening to Bach. Let's not bug her.*'

Most of the other mutilations would've been, to the poor soul who first stumbled on the scene, concealed by the victim's garments.

Blood had sullied the skin of the arms, certainly.

But the stockings made it tough to spot the gouges to the thighs and the calves.

Unless one knew to look for them.

'A split face, however, will *always* stick out. Not to mention the hatchet was in it.'

Postmortem, that wound. Dziurzynski's money was on it having been done while the body was already in the chair.

'Last blow? Probably. But who's to say? After all, person who'd drive a hatchet into an innocent woman's face might not be above inserting it back into the wound after inflicting umpteen others. It's never a good move to presume about hatchet murderers, in my experience.'

Gould admired his cocktail of medications. Such a deft mingling of contraindications. Keeping him arm's length from the detective-inspector's antics.

Which he was certain this carnival-barker act was.

An *antic*.

Lord only knew how his constitution would hold up. In the normal run of things.

If he'd had to face the unnatural naturally.

This aftermath.

These images.

Descriptions.

As it stood, he could play it as anthropologist.

Interviewer.

Dziurzynski his subject. Across table.

Babbling her fascinations into a patient microphone.

Reel-to-reel collecting everything.

Whirl.

Whirl.

Even now, from habit, he ticked mental notes.

Favorite words from those she'd use.

Admired her annunciation.

How she'd avoid repeating the same terms.

Unless repetition made repetition seem non-repetitious.

Dziurzynski seemed to pay him not the least little mind. Or no more than an abstract camera to newscast down the barrel of.

So, to Gould, watching her, listening, was as through a monitor.

Two monitors.

Each eye offering different angle.

One for coverage.

One for detail.

Switch.

Switch.

In his coat pocket, as her account of the violence pressed on, the fingers of his right hand pressed together. Tip of middle a conductor's baton. Wrist tilted this way. That. Measuring out tempo. Matching melody of speech pattern to what was being described.

Generating his own transcript.

Or *refining* one.

Smoothing down an amateur account from raw takes to seem an expert, erudite rendering of pristine reality.

May even have been humming.

Wasn't certain he wasn't.

Wanted to be. Humming.

To be. Certain.

Abruptly, Dziurzynski was crossing her arms.

Had heaved a bulbous breath.

Up. Down.

An honest galumph.

Pointing at the record player.

'The record player ... record player ... the record player, Mister Gould. One of the two reasons I specifically wanted to speak with you.'

He felt his jaw clamp. About to react with vexation. As though he'd been at work on a studio mix and a technician had chimed in there'd been some technical glitch due to which he'd be required to redo hours of edits.

Cleared his throat.

Able to comport himself as though simply shaken from the residual carnage all around. Yes. The look of bother on his face, he felt, made sense if he suggested it was there for that.

Beating him to the punch, Dziurzynski waved her hands limply, shoulder height. As though doing so would scrub physical details of the room from vision.

Was sorry. No need for all her chatter.

Bad habit.

'A track is always churning in my head.'

Did he understand?

Crime scenes.

Made little storybooks of them.

Adding.

Altering.

Reworking.

Truth be told, often by the end of a case it'd occur to her she'd solved it based on utter *fantasia*. None of the facts she'd followed matching reality.

Sleuthed a fairy story, did he see?

But nabbed the culprit, regardless.

'It's too easy to get caught up in the macabre. I make it more macabre so it seems less. When I look back on my life.'

Still, it was no excuse for imposing her melodramatics on anyone else. Promised Gould this was serious business. She derived absolutely no pleasure from it. Therefore had to find a way to take pleasure in not taking pleasure.

Otherwise, what was her life?

What was anyone's?

'Think of the amount of pretend which goes into simply *exist-*

ing. The dead woman, for example? Much of her life was probably pretend. Like *yours*. Like *mine*. I try to keep pretending. On her *behalf*. Maybe she's not even dead, you know? It gives me comfort, ideas like that. To believe she might believe such things. Is listening in on my little tale. Thinking nothing more of it than *Goodness, yes—how ghastly it would've been to be painted all over one of the rooms I'd spent so much time cleaning.*'

To Dziurzynski, the record player was the puzzler.

Certainly, a guest might request such device be lent.

But the victim's suite had stood vacant at the time of the murder. For the days leading up, as well. Would have stood so for days after. At which point a guest who'd made no request for a record player would arrive.

'Another room has already been secured for them. In light of … well. So how did your record player wind up in that corner? That's the puzzler …'

'*The* record player' Gould corrected.

Dziurzynski eyeing him quizzically.

'As opposed to *my* record player. *That* record player, itself, merely lent to my suite. To *the* suite. So not, in fact, *my* record player, full stop. *The*. Record player.'

Dziurzynski kept face at performative scrunch. Eyes tick tock tick tock. As though probing for some glitch in her previous statement.

'The record players … are one and the same. *The* record player. *Your*. Record player. Had I not made that clear? *The*. *Your*. In grammatical context, in our present situation, are the same.'

To Gould's recollection, the detective-inspector hadn't the foggiest notion where the record player had come from. Had verbalized as much. Not half-hour previous.

In no way meaning to offend, Dziurzynski wanted to correct him there. She'd said no such thing.

Pulled yellow pad from pant pocket.

Brandished it, unopened, in the air between them.

As though doing so proved her assertion.

Then, snapping the fingers of her free hand, chirped 'I'll bet you mean when I'd said I wondered *how* the record player had gotten to the victim's room. Which, if you'll pardon me, isn't the same.'

'... *isn't* it?' Gould queried, dubious, after honest consideration.

Hardly mattered now, eh?

Point being: Had Gould noticed his record player missing?

No. But he hadn't noticed *the* record player present, either.

Yet his suite, per him, was equipped with one?

His suite, allow him to explain, *always* came equipped with one.

'Even when in town for ...' Dziurzynski flapped open her pad, slowly thumbed through pages '... *business not remotely to do with music*?'

'Even always.'

Another curious thing?

The record player had been set precisely where a record player would traditionally be. If arranged by the hotel. Prior to a room being let.

'A room ...' Dziurzynski whispered, ominously narrative '... like Glenn Gould's room.'

Gestured at their present surroundings.

To drive home how the layout of the two suites was identical.

'Perhaps the record player had ...' Gould offered idly '... through some madcap *fluke*, wound up in the incorrect suite. From the *get-go*.'

Dziurzynski seemed excited by this prospect for a moment.

'Thing'd never ever *been* in Gould's suite …'
But just as abruptly deflated
'… except in that scenario: why doesn't it have *blood* on it?'
Was Gould catching her drift?
'The device …' he nodded '… had been *brought* from my room, you believe.'
'*Postmortem.*'
Gould stared at Dziurzynski.
'*Probably* postmortem' he said with an air like repeating verbatim.
She stared back.
As though waiting for Gould to say something else he'd promised he would.
Until her eyes drifted up. Dotted back and forth.
Lips moving slightly. Little pops.
Then, seeming to realize it was in fact her turn, she asked 'You didn't … *bring* the record player in here, did you? *Pre-mortem*?'
Was the detective-inspector suggesting he had?
'Not really. But maybe.'
'For what reason … and *how*?'
'Perhaps for a *liaison* … with the … *victim* … using … her *key* ..?'
'Certainly not. And if that is the smutty direction we're tacking in, with your permission, I'll thank you for your time.'
Gould pivoted to exit.
Behind him heard Dziurzynski stating aloud broadly 'No, of course … she really hadn't *liked* you …'

Catching him up as he entered the corridor, Dziurzynski apologized.
'A terrible trait. Thinking aloud.'
Regardless, before Gould retired, there was one further matter.

Gould understood the record player to've been the second of two matters. The room, itself, having been the first.

No no. He was wrong, again. Or else things hadn't been made clear. This time, Dziurzynski supposed, the fault being her own. But it hardly amounted to anything they ought have a falling out over.

'Your mind is elsewhere, as you've said. In point of fact, the record player had been the *first* matter. The second is the *newspaper review*. Crumpled. Shoved in the mouth of the cadaver.'

Before Gould could process this rather grisly image, Dziurzynski had opened her yellow pad. Flapped through pages in what seemed to him a childish, even phony, way.

'You *did* know a Paul Henry Lang, is that right?'

The detective-inspector didn't lift her head following the question. Nor did she stop rummaging through the pad.

Gould was uncertain whether he was meant to respond. Only when Dziurzynski cocked her eyes up and asked '... Mister Gould?' did he acknowledge, yes, he knew Lang.

'Of course. A critic.'

'Of *yours*?'

'Of music.'

'Of *yours*?'

'Of my performance of some of it.'

'*Critic* in this case meaning *not-a-fan*?'

'He was ... *critical*. At times.'

'Negative?'

'Critical. Which is excusable. He being, after all, professionally a *critic*.'

Dziurzynski flipped between two leafs of the notebook ... again ... again ... running her fingers over each studiously ... face set intently ...

... although Gould could swear both sheets were blank ...

... and that she'd positioned herself purposefully ...

... so he'd notice ...

'... Mister Gould? Are you feeling quite alright?'

He blinked.

Looked both ways down the corridor.

Momentarily wordstruck.

Cleared his throat.

Would this be much longer?

As he was certain he'd mentioned, he felt ... fatigued.

'All of this ... *business* ... perhaps only now hitting me.'

'Understood. If you could spare but one moment more. I promise there's just the matter of the newspaper review crammed into the victim's mouth.'

She paused.

Regarded him pointedly before seemingly referencing her pad '... review which goes on about how you bungled some Brahms Concerto rather egregiously ... a conductor named Bernstein made an apology to the audience ...'

'Bernstein didn't *apologize* ...' Gould began '... he merely explained, *beforehand*, that ...'

Dziurzynski nodded but didn't look up or pause even a beat before continuing overtop '... then it says you are ... Gould is ... I quote ... *indeed a fine artist, unfortunately at present suffering from musical hallucinations that make him unfit for public appearances.*'

Dziurzynski now regarded Gould.

Her face void of expression.

Until Gould nodded.

To which she winked.

'That's about your *final* performance, yes?'

'One of my ... final ... I suppose, yes, for sake of how you mean it. Yes.'

'It's not a very *nice* thing to say.'

'I don't suppose he reckoned there was compelling enough jurisdiction to entertain his finer angels.'
'It didn't bother you?'
'To each their own, it has been said.'
'Do you think Paul Henry Lang knew that?'
'He was likely paid handsomely to avoid taking it to heart, if so.'
'That's why you left the concert beat, is it?'
'Because of Paul Henry Lang? No.'
'Because of musical hallucinations?'
'Not at all.'
'*Any* ... hallucinations?'
Gould took a long breath in. Held it. Long breath out.
'No.'
'That was ... two years ago?'
'Roundabout.'
'Long time.'
'To hold onto a scrap of newspaper?'
'... or a grudge' Dziurzynski admitted she'd been thinking. 'But even the newspaper, yeah ... quite awhile for that, too.'

Suspect him?
'Absolutely not, Mister Gould.'
To the contrary. The detective-inspector suspected nobody.
At present.
Rest assured.
Now followed at his heels as he brusquely cold-shouldered her. Barged with him through the door to his suite.
'Please sit down, Mister Gould.'
Ushered him to the chair by the bookshelf.
Gave a respectful berth once he'd slumped harshly to it.
If anything she'd said—

'*Everything* you have said—'

Then if everything she'd said had upset him, let her disabuse him of any ill intent, now. Might she?

'I have answered all of your—'

He had. No denying it. She'd imposed on him terribly. Clearly he was distraught. It was furthest from her mind to badger. Notwithstanding, the following needed to be made plain. If only to spare him future grief.

'Glenn Gould, *here* …' she gestured arms wide '… in this hotel. Glenn Gould, *here* …' brought her hands together in a light clap, pointed at his slouching figure '… in this suite. A dead body …' gingerly nudged head toward the door '… *there*.'

Gould wet his lips, but said nothing.

Skin beneath left eye fluttering a pulse.

'Dead body and Gould knew each other.'

'*Cursorily*' he faintly hissed.

'Rumor had it Gould was *disliked* by dead body.'

'*Libel*, at best' he all but growled.

'A record of Bach is playing …' she pointed toward the door '… Gould is the performer …' she pointed at him '… Coincidence?'

Turned palm up like a shrug.

To this Gould nodded.

Once.

With vigor.

Straightened his still seated posture.

'Record player supposed to be *here* …' Dziurzynski gestured vaguely toward the room corner behind her '… instead is *there* …' let her arms go slack '… Coincidence? Maybe.'

Gripped hands together, tightly, shut her eyes, dropped chin toward chest, then rolled head along her shoulders.

'A piece of newspaper, two years old, with an article about Gould printed on it, found *interior* the victim?'

Stabbed two fingers at her mouth.
Stared at him soberly.
'While *record* ...' snapped her fingers '... *record player* ...' snapped again '... while *Gould* ..?'
Petulant, Dziurzynski turned and walked a few paces off. Roughed her unkempt hair. Wiped back of hand across nose and snorted.
'It's a glut of coincidence. On that might we agree?'
'Provided I am permitted to remind the court the plural of *coincidence* isn't *murder*' Gould purred. Effort expended to keep his tone even-keeled.
'Except there has *been* a murder.'
Gould moved as though to interject, but Dziurzynski held up a hand to halt him.
'Yet even still: the plural of *coincidence* is certainly not *j'accuse*.'
Gould held a glare.
But realizing he was being drawn out, allowed its imperative to slacken.
Instinctive.
Redoubled efforts to withdraw.
Cocoon.
Play possum.
'Someone doesn't do what was done in that suite for no reason ...' Dziurzynski had begun while Gould attempted to be swallowed in placid, medicinal haze '... and didn't include you at a whim. Whoever is responsible has manufactured *seeming* coincidence. Done so painstakingly. The more of these coincidence we gather, the closer we inch to comprehending their honest calculus. Disparate pieces, Mister Gould. Which aim to present a picture. A picture, for whatever reason, Glenn Gould features in. Prominently. At this stage? I've nothing like a full picture to regard. Therefore? Other pieces exist. Not *missing*, simply not yet

in hand. I guarantee it they are *forthcoming*. Meantime ... what do I have?'

Gould had scarcely taken in the detective-inspector's thrust. Loathe to let on, however, he asked with perplexed but genial affect '*What* ... do you have?'

'*You*. Mister Gould.'

Dziurzynski well understood what a pest she'd made of herself. In future, vowed to be less importunate. All apologies.

Gould, not wanting to unwittingly stir further banter or controversy, bowed his head. Reiterated his complaint of fatigue.

Dziurzynski could well imagine.

To further show herself conciliatory adopted an air of vulnerability, all but confessing to Gould that 'While this business is where I live *my* life, I need to respect it's where you'd prefer *not* to live yours. You've been a terrific resource, thank you.'

Before shoving off, there simply remained the matter of Gould's promise to jot down his whereabouts.

From yesterday.

Five o'clock onward.

'Sure would come in handy.'

This time, Gould was sorry, but had to insist the detective-inspector quite explicitly claimed to already be in possession of the requested information.

'The sort of thing learned *even in the remedial classes,* if memory serves.'

Had, in fact, rebuffed his spontaneous offer to tender it, less than one hour ago.

Nothing had changed, of course, in Gould's willingness to provide the affidavit itinerary. However, such transaction would now need to wait until after he'd rested. Recuperated.

Promised he wasn't about to run off.

Dziurzynski admitted it. Gould was entirely correct. She'd worded things all amok.

One of her flunkies, yes, had done the yeoman's work of cobbling together a timeline of his recent movements.

In fact, Dziurzynski was now determined to save Gould any further heartache. In that connection, the best course of action was for her to simply bring the already extant document to him.

He'd give it a squint. At his leisure, of course.

Confirm.

Annotate.

Just so there couldn't be a crumb unaccounted for.

'At which point, I'll leave you in peace.'

'Why is it, detective-inspector, I find such promises from you coquettish?'

Well, of course it was unavoidable he'd remain a person of interest. It'd be best he keep cognizant of that.

But other than this final trifle, Dziurzynski wanted Gould to understand *she* was at *his* disposal. Wouldn't act for a moment as though it were the other way around. Indeed, he was to think of her at his literal beck and call.

If anything troubled him.

Anything occurred to him.

'If anything ... happens.'

'*Happens?*'

Not desiring to cut into or sour his respite, and only because he was asking, Dziurzynski took this opportunity to give him her concise read of the present scene.

'This nasty business across the hall is an opening salvo. Directed *from* the killer. *Toward* you. For what reason? Impossible to know ... until something else happens.'

Frankly, Dziurzynski was surprised this was the gambit. Such flagrant hoopla right at the starting bell seemed incongruous.

'Out of courtesy, detective-inspector, pretend I'm not a deranged individual nor versed in such person's culture or idiom—*incongruous* how?'

This spectacle of the dead woman, the record, the article?

It already includes the police.

The public.

An invitation to onlookers.

All the earmarks of an *expansion*.

'Before so bombastic an expression, Mister Gould, the killer typically would've enacted something more private. Intimate. Something only to do with you. To make *you* aware of them.'

Gould couldn't help his bemused grin.

'Our killer is an *auteur* then, is he? Bucking the system. *Le enfant terrible* of his art form?'

Knew his eyes betrayed a glint of what someone smitten would call *devilish*, someone not would call *smug*.

Dziurzynski gave a brief chuckle.

Winked.

Resumed a somber tone.

'Something else *will* occur, Mister Gould. I believe you'll be *contacted*. By the killer. A letter sent. A telephone call. When that happens, I'd be obliged if you'd let me know. Save me from having to come asking.'

He nodded.

Watched her back out the door.

Watched it close on her smiling.

The quiet. The alone.

Gould couldn't comprehend it feeling oppressive to him. Seeming so remote from isolation.

But here he was. The sensation exactly that.

Oppressive.

Worse. He didn't feel *alone*. Rather the object of some party's voyeurism.
Multiple parties.
Eyes peering at him.
Surreptitious.
Nor was it silence he heard. Not even in the form of the glib chatter of his interior monologue.
No.
Rather his own imagined voice unrelentingly assailed him with the events he'd experienced since waking.
Dziurzynski's voice.
Waitress.
Taxicar driver.
Motel manager.
A chorus, cacophonous, directing his attention to matters he'd just as soon consider nonexistent.
It'd been, what—ten hours?
Shy of ten hours?
Eight?
Only a fleck of time since his eyes had opened in that motel.
During which he'd endured trauma after trauma.
His very waking in that room had been an insult.
Every moment since, his only desire had been this room.
His own company.
Quiet.
Alone.
So why wouldn't he let himself have it?
To anyone observing, he'd every semblance of quiet.
Profound quiet.
Quietus.
Serenity. Peace.
Reclined in the plush yawn of this armchair. Slouched almost cavalier. One leg draped over the furniture's arm. Two fingers,

spread as though limp open scissor blades, pressed against forehead while tip of thumb alternately caressed or gave soft tip-taps to his somewhat slack lips.

The very portrait of placidness.

Self-contentment.

How ordinary everything ought be now.

See how everyday it looks?

Sounds?

The hotel room.

Nothing about it a stitch different than it'd ever been. No portion altered from how it'd appeared yesterday. Day before. How he'd have expected it to look today.

The only thing altered was himself.

Entirely against his will.

Why should he go along with these intrusive circumstances?

Surely, by the time he woke tomorrow, all could press on exactly as it had been set to.

If he willed it so.

Return to the studio.

His radio documentary.

As he should have, today.

No one could debate there exist individuals who'd suffered horrors unimaginable but who find no daily need to revisit them. Who refuse them a locus of control.

This day would one day be five years old.

Ten years.

Two decades behind him.

Incidental.

Certainly not *defining*.

If it would be *eventually*, he'd treat it, *tomorrow*, as though it already *was*.

Yet here was his own voice. Challenging him.

Gnashing, rabid behind the glazed torpor of half-closed eyes.

Arguing his obligation.

Arguing his survival.

Arguing the impossibility of his life continuing without having addressed head-on his experiences today.

Christ's sake, he didn't even know where he'd been during the hours Dziurzynski would soon bring him written record of. An accounting of hours of his life she'd ask him to call accurate or inaccurate.

Would he simply accept whatever was written?

Splice the chain of events leading him to that diner into his memory?

Treat it as a more palatable, erudite take than another?

A version of these hours, studio cobbled, so that no audience would know it composite?

So he, himself, might forget it was?

'Yes ...' he murmured '... yes, I will.'

See how he'd already accepted the diner as part of his life?

The taxi?

Renting that motel?

Doesn't even agitate him how the events were given him, secondhand. Learned in reverse.

Does Glenn Gould *remember* these things?

No.

But they *happened*.

Seamlessly, he'd fused them to his existence.

What was the alternative?

To believe he'd interacted with three liars today?

A conspiracy of deception ensnaring him?

Ought he, from this moment forward, mistrust anything but his own impressions while at the same time not trusting himself when he chooses which impressions he chooses to trust?

'Preposterous' he muttered.

In fact ... had the record player ever *been* in that corner?

Gould moved to where, in the identical suite, the walls would be abattoir. Arranged his hands as though holding invisible object. Gestured as though lowering it to a pedestal.

Which wasn't present, either.

Meaning the fixture the record player had perched on relocated from his to the charnel room, as well.

Taking uncertain strides to stand equivalent to where he'd been positioned in that other room while Dziurzynski had descripted the violence and offal, Gould surveyed his surroundings.

Perplexed.

Genuinely didn't feel anything was missing.

Despite he'd been guest of the hotel these several weeks.

In this exact room.

'What, precisely, is your point?'

The record player and its station could've been filched the day he'd checked in.

'No they couldn't have, Glenn. *You* might not've noticed them gone. But the *staff* would have.'

Who'd suggested the record player in the victim's suite belonged to this room?

'There'd been no need to *suggest* it. There'd been a label affixed. The property ledger consulted.'

He shook his head.

Not wanting dialogue.

Contradiction.

Flatted back against the door.

Shut one eye.

Traced the room slowly, this side to that, with a finger pointed from the end of his limp-bent arm.

As he'd told himself: nothing about the room seemed different than yesterday. Than any day else he'd dwelt in it. Days during which he'd paced its length in thought. Had teetered, sawing the air, in that very corner.

Yes. He knew he'd done that.

Yet ... if someone hadn't insisted a record player was absent, he'd never have expected to see one.

'What, precisely, is your—'

Shook his head. Wincing the question away.

Traced the room a second time.

Outstretched finger stopping at the typewriter.

His typewriter.

Brought back from the motel.

Blinked.

Brought back from the motel where it'd produced writing he'd no recollection of composing.

Blinked.

Drifted his focus to the pile of correspondence.

Blinked.

Everyone at the motel had called him ... *doctor*.

Blinked.

Traced his finger to point at the stacked envelopes.

Blinked.

Blinked.

Arm went slack.

Then, in his hand, grey envelope.

Return address: Dr. Herbert Von Hochmeister.

Zipped the finger he'd been pointing with beneath the envelope's adhesive flap. Discovering the thing was entirely empty.

Probed fingers all through it.

Examined front, back, inside of flap and cavity for any indication of writing or content else.

Finding nothing, moved to set it on the desk blotter.

Moved around desk. Tilting his head side-to-side.

Rather absently opened the small left side drawer.

Empty.
Opened the larger center drawer.
Where he discovered a set of typewritten pages.
Dense with words.
Envelope still in left hand, he took this document up.
Brow knit in attempt to recall what he'd been writing ... when ... he'd been writing it ...
Winced in a spasm.
Hand holding papers brought to his temple.
Resting there while a wave of vertigo passed.
Sniffling, he tottered toward the room center.
His focus returning to normal as his eyes fell on the opening paragraph of the first page.

> I had scarcely begun the first supper show of my gala season at the Maude Harbor festival when, as was my habit, I glanced toward the boxes. And there, seated on one marked LIVE BAIT—DO NOT REFRIGERATE was a vision of such loveliness that it instantly erased ...

Gould could tell he was still reading, but a gargling of blood had begun in both ears.
Taste of citrus lined his cheeks.
Both eyes beginning to sting as though wood shavings had sprinkled on them.

> ... realized at once that my future, my fate, my destiny belonged to the dazzling enchantress who now, with sure demure grace, hid her bubblegum beneath the crate of worms on which she sat ...

Pacing now.
Unaware he was. But not unaware.
Steps rubbery. Seasick.
Sitting now to the armchair.

Unaware he was. But not unaware.

> ... I resolved to address every note of my performance to her and her alone and to inquire into the county's statutory-rape provisions at intermission.

No idea how long he'd been seated when the knock to the door jolted him to attention.

No idea how long the papers he'd been reading from had been on the carpet.

Torn to pieces.

Shreds of grey envelope mingled with the scraps.

———

Gould insisted it was no intrusion. Far from it. The detective-inspector had duly informed him she'd be returning.

That was gracious of him to allow, Dziurzynski said with a courteous roll of her hand, palm-down to palm-up.

She'd been anxious.

May well've left him under the impression it'd be morning before she'd swing by.

Then had thought *Why not slip the paper beneath his door?*

'But look here ...' she gestured at the floor '... no space at all.'

Gould nodded. Though with the door held open, Dziurzynski's claim was unverifiable.

A fact she seemed to ignore.

Just chuckled, sniffled, asked 'Have you ever seen a door like this?'

As though in on a joke, Gould idly offered how he imagined, somewhere in his storied travels, there'd been such a portal, though he'd be a monkey's uncle if he recalled in what exotic clime.

Well, Dziurzynski wasn't pleased.

Thought it should be against some law.

As the door closed, Gould considered, in the spirit of fun, pointing out to the detective-inspector how it, in fact, didn't go all the way to the ground.

But let the matter drop.

Best stick to his fatigue narrative.

Otherwise his antsiness over the shredded paper he'd hurriedly dumped in the wastebin, wastebin then shoved with side of his foot beneath the desk, might creep into his observable behavior.

Couldn't help his eyes still ticking involuntarily to the carpet in search of stray pieces.

Almost pained him to turn his back toward the door.

Following Dziurzynski as she drifted toward the desk.

Knowing she'd have a clear, wide view of the area of floor he was concerned with.

'You *always* sleep in the get-up?' Dziurzynski suddenly inquired, at the same time flourishing the sheet of paper she carried.

The ill-matched action and query rather unfooted Gould.

'… the *get-up*?'

Pantomime of gripping a fencing foil, whisks of swordplay from wriggled wrist of free hand, Dziurzynski explained she meant 'All that *junk* on ya.'

Gould couldn't vouch for *always* '… but just now I'd dropped dead from my feet into opiate slumber, right where you'd left me and exactly as clothed.'

Gestured to armchair.

Crossed his arms.

Shrugged.

Scratched chin to rough fabric of coat shoulder.

'What've you, got the *dropsy*?'

Gould grinned.

'I'm lousy with the sleeping sickness.'

'How ghastly. And what a bum deal for you. Me here, exactly before you close your eyes. Me here, exactly as you open them.

You must not've got a thing done in the interim between my party crashings.'

'To the contrary, I accomplished the exact task I'd aspired to.'

'Exact task?'

Gould nodded.

But squinted, confused, as Dziurzynski kept regarding him.

Her nose wrinkled.

As though she'd not took his meaning.

'I ... *passed out*, detective-inspector. The literal *moment* you were out the door.'

She rolled her eyes cartoonish, flapping hands in profuse apology for being caught woolgathering.

'In an event, here is the result of my minion's truffle hunt.'

Gould accepted the paper cordially.

Was taking a breath to bid her good evening when she stomped, gesticulating at the base of the door.

'It doesn't go all the way to the ground, after all!'

Gould took a moment to recover from the jolt of her tone change. Stammered vaguely how perhaps on the other side it did.

'... I've seen doors ... brass affixed to their bases ... or the corridor floor might ... be *higher* ...'

Dziurzynski dropped to knees.

Bent forward.

Pressed cheek flush to carpet

'Nope. Not even *close* to the whole way. If someone was of a mind to, they could see right on in.'

Dusted herself off as she groaned back to her feet.

Puffed her cheeks.

Let the air slowly leak out through puckered lips.

Said now she felt even shabbier for having disturbed his repose.

'This time, I promise, sleep tight.'

The good job was this document confirmed Glenn Gould hadn't perpetrated a hatchet murder.

The timeline, prim and numerical, cleared him of all possible suspicion.

He *couldn't* have personally enacted this horror.

Not, he reminded himself, that he needed to have this confirmed.

Though, he corrected himself, in the strictest sense, yes, he most certainly did.

The victim completed her duties at five.

Was thought to've been seen vital as late as fifteen past, though no firm confirmation of such could be made.

As to when and under which circumstances she'd entered the fatal suite, no theories had developed.

It was proved the murder, itself, transpired between seven and ten.

Per his habit, Gould had departed the hotel yesterday, few minutes before eight in the morning.

Been at the recording studio until approximately four.

Returned to hotel shy of four-thirty.

Was present in his room as of five-forty-five. This verified by a desk clerk who'd received a short call from him. Indeterminate purpose. Gould, to the clerk's recollection, not stating any particular business nor leaving request.

Exited hotel once more, approximately seven-thirty. Confirmed by a separate clerk from who Gould had inquired about his correspondence. Seemed he'd examined the batch given him. Asked clerk to replace the lot in its appointed cubby for retrieval upon his return.

Out the door, on foot.

Proceeded to briefly visit a bookstore, four blocks from hotel premises. No transaction tendered. Despite a lengthy chat with the bookseller stocking shelves.

From there, returned to his room, direct.
A meal was ordered.
Brought to him approximately eight-thirty.
Observed by custodial staff placing tray into corridor, quarter past nine.
By nine-thirty, had driven his car from the establishment's attaché garage.

In addition to the timeline proving it impossible for Glenn Gould to have butchered a woman and theatrically arranged a record player on which his most famous recording had spun, its contents fit exactly with his own knowledge of how long a trip to the diner where he'd spoken to the waitress would take.

Arrival by ten, no trick.

Troubling though it remained how he possessed no memory of the events he read over, nor of any event from diner until waking, all the pieces gelled without flaw.

However ... the timeline continued.

Without indication of his arrival to diner.

No mention of his car left in the restaurant's lot.

Nor of taxi being summoned.

Arrival at motel.

Instead, the matter was summarized thus:

Glenn Gould returned to hotel garage around one in the morning. Attendant on duty explaining how, as on other occasions, they'd chatted about the joys of night driving.

Once inside, Gould sheepishly inquired of the overnight auditor whether he'd be blacklisted for requesting the kitchen send up a meal 'past the witching hour.' The phrase recalled by the auditor, exactly. Because they'd then discussed whether *midnight* or *three-in-the-morning* was the time commonly considered the devil's.

Meal sent.

Food entirely in line with his diet.

Signed for, just past Two am.

All this on the official document Gould, for the fourteenth time, ran his finger along every word of. As though pinning them to place so no context or import could shift.

Most of all, he read then re-read then re-read then recited aloud how Gould had left the hotel, this very morning.

Few minutes before eight.

Arrived at studio.

Told the technician, after only an hour, he'd an important errand to run.

From which he'd returned, two hours later.

Worked another brief while.

Cutting his usual day short.

The last entry noting Gould's arrival to the hotel.

That afternoon.

From which time he'd been in the direct visual custody of Dziurzynski.

The detective-inspector's card.

Gould hadn't noticed she'd left it. Whenever she had.

Could've been any time.

Probably just now, however.

She'd drifted over toward the desk.

Or ... hadn't she given him a card, sometime early on?

He'd set this here, himself?

No.

Or yes ... *but didn't matter*.

Yes.

Or *no ... but didn't matter*.

Gould slumped to the typewriter chair. Set the itinerary down, dismissive. Stewing over how it being in his possession gave the detective-inspector ready excuse for another unannounced pop-in.

Or had he told her, in future, to please call ahead before any interaction?

No. Just should've.

Though ... what *difference* would it make?

She was murder-police. Wouldn't be bound by any adherence to quirk of courtesy.

On the card front, above her name, Dziurzynski had handwritten *Call anytime*. Below it *Room four-four-four*.

Gould sucked in a reverse hiss as it occurred to him this meant she'd taken a room in the hotel.

'Why *shouldn't* she and what could it *possibly* matter to you?' he asked. Already tipping his head in resigned agreement with the import of the rhetorical.

Lifted the card to discover it'd been set directly overtop Dziurzynski's typewritten Bwahahahaha.

Obviously a purposeful thing to've done.

Hadn't set card above the writing or beneath. Proving she'd actively opted not to simply hand the card to him. Instead, had chosen to play her little prank. In continuation of the original odd gesture. Which now felt less random a thing for her to've done.

The more he drilled down, the more vexed he became.

This document she'd left him with was a homework assignment. If it went overdue, she'd seek him out, truant.

Even if he brought it to her, such action counted the same as her popping in.

One more nimbly forced interaction.

Say he left it with another officer or the hotel front desk?

She'd deem it within reason to politely waylay him.

Verify, firsthand, he'd not left anything out.

Present him the prop of a new, official version.

Incorporating his updates.

His signature required.

After all, he wouldn't be allowed to simply say 'That's right' without adding so much as one remark of anecdotal nuance.

Was … this … really what he was thinking about?

In his present situation?

'I already told you …' he calmly addressed over the desktop '… tomorrow, none of this will have happened.'

Sighed.

Let head tilt back.

Catch painfully.

Drift more toward one shoulder than the other.

'Besides …' another perspective kicked in, this one speaking more mumbled '… why *trust* the paper?'

Possibly, it was entirely inaccurate.

Though the first half … those elements … seemed correct to him. Outlined exactly how any given day of his *may've* gone.

Had benefit, also, of they distanced him from the crime.

Those contents described, so to speak, exactly how he'd have been able to prove himself unconnected to the violence if he could have.

'You trust the part you *don't* remember … and dismiss the part you *do*?'

This gnawed at him.

How he knew for certain he hadn't spent the night in this hotel.

Hadn't been at the studio, today.

Maybe … all his activity the previous day had been verified … up until he'd taken his car from the garage … at which point … Dziurzynski's trail had gone cold.

A *guess* had been presented him?

Meant for him to *correct*?

A … *deception*?

It felt criminal, thinking in this fashion.

'Doesn't that simply mean you feel you're a criminal, Glenn?'

What did he mean?

'Isn't *this* ... just how you think?'

———————

Blood-pressure cuff deflated.

A sound like the rattle of breeze through dead, brittle leaves.

The hiss and crackle of radio static.

Chill carbonation of blood-flow returned to Gould's palm, finger lengths, tips, while he reached absently for the small notebook kept on the bathroom counter.

Uncapped the pen bound to it with green rubber band.

Glanced to the medication bottles, all lined up.

Clicking tongue against roof of mouth as he mentally inventoried which pills he'd swallowed since returning.

Flipped through notebook to add the new entries.

It taking a moment to consciously register why the date he'd jotted seemed odd.

Wasn't that today?

Flit of eyes to the previous entry of medication intake and vitals showed *twenty-two*.

Yesterday.

Making today the twenty-third.

Which is why he'd written *twenty-three*.

Yes ... having absently glimpsed the most recent date in the notebook, he'd set to start now, the day after.

Except, it struck him, today was *definitely* the twenty-second.

Meaning his latest entry should've been from the *twenty-first*. Made upon *returning* to the hotel from the studio.

Before his lost time.

Possibly ... an entry from that evening ...

Either way, what he'd been about to write should've been the first and *only* entry thus far today.

The *twenty-second*.

But there were notations all throughout the space allotted for the evening of the twenty-first.

The night.

The early morning of the twenty-second.

Today.

These most recent from a time, per the itinerary, just before he'd left for the studio. This morning.

Medication dosages.

Pulse.

Blood pressure.

Remarks jotted, per his habit.

Personal abbreviations.

Handwriting, unquestionably, his own.

But *today* he'd been at the motel.

The diner.

On the road.

Meticulously checked dates going back many many pages.

No sign of a blip where he'd wound up a day ahead.

Irrelevant, anyway.

Knew he'd made entries after getting back to his room, yesterday. At least five-o'clock.

Say he'd been responsible for the late night entry, the timestamp on the most recent *actual* notation in the book showed *seven-forty-five*.

In the morning.

Flagrantly incorrect, even allowing for a mishap with the date.

Found himself re-inflating blood-pressure cuff.

Sqwik-sqwik-sqwik.

His mind fritzed.

Unable to square this development.

These markings in his own chicken-scratch.

Heard the crackling shush of cuff releasing pressure.

Knew he was squeezing bulb to reapply.
Sqwik-sqwik-sqwik.
Shush. Crinkle.
Staring blankly at the reflection of his blank stare.
Sqwik-sqwik-sqwik.
Shush. Crinkle.
Wondering what, if anything, his reflection thought he was thinking.
Sqwik-sqwik-sqwik.
Watched himself blink.
Shush.
Crinkle.
Counting pills revealed exactly as many as there ought be, were the notebook accurate.

No idea why he'd expected anything different, of course.

Had someone tampered with his notes, it was a cinch they'd discarded the requisite caplets, as well.

Disquieting, the natural ease with which such consideration presented itself.

Tampered.

Yes. An *intruder* had *tampered*.

Well, why not?

Only this morning he'd considered, despite all evidence to the contrary, how he may've been abducted. Spirited off hotel grounds.

Except he'd dismissed that possibility.

Despite no recall, considered it indisputable he'd been at that diner.

Spoken to that waitress.

Summoned that taxi.

Checked into that motel.

Where'd he stayed overnight.

Now, likewise, he could accept, despite zero memory, how yesterday he'd done everything the paper Dziurzynski tendered him claimed.

Up until leaving the hotel garage.

Quarter-past nine.

But he knew, recalled, could *recount* every moment since waking, today.

None of which had been spent writing in this notebook.

Knew having done so at the times the notebook indicated was, physically, impossible.

It hadn't happened.

… and yet …

He wanted it to have.

Wanted to live as though it had.

Wanted whoever had done to him whatever they'd done to be stopped.

Without ever needing to know what whatever it was they'd done to him was.

Without ever knowing why.

Dziurzynski was dressed, top-to-toe, differently than the hour previous.

Yellow-and-green striped blouse.

Plaid, fitted suitcoat.

Houndstooth pants, dyed burgundy.

Grey boots, svelte and snakeskin.

Gould hoped he'd not encroached on her personal time.

'Naw, I don't go in for that kind of thing' she chirped while plopping down in the armchair quite blithely.

Ran fingertip over spines of the nearby books.

Wondered aloud who curated each room's little library.

Gould let his affect shift to match her devil-may-care.

'There are some things I should tell you ...' he began, almost a chuckle. Casting a glance for someplace he might sit.

Dziurzynski stood.

Beckoned him take her place.

'Can't sleep?'

Supposed, in fact, his desire to sleep was at the heart of his summons. As he sat, explained certain notions Dziurzynski had proposed were rankling him.

'The gravity of these circumstances which have ...' he rooted for an appropriate word '... *engulfed* me taking a toll.'

She adjusted her posture, upright.

Folded her hands, attentively.

'I might've received a telephone call ... from the killer ...' Gould said, feeling himself go somewhat numb.

Dziurzynski nodded.

Squinted.

Tilted her head wordlessly to prompt him along.

Gould explained the telephone had rung. While she'd been out of the room. Before showing him the housekeeper's crime scene.

'A *man* ... I think ... a whispering *voice* ... I didn't exactly *understand* it ... *process* it at the time ... but now am ... *concerned* ...'

Again nodding, Dziurzynski, seemingly only vaguely concerned herself, inquired what it was the man had said to him.

'Nothing of any *substance* ...' Gould awkwardly explained as he fidgeted '... just a man ... I *think* it was a man, that is ... *whispering* ... asked were the police with me ... told me to say nothing to them ...'

A moment passed, stone silent, before Dziurzynski asked had that been all.

Gould cleared his throat. Flapped his hand to affirm.

'Were you with the police. You weren't to speak to us, if so. Nothing *else*?'

Gould shrugged with both shoulders and again cleared his throat.

Dziurzynski puffed a few breaths.

Then, quite offhand, a touch of boredom in her tone, practically sighed the words 'You've nothing to worry about, there. That call was placed by a cohort of mine.'

Gould blinked.

Dziurzynski cracking her neck before continuing 'You said some *things*, however. What *else*?'

Too flummoxed to entirely grasp his outrage, let alone explicate it, Gould flowed right along with the detective-inspector's query.

'I ... said ... *something*, detective-inspector. *Thing*. Which, it seems—'

Begging pardon, no. 'You said *things*.'

Pinched tongue between her front teeth.

'I said some ... *thing*' Gould insisted. Growl roiling at throat base as he regarded her childish expression. 'That notwithstanding, perhaps it would be best you explain *yourself*. I'm admittedly gobsmacked. Please make me understand how—'

'It's important ...' Dziurzynski groaned, remarks addressed over her shoulder into the empty suite '... *you* understand you *understanding* means *nothing* to me.'

With his own aggressive huff, Gould clapped his hands once.

'Fine and dandy. Yet it might behoove you to explain yourself, regardless. Or shall we impose upon your superiors?'

'You think I fear the boss-man'd not take my side?'

Dziurzynski cocked her eyes with a *tsk*.

'The boss-man'd ... take my side, Mister Gould. If I dreamt for an instant otherwise, I'd *convincingly* claim to have no clue what you're *accusing* me of. As it happens, however, we've no need to get contentious. I'm pleased to explain myself, here and now. There is this woman, for example. Killed. *People killed*, Mister

Gould, being all. That matters. To me. With respect to uncovering *who* killed them? Frankly ... I'll do ... whatever ... tickles my fancy. I mean, imagine what sort of shady customer you'd come across had you kept keeping such a thing from me, eh?'

'If I'd ...' Gould began to rise from his chair, sank back at Dziurzynski's gesture he stay put '... *kept* ... keeping it?'

'Was hardly the first thing out of your mouth, eh? When did you say the call had come in?'

'I'd scarcely ...' he stammered '... a moment ... to consider it ... under the circumstances ...'

'I suppose that's debatable. Though I do make every effort to time these tactics out just so. It's important I *trust* you, after all.'

Gould held a glare.

Breathing high pitched.

Up and down his nose.

Mouth open. Snarled.

One finger reflexively taking pulse at the opposite wrist.

Dziurzynski, meanwhile, had moved toward the door.

To all appearances intent on exiting without further remark.

'Important ... you *trust* me?'

She turned.

Face shaped to suggest this was an odd thing to ask.

He stood.

Took several centering breaths before adopting a cordial posture.

'And do you ... *trust* me?'

She squinted. Wet her lips. Wiped side of thumb across them. Rubbed this with tips of index and middle finger. The gesture almost feline.

'No, Mister Gould.'

Bowed forehead to indicate their audience was complete.

'I *absolutely* do not.'

... HANDS SCOOPED MEALWORMS ... WAX WORMS ... Butterworms ... Red worms ... Handful after handful ... Frantic ... Nightcrawlers, leeches squirming up coat cuffs ... Shirt cuffs ... Paste of them plump under fingernails ... Weight of knees pressing down through cold trouser fabric ... Mashing piles of discarded louse ... Crushed ... Smeared to paste over wet dockwood ... Fingers scouring pulpy inside of barrel overturned ... Scraping maggot life free from the cavity ... The grittiness and tang from repeated regurgitation crackling like firewood at the tip of his throat ...

Hours after opening unrested eyes from it, the dream yet possessed Gould.

He'd awakened, yes.

Safe and sound.

Own hotel.

Verified date and time, straight away.

Knock of scheduled Room Service promptly struck.

Light meal.

Valium. Trifluoperazine.

Aldomet. Clonidine.

Pop pop gulp gulp.

Showered behind locked door.

Cloistered in curling drafts of steam had dressed.

Cleaned teeth.

Coat. Hat. Scarf. Gloves.

Shut into car.

Locked doors.

Radio clicked, radio tuned.

Merged with the anonymity of morning traffic.

… Girl's face … What remained of a girl's face … Mouth open … It seemed in too many directions … Stuffed with creek chub … Suckers … Shad … Beetles scrambling out … Grasshoppers flitting … Ants, roaches, crickets, vermin all manner writhing upward from throat after dropped down in fistfuls … Pulsing mounds of them clogging any free space around the flayed, folded body … Barrel crammed fat with disarranged torso … Head unjointed from neck … Eyes opened … Now splattered with freckles of the bile he'd sprayed … The last acrid pellets strangled up from a final dry heave …

Regardless how much he withdrew, how thick he cocooned, clothing, medication, white noise, mumbling, Gould's perceptions wouldn't wash of these images.

Sensations.

All the more troubling was how the dream had played out in dread silence.

Not even vacuum or signal hiss as canvas.

So his memories, now, of any certain scene spliced from it seemed to blot the world around him mute.

He drove as though a head bobbing into and out from a turgid lake surface.

His inability to control the intrusion of this images or that, the duration of one tactile remembrance versus another, made the journey to studio this morning akin to drowning.

… Stone … Large … Heavy … Too large, too heavy to carry … Lugged … Legs wide spread … Body doubled-over … Arms dangling and taut … Veins up to elbow thick as sumac, veins of neck strained tight as collarbone … Groaning the unwieldy mass toward waiting barrel ... Now upright ... Circumference meaty with smear of insects and minnow he'd trodden on ...

The sleep he'd spent the previous day begging toward had been robbed of him.

Transformed into assault.

Not even a nightmare had awaited him, it hadn't seemed.

Rather the hours asleep were as though he'd been ushered into a more visceral awakeness.

Every moment there ugly.

Endless.

An existence of terror it'd felt like he yet desired sleep to escape.

... Sullied hands ... Frozen ... Swollen ... Bleeding ... Fisted from pounding barrel-top to fit ... Pain in his chest arson ... Sinewy drool slung down his front ... He could rid himself of nothing else ... Whatever was hocked up, expectorated now clung ... Wriggled back into him ... Down him ... As he struggled for breath ...

Was that what today was, then?

A dream he'd escaped to?

These images barnacled to his mind the reality of what would await if he ever regained consciousness?

Images too real to bear.

... Images ...

... like over there ...

That was Glenn Gould.

Leaned rakish.

Watching.

Everything.

Encouraging.

Everything.

Looking ... right at him ...

... while he struggled with barrel to the dock's edge ...

... in panic ... panic ...
... panic ...

In the dream. Panic.
In the dream, only.
Not here. In this car.
Gould's rationality was able to keep any present panic phantasm. Bar trespass from its ethereal realm into his physical.
Aloof. Gould kept aloof.
Logical.
Knew the blame for any fraying to his nerves, beyond the typical walking nervosa he daily endured, lay square at the feet of that detective-inspector.
Exposing him to such horrors.
Depriving him of sleep.
Toying with his perceptions.
Winding him up to play some designated role.
Plying his behaviors in accordance to her manipulative dictates.
After what she'd put him through, how would his slumber not be packed tight with such nastiness?
Being dreamt, how would scenes so jarring fail to persist into his waking life?
He'd weather them. Let them fade.
Stay the course.
Live exactly as usual.
If such action would profit him, yes, he'd gleefully call Dziurzynski's bluff. Report her overreaches of authority to those superiors she'd so complacently claimed would be indifferent to her machinations.
To bother himself with such, though?

No.

Forcing a reprimand would only serve to keep him entangled. Invest his energies into a situation he'd just as soon leave behind.

Probably it'd be what she wanted.

Tantamount to volunteering for a stint as her chipper little deputy.

Or sounding board.

Or ... *bait* ...

Lord only knew what tangled notions Dziurzynski entertained about how to conduct investigations. Whatever askance viewpoint she maintained with regard to her responsibilities, however, it wasn't Gould's job, nor at all his inclination, to assist in ferreting out a criminal.

Why ought it be?

Let alone a murderer of so animalistic a bent!

That the detective-inspector had, however tacitly, suggested he should feel it his humane duty to hazard personal safety in order to uncover a culprit in this poor woman's murder was not only false but, frankly, offensive.

Derelict of her own duty, he'd go so far as to argue.

Wasn't a whit the fault of Glenn Gould how some maniac had cottoned to his iconography, utilized his paraphernalia as window dressing for abject insanity.

If anything, as Dziurzynski herself should attest, this made all the more compelling an argument to keep Glenn Gould from venturing one centimeter nearer the macabre business.

Not, he might remind the court, that he'd any assistance to offer.

Truth be told, Dziurzynski knew where he'd been better than he did ... up until she didn't ... but where she'd veered off the mark, he could pick up the slack ... yes ...

What he meant was, between them, it was well proofed that where he *hadn't* been was hatchet killing his housekeeper.

The detective-inspector's own efforts *definitively* showcased as much.

Yet even after knowing he wasn't party to any mischief, she'd thought fit to spin her kindergarten deceptions!

Justifying her torment of him with talk of *trust*!

Gould had been in his parking space ten minutes.

Subvocalizing many of these thoughts.

Addressing others to rearview or vehicle side mirror.

Took pulse at carotid.

Tried to clear his head.

Nothing about the detective-inspector added up …

… but he'd leave her to heaven.

Could fend for himself.

Careful track of his movements.

With vigilance and the presence of investigators all around, he could hardly *go missing* again.

Of his own volition or that of some lurking madman.

No doubt he was being followed.

Perhaps by multiple parties.

Of varying intents.

If he kept himself under lock and key, it was little matter.

Cops 'n robbers would nullify each other.

… If someone wanted him dead, after all …

Took pulse at carotid.

… so clearly they didn't.

The technician, despite rumpled clothing and unkempt fringe of male pattern baldness, exuded the same air of trim athleticism as always.

Straight away hupped to his feet.

Inquired of Gould had everything worked out yesterday?
Not his place to pry, of course.
Please excuse him if the question was presumptuous.
'Nothing in all the world to apologize for.'
In fact, Gould begged pardon for having been so harried.
'My goodness, I can't even recollect, proper, whether I'd accomplished a jot on the project.'
Gould hoped the dear fellow's time hadn't been entirely wasted.
'*Yes*, by the way ...' he added, offhand '... all is quite well. Kind of you to've followed up.'
It didn't escape Gould that the technician had been spoken to by the police within these twenty-four hours. This innocuous query whether *everything worked out* likely meant to reference such intrigue.
The chap, however, readily took the hint Gould was replying only with regard to how he'd dashed off on some errand and afterward truncated their workday.
'You actually got quite a bit done' the technician remarked, drumming fingers to desk while retrieving documentation.
So how will this work? Gould wondered as he nodded, accepting the logbook being tendered him.
What possibly could've been accomplished in his yesterday's absence?
It was peculiar enough how this individual who'd sat beside him for several weeks was readily behaving as though he'd been present in studio the previous day.
Say it were a ruse ...
Pretend the man was being *instructed* to behave this way or else had been *compensated* to do so ...
Altogether outlandish considerations, but Gould needed to float them rhetorically.
Even then, this documentary was nothing another party could

fake. Not so much as a scrap of. The technician himself, with access to the raw materials, couldn't hope to render a product appropriately.

Not to the extent Gould would fail to immediately see through the counterfeit.

To his understanding, the piece was, and would most likely remain, wholly unique in the realm of radio broadcast.

But the markings in the log, dated yesterday, were all intricate and undoubtedly rendered in Gould's penmanship. The sight of them enough he was almost moved to reconsider the sanctity of his own perceptions.

Was it, in fact, his motel escapade which he ought be doubting? A misfiled dream … a *delusion*?

Lightheaded with limbs turning gummy, he read over certain of *his* scribbles.

Precisely what he, most likely, would've remarked.

Was almost able to glean from the notations alone what the portion of recording would sound like …

… had …

… sounded like …

With a hiccoughed breath, Gould let the log flop to a raised portion of countertop, near at hand.

The technician eyed him with concern but didn't venture comment.

Citing the strain he'd been under all throughout the most recent session, Gould announced he'd like to review, perhaps re-do, any and all work which had been rendered, yesterday.

'Like me to patch it through for a full listen?' the technician offered, all in one motion whisking a stick of chewing gum from shirt pocket to mouth, flicking its wrapper away.

Gould took a stance of consideration.

Arms wrapped so far around himself he felt his fingers might meet between shoulder blades.

Paced with lips puckered in a cartoonish fashion no doubt the technician would think was meant as a joke.

In fact, sensing himself scrutinized, he all at once broke posture. Clapped gloved hands. The knit of the garments muffling the bang he'd meant to seem definitive.

'Yes. Let's see what I've been up to, shall we?'

———————

But Gould wasn't ready.

No … no more could he thoughtlessly inch forward. Glissando automaton here-to-there.

No no … this moment about to be endured was one of genuine *crisis*.

He shouldn't have come to the studio without precautions.

Shouldn't have allowed himself to be led.

Sequestered in the single occupancy restroom, his hands gripped clammy around edges of sink basin.

Light switch left off.

Eyes shut.

So shut the pressure seemed to produce illumination.

Eyes opening to a darker darkness than what closing eyes had caused. Daubs of shapeless green, grey, mustard-yellow drifting along the murk.

He ran the faucet a trickle.

Something in the way the darkness hung resin-like mingled this steady shush and his exhalations, multiplying the sound.

His ears clogging.

As though dozens upon dozens of himself were crammed in the pitch black alongside him.

Each wanting to whisper a thought.

The documentary.

This documentary.

His documentary.

The Idea of North.
Inimitable. Uncanny.
His alone.
Only ever meant to be comprehended by himself.
If *even* by himself.
An extension of his apartness.
The proof he could reach the world, shape it, but never be reached back.
A promise to himself how if he could achieve such remove intellectually, artistically, then, too, he could physically attain its equal.
Gould had conducted the interviews, himself.
People. But no one.
Not to anyone listening.
Five voices.
Nurse. Geographer. Government Official.
Sociologist. Retired Surveyor.
Anonymous instruments.
Had spent the hours, days, weeks, months, clipping excess Ums and Uhs, throat clearings, and stammers from raw recordings. Toiling to fashion each remark into serene, unfaltering melody.
To think of someone else mixing the recording correctly was patently absurd. Would be as though another composer had wandered in, seen a violin, noticed a handful of tempos, volume registers, time-signatures, and from those clues deduced an exact Concerto.
More. More absurd.
As though someone who'd only heard of *Tarantellas* intuited an *Opera* from a Latin libretto left on the seat of public transit.
This experiment was an intricate, contrapuntal composition. There existed no map or index outside Gould's own head. To any other party, the logic and craft of the composition could only be taken for whimsy.

His whimsy.

The ideas overlapped where he deemed overlap, voices kept individual where he so decreed, mixed all in cacophony only *if*, *when*, and *as* it humored him they might.

To a listener, even when experienced in its fullness, the venture might well come across incomprehensible. *Pointless*. No different than idling in a crowded train station. Eavesdropping. This conversation. That. Unable to fully focus or filter out unwanted germs from the surroundings. Connect to any narrative or personality. One's own *thoughts* an intrusion.

So ... *what* did he fear?

That the playback would be *unrecognizable*?

Certainly, he'd not be alarmed by that, as it went without saying.

Someone else had edited, mixed whatever he was about to audit.

The next half-hour would confirm a third party was circling him.

Breathing down his neck.

With aims perverse.

Perhaps *mortal*.

Though, of course, that much was *also* already confirmed.

What did he fear, then?

That the recording would be *flawless*?

' ... despite ... I wasn't here ...' he mumbled.

Mumbled barely.

Pretending the voice originated from the drain he couldn't see in the dark.

Able to convince himself.

Yes. Those words had groaned from down that cold, twisting aperture.

> ... the person that makes the trip ... is going to realize before long he's going to be up against himself ... up against his own sad self ...

The booth coiled around him.
Soundproofed. Windowless.
Serpentine. Slithering.
As vertigo became more pronounced, he pressed palms against cushioned wall to confirm the permanent position of things.
Felt no more anchored.
Indeed, ever further adrift.
The room exhaling toward him as it seemed to inch counter-clockwise, then sinking under his touch like the belly of a snoring canine.
Nausea grew.
The floor swayed lazy toward ceiling, hung, dropped backward, then arced toward ceiling, other end, hung—each lap of its pendulum threatening eventual loop-the-loop.

> ... Can a man get along with himself? In this solitary life ... of the hermit ... the solitary life ... of anyplace where he secludes himself ..?

He'd *heard* this.
Precisely *this*.
Not merely the same phrases while he'd whittled more expansive raw reels down. Nor did he simply recollect the verbiage from transcription.
He recalled this final product.
Word. Syllable. Intonation.
Every volume shift to achieve his desired effect on a listener.
Fade in, fade out in synchrony.
The ingress, egress of each speaker's proposition.
One muffling another or one being scrubbed free.

Audience ears attempting to retain focus on a dwindling speaker's narrative while a new speaker's passion crept in.

Became dominant.

Robbed them of the slightest recall of what they'd fought to remain coupled with.

Yes.

Those tensions he'd aimed to concoct were in evidence.

His architecture.

Meant to turn minds elastic.

Ushered into and out from erudite speech then left without precise memory. Lacking ability to reproduce it any more exactly than they'd be able to a symphonic passage.

> ... You're excluding the rest of the world ... and you've made your own world ... and probably what you'll never know and what nobody else will ever know is whether you're kidding yourself ...

No one else could've rendered this.

Even if he'd loomed over the shoulders of a surrogate while they drew instruction from his lips, they'd fail to execute the subtleties. To elicit or preserve the sounds only he knew to listen for.

> ... Have you really made your peace ... have you made a peace because the only other alternative to the peace is a kind of crack up ..?

Pulse rate freewheeled.

Felt screwed to his chair at the console in booth center.

Arms twined around head.

Face buried in elbow.

Coat fabric clenched between teeth.

> ... it all depends on whether you think you're answering a challenge ... or escaping from yourself ...

No.
He was falling folly to his own psychology.
Convinced of the recording's perfection due to *strain* while honestly *unable* to process its input, digest it *realistically*.

> ... Are you in fact escaping in any real way ... by retreating North ... by retreating in any direction ..?

Flitted eyes from logbook to personal studio journal.
The assorted hieroglyphs there.
Scribbles not even someone who'd studied previous example of could've deciphered. Certainly not enough to've gained fluency in. Duplicated.
Yet every letter, squiggle, dash made by whomever had been present yesterday matched the arcane shorthand.
All of it exactly as he'd have produced.

> ... I think we all create in our own problems ... if we haven't got some to discuss ... we would sooner be kicked than remain unnoticed ...

Tore a scrap of paper free.
Let the airborne speeches sieve through him.
Unconsciously notated as he'd have done during final playthrough, yesterday. Scribbling until the aural excerpt reached terminus.
Sat in silence while he translated his abstract jots to full remarks.
Set paper scrap above the logbook entries made by whomever had been present yesterday.
The two sets of writing were twin.
Down to the misspellings.

'I daresay the once was sufficient, but thank you kindly' Gould purred into his console mic when the technician piped over booth speaker to inquire whether the recording should be run, again.

His attention, meantime, had shifted.

Fixated on a logbook entry indicating he, or whoever had been present in his place, had made a recording, the previous day.

Maude Harbor. Initial.

Quite the sore thumb of a designation.

Never had he labeled raw materials by letter in such pulp magazine manner.

Someone had taken pains to be certain he'd notice these three words.

Their peculiarity.

Maude Harbor. Initial.

He wrote down the words himself.

Held his present rendering to the side of the logged version.

Nodded.

Any disquiet produced by the eerie match-up of his own and this Other's penmanship apparently diminished with each repeat incidence.

Pressed button to patch through to technician.

Lifted finger, immediately.

Tightening hand to fist and drawing in a sharp breath.

Technician chimed in without a beat skipped 'Mister Gould?'

He replied, first without depressing the console button then recalling to do so, how there was nothing.

'I'd had a question. Answered it myself.'

Chuckled at this phrasing.

Absurd how many ways it might technically be accurate, at present.

More germane, though, was how any response to what he'd intended to ask would've been irrelevant.

Say he'd inquired 'Are the materials I recorded yesterday available?'

Most likely, the answer would've been a befuddled *Yes* with undertone of confusion over why it'd be any other way.

If the technician had pled ignorance?

'...*which* materials were those?'

That would simply mean Gould's tormentor had rendered whichever recording without making mention of the task.

Such behavior not particularly odd, at all.

No matter, the entry was explicitly a message directed to Gould, alone.

So far as he figured things, it made sense.

Was ... what he would've done ... were he the one out to get him ...

Odd as such consideration may seem, it was no use ignoring it.

After all, what scheme would've been aided by making the technician aware of whatever this *Maude Harbor* material turned out to be?

The existence of it would be nothing to do with them.

No more than any other piece of material.

All of which Gould would've recorded, logged, and stowed in his secure workroom, personally.

In fact ... now he was curious. Even a bit giddy from a desire to sleuth the matter further. To check the quality of his deductions.

Depressed intercom to ask 'Could you set up the *Maude Harbor* reel for me? I'd like to review it, as well.'

Technician popped on, lickity-split, but only to hew-haw about had Gould left something with him, today?

Or else which *specific* material was it needed be cued?

Something from his *workroom*?

'My mistake, entirely ...' Gould replied, grinning ' ... I'm getting ahead of myself ...'

Could right picture the fella tapping amongst whichever materials were stacked near at hand—surveying the floor, combing counters and cabinet tops, opening locked drawers

'... Don't give it another thought.'

The *Maude Harbor* reel would be inside a locked room.

Shut to a combination-secured cache.

Which meant whoever was playing imposture not only possessed duplicate key to the former but seven-digit code to the latter. Knew to spin dial left all the way twice to begin.

Surely not an impossible set of items and knowledge to acquire ... but only rather clumsy methods, leaving much to random chance, readily occurred to Gould to bring the tasks off. Techniques which flew in the face of the precision so evidently displayed in every aspect else of this intrigue to date.

Jolted dead to a halt at the sight of detective-inspector Dziurzynski lounged in the technician's chair, Gould stammered a moment then went silent.

Perplexed, he watched as she kept fervently occupied with a game of balancing pencils on the edge of her yellow leather pad.

Without altering her focus, she playfully mentioned, in semi-whisper, how much trickier the task was than usual due to whomever sat there 'sharpening the buggers down to all lengths.'

Next breath, she snatched the pencils with free hand.

Set them down.

Slipping pad to blouse pocket, right after.

'Why does he *do* that, do you think?'

Gould suggested she petition the horse's mouth, direct. Explained the technician should be along, presently.

'Such matters are outside the realm of my expertise.'

'Matters of the mysterious human psyche, you mean?'

'I meant, specifically, matters of any man's fetish for different lengthed pencils.'

Dziurzynski raised eyebrows tick-tick, mock lascivious. Then, before Gould could voice his visible disdain over the gesture, broadly announced how she'd chatted up the technician about it, already.

'He gave a *terrific* answer. I even wrote some of it down' she winked, tapping two fingers against pocketed pad. 'What I'd wondered is why *you* thought he did it. But now I know. You've no clue. Or interest. In the length of the fella's ... pencils.'

Curtly insisting he was quite occupied, having already lost a day to recent events, Gould bid the detective-inspector good morning.

'I'm starting off poorly ...' Dziurzynski stood, gesturing Gould to remain '... but it's a defense mechanism. Since girlhood. A *foible*. One of umpteen. I try to dodge out of serious matters by means of affable banter. Hoping enough jabber might spare me having aired what has every right to be aired.'

She came around the counter.

Leaned to it.

Hands tucked to pant pockets.

Rocking ball-of-foot to heel.

Her eyes cast down, timidly.

'I need to sincerely *apologize*, Mister Gould. For my behavior. Yesterday. Last night. Would you allow me this?'

There was absolutely no need. He promised. She'd explained herself to his satisfaction.

'Consider any hatchet buried' he added with a nod.

Blushed when he caught the *faux pas*.

Dziurzynski claimed the opportunity of his embarrassment to press on.

'I take your grace in the spirit it is offered. But, in fact, there *is* need. *Official*. Because you were correct. I went out of bounds.

Those snakes-and-ladders of mine were atrocious. Therefore, I invite you to be present while my actions are reviewed by committee. As the recipient of my unprofessionalism, your being on hand is ideal. After all, what good's my reprimand if only in the abstract? You'd never *know* it happened. Wouldn't *believe* me if I told you. And, Mister Gould, it's of *paramount* importance we maintain open boarders, you and I.'

Entirely uncertain how to proceed, Gould reiterated his forgiveness. Wanted nothing more than to have such business behind him. Assured her that, when requested, he'd continue to make himself available to aid her investigation. Within reason.

'I was somewhat run down when we met, detective-inspector. May've come off as though nothing mattered to me in the world outside my own creature comforts. In actual fact, had my sea-legs been under me we'd never have come at loggerheads.'

Any inquest into her tactics, so far as Gould was concerned, would be irresponsible. A disservice to the victim. If such disciplinary affair was meant for his benefit, he'd have her understand how an undertaking of that variety would be more traumatic to his sensibilities than had any behavior it might redress.

'Please, if possible, have any hearing called off.'

That was swell of him.

Even better if he might put such magnanimity in writing.

Dziurzynski followed Gould into the corridor which lead to the workroom where his materials were stored.

'Remember how we were talking about Paul Henry Lang, that time?'

Gould swallowed. Sniffled. Quizzed his nose in rabbit wrinkle '... *talking* about?'

'Paul Henry Lang ...' Dziurzynski nodded, running one finger along the textured wall as they proceeded, trilling four against it when she said '… your *critic*.'

'Is *that* what we'd settled on his being?' Gould quipped, puff of air out his nose, maintaining affect of jovial rapport.

'As opposed to ..?'

Ignoring the door he'd intended to enter, Gould carried on in the direction of a small cafeteria.

'I recollect a round or two of semantical *jousting*. Though suppose the matter did wind up all the same.'

'Semantics so often wind up so, don't they?'

An awkward silence crept in at cafeteria entrance.

'Lang's *article* …' Gould prompted, holding the door, gesturing Dziurzynski ought go ahead.

'His *article* ..?'

'… I recall our speaking of it …' Gould offered, now standing in place, hands folded patiently.

'Article was kinda of mean—wouldn't you say so, in candor?'

Again huffing amusedly down nose, Gould lifted hands in fatuous gesture of apologia, admitting 'I have, myself, been known to refer to sundry members of the musical press as *hacks*. Smack to their faces. So stones, perhaps, I ought not cast.'

Dziurzynski raised chin to indicate Gould should feel free to walk on. He, however, merely glanced toward the tables, counter, coffee pot, cabinets, then returned his focus to her.

'Would you care for coffee, detective-inspector?'

She made noncommittal waggle of both hands.

'I'd just as soon answer whichever questions before settling in, then. No need to hold you up.'

The main thing she needed was to clarify he didn't know Lang. In a personal way. Never had occasion to communicate. Letters. Telegrams. Telephone.

'Smoke signals, séance …' Gould puckishly rolled hand at the wrist '… no, not at all.'

So absolutely, *positively*, at *no* moment in the *recent* past had the two of them discussed *seeing* each other?

For either professional or personal reasons?

'Zero scheduled assignations you'd know about, Mister Gould?'

'Has ... someone proposed otherwise?'

Dziurzynski squinted.

Touching at the pad in blouse pocket but not moving to withdraw it.

'In fact someone has done.'

But her telling him so didn't ... alter his *own* recollection ... of recent times ... did it?

'Not a jot, detective-inspector. I *distinctly* didn't know the man.'

'Apart from his hackwork?' she winked.

Gould shrugged. Supposed that was fair enough.

'Someone, you were saying, has come under the incorrect impression he and I were ... close?'

At any rate, *someone* had mentioned to *someone else* how Lang had mentioned he'd spoken to Gould *directly* and word of it had found its way to her.

He swayed two fingers upward, conductor's gesture of pause 'In the ... recent past?'

Brought hands together as Dziurzynski confirmed.

Edges of index fingers tapping pursed lips.

Brow set contemplative.

'Seems, according to this individual, Lang was under the impression he was to be interviewed. By you.'

Gould couldn't help his eyes popping wide.

Dziurzynski laughed as her response mimicked his.

'That ... ring a bell, Mister Gould?'

Excuse him. Truth be told, Gould couldn't dream what would possess Lang to utter such a claim.

'Why on Earth would I've been interested in *interviewing* that hack?' he mugged.

Not a whiff of detail on that front, Dziurzynski shrugged back.

Fact had simply come up.

Course of the investigation.

Thought maybe Gould would know.

Seemed not.

Guess nobody did.

'Or *could* ...' the detective-inspector added '...if it hadn't *happened*. Coffee any good here?'

Very astute question. Bravo. First one Dziurzynski had asked herself.

'Especially because I have *enough* going on' she winked pistol pop gesture across table. 'Why couldn't these other cops, as you might've suggested, petition the horse's mouth, direct? You'd make a slick gumshoe, Glenn.'

Flattered, he was sure.

'But why, in actual fact, *haven't* they asked Lang what it's all about?'

'Just a law of physics thing ...' Dziurzynski explained offhand, scratching tip of her nose with nail of her pinkie '... at present, no one can get a bead on the guy.'

Not that anyone had been looking more than since yesterday or so.

'Few phone calls made to smoke him out. Some door-to-door. Flat-foot floogie sort of stuff.'

Such efforts were where the report of the alleged interview appointment had originated.

'So that allegation isn't ... *very* verified?'

'The interview? No. That bit's been confirmed. At least insofar as Lang *thought* one was in the offing. Or better say: it's as verified as could be without, you know, asking him.'

Dziurzynski made a face at her current sip of coffee.

Rubbed her tongue aggressively with three fingers.

Roughed them dry in her hair.

Gould's face must've betrayed more disgust than he'd intended, because she spent the next five minutes explaining a medical condition.

'Membrane of my cheeks act up, sometimes. This time it's my tongue. Suddenly everything'll taste of *radishes*. My doctor said. I had to eat a radish for the first time to believe him.'

Her apologies for not handling the affliction more demurely.

Moved as though to take another sip.

Instead abruptly addressed Gould, direct.

He agreed with her, then, how Lang being in town was a pesky coincidence?

Gould blinked. Left eye squinting, confused.

Had thought no one knew the whereabouts of Lang.

'Not right this minute, nobody does.'

But it was confirmed, with certainty, it'd been he who'd checked into a hotel in town. Few days ago.

'Under his name.'

'Who *else's* name ...' Gould's eyes cocked upward, centered, hands in front of him, palms out in gesture of *Hold on* '... might he have taken the room under?'

Dziurzynski crossed her arms.

Seemingly stumped by what he was asking.

Soon nodded.

Sip of coffee.

'No no no ...' what she'd meant was '... someone *else* might've checked in under *his* name. Similar to how some fella might claim *I'm Glenn Gould* when taking out a room while meantime being anything *but* Glenn Gould! Or, for that matter, how another fella who *is* Glenn Gould might up and check in some place but claim they're very much *not* Glenn Gould, at all.'

People played all manner of pranks at hotels.

'For chuckles' is what she thought.

In this case though: Paul Henry Lang.

Without a doubt.

Photo verified by various professional folks.

Telephone calls logged from his room.

Local and to pals back home.

'He was very excited about it all, though still in the dark to specifics.'

'I have a very good understanding how he felt …' Gould meekly sighed, trilling fingertips of one hand on gloved back of the other.

Dziurzynski leaned in, adopting a tone of confidentiality.

'You find this … *exciting*?'

'Understand about being *in the dark*' Gould wryly answered her after letting a purposeful beat elapse.

Elbows on table, fingers laced, chin rubbing side-to-side over them Dziurzynski said now she felt in the same boat, too.

'What do you mean *in the dark*, Mister Gould?'

Pressing at left temple with thumb knuckle, other four fingers spread wide, Gould admitted he'd wound up in the weeds.

'Why … was anyone … trying to locate Paul Henry Lang?'

See?

There's another crackerjack question.

At this rate Dziurzynski was apt to think he had aims on her job.

It'd been a nearly identical scene.

   Hotel suite.

   Record player.

Goldberg Variations on repeat.

There'd even been a tooth on the carpet. Evidence indicating the mouth it'd come from had been forcibly bashed into the sharp corner of the mantle. Gums blunted viciously into marble a handful of times.

Hatchet was on hand, as well.

Thing left a gory mess.

Flesh and coagulate caking it, blade-sharp to flat-face to leather-grip handle.

The rooms were a horror-show, stem-to-stern.

Blood every conceivable place.

Walls. Ceiling. Bedcovers. Carpet. Doorknobs.

All revealing quite unambiguously how the victim had been butchered with leisure.

Which isn't to say the violence had lacked marked ferocity.

The initial impression of the crime scene all but demanded a description of *feral*.

Rabid.

Venomous.

Victim must've attempted to evade attacker.

The placement of certain objects indicated they'd been throw with unrepentant force. Others likely shattered when the fireplace poker had been swung in defense. Tears to an overturned armchair's upholstery in conjunction with flecks from chips to the tile floor and a gouge to the dining table's rosewood found embedded in the object's wrought iron attested to at least one desperate bout of *Stay away!*

Also?

Must've eventually crawled. In vain hope of survival.

Certain smears, poolings of blood, and towels plump with sanguine dampness discovered in the washroom suggested at one point the victim tried to close themself in.

Unsuccessfully. Obviously.

More than apparent they'd been dragged out.
Wriggling fingerprints in crimson.
Similar, also, to the housekeeper affair:
Despite the perverse abandon on display, it was abundantly clear that orchestral precision had been applied during the massacre's preparation.
Why no reports of anything having been overheard?
Judging from blood spatter and residue of flesh torn from the gums, there'd been trauma enough to inflict substantive damage to the victim's oral and nasal cavities.
Pretend the attacker had got the drop on the victim, entirely by surprise—suppose the jaw had been broken, at least, during an initial assault, poor soul unable scream out for aid?
This didn't mean the overall damage to the room would've produced any less preposterous a clamor that it must have.
Here's what, though:
Victim's suite was situated top floor, corner.
Two rooms next to it, three rooms across the hall, three rooms below it, same side, three rooms below it, across hall—*none* of them housed a *single* occupant at the time the violence transpired.
By chance?
Not hardly.
Whole batch had been *reserved*.
One week prior.
For several days.
Paid in full.
Cashier's check.
All arrangements conducted over the telephone.
Payment delivered via courier.
How about that, eh?
Names of who'd be staying in each room had been supplied. Hotel had prepped keys. Whole shebang. There'd even been instructions given how the occupants weren't *of a group* so had no

business knowing about each other, were any of them to make inquiries.

Needless to say, no other party assigned to the eleven excess rooms had ever arrived.

Quite the song and dance to get Paul Henry Lang, illustrious critic, cordoned off!

But for the detective-inspector's money, the real gem was how the crime scene could've remained inviolate, even yet.

The unredeemed rooms stood vacant.

Instructions the occupant of the victim's not be disturbed by cleaning staff.

Instructions which, by all indication, had been delivered *post-incident*. In a call *from* the victim's suite.

But the hotel had been alerted of the fiasco anonymously.

Authorities in that jurisdiction summoned to Lang's suite.

Almost precisely as the housekeeper crime scene at Gould's hotel was first being discovered.

'If not for having to show respect over how someone's most likely dead ...' Dziurzynski confessed, *sotto voce* '... I'd call the entire production *virtuosic*.'

Gould had grown visibly tense during what he'd bitterly dubbed Dziurzynski's *one-man-show*.

Seethed, internal.

Each time cafeteria door opened would briefly bare teeth.

Accompaniment to slight inward hisses.

Tighten his posture.

Shoulders curling as arms crossed.

To anyone watching, it might seem as though he were shyly attempting to fold himself in half. Perhaps in half, twice over.

'Ought we be …' he finally ticked head, wide-eyed, in the direction of an arriving party '… airing country matters … *corum populo*?'

Dziurzynski had previously lowered her voice. Twice. Brought chair around to first sit side-by-side with Gould, now straddled the thing, turned reverse, craning forward overtop its backrest, semi-diagonal to him.

All, he assumed she'd claim, to be certain what was between them couldn't be readily eavesdropped.

The overall effect, however, especially as the room continued to crowd, was the two of them had become *increasingly* conspicuous.

Disguising it as a scratch to his eyebrow, Gould made casual gesture meant to indicate he felt they ought vacate the room.

Presently.

Please.

To this, the detective-inspector rolled her eyes in a chummy way. Seemed genuinely bothered, herself, how yet another person was entering.

Muttered something indistinct.

Did a nudge-nudge motion with her head.

Stood quite suddenly.

In half-dozen long strides was to the cafeteria door.

Through it.

Taken off guard at the abruptness of this departure, Gould hesitated over what to do with the Styrofoam coffee cup still on the table.

Finally left it.

Stood.

Head down, slunked toward the door.

Nauseous.

Aggrieved.

Felt every gathered eye poking at him like hypodermics.

The moment he joined Dziurzynski in corridor she, seeming already mid-statement, said 'Another word for it all might be *barbarous* ...' and held up both index fingers '... or else *bestial* ...' ticking them left-right left-right '... or even *subhuman* ...' a bit slower each time until Gould caught on she was asking which way they should go '... or ... had I already said *barbarous*?'

'For privacy ...' he waffled after agreeing *barbarous* was a fine word '... it might be best we cloister ...' then made a testy gesture of both hands in the direction they'd previously come.

'To get at the heart of your question ...' the detective-inspector stage-whispered as they walked, Gould certain she was dragging her feet despite making truncated chops of the air between then with hands and wrists as though in a hurry ' ... nobody would have *thought* to look for Lang if not for all that brouhaha. Even now, we wouldn't need to be looking. If only his *body* had just *been there* in the suite. As it stands ...' puffed one cheek, let out a pop of breath '... there's not a *bit* of it. So we gotta see *Why is that?*'

Gould nodded.

Reluctantly entering key into lock of his workroom.

'Of course there was the *tooth* ...' Dziurzynski added with a shrug as the door opened to damp sounding swish of breaking suction '... but we can't just assume lineage of teeth we find on the carpet.'

Yes. Gould could quite imagine the unruly minutia of police work.

'No doubt even with dental pedigree established, you'd prefer arms and legs. *The more the merrier*, I surmise is the departmental motto.'

Dziurzynski laughed.

Unselfconscious.

Even girlish.

Whisked yellow pad out, snatched pen from a container nearby.

'If I *credit* you …' she giggled, not looking up while making her grinning scribble '… can I *use* that one?'

The detective-inspector held hands politely behind back. One gripped round wrist of the other. This other softly fisted. Slowly swaying side-to-side. A bit like a kitten tail.

Which matched well her inspection of various controls on the primary panel of the reel-to-reel recorder in Gould's private workroom.

Nose all but touched one dial.

Seemed ready to gently brush forehead or cheek along a series of switches.

Peppering innocent queries about how the 'contraption' did 'whatever it does' between talk of the Lang crime scene.

Gould felt almost convinced she was more interested in the process of audio editing than anything attached to her official duties.

Nevertheless was wary.

Puzzling over why he'd be made privy to so many specifics.

Maintained calm.

Let her continue as she pleased.

Waiting out the instant he might, without brusqueness, explain that, while he appreciated the updates, it was time for Dziurzynski to go.

Absolutely, he agreed how the lack of any corpse was a profound curiosity.

'Literally every *inch* of the suite has been examined to *exhaustion*?'

Including the ceiling.

With a fine-toothed comb.

In case some portion had been removed then redone.

Every last preposterous notion had been given due diligence!

'After all, there'd quite recently been a situation wherein the killer of several individuals had stowed bodies inside of walls. Smashed in the original facades. Redone masonry. Plastered. Painted. Coppers are on high alert for such chicanery now, you can rest assured. Real egg on our face if someone *else* got away with that, Mister Gould.'

'But the working hypothesis *is* that Lang was murdered?'

Dziurzynski huffed. Took a seat. Petulant.

'Even taking that as read, the absence of carcass changes the *nature* of what's being investigated.'

It's one thing to rent a bunch of rooms with aims on ensuring privacy during the commission of a homicide.

But to cart a body, which must've been in a state of unthinkable gore, out of a stately hotel?

Even in the middle of the night that's harder than it sounds!

Not impossible, of course.

'Could be ruthlessly *dismembered*. Portions wrapped in plastic. Plastic bundled in duct tape. Several packets at-a-time enclosed inside articles of luggage. Ferried to an automobile.'

Problem there?

No one had exited the hotel through the *main* doors in the wee, wee hours.

No cars in or out of hotel garage during the night.

'Likewise no mysterious persons sighted by dutiful watchman loading up an already parked car, van, what-have-you.'

In fact, all authorized vehicles, hotel-owned, rental, or guest-brought, remained present and accounted for.

Meaning?

A third-party would have to've driven their own vehicle, parked off site.

Two side doors to the premises theoretically could've served as entrance and exit.

But with such scant window of time wherein a lulling vehicle outside was *unlikely* to be witnessed it rather beggared belief.

'So let's say someone decided to *do* all that ... *why* did they? If the idea was to *vanish* the body, it'd be a *zillion* times easier to lure Lang someplace *else*. Slice him up a trick. Lug him into a truck. Drive out of the area. Dump his leftovers off some anonymous pier. Right?'

Gould didn't register immediately how this was a direct query to which the detective-inspector expected his reply.

Eventually, clearing his throat first, concurred.

'Indeed, it seems a lot of effort had already gone into, as you say, *ensnaring* the man. Making him a ... sitting duck, so far as things go. I imagine it'd make sense to've called it day. Leave him there. If the idea behind summoning him, in the first place, was nothing more than wanting, if you'll pardon another colloquial, to rub him out. Top floor of a hotel seems, indeed, the *worst* real estate imaginable from which to alight with a cadaver.'

'Well exactly. Thank you. You always put matters much more *eloquently* than I ever could.'

'Let me float you a *For Example* ...' Dziurzynski said with sudden animation, finger snaps and fist percussive into her palm after each. 'The reason there's no corpse? No one's been *killed*. Or even *injured*. Not *Lang*, not *nobody*.'

Gould perked to attention briefly from the inertia of her enthusiasm. But as he processed the statements, his brow furrowed. Posture wilting.

'Are you meaning to say ...' eyes narrowed, sting of vexation '... you've been winding me up here, *again*?'

The detective-inspector froze.

Percussive clunk of heel hitting tile seemed to echo from the sudden silence between them.

To all appearances she felt blindsided. Wounded. The unchecked vulnerability in her expression so affecting Gould took an awkward swallow. Mind backtracked. Uncertain which words had just come from his mouth.

'I've apologized to you in good faith, Mister Gould. Invited sanctions on myself. Which I'd understood you to've graciously deemed unnecessary. If there remains some point you're yet begrudging me, it might be best we do proceed with having your grievance aired in front of—'

'Detective-inspector, you misunderstand ...' Gould interjected, gloved hands clasped, gentle circular motions at chest to portray the heartfelt nature of his address '... or rather I misunderstood. You made it distinct how you were positing a rhetorical. I regrettably took wrong-headed affront.'

Dziurzynski's only aim was they become *simpatico*. Had been conversing in candor so there might develop a trustful rapport between them.

Yes. Gould knew this.

Again begged her patience.

The entire affair was a lot to digest, let alone riff on *in abstracto*.

She looked sincerely on the verge of shutting their conversation down.

Gould, as a somewhat ham-handed olive-branch, diverting their interaction to discussing, in pedantic detail, a certain dial on the reel-to-reel console she'd previously inquired about.

This seemed to have the desired effect of re-stabilization.

Not a moment after delightedly thanking him for the fascinating information, Dziurzynski returned to her postulate.

Gould positive she spoke in the exact tone of voice as before the snafu.

Stood in the precise posture.

Began with exact hand gesture.

As though a recording rewound.

'... *Lang*, not *nobody*. The room, the curious circumstances under how it was rented, entirely a blind alley. To what purpose? In order we'll conclude *privacy was needed for the murder*. However: this same privacy could've been required in aid of wrecking the joint up, merely. Could've been Lang himself had done so!' she added with victorious clap, as though the notion had struck her spontaneously.

To illustrate his engagement, cautious not to sound derisive but rather an attentive participant in her ... *game*? ... Gould raised hand, calling for a point-of-order.

Hadn't the detective-inspector described an 'excess of viscera as well as sundry signs of physical violence?'

Seeming suddenly quite fond of the notion, Dziurzynski replied how 'Any blood could've been *planted* by Lang, too—why not?'

Collected by way of self-inflicted laceration or via syringe over whichever period of time.

Slathered, spritzed, towels sopped swampy with it at the hotel.

'Easy trick, really.'

Apart from the B-movie scope of the bloodshed, what was there?

One single tooth?

Flesh from gums smeared to the mantle?

'Listen to this: self-inflicted, as well! Coulda cut out a portion of his mouth under *controlled* conditions. In order to mash it against the marble. Meanwhile, knew next day he'd bludgeon your housekeeper's teeth out. Therefore, when *his* crime scene was discovered it'd seem a no-brainer whoever'd done the poor girl's slaying had done the same things to him.'

Noting Gould's expression of respectful incredulity, Dziurzynski held up her hands, pumping palms in his direction.

'Okay okay ...'

Admitted it was a lot to suppose.

'Though I once worked a case ...' she sniffed with a hint of defensiveness '... where it turned out a woman'd cut off her own arm with a table saw. Right above the elbow. In order to have a stray dog dig it up. Left an impression, I guess.'

'Many of my colleagues ...' Dziurzynski explained, leaning back, careful her elbows weren't at risk of disrupting dials, knobs, switches on any of Gould's equipment '... believe murder a *simple* proposition. The *likeliest* line from A-to-Z a cinch to nab them their culprit. I say? *Way wrong*. Murder is gonna be the most *convoluted* kerfuffle imaginable. Not even imaginable! A happenstance so outside typical human experience the truth of any instance would sound farcical if laid out by barristers to jury-folk. Thus, most prefer to consider it commonplace. Many in the *intelligentsia* go so far as to posit how all of us are a mood or mitigating factor away from pressing snubnose to some stranger's ribs ... *Blam*! Even you and I, Mister Gould!'

But *Gould* wasn't about to be a killer, right?

Well, neither was *she*.

Not for love nor money.

The both of them, therefore, exemplary of her point.

'You think you've got your villain in the bag?' she continued, leaning forward, address quite emphatic, accented with pointed fingers, ticks of head. 'Reckon their motives, chain of events, evidence all makes sense? I *promise*, it's only on account some *actual* villain took pains to make it *seem* so. Weaponized this phony-baloney of there being mere thin line between *Civilized* and *Savage*. Killed for whichever goblin rationale. Got away with it by orchestrating a fairy-tale.'

All this collecting alibi and forensic table-scraps?

These hours compiling timelines and pouring through bank records?

Learning when a telephone was dialed?

Whose signature it is on something?

'The more ironclad the case against a suspect …' Dziurzynski clapped her hands definitively '… the more *uneasy* I become. Hook-line most buy in that Phil strangled Herbert because Herbert tried it on with the missus, for example. But does that make *any* kind of sense to you, Mister Gould? Killing someone for the reasons we *say* people do?'

Chuckling, Gould rubbed his hands, weighing the question judiciously.

'It's quite a vision, detective-inspector' he eventually allowed. 'Nary a guilty feather among the jailbirds, eh?'

'Oh, the prisons, I think, are ninety-percent populated with unwitting patsies' she nodded, no nonsense. 'Meantime? The streets are awash with the self-congratulatory guilty. See over there?' she gestured randomly. Stuck out her tongue when Gould actually looked. 'I know there's no one, *literally*—but if there was?' She paused. Nodded for emphasis. 'God only knows what they'd be hiding.'

'I can't help but feel my crank being given a jolly fine yank, detective-inspector. Surmise your tongue will poke like a gopher through either cheek, any moment. Yet, at risk of looking dunce, may I inquire … what about *confessions*?'

'Mister Gould …' she *tsk-tsk*ed with her fingers '… a confession is far easier to *manufacture* than a murderer is to *catch*, wouldn't you think?'

She winked.

'Besides which, the first thing any investigator worth their salt has to do is look at confessions askance. If we're to believe someone *dunnit* simply because they say so … aren't we bound to believe, with equal vigor, the person who passionately says *wasn't me*? Confessed to or not, we have to go prove it! Using the confession as *blueprint* ...' she glibly shrugged '... usually the confession's all we'll try to prove.'

Those prisons they'd spoken of were filled to the brim with people bellowing *I'm innocent*.

Many such bellowers had already confessed.

Since then, recanted.

Other confessions came after years of bellowing their opposite.

In the end, waters too muddy to much wallow in.

'No, Mister Gould ...' Dziurzynski said through a yawn, standing, twisting to work out a kink in her back '... it's best to believe people capable of far worse than could ever be *proven*.'

Despite being presented a perfect curtain line to bring amicable closure to their *tete-a-tete*, Gould felt himself irresistibly drawn in. Intrigue over Dziurzynski's flagrant, even alarming, unorthodoxy percolated the way it might've were she an interviewee who'd chanced upon some captivating tangent.

'In circumstances such as present with Lang ...' he found himself prompting '... how *does* an investigation find footing? Through the aperture of your espoused philosophy, there seem insurmountable roadblocks.'

Well, if she had it her way, she'd spin a culprit from whole cloth. Cobble up whatever evidence would snare them.

'That's unrealistic, though. Can't arrest the Boogey Man based on gossamer.'

But happy chance might have whichever scenario she'd invent intersect with some person the public would acceptably incarcerate.

'I'd feel *glum* about it, of course. Get a rotten heart every time I go ruining some innocent's life.'

Next best thing?

She'd pick someone directly in orbit of the crime to suspect. Work tirelessly to run them to ground.

'Think something along the lines of my previous hijinks with you.'

Better still?

Select a party only *tangentially* associated to events.

Turn over every stone possible to root out some reason they'd be responsible.

Best yet?

'There's always the chance the victim's behind it.'

'Lang, for example' Gould nodded, the detective-inspector clicking finger-gun in assent. 'You do ... think there exist such things as *legitimately* guilty parties, correct? Or do you assert any arrest you've ever made is *illegitimate*?'

Dziurzynski twisted lips in a flirty pout, Gould chuckling despite himself.

'Or perhaps better say ...' he grinned, tapping thumbs together while working to rephrase '... assert that such arrests were only *acceptably* legitimate.'

It's more complex than Gould was steering it, she began after a considered bit of hesitancy.

'Have I ever arrested the *perpetrator* of a murder? Loads of times. But that just means George stuck his sister's penknife in the gizzard of Billy. Too bad, so sad. George is in prison. For that crime. Is *specifically* guilty of it. But that's *never* the *whole* story, I promise. *Somebody* ...' Dziurzynski made a tentative wobble of one hand '... let's call them *Somebody Else*, to make them distinct ...' she waited for Gould to nod indication he was with her '... *Somebody Else* got away with that same crime. *And* got away with *getting-away-with-it*.'

Gould ruminated on Dziurzynski's remarks.

Sincerely contemplative.

Dziurzynski held soft eye contact.

Tilting head slowly left-to-right.

'Which is why ...' she barreled ahead exactly as Gould took a breath, addressing himself to motion in preparation to put forward a follow-up '... questions about *alibis* are so abhorrently tiresome to me. *Where-were-you-when? Who-saw-you-there?* Fat lotta good the answers do me.'

'You disregard alibis as you dismiss confessions?'

Again, Dziurzynski made non-committal finger waggles.

Clucked tongue to teeth while probing for a way to explain.

'Here's an easy example ...' she finally ventured, leaning forward severely, arms limply dangled between legs spread wide '... *you* have an alibi for the *housekeeper. Probably* one for *Lang.* But so *what*? It's like I've said since being a kid on the playground and knew some little cuss had filched my strawberry eraser. All their alibi meant was now I had to think *Who might their confederate be?* Nowadays? I go the extra mile of extending that to *Who might they be confederate to?*'

'I imagine ...' Gould reflexively cut in, able only barely to maintain his placid demeanor '... you'll just about *here* want to know whether I *do* have an alibi for the time of Lang's ...' he briefly pursed lips, deciding which phrase might be most apropos '... *possible disappearance*?'

'It's not so much me asking, please understand ...' she now slouched back, folding hands in lap, crossing legs ladylike '... so much as it has to be asked.'

On the telephone. In conversation. With a dear friend. A customary thing. Spoke for nearly seven hours. Eight in the evening until roughly three.

Would she like the name and contact number, now?

Wouldn't be necessary.

Those particulars had already been verified.

Exactly as he'd so graciously detailed.
His hotel's phone records proved he'd initiated such call.
When it ended.
Dziurzynski had personally rung the party he'd dialed to confirm the gab session genuine.

'Chap couldn't *exactly* alibi you ...' she added, unable to suppress her grin '... as he admits he'd fallen *asleep* for a lengthy chunk of your ... *discourse*. However ...' she continued, at a bit of a rush, as though regretting how Gould might've been embarrassed by her prior remark '... you'd been yakking away when the follow regained consciousness.'

Finale of the call was confirmed conversational.
Everything tracked.
What she needed now was for Gould to listen to her, in dread earnest.

As much as she'd thoroughly enjoyed meandering down some esoteric side roads with him, she was duty bound to soberly emphasize how, in actuality, she felt increasingly confident that whoever was behind this murder and mischief had endgame aims on him. In point of fact, felt uneasy how the timelines of both incidents currently under investigation lined up flush to clear him of all involvement.

'Almost as though the perpetrator wanted there to be *specifically* no doubt it *hadn't* been you ... but nonetheless wanted you tethered into the thick of things.'

The Lang scene being discovered in tandem with the housekeeper scene, despite a full twenty-four hours between commission of the crimes, was a hyper-particular showcase of prowess.

'It's too much to entertain a snowball's chance there won't be more to come. Either further *past* murders await their reveal or *new* victims are being actively corralled.'

Let her be blunt:
Gould was still alive. On purpose.

This didn't mean his purpose was to remain so.

'If what I believe is correct, Mister Gould, there is someone very dangerous standing behind you, in the dark, breathing down your neck. They've proven themselves not only vicious, but *calculating*. Patient. In one way or another, however unwittingly, you are their link to whichever macabre impulse fuels this bloodthirsty endeavor.'

Let Gould answer her. Equally blunt:

This had all certainly occurred to him.

Without professional aid.

What was Dziurzynski suggesting?

He disappear, himself?

That hardly made sense, did it?

'My doing so may be exactly the plan of this madman. In which case, in their eyes, such action leaves me more vulnerable to whichever their next steps would be.'

Or?

Fleeing would accomplish *nothing*. Except having the monster pause. Waiting until Gould resurfaced to resurface, as well.

'By which time my life and livelihood will have been sorely molested. With me found in no less dangerous a position than now.'

Dziurzynski nodded.

'There needs no ghost come from the grave to tell me I am under police protection, at present—yes, no?'

Dziurzynski nodded.

Gould gathered breath.

Wet his lips before continuing.

'I will be *here*. I shall be at my *hotel*. I'll drive the same route *betwixt*. Daily. I feel my safety could in no other circumstance be more finely vouchsafed.'

Again, Dziurzynski nodded.

Stood.

'You will, of course, keep me privy to any intrusive developments? However slight. So much as a crumb on your bedspread from a cracker you don't quite recall?'

'I will *continue* to do so, detective-inspector, most certainly' he replied. As though answering exactly her question.

Gould stared at himself.
 Toilet mirror.
 Closed eyes.
 Opened them.
 'Well, Glenn …'
 Undid blood-pressure cuff.
 '… you had *every* opportunity …'
 Jotted down the reading.
 '… to *ask* those questions …'
 Popped *Clonidine, Septra*.
 '… and she *offered* quite flatly …'
 Popped *Valium, Fiorinal*.
 '… to be presented for disciplinary charges …'
 Popped *Thorazine*.
 '… but you opted *instead* to play the neighborhood gallant …'
 Jotted down which pills he'd swallowed
 '… so perhaps it's your *own* motivations …'
 Closed notebook, twisted green rubber band three times around, pinned pen snuggly beneath it
 '… you should be *questioning*.'
 Closed eyes.
 Opened them.
 Stared at himself. Toilet mirror.
 Why had he closed his notebook?
 Hadn't he meant to compile a list of questions he'd neglected to put to Dziurzynski?

Of statements she'd made.
Which'd seemed pointed. Peculiar.
Been left unexplored. Unchallenged.
Stared at himself. Toilet mirror.
Which questions had he neglected to ask?
Couldn't focus enough to recall any, specifically.
But felt a dozen squirming behind his eyes.
Nor could he recall which phrasings had stuck out to him.
Spoken as though to bait reaction.
The bizarre manner in which the detective-inspector had chosen to present him information resulted in only confusion when looked back upon.
Almost reverse chronological, so far as importance, hadn't it seemed?
Overlapping of conjecture and fact.
Breaking interrogatory flow with miscellany and little spats.
Their interactions coalesced into a sort of mental sludge.
Whose signature it was on a thing …
He nodded, lips tight, lower curled under upper, warm breath blowing down over his chin.
That was something she'd said.
Signature on *what*?
Or had that only been mentioned during one of her digressive extrapolations?
Shook his face.
Insidious how she'd materialized out of thin air.
Precisely when he'd been jolted by the perfection of yesterday's edit. The notations left in logbook. The *Maude Harbor* reel.
Conniving, the methods by which she'd sequestered him in the cafeteria.
Surrounded by gawkers.
Pummeled with asinine conjectures.
His last nerve worked raw.

Then maneuvered to transgress his workroom.

Plopped herself dab in front of the safe-box some unseen hand was maneuvering him toward …

Though … Dziurzynski … couldn't have done any of that *on purpose*. Possessed no understanding how the recording had unsettled him. Not aware how the penmanship in the log had deepened an in-progress dread. Couldn't even have surmised he'd grow queasy at the possibility of a crowd peeking ears into his affairs.

'It was *you* who walked her to the cafeteria, Glenn …' he heard himself calmly explaining '… then into the workroom. All she'd done was seek you out to apologize. Invite you to initiate formal proceedings based on your obvious anger, last night.'

No. That's wrong.

Clenched eyes shut. Hard.

Slowly opened them.

Her apologetics were a *feint*.

Obviously she'd been intent on bringing up the business with Lang.

Dogged his heels to buttonhole him with it.

'No …' he stared at himself mouthing the word '… no …'

If he'd maintained his honest affront, consented to, or indeed *insisted* on, the proposed disciplinary committee, she'd have left.

Let him be.

'You *invited* her to tell you about Lang' he watched himself say.

'To *keep talking to me* …' he corrected the reflected version of himself '… about *whatever she decided to*. I didn't know it'd be about Lang. No idea there'd be anything *about* Lang it *might* be.'

Even if true, that hardly challenged his reflection's thesis, did it?

He'd had ready chance to deflect the detective-inspector.

Instead, entreated her to stay.

Plied her with questions.
Choked down his bile at times to preserve cordiality.
As though he'd ... wanted to *know* ...
... what *she* knew ...
... what she was *doing* ...
... with the *investigation* ...
'But why would you want that, Glenn?' he had his reflection ask.
Wanted to retort 'I wouldn't.'
But found himself simply still there.
Staring.

———————

Yet unable to clear the specter of Dziurzynski's intrusion from mind enough to confront the pressing enigma of the *Maude Harbor* reel, Gould strode down the corridor toward the technician's room.
Was greeted warmly when he entered.
Did he have something to patch through to the booth, already?
'No, thank you.'
Just a question. Nothing business related.
The technician had spoken to the detective-inspector, correct?
'What time had she arrived?'
The technician wasn't certain it'd been a detective-inspector he'd chatted with, *per se*. Guy had said 'officer' to the best of his recollection.
'His card's just here' he added, briskly snapping something from where it'd been taped to a rise of the counter's interior.
Divining the technician was referencing his police interview the previous day, Gould corrected him.
'I meant just *now*. This morning. Dziurzynski. A *woman*.'
The technician's face scrunched quizzical.

Let slow breath through teeth as though regretting to say so but ... no, he hadn't spoken to police since yesterday. If someone had popped in so far this morning, it must've been while Gould had been finishing off in the booth.

'I stepped out, myself ...' the technician shrugged '... just after you'd told me you were wrapping up.'

Gone all of twenty minutes.

Booth had been vacant upon his return.

Betraying as little suspicion as he could manage, Gould suggested perhaps they'd had words when she'd departed.

Only quite recently.

Hadn't he seen a woman come back through?

'She'd have been dressed quite ...' he rolled his hand, struck for appropriate descriptor '... *spiffily*.'

Wait ... did Gould mean the woman who'd popped in *yesterday*?

'While you were out?'

If so, the technician didn't recall her having mentioned she'd anything to do with the police.

'I thought she said she'd meet you in front. Told her you'd not arrived back from an errand, but I expected you.'

Gould nodded at this.

Betraying no sign of hesitancy or confusion.

Then, upon the technician assuring him no one apart from a colleague or two had come around *today*, thanked the man kindly.

Excused himself back into the corridor.

Fuming as he shouldered through the door to his workroom.

Went without saying there'd been no flirtatious chit-chat regarding the technician's pencil length. Only another nonsense game of play pretend.

Was Dziurzynski *pathological* in her penchant for bald-face deception, from matters trivial to those of immense consequence?

Though ... wasn't that going a touch far?

What ... had actually *happened*?

Gould clenched his jaw against having to admit going off half-cocked.

Dziurzynski had claimed she'd traded words with the technician. But only in response to Gould getting testy with her.

And ... so what?

Innocuous, at worst.

Plus, afterward she'd apologized for the ... bad habit of being overly affable in certain circumstance. Immediately on the heels of that had apologized for the previous night's far more egregious behaviors.

Apologies he'd accepted.

Quite disingenuously.

Dishonestly.

Not that he needed to be held to the same standard as a detective-inspector.

Regardless: was he to believe she'd coincidentally arrived during the miniscule interval the technician had been absent?

Had decided to exit the building not the same way she'd entered?

It wasn't as though the door leading from corridor into and out from the technician's area could be mistaken. Upon her departure from Gould's workroom it was meters away.

Very end of the hall.

Orange.

No mistaking it.

Certainly she may've started down toward the cafeteria, realized it after a moment, decided to seek an exit further on.

There were exits further on, after all.

'Of course I've considered that!' he snapped at the empty air.

It simply seemed she'd ... *conspicuously* ... decided to arrive and depart as though a wraith.

'Many people had been in the cafeteria, Glenn. You, yourself, remarked how she'd gone out of her way to secure their attentions with various antics.'

'Yes …' he nodded, absolutely in agreement '… that's very true …'

Sat silently, a moment.

Then heard himself saying '… might I venture for *clarification's* sake …'

Sat silently, another moment.

'… were you … suggesting you'd been talking to *yourself*, that whole time?'

Pouring through bank records.

That'd been verbiage which'd raised alarm.

Not that he was pleased with himself for choosing the expression *raised alarm*.

Because it's not what he meant.

Pouring through bank records.

Was verbiage he'd *taken note of*, is all.

Served to reason this'd been uttered in relation to the curious provisions undertaken to assure Lang's suite would remain perversely isolated.

To wit: if the suites in Lang's hotel were, indeed, comparable to those in Gould's, eleven of them paid for in advance and for multiple days would require a rather plump sum.

Cashier's check.

Not traceable, he didn't think.

Though not *not-traceable*, he couldn't help but reason.

For purposes of law enforcement.

There must exist methods of ferreting out where a check had been cut.

Interview any individuals who'd been on duty at the time of transaction.

There's your description of someone to suspect.

Any nitwit would tell anyone listening how Lang's assailant-cum-executioner wouldn't have sidled up to his local bank teller, plonked cash monies down.

Would've solicited some patsy.

Likely unaware of what horror the milquetoast transaction was attache to.

Hence Dziurzynski's loaded talk about confederates.

Shoehorned in quite inelegantly, to his recollection.

What would remain to uncover?

Where the money *originated*.

Once a party had been found to suspect, it'd be incumbent upon an investigator to *pour through their bank records*. Hoping to espy some flagrantly large withdrawal or a clever series of small ones adding up to the bulk.

'You'd make a slick gumshoe, Glenn' he couldn't help grin.

Recalling that quote, wondered how closely he'd hemmed to the detective-inspector's ideal script.

Crumb-to-crumb she'd ushered him.

To lead him, now, thought-to-thought.

Coerce him into thinking this way.

Criminally.

Utterly scandalous, her machinations.

Dziurzynski wanted him to feel compelled to check his financial records. Something he'd obviously have every right to do.

Once he had?

She'd wend some conversation around to inquiring why he'd gone to the bank.

Wasn't such trip outside his plan of only venturing from hotel to studio and back?

Nothing *suspicious* had prompted the break in pattern, she'd hope.

Or if, instead, he gave the bank a ring?

She'd claim there'd been reason to have requisitioned details concerning his hotel phone activity.

Or else the phone here in studio.

Had remarked the call.

He hadn't noticed anything *fishy*, had he?

It was well documented by now the detective-inspector's reasons for prying had no need to make *rational* sense. He'd all but personally signed off on her doing as she pleased. In the name of Justice.

Why would he suddenly clam up about giving her a peek at his ledgers if she insisted it would aid the investigation?

After all, he'd forgiven her for posing telephonically as the very murderer she was pursuing!

Loathe to admit such to himself as he may be, Gould's present trouble was his own desire to check his finances.

Of course he hadn't disposed of Lang's carcass nor butchered a housekeeper ... but neither had he driven to a motel, had gossip with a waitress, or been in this very studio the previous day.

His car had been utilized, though.

His hotel suite entered.

Not at all unreasonable to presume someone could've been accessing his accounts. Doctoring them up how they pleased.

'Someone who *looks* like you?' he mumbled, reflexively trying to dismiss the notion with a snort. '*Sounds* like you? *Thinks* like you?'

How easy would it be, exactly, to impersonate Glenn Gould?

A costume. Handful of mannerisms.

Would that be all it took?

Did his idiosyncrasies and the very elements which fashioned him so inimitable allow him to be, in the eyes of the general public, recreated, slapdash?

The *Maude Harbor* reel was markedly unimposing.

At most, the slight spool could contain fifteen minutes worth of audio.

Arranged to the player, headphones cupped over ears, Gould toggled the switch for playback.

Wanted this over.

Done.

Behind him.

As leaving the matter ignored would no more end it than would his pressing ahead, he'd run out of methods to hesitate.

Slight hiss of emptiness.

Nearly a minute.

Gould's eyes during that time flitting to the device controls.

Searching out defect.

Then, abruptly, a voice.

Distorted, loud, indecipherable, mouth too near the microphone.

The next moment drifting too distant.

Sounds of paper shuffling.

Scrape of chair legs.

Throat cleared.

Another twenty seconds silence.

Then a voice, properly arranged at clean distance from mic, began a smooth address.

> I had scarcely begun the first supper show of my gala season at the Maude Harbor festival when, as was my habit ...

Glenn Gould's voice.

His voice.

Unmistakable.

Except not his voice.

He'd never said this.

The words the same as had been on the sheets he'd discovered in his hotel.
Words which continued as his head began to swim.
Ears ringing. Clogging.
A high pitched muffle he couldn't keep but straining to listen through.

> ... despite the elegant and fashionable turnout, there was but one face that I longed to behold, one voice from which I longed to hear a confirmation of my own view of my greatness ...

Despite his certainty of the recording being forgery, the words spoken triggered lush replay of incident.

> ... and that, alas, was denied me; my beloved was nowhere to be seen ...

Distinct sensations.

> ... I perceived, in the front of the skiff ...

Aural. Olfactory.
Visual. Tactile.

> ... dimly outlined by the glow from the town across the bay ...

Details flashing through his mind of scenes.
Numerous.
A reality birthing from the soporific words of the recording.
Too lavish to be *unreal*.
To be anything but *actual*.
Recollected. By him.

> ... the precious figure upon which I longed to cast my eye ...

But the sights, the scents, sounds, sensations announcing themselves entirely and all at once were not of any water.
Any boat.
Any girl.

> ... and it was clear to me at once that in the few hours since our glances intertwined, she had undergone a momentous metamorphosis ...

Memories as though seen through a window.
Sensation of chill through his body.
Of breath turning pane grey.
Obscuring the sight of what was described.
Grey fading clear.

> ... The coy, girlish ways in which I read such promise of fruition as I scaled the Scarlattian heights were now transformed ...

Memory of shivering hands.
Working some length of metal.
Stealthily prying loose a door.
Of clenched jaw.
Headache.
Attempting to silence the chatter of his teeth.

> ... the shy, uncertain, awkward adolescent of the afternoon had, in truth, become a woman of the evening ...

Music.
Chatter.
Laughter from down a dark corridor.

... There was, of course, but one explanation ...

Yes.
He recalled.
Being crouched tense in the gullet of that corridor.

... and I was humbled before the mystery it implicitly conveyed ...

Listening.
Creeping forward.
Until he could see.

... Clearly, the hypnotic spell cast by my concert had worked its wonders ...

There were figures.
A woman.
A larger man.
The girl ...
... and ...

... released from its cocoon the magnificent butterfly who now alit upon our rock.

... *Glenn Gould*.
He remembered.
He saw. Had *seen*.
On the carpet.
Glenn Gould.
The recording continued unspooling.
As his eyes shut with enough force it caused him to rise.
Headphones coming away from him.

As he staggered.
Reaching forward for support as his knees gave out under him. Blind hand finding no surface to bolster against.
Blood pounding at his temples.
Distortion. Clatter. Muffle.
As he lay on the floor.
On his back.
Mouth open wide.
Leaking breath.
Like the sound from the whir of the spool continuing to unspool without anything further to say.

CAR PARKED. NOD TO ATTENDANT. Hotel lobby. Bustling. Front desk. Was there correspondence? 'Thank you.' 'You're quite welcome.' Elevator. Gould's floor. Hush of corridor. Key to lock. Crunch of latch turned. Suite entered. Soft clatter of security chain.

Silence.
Normalcy was the word of the day.
Normalcy.
A mask of it.
Proceed the same as always.
What difference between façade and authenticity?
To anyone looking, he'd seem the same.
To anyone looking, how one *seemed* was how one *was*.
Gould seemed, therefore Gould was, the same as Gould always seemed, always was.
Same as he *ought* be.
No one could reasonably suspect him of anything outside the ordinary if all they observed was the ordinary. None could imagine him thrown off-kilter if all they observed was perfunctory conduct.
Normalcy.
The same as always.
Yes.

Gould chuckled, the more he considered it.

Hardly a new endeavor.

Donning the same mask as always.

It simply covered something different, now.

His natural state was perpetual contrivance, wasn't it—whatever was happening, literally, deemed secondary, always, to whatever he decided was.

Whatever *might* be.

Might *be said to be*.

Parts of the world he moved through, portions of personal interactions, pieces of any communion he deemed less than palatable were snipped from the record.

Always.

What was happening around him, now, *to him*, now, would be, likewise redacted.

What was happening?

Gould was being *watched*.

Knew exactly by whom.

Knew, also, by God only knew.

What he'd decided?

Behave as though he wasn't. Reduce his acknowledgment of the surveillance to background crackle.

Excise it, entire, if possible.

The truth was: he'd currently be under this dual observation whether cognizant of the fact or no. If unaware, life would be proceeding per his typical whims. His observers able to intrude with their intents, same as could any random happenstance.

In other words?

His life would be the same as anyone's, any time.

Therefore?

Admit it was still exactly that.

Continue existing in accordance to his dictates, unfettered.

It profited him nothing to guess at, interpret, buck against whichever attentions were being leveled by his observers. To do so, in fact, only caused *disruption*.

Physically.

Psychologically.

If he lost control of his faculties, he'd deliver himself to the mercy of these third-parties. In effect, cede personal jurisdiction to them.

Good God ...

... was this the chop-logic lunacy he'd been reduced to?

Flapped hands around in disdain. Irked that his mind wouldn't stop calling him out on his own semantics. Demanded to the empty air he wasn't burying his head beneath the sand.

There was no resignation in this decision!

Far from it.

It doubled as a sensible posture of defense.

Whoever was tormenting him counted on his becoming unglued. Their *modus operandi* seemed to revolve around adding discrepancies into his days in hopes he'd consider the intrusions, the *anomalies*, to be the constants, the *actual*.

To refuse to engage reinforced the most pertinent reality:

Glenn Gould was in control.

Of himself.

His movements.

Activities.

This very afternoon had proven as much.

Assailed by discovering the progress made to his documentary during his absence, accosted by Dziurzynski's mind games, agitated by the bizarre recording left for him to discover, he'd nevertheless put in a full day's work.

Hadn't even lost composure enough to destroy the *Maude Harbor* reel. Placidly recorded over the full spool with empty air.

Left canister in the safe-box.

Jotted in the logbook: *Maude Harbor—project discarded.*

Little securities. In private.

While present in the room alone, for example, he'd wedge the desk chair underneath door handle. Bar entry even to those with a key. Overnight, perhaps move the armchair or small bookshelf to bulwark this precaution.

The windows?

Locked.

Even were they jimmied from exterior, his suite was situated several stories up. No fire escape or ledge immediately outside.

If an assassin found themselves dead set on trespassing enough they'd scale the sheer brick, Gould'd be gentleman enough to allow his number was rightfully up.

Whenever he departs?

Matchbook on doorknob.

Would know if anyone had come or gone after him ...

'None of this ...' a voice seemed to wryly cut in '... seems like anything you'd *normally* do, Glenn.'

Briefly snarled at the intrusive remark.

'Nobody can *see me* right now' he muttered in retort. Accused himself of obstinately missing the point. 'I hasten to add ...' he huffed '... how these little *insights* of yours are the sort of feckless nattering that will get us acting out-of-sorts.'

'But no one can *see you* right now ...' Gould couldn't help having himself retort, just as nimbly '... as a wiser man than myself only recently said. I'm simply ...' he sighed, long suffering '... attempting to shepherd you back to your afore-quoted desire for *normalcy*.'

Well gosh, he certainly appreciated that. However—

What about his pills, for example?

Stopped short at the query.

Froze precisely where he stood.

Throat constricting.

Eyed the satchel he'd set on the armchair upon entering the room.

Gaze drifting from it toward the washroom.

'... what *about* my pills?'

He'd lost time. Awakened in some mutt motel. Partaken of interactions he didn't recollect with individuals he failed to recall ...

Gould's focus blurred as the gravity of his present consideration sunk in.

'If your *studio* can be entered, Glenn ...' he felt he was being told by a voice almost piteous '... exited, *combination* locks unspun, it only serves to reason someone might have tip-toed into and out from your medicine cabinet, eh?'

Wasn't it wisest to suppose every pill he hadn't gobbled down might be spiked?

Mind seized up.

Swayed where he stood.

Blinking an inordinate amount though entirely oblivious to his doing so.

Part of him tried to maneuver out of entertaining such a monstrous scenario.

Drugged?

For heaven's sake, it would have to've been a precision operation. He'd taken several pills of different variety since his return from the motel. To no ill effect.

Was some fiend supposed to know he'd take just the exact right pill at the exact right time to go down for the count?

Doctored it and no others?

'Preposterous ...'

Then again, he was a creature of habit.

Easy-as-pie someone might've strolled in while he'd been otherwise occupied. Replaced every pill in a given bottle. Certain at least one would be swallowed. Swapped the proper medications back in after the deed was wrought.

Exact same switcheroo might've gone on today.

Trap set.

Aims on having him spirited away, tonight.

Bristling, he snorted such consideration aside.

'It's not only too early to refill any of these prescriptions …' his hand drifted in the air at hip height, conducted the words to drift out serenely '… but also, to do so is the manner of *glaringly* out-of-the-ordinary activity which would invite scrutiny from my police watchdog and would hip *le tueur caché* their villainous jig was up.'

This didn't mean, however, that, in his present privacy, Gould was averse to a thorough inspection.

Emptied each bottle to countertop in turn.

Several capsules could've been opened.

Different substance inserted.

Resealed.

How this would be accomplished was beyond his comprehension …

'…. but nevertheless …' he heard himself curtly interject '… these are pills you habitually take every night. In this room.'

Gould stared at the pill currently resting in his moistening palm.

'Then I won't take them anymore' he firmly announced.

Tried not to quip 'Holding fervent to that regiment of prescribed *normalcy*, eh?'

But obviously did.

Found himself slumped in the armchair.

Felt waterlogged. Cotton mouthed.

Certain his hand had developed a minor tremor it would purposefully conceal whenever he'd concentrate to observe the malady.

Legs crossed. Uncrossed.

Crossed.

Didn't realize he'd closed his eyes until he languidly opened them in response to the telephone ringing.

A syrup thick sensation of waking from dense slumber restrained him from rising. Attending to the phone.

Which stopped ringing.

Began again after just a moment.

Stopped.

Began.

Stopped.

Began.

Sluggish and irritable, he eventually stood to traverse the suite carpet. Intent not on conversing with whoever was pestering him, but on removing the receiver from its cradle.

Unplugging the device, entire.

Burying himself in the bedcovers.

Fatigue so heavy over him, in fact, he laughed.

Not quite a laugh.

A hiccough.

Certain he'd succumbed to his previously theorized dosing of illicit sedative. Despite having not swallowed a single pill since the *Valium* before departing his studio.

Yes.

Any moment he expected to impact the floor.

Face first.

Stare weakly as out-of-focus feet emerged from hiding.

Approached his flaccid torso.

Would feel his wrists gripped.

Or his ankles.

Shush in ears and rug-burn over cheek as he was dragged off.
Sat to desk chair.
Blinked.
Working to recall what train of thought had brought him there.
Just as the telephone began to ring, again.
Without truly intending it, he clumsily snatched up the receiver.
Held it.
Watched it numbly bob up-down-up-down in his rather limp hand.
Elbow rested to desktop.
Squinting as faint murmur of voice emanated from the lower bulb.

'… Mister Gould ..?'

Mumbling an apologetic, almost embarrassed 'Yes, hello' Gould rubbed his free ear with cupped palm.
Dug finger in.
Further than he'd meant.
Winced from a jolt of sharp pain.
The voice over the line seemed yet distant. Or else muffled. As though the speaker were purposefully filtering themselves through fabric.
Suggesting something was the matter with their connection, Gould stammered it might be best for the caller to ring through, again.
But even while he said this, the muffled voice primly assured him 'I can hear you fine and dandy, Mister Gould. Nothing the matter with the *phone*. But is something the matter with *you*, may I ask?'
There was some quality to the voice, though it remained muted, Gould found deeply unnerving.

'The matter with *me* ..?'

'You do remember what you've done, Mister Gould, do you not?'

Viced shut his eyes.

Clenched jaw.

After a moment, during which the voice kept silent, he let pass an angry chortle. Felt his teeth click sharply. Swallowed hard. The damp squish magnified by the receiver.

'*Detective-inspector* ...' he seethed, clearing his throat, practically a growl.

'This *isn't* the detective-inspector, Mister Gould.'

'... is it not? I suppose, then, this the dutiful flunky. *Dutiful flunky* ...' he asked through bared teeth '... would you be so kind as to put your mistress, the detective-inspector, on?'

'This isn't ...' the voice seemed to be stifling amusement '... the *dutiful flunky*. I think—'

But enough was enough.

Gould blurted he wasn't certain which was the more irritating aspect of this present intrusion—that it was happening to begin with, or how mind-bogglingly insulting it was for Dziurzynski to believe he'd let such an unmitigated outrage slide a second time without retaliation.

'*Retaliation*?' the voice seemed curious if not giddy.

'Tell your mistress I think it's time we reevaluate our open-border policy. In fact, inform her, since she'd so warmly *invited* me do so, I shall presently move to initiate the previously discussed proceedings against her for these *imponderably* disreputable behaviors.'

A pause held.

Gould shaking where he sat.

Tensing against coming hyperventilation.

Uncertain he'd have energy for another outburst if Dziurzynski had her cohort retort some snide way.

'I can pass the message along, Mister Gould ...' the voice eventually ventured, tentative, then tranquilly, almost a shrug, added '... but this *isn't* the detective-inspector. *Nor* her dutiful flunky.'

Proof?
  Gould regretted he'd asked.
  Had ... he asked?
  Regardless, here was the voice.
  Proving.
  'Were I Dziurzynski ...' it began '... I wouldn't know which *motel* you'd woke up in, just these two days prior. Nor how hat, tinted glasses, and the like had been left with that *cutie-pie* waitress. Or is the better term for her ... *jailbait*?'
  The voice sloppily purred this last question.
  A performative quality to it.
  Slurp made over distinct.
  Sound of sucking up saliva just before it dribbled over lip.
  Even through whichever gauze muffler the effect was pronounced.
  Gould couldn't help picture the lascivious leer, flared nose of the speaker.
  'Certainly *Dziurzynski* wouldn't know the name of the cab company. Nor the *accent* of the motel proprietor. And goodness me, Mister Gould, our poor civil servant wouldn't be privy to what words you'd found on that *typewriter*. No ...' the voice made a thoughtful few puffs of breath, connection crackling with them '... I think you can trust that I'm not who I say I'm not.'
  Gould took a bad swallow before attempting to ask who was speaking.
  'It might be time we meet' the voice meanwhile pressed on.
  '*Who* is speaking?' Gould was finally able to manage.
  After what might've been five minutes.
  Might've been not quite a single beat.
  Sense of orientation in shambles.

'That is ... the very subject we need to *unpack* ... isn't it?'
Laughter. Between each portion of this question.
Laughter like from a television heard through a wall.
Then muffled snort. Long composure-recovering breath out.
The voice continuing 'I might ask you the same question, in fact. But think the effect will be so much *cleaner*. Face. To. Face.'
'Meet where?'
'Oh bah!' the voice poo-poohed. 'Mister Gould, whether *affliction* or *charade* this is becoming quite tedious. You know right well where.'
'I haven't the foggiest ...' he lied, already picturing the motel '... so why not you come over here. As my guest. I trust you know to let yourself in. *Mi casa es su* or at least so it seems you believe.'
Another chuckle.
'Well...' the voice clucked sardonically '... while the invitation is jolly courteous and I'm always loathe to *insist*, the business needing discussion requires the pertinent *materials* be on hand. To ferry them, alas, would be prohibitively cumbersome.'
Before Gould could press for details concerning this ominous pronouncement, the voice sighed. Another gravelly crackle in Gould's ear.
'You're troubled over how you'll get out of your pen. What with being so prized a hog. The eyes, the ears of these rascal policemen so despotically surrounding you.'
Again, Gould took a breath in preparation to respond, but the voice had already trudged ahead, accusatory.
'Or are you thinking to shoot dirty pool with me, Mister Gould? Alert your detective-inspector fiancée to this call?'
Gould let silence hang a long while, uncertain whether he was meant to respond.
'I wouldn't dream of it' he finally assured.
'Now ... why *is* that?' the voice seemed genuinely puzzled. 'I

can't shake the sinking suspicion you're trying to show me down the garden path, Mister Gould. Is it *that*? Or is it …' the voice took a tone of grave seriousness, lowered an octave '… that you're worried what'll happen were she to learn you weren't where she seems to *think* you were … weren't where you *know* you *weren't* … at … *certain* … times?'

Gould attempted to wet his lips.

Found the usual plush of their skin cracked and rough.

His tongue severely dried.

Touch of the one to the other abrasive.

'Who …' he barely was able to croak after four unsuccessful attempts to gather enough saliva to swallow '… *is this*?'

'To repeat ourselves, Mister Gould …' the voice patiently cooed, almost flirtatious '… that is *exactly* what we so dreadfully need to *discuss*.'

Regrettable though it was, the voice would have to cut things brief. Told Gould his 'on-again-off-again' was arriving to the hotel, presently.

'No doubt with batted eyes she'll make her way behind closed doors with you—and I'd never stoop to so unmannerly a low as curtailing your turtle-doving. Write this down—do you have a pen?'

Gould, after standing in alarm, slowly retook his seat.

Asked exactly what the voice meant.

'Dziurzynski … is on her way?'

'Her car has just this minute pulled into the garage. She'll probably have something to *tell* you. Or will tell you something whether she has something to or not, eh?'

'Where are you, exactly?' Gould inquired, turning his head, squinting, as though he'd discover some cleverly concealed person within spitting distance.

'Across the street. Public telephone box. Have to play things a bit cloak-and-dagger. Just in case you're feeling cheeky enough you'd ask your betrothed to run a check.'

Gould let out a breath of protestation.

'I know, I know ...' the voice placated '... you'd never *dream* of it. Now, if you please: *write this down*.'

Gould uncapped a pen he retrieved from the desk drawer.

'What is it I'm *writing*?'

Whisked several sheets of paper over from the stack near the typewriter to the desk blotter ...

... not recalling having stacked paper by the typewriter ...

... nor having opened the typewriter ...

... nor having inserted a sheet ...

... nor typing anything on it ...

... despite seeing at least a paragraph ...

The voice, breaking Gould's concentration from such little mystery, cleared its throat. Then, instead of answering his question direct, began reciting a liturgy of what steps Gould was to take in order he might slip from the hotel, police unawares.

Spoke with careful enunciation.

Steady clip.

As though conscientious to correct for the filter it spoke through.

Gould hurriedly tested his pen with a shaky scribble.

Discarded it.

Uncapped another.

Tested.

Rushed to catch up with jotting the dictums.

Tense from not wanting to interrupt despite being anxious some point may've been missed.

The initial bit of '*la grande liberation*' was more-or-less at Gould's discretion.

'A good job ...' the voice reckoned '... would be to order a meal from Room Service, the usual time. Or a touch later than usual, might be better.'

Perhaps put in an appearance with the front desk.

Ask them to call down to the kitchen.

'Give bleary mention of turning in for the night. *Do Not Disturb*. All that.'

By all means, Gould should feel free to eat, too.

'At least *do away* with the foodstuffs, if you've no appetite. But no need to trouble yourself leaving tray in the hall.'

He ought exit via one of the building's side doors.

'I'd recommend donning something less conspicuous than your trademark zoot suit, at least until you're in the car.'

Such vehicle would be parked, several blocks distant.

Key on top of left rear tire.

'Extra room key, too ... though you do still have *yours*, yes no?'

Gould made noncommittal sounds, free hand drifting to coat pocket to verify while the voice rolled on, obviously not having expected actual response.

'Nothing else of *consequence* ...' it said expansively, then staccato added, emphatic '... other than you should ideally arrive around two in the morning. I have ...' the voice chuckled as though confessing a private peccadillo '... a few *things* to do until then. But it'd be for the best my already being present when you arrive.'

Gould nodded. Scribbling *Two A.M.*

Triple underlined.

'All joviality and banter aside, for a moment ... you do know not to tell your lady friend about this conversation, Mister Gould? I can *trust* you, can I?'

'You can trust me' Gould blankly responded, neither statement nor question.

The connection having severed by the word *trust*.

Not until the knock to the suite door sounded did Gould realize he was still staring at the papers he'd taken dictation on.

Mind numb.

Vision blurred.

Reading nothing.

Now folded the sheets in half, in half, in half.

Stacked them.

Shoved the lot down coat pocket.

Three more polite raps to the door.

Took up several blank sheets from the pile, in case some impression of his writing could be lifted.

Folded folded folded those.

Shoved them down pocket, too.

Buried the remaining pages from the desk into the center of the larger pile near the typewriter.

Blinked.

Was set to give a peek to whatever was written on the page pinned to the roller when another knock sounded.

Dziurzynski was wiping at the polka-dot tie she now wore, the dark orange circles of which matched exactly the shade of her crushed velvet blazer. Pants oversized. Deep green baby-corduroy. Cuffs rolled twice to keep from covering entire the tips of the wine colored footwear Gould briefly made out while moving a polite step back.

Thanking him and giving general apology, Dziurzynski made no eye contact as she entered the suite. Wholly fixated on whichever issue with the tie.

'You were right about cigarettes, all along ...' she laughed with a tinge of exasperation, final slap slap to the accoutrement before giving up her ministrations '... look here! A hole's burnt right through! Poor ciggie couldn't have been touching the silk but three, four seconds tops.'

All she'd been doing was her job, to boot!

'Taking a moment to *think*, eh?'

Well, here's the thanks she gets!

Puffed a petulant breath up as though to clear hair from her eyes, despite it being pulled back in prosaic pony tail.

Gould offered condolences. Glad she'd dodged the pesky cancer, at any rate. Entreated her to take his sage warnings full to heart, with this as the surest sign.

'I can tell just from looking the cravat must've set you back two days salary, if a cent.'

Was there something specific he could do for her, though?

She blinked.

Eyes keeping wide, after.

Puckered lips, question mark.

Slowly inched her leather notepad from rear pant pocket.

'You ... *called* me?'

'I *called* you?' he echoed back, matching expression to hers.

'I was *told*, at any rate ...' flipped through her pad, eyes locked to his '... you had called for me.'

'*Told*?'

'Had you not?'

'*Called for you*? I had not.'

Dziurzynski tapped finger to a spot on a note page.

Thump thump thump.

Still not breaking gaze.

Snapped pad shut.

Slipped it to blazer hip pocket.

'To meet you. Right now. My note said.'

'*Right now* ...?' Gould furrowed brow, not getting her drift.

Six o'clock. Is what had been related.

Who ... had told her this?

She'd been told he had.

'I had?'

'So I was *told*.'
He'd left word he was on the way to hotel from the studio.
She ought drop by for a chaw.
'At … six o'clock …' Gould mumbled, slow nod, squint.
She sniffled, snapped fingers at him, thumbs-up like he'd meant he remembered.
To which he shook his head.
Bewildered and a bit aggravated.
'What was I meant to be meeting you *regarding*, detective-inspector?'
'That was …' she clucked tongue aw-shucks '… what I reckoned you wanted to meet me regarding.'
'What … was?'
'To let me know what you'd wanted to meet me regarding.'
Wink.
Gould rolled his eyes. 'Yes. Quite.'
Well, if he had nothing to say, it must've been a silly miscue on the part of some underling.
Was glad she'd stopped by, regardless.
On her end, something had arisen she'd adore his insights regarding.
'It's not that I've *nothing to say*, detective-inspector …' Gould interjected with restrained curtness, wanting the point to be made clear '… so much as it's I *didn't request your audience*.'
Then he … *did* have something to say?
'Not a thing'
Well, there he had it.
Amounted to the same.
Was there someplace she could sit?

———————

Had she ever hipped Gould to what made her so fine a detective—ranked her a band apart from the more traditionally admired in her orbit?

'It's a certain *je ne sais quoi* as the expression goes.'

Perhaps he could relate.

'Even colleagues who claim they *admire* what I do, after it's been done, don't truly *understand* it. I doubt most of them believe anyone else does, either.'

There was an air to her which, when combined with a demonstrable handful of results, inspired a cultishness in some fellow snoops and members of the Press Corps.

'None of them want to be the bold sort who'd wave me away as a *charlatan*, you see? Therefore, and especially, when someone in authority, of esteem, talks *baldly* of me, expresses how they think I'm a *spook* … a … a a a …' she tick-tick-ticked tongue to teeth, eventually settling on the expression '… *degenerate down by the canal* my devotion in the ranks of those who've already dubbed me one-of-a-kind grows tenfold! However …' she shrugged, scratching the back of her calve with the toe of the shoe on the opposite foot '… in my private heart I know it all to be orchestrated hokum. I'm seen as a dime-magazine *eccentric*, eh? Those without authority in my practiced art love me oodles. As do onlookers. As do *just enough* genuine articles wanting to stay in the good graces of amateurs and those-who-know-nothing. I'm a motely ol' snake oil salesman, you see?'

Not at all following her line of thinking or finding himself remotely concerned with attempting to, Gould claimed he apprehended her point quite clearly.

Admitted, nevertheless, to being stumped.

Was this humblebrag what she'd felt it so imperative to get his two cents regarding?

Dziurzynski blushed.

Supposed she'd lost her thread.

Thanked Gould for being gallant with his concurring.

'You're adorably kind hearted.'

'I'm many things, detective-inspector, though some of those inadvertently. Please continue.'

He took a seat in the armchair while Dziurzynski paced, dotting her finger in the air as though tracing a recipe backward.

'Why I'm so fine a detective!' she suddenly clapped, pointing at Gould then nodding by way of graciously acknowledging his patience. 'Take these silly *crimes* going on now, for example. Most people? They're gonna straight out the gate assume the perpetrator has a whiz-bang *masterplan* going on, I bet. Not only that, they'll reckon each step is linking *perfectly* to the next step, in real time. Now ... do I *deny* they have a masterplan? Of course not. Who *doesn't* have a masterplan, after all? Do I even postulate the revealed steps aren't going precisely in accordance to some intricate *schema*? Nope. Because, again, that's not so tough to swing, is it? Plus, dead bodies inspire a tremendous confidence in the ingenuity of some inky madman, eh?'

After a pause, Gould realized he was meant to throw another log of enthusiasm onto the fire. Concurred with her entirely, thus far.

'Now ...' she took a seat at the writing desk '... do I believe their plan makes a lick of sense, outside of their own head? Has a context or apparatus even the perpetrator could articulate to the satisfaction of the *non-deranged*?'

She slapped both palms to the desk.

Paused.

Whispered 'Not on your life.'

A killer like this one operated while terrified of being caught, was her opinion.

'Not on account of prison life or execution, but because when they're caught out all their big ideas will turn out to be nothing but a kid making up a story as they go. Little guy might've worked out their tale very intricately, developed the underlying philosophy with tender love and care, point-by-point ... but the moment a grown-up asks *So what?* it'll be reduced to a smithereens of *goo-goo-ga-ga*! All these hotels and hatchets and newspaper scraps and what have you won't *mean* anything. The crimes, for all their *elaborateness*, won't be any better or worse than a common street stabbing.'

Gould supposed not. Frankly, wouldn't know with what criteria two such things could be audited.

'Like I told my daughter when she was a child and would still speak to me ...' Dziurzynski continued after a nod '... if a person is willing to stoop to anything, money is easy to come by. Shoot that clerk in the face! Empty the till! Run for it! But when *you're* caught? No one is apt to say *your* plan was jolly clever.'

Gould squinted.

'When *the killer* is caught' he offered, nose wrinkling.

What had she said?

'When *I* ...' he gestured at himself, doffed his forehead a puckish bow '... am caught.'

'Oh, but I'd just meant *supposing you were the killer*' she explained through laughter, as though correcting a bonehead misimpression she'd left. 'In which case, the point stands the same as if you aren't.'

'The more *intricate* a plan, the less I think it's *clever*. It's *meticulous*, perhaps. But keep in mind such word has root in the Latin. *Metus*. *Fear*. And what *scares* us, Mister Gould? Frightens us more than *anything*?'

He shrugged.

Watched Dziurzynski swipe a sheet of paper from the pile near the typewriter.

Begin folding it into a paper airplane.

'Eventually being asked *Why?* And why is *this* terrifying? Because we'll have to have something to reply. Knowing full well we'll be reduced to blathering incoherently in defense of an illusion we don't even have faith in. Or else, having been caught, one which defending will seem *idiotic*. Our best bet? Keep the nonsense going! Making it up as we go. Keep 'em guessing, eh? Kill kill kill and kill again. The plan, or its semblance, is just there to make it seem like the plan is there for a reason.'

Dziurzynski tossed her airplane.

The thing cresting pathetic off to one side.

Impacting the carpet without elegance.

Gould could almost picture the cartoon curlicue scribble its dismal trail had left.

Dziurzynski's lower lip turned out, accenting the moment as something between purposeful and dumb luck.

'You don't ...' Gould sniffed, speaking tentative, leaned forward where he sat, elbows digging into thigh fronts while knuckles of lightly fisted hands tapped ellipses between each portion of phrase '... believe ... there is *rational* ... or even *any* ... connection between ... these crimes? Is that your general thesis? One slaying is perpetrated merely to lead an investigator to another but the both combined will lead *nowhere*? A sequence of ... red herrings ... diverting focus from ... *nothing*?'

Dziurzynski nabbed another sheet of paper.

Stood as she folded it.

Paced with her back to Gould.

Peeked out the window curtain.

Nodded her head.

Let the curtain close.

Turned to face him, again.

Tossed airplane.

It cruising lamely off any course, same as previous.

Clunking to carpet.

She giving no reaction this time.

'When you put it *that* way …' she sighed, crestfallen, turning around the chair by the typewriter and plopping to it, mounted reverse '… I suppose it sounds quite silly.'

Let her arms dangle, childlike, over the chair back, as though trying to reach the carpet with fingertips.

'I guess I was just really hoping it didn't have anything to do with you.'

Like maybe a *new* crime would happen—did he get what she meant?

A snazzy new *clue* would show up.

Leading further away.

So he might be left to his peace and quiet.

His radio programme.

'Your gloves, your cookies …' she said, flicking a half-empty box of Arrowroots next to the typewriter '… your memoirs and all of that.'

Sighed. Deeply.

'You're probably right, though' she continued with a firm nod. Sitting upright. Standing to turn the chair normal way round before returning to it, legs crossed. 'I bet you're the key to *everything*.'

Puffed a beleaguered breath.

'Or someone really *really* wants it to seem that way.'

Scratched ear with her shoulder.

'Which, you know, could easily amount to the same.'

Changing the subject, or rather returning to the reason she'd have popped in even hadn't he invited her, she wondered if she'd be permitted to ask him something quite blunt.

'Provided I might first, *again*, addend the transcript to emphasize I'd *not* invited you—feel free.'

'Yes yes yes.'

Editorial taken to heart, she promised.

This point of his, though, paired well with her query. Deepened its import, in fact.

'Had Paul Henry Lang ever struck you as a fella insane enough to do a thing like this?'

'By *this* you refer to ...?'

'The commission of these murders.'

'No *fella* has ever struck me so kooky, detective-inspector.'

She withdrew pad from blazer pocket, pen from shirt breast, reciting the word *No* as she jotted it. Seemed to circle it twice.

'Or to call one of my underlings on the telephone ... claiming to be you?'

Catching her drift, Gould felt he should point out how uncanny it would be had 'a fella' decided to do that if 'said fella' hadn't *also* committed the associated crimes.

'But to answer your question: *no*.'

Dziurzynski admitted it was a fine observation he'd made.

'Though you do seem ... fairly easy to *imitate*, don't you think? One of those whom a caricature of would suffice in place of the real McCoy?'

Holding up hands to stave off Gould answering, she perked up.

Composed herself.

'I've been working on my *you*, for example.'

Glanced around as though for a prop or some scripted material to utilize.

Landed on the typewriter.

'Let me just use this, eh?'

Gould involuntarily tightened where he sat.

Mind shunted violently to find suitable excuse for blurting out she mustn't read whatever was written on the typewriter page, but was able to calm himself.

Nodded with a sociable grin.

Curtailing what would've been a disastrous moment if forced to explain.

Postured somewhat like a praying mantis, Dziurzynski cleared her throat. Rolled one hand repeatedly overtop the other while speaking to give emphasis to Gould's sometimes insect-like attributes and mannerisms.

'Tonight in the role of *Glenn Gould* ...' she coughed, recalibrating her voice to better approximate his '... we have ... *me*.'

After a final ahem she began reading from the page.

'*I had scarcely begun the first supper show of my gala season at the Maude Harbor festival when ...*'

A queasiness loosed itself through Gould.

Flow of his blood tainting sour.

Inside of cheeks seemed to shrink, to prune from being sucked harshly inward between his clamped teeth, pinched together so forcefully he didn't know if he'd be able to speak when next addressed.

Meantime, Dziurzynski chuckled, glancing up a peck to Gould for approval of her impersonation

'*... as was my habit, I glanced toward the boxes. And there, seated on one marked Live Bait—Do Not Refrigerate was a vision of such loveliness that it ...*'

She abruptly broke off.

Supposing he got her meaning.

'You have a ... *distinctness*. It almost *begs* for mimicry.'

What did he think?

She had the essence down, eh?

Even sounding still quite like the woman she was.

'If a man were to put work into it, speak over the telephone, say, they might *easily* come across as Glenn Gould as you please! Enough someone would swear to it in open court, I'd wager.'

To buy himself a moment in which his jaw would hopefully loosen, Gould shifted where he sat a number of times.

Jovial.

Matching the cartoony demeanor the detective-inspector had taken pains to adopt.

'Over the wire ...' he eventually seemed to be admitting through boyish reluctance '... I may not be as one-in-a-million as I've always strived to maintain, flesh and bone.'

To which Dziurzynski didn't reply beyond an acknowledging 'Hmn ...'

Too busy jotting something on her notepad.

Pronounced squint to the typewritten material before her.

Was Gould familiar with the name *Doctor Herbert Von Hochmeister*?

Dziurzynski rose to her feet while posing the question. Groaned out a kink in her lower back.

'*Which* was the name?' he asked, affect of not having quite heard.

Meantime the detective-inspector continued twisting her torso one way then the other. Seemed to genuinely want it rotated entire.

'*Doctor Herbert Von Hochmeister*' she repeated, a bit out of breath.

Touched her toes.

Tapped them with fingertips of one hand and notepad held in the other, a bouncy one-two-three motion, as Gould answered her Yes.

'*Yes*?' she echoed him and afterward tucked notepad away.

An action Gould couldn't help be set on his guard by.

Did he ... *know* a Doctor Herbert Von Hochmeister?

Had never met the man, no.

How did it chance he knew the name, if she might inquire.

'Quite exactly by chance, in fact' Gould replied, casual. Adjusting his position in the chair so he lilted one way somewhat foppishly.

Waited for Dziurzynski to begin follow-up query before, overtop of her, explaining how he 'received a letter. Day before last. *Here*. Delivered to me amongst my other correspondence.'

He meant the day of the housekeeper's murder, did he?

Not to be a pedant, but from his understanding it would've been the day *after* that tragic circumstance.

'The day we first met, in any event.'

Dziurzynski nodded.

Seeming quite pleased.

Her memory hadn't played her a trick, then.

'*Trick*, detective-inspector?'

All cards on the table, let her begin by confessing to a touch of surprise over Gould admitting, so candidly, he'd received contact from Von Hochmeister.

'A pleasant surprise' she insisted, waving her hand as though batting off some objection or affront Gould hadn't given the slightest hint the expression had caused.

She thought she'd seen such letter 'or the envelope, anyway' during their maiden chit-chat.

'You are nothing if not keenly observant' Gould supposed.

'What was the *content*?' if she may be so bold as to inquire.

His pleasure to relate, provided she didn't mind him first asking her reason.

Waggled fingers of both hands, shook her face rubbery.

'Yes yes yes' he was quite correct.

She still hadn't yet got to her own point!

Things had been so busy 'what with all of the murder and such going around' and having to flit between crime scenes like a honeybee that only this afternoon had she occasioned to give examination to much of the evidence from Lang's suite.

'Today, *after* we talked?' Gould floated for context.

'About two hours ago' Dziurzynski replied absently, sniffling, Gould not certain whether in reply to him, specific, or as simple continuation of her previous statement.

Say—Gould didn't *have* that envelope handy did he?

'No.'

'Or the letter, even better.'

Unfortunately, he was able to furnish her neither. Swiftly added how he doubted anything illuminating would've come from any inspection.

'A card inviting me to participate in a forthcoming forum. Von Hochmeister is a musicologist, from what I gathered.'

The envelope, with contents, had gone into the trash.

'Here?' Dziurzynski asked, pointing to the wastebin, currently empty, nearby the typewriter desk.

'Just there, yes.'

She frowned. Snapped her fingers bad luck.

'What did you *mean*, detective-inspector ...' Gould held up a finger to not let her meander over to some *non sequitur* point without the matter being addressed '... by saying it had *surprised* you, my admitting I'd been in possession of this material?'

Had she used the term *admitting*?

Quite pointedly, was Gould's recollection.

Gosh. She scratched her forehead with thumbnail roughly, wiped hand at her hip. *Maybe* she had.

But see it her way and he'd have to grant her begged pardon, no doubt.

'You aren't, Mister Gould, anyone who'd be *rightly* catalogued an open book.'

The name had come up in connection to the hotel where Lang had met his unfortunate end.

'I frankly thought it sounded phony baloney ...' Dziurzynski giggled '... but apparently he's a *musicologist* is what you'd said, Mister Gould?'

'According to the invitation present in the envelope I received' Gould put the fine point on. Reiterating he'd never seen the name before and noting, by the way 'I'd thought the name sounded a tickle on the queer side, myself.'

Yes, it sure did, eh?

Dziurzynski repeated *Von Hochmeister* aloud some half-dozen times. Made a raspberry sound, grading it with disdainful thumbs-down gesture.

'Name or pseudonym, it remains perplexing. All the moreso, now. You're sure you don't have that invitation lurking around? Don't recall any specific phrasing?'

Nothing lived in his memory. Except how 'It didn't seem anything but boilerplate, in itself.'

What Dziurzynski wondered was if, perhaps in conjunction with *other* evidence, whatever'd been *written* might be instrumental in the dot-to-dot.

'Or the paint-by-numbers ...' she momentarily paused, wanting her analogy to hit correct '... or the whatever sort of thing is best to say.'

Gould took her point.

A jigsaw.

Mixed with a scavenger hunt.

'Exactly' she laughed. 'I'm on emu duty. Moving crumb-to-crumb.'

A picture was being presented, as she'd once suggested, with pieces doled out explicitly to keep it indistinct.

'Rationed *meticulously*, in fact ...' Dziurzynski now seemed deep in sincere contemplation '... and we all know such has its root in the Latin, don't we?'

Did he catch her drift?

Why would whoever had been present at Lang's suite have left so tantalizing a clue as this?

Envelope ... name on it ... sent to Gould ... with nothing of value inside?

'Or something of no *apparent* value. Nothing which stoked *curiosity* enough in you to elicit a reaction. Tossed in the rubbish, hardly a second thought.'

Seemed clumsy for someone who'd taken the time to lodge a two-year-old concert review in a young woman's larynx.

'You aren't being *threatened* are you, Mister Gould?'

The abruptness of the remark caught Gould off guard. Stabbed in his direction so suddenly that to consider it accusatory wouldn't be at all out of line.

He balked, blinking rapidly, it taking half-a-minute for him to stammer out his eventual 'I haven't ... any idea what ... you ... mean by ... *that*.' An expression so puny and noncommittal his face flushed with self-directed anger as he more steadfastly insisted 'No, I am *not*. Nothing of the sort.'

Don't get her wrong.

Asking to be polite.

Nonetheless, it behooved her to hypothesize 'It might've been a *threat* in that envelope. Or something your silence has since been *solicited* regarding. Hold your tongue under hazard of *penalty*, you see?'

He did see.

Calmly said so.

With calm nod to accompany.

'I travel under no darker cloud than previous, detective-inspector. Much though it perhaps disappoints you to discover.'

Now now now. No call to get feisty or cross with her, please. She'd inquired with his own best interests at heart.

'You'd not want to be threatened into *complicity*' was her point.

'That ... sounds somewhat like a threat, in *itself*' she might have to admit.

'Yes ...' she supposed with a chuckle, not a single beat missed '... I might have to do just that.'

'Have I ever told you what makes me so fine a detective?' Dziurzynski asked, dusting a finger playfully along the desk as she idled past it. Tipping the amassed correspondence stacked beside the cookie box before continuing to amble a wide arc of the suite.

'You had ...' Gould grinned after a tense swallow, watching her progress '... *preambled*, at any rate.'

Narrowed his eyes as she traced finger now along the wall in slow approach to the suite door.

'No doubt it is an exhaustive subject. To be codified in multiple volumes, one day. I'll keep copies on the nightstand. Inscribed, I'd like to assume.'

'I'm good at *people* ...' the detective-inspector continued, not so much as a blink of response given Gould's quip despite its blatant tint of antagonism '... like you are good at *piano*. But I don't play people like other people might. As you never did the clavier. I play people, Mister Gould, like you might play Bach. In that I don't follow their instructions. As you don't follow his. But then ...' she gazed at him direct '... *all creative artists claim, when challenged, that they have nothing but disdain for the limited vision of their present audience, that posterity will be their judge.*'

Gould stared at Dziurzynski staring at him.

Coyly looked over his shoulder as though someone else might be there for whom a private meaning in her address was aimed.

Eventually folded hands to his lap, smiling with eyebrow cocked.

'That was very ...' he offered dubiously '... *well remarked*, detective-inspector. Von Hochmeister perhaps ought have invited you to do the keynote over myself.'

Dziurzynski seemed genuinely puzzled.

'You don't remember saying that?'

'Saying ... *what*?'

The remark he'd remarked on, she explained 'Was a direct quote.'

Perhaps he'd missed something. If so, forgive him.

'Neither the subject of *posterity* nor the woeful limitations of *audience* have been volleyed between us' he felt certain.

Still wearing an expression of naked bewilderment, she nodded. 'I'm honestly *never* certain, Mister Gould ...'

'*Certain*?'

'About you.'

'*About* ..?' he prompted with absent drift of thumb tip wetted by lower lip to nose.

'Frankly, I'm sometimes not certain you're certain you're speaking to me when we're speaking.'

'An admirable, perhaps aggressively Socratic, mindset to adopt ... though beyond saying so, I'm not certain what to reply.'

'When I speak to you tomorrow, will you recall this we've said here, today?'

Briefly parting his lips, reclosing them, folding arms and blinking to signify the loss he was at, yet again, Gould didn't respond.

If she were to ask him, for example, what she'd just been saying could he, for the sake of a lark, humor her with recounting it.

'How we are weirdo peas in a pod ...' he replied '... or so I'd interpreted your drift. You attempt to play me like I, some say, subjugate Bach. Or else attempt to subjugate me like I, some say, play him.'

Fair enough, she supposed.

Was sorry again for so long an intrusion.

Though, in her defense, she *had* been told it'd been his idea she drop in.

'A bumbling miscommunication for which, believe me, heads will roll.'

Gould found himself nibbling his lower lip. Who knew for how long. Trying gingerly to remove some layer of dead paste via gentle scrapes of upper front teeth. Pinches down.

Each time he completed an administration of sharp tips to some spot, though, it seemed another dollop of gummy excess would arise.

In fact, he was sure he'd removed the same gluey chapped splotch six times.

Stood up.

Ran gloved back of hand over lower lip turned out.

Then over lips puckered kissy.

Moved to restroom mirror.

Expecting he'd find raw discoloration or areas near to bleeding. But his lips appeared normal as he dabbed them with fingertips wetted from trickling faucet.

As he swallowed *Valium*.

As he swallowed more.

Writing desk.

Stack of correspondence spread like a flourished deck of cards. Envelopes from today but from yesterday, as well.

From the day before.

Flagrant how the only envelope *not* present was the grey with the Von Hochmeister return address.

'So you know without my having to break the news what Dziurzynski is thinking …' he didn't mutter but pretended he had.

Retorted in a hiss how she'd made it quite *clear* what she was thinking.

Suspected he was being threatened.
Which, he supposed, he was.
Could she know that?
Know it.
Not merely *surmise*.
Rather than address such question, Gould redirected the debate to whether he was, *de facto*, being threatened.
Who was to say he wasn't knee deep in another of the detective-inspector's gimmicks?
This recent call, timed for mere moments before she arrived, one she'd solicited, perhaps.
He recalled her peeking out the window.
Moved to exactly where she'd been positioned.
Parted the curtain, same as her.
Sure enough: two public telephone boxes in easy view.
Was parting the blinds as she had some subtle way of cluing him in?
To ... *what*?
Her own *trick*?
If she'd wanted him to know something, why not be straightforward?
'Because she desires fervently to trip you up' he subvocalized.
Trip me up?
'Have you tip your hand?'
What hand?
'She *suspects* you, Glenn.'
Of what?
'Of *something*.'
Ridiculous.
She'd herself done the work proving these killings weren't his. Couldn't have been.
What remained to suspect him of?
Complicity.

'In what?' he demanded, aloud.

Something he imagined being whispered in his ear.

'This is ludicrous' he announced flatly to the empty room, swatting the air with violence.

But if the envelope with return address of this Von Hochmeister had some connection to the Lang suite, what could it possibly mean?

Had Paul Henry Lang sent him that envelope?

Before ... being killed?

Before ... faking his own assault?

Had whoever'd assaulted Lang, murdered Lang, sent it?

What purpose would any of these actions serve?

Whatever purpose ... could the envelope have some connection to these other intrusions—this bizarre appearance and reappearance of writing about ...

'... *Maude Harbor* ...' Gould mumbled aloud.

Eyes flitting to the typewriter.

Gripped a hand over eyes.

Gripped hard.

Growling.

What had happened in *Maude Harbor*?

'I gave a concert.'

He nodded. Repeated.

'I gave a concert, there. Of Scarlatti.'

Nodded. Repeated.

Added 'That's all.'

But even as he did so, couldn't stop memory of the muffled voice.

You do remember what you've done, Mister Gould, do you not?

Nor the images which'd flashed through his mind while that reel in the studio had spun round.

The writing. Begin with that.
　Tangible.
　Same exact text as had been found in the drawer.
　Here. In front of him.
　Again.
　Gould hadn't written this.
　Not the first time.
　Certainly not now.
　So how had it gotten into his typewriter?
　First suspicion was Dziurzynski.
　Perhaps the same text had been present at the Lang crime scene. She'd arranged replica to observe his reaction.
　Alternately: who was to say the detective-inspector hadn't gone through his garbage, pieced the original back together?
　Hadn't she pointed at the wastebin, just now?
　Might've done so to goad.
　Thinking to lord something over him.
　Keep him at tenterhooks.
　Possible ... possible ...
　Though either scenario made little sense.
　Not, he reminded himself, that *making sense* was the detective-inspector's identifying trait.
　Possible ... possible ...
　Wanting to take things a step at-a-time, he focused down.
　Had some version of the text been present in Lang's suite, why would the detective-inspector have suspected it to have association with Gould?
　Nothing in the few hundred words currently on display identified him. Nothing, in fact, he could recall from the longer version he'd destroyed identified him, either. Nor revealed the purpose of the words, full stop.
　Could've been a short story.
　Or a bit of memoir Lang had been cooking up ...

It occurred to Gould to test a few keys before adjusting the alignment of the paper.

Tack. Tack. Tack.

Yes.

Typed on this very machine.

Without doubt.

Information which did nothing to eliminate Dziurzynski as the typist.

Though that prospect seemed more and more dubious as he dwelled on it.

Was he proposing she'd entered his suite surreptitiously ... or under some vague pretext of the law ... in order to type this document ... so she might later show up ... claiming he'd invited her ... all so the stage would be set to read the words in impersonation of him ..?

To what end?

No.

This line of thinking contained multiple points of failure.

'And why are you focusing on this *trivia*?' he demanded of himself.

Dziurzynski was cognizant of the name Von Hochmeister—what difference could it make how?

'Isn't it quite obvious what's going to happen next, Glenn?'

The forcefulness of this interjection caught him entirely by surprise. Wiped the slate of his thoughts blank.

'What ... is going to happen next?' he eventually asked.

Timidly.

Childish.

Taking seat in the armchair as though to be addressed by a figure in authority.

Gould had confirmed, officially, the presence of the Von Hochmeister envelope in his room.

How long until Dziurzynski rousted one of her underlings to

begin searching for signs of the man—if she hadn't *already* done?

How long until they take the obvious step of opening a telephone directory?

Begin dialing hotels.

Motels.

Confirm a Von Hochemeister—*herr doctor*, no less—had taken a room out, forty-five minutes' drive from Gould's very location.

How long until a *description* was given?

Startled look crossing some investigator's face.

Photograph held up.

Of Gould.

'Is *this* Von Hochmeister?'

How long until 'Yes, yes—that is the doctor, himself.'

How long?

Hardly mattered.

From there it'd be mere hop-skip to Dziurzynski realizing Gould *hadn't* been where he'd been thought to be. During the *crucial* hours he needed most to account for.

From that ... how long until ...?

He blinked.

Cleared throat.

Eyes drifting back to the typewriter.

To words someone had written.

He had destroyed.

Someone had written.

Words it soon wouldn't matter were he to tear to ribbons, again.

Or again.

Or again.

Considering all this, Gould couldn't possibly be calculating to slip out during the wee hours so he might liaison with whoever it was had beckoned him.

'For the love of Christ ...' he hoped aloud to've *never* been entertaining so reckless a notion.

Hoped.

Aloud.

Despite knowing full well he was presently working out how best to diligently swing the departure.

Look at Glenn Gould.

Folding coat around gloves, hat, scarf.

Bundle stuffed snug in as small a carry bag as he could manage.

There he is.

Laying out the tan suit he'd wear.

Tan suit he'd *disguise himself in*.

What a phrase!

Couldn't help but chortle. Earnestly amused.

Part of him reasoned thus: were his days numbered, there was little call to walk the plank without protest. To totter automaton to his gallows.

Instead?

Fight back.

At bare minimum refuse to perish per some third party's programme.

But what *was* it to refrain from protest?

What *was* it to fight back?

How was he meant to sort the one from the other—to decide for himself rather than bow to decisions exterior?

Decision belonging to his faceless tormentor.

To Dziurzynski.

'My *tormentors*, perhaps better say.'

Couldn't help sense something altogether more *personal* at play than shilling-shocker games of cat-and-mouse.

As things stood, he was clearly the victim of a bourgeoning frame-up.

Hadn't killed the poor housekeeper.

Lang.

'Or anyone else.'

Could, with clean conscience, ring Dziurzynski, this very minute. Make a clean breast of all which had transpired these several days. No detail spared.

She likely wouldn't be particularly startled by it.

Once he'd unburdened himself of the nightmare, his last act before moving on might be to aid her in apprehending the butcher she sought.

Have her keep close tabs on him while he went along with the voice's outline.

Set it up so she or some agent of hers be planted at the motel, ahead of time.

Part of him reasoned, however: were he to fight back, it was best to ascertain as much information as possible.

It was, yes, precisely true he was victim to a frame-up.

So why hadn't the trap *sprung*?

What could be waiting in the wings?

Whatever it was, could it paint him in any *less* believable a light than he'd come across were he to announce the reality of the past forty-eight hours, this exact instant?

Hadn't he already considered how if this lunatic wanted him dead he'd be dead?

Add into this equation how it was more than evident that if they'd wanted to *indict* him, no question, in murderous horrors they could've done so any old time it tickled them to.

There was *unknown* motive else, then.

Without question.

The more he paced, turned the matter around, the more evident it was his position remained unaltered.

Maybe the person who'd contacted him *desired* that he bring the detective-inspector into his confidence. At this very juncture. Timed events so Gould would feel compelled toward precisely that.

Had contacted Dziurzynski's deputy, claiming to be him.

Arranged his own call to be received just moments prior to her arrival.

To *maximize* stress.

Confusion.

Why not?

If he could imagine himself walking into a trap were he to arrive to the motel alone, it also served to reason he'd be stepping into as sinister a snare were he to alert the authorities.

Only one path forward allowed him any semblance of volition. Opportunity to look whoever this manipulator was direct in the eye.

Ask his own questions.

Understand his fate according to terms he, himself, would set.

Gould, it so happened, did eat the food he'd requested the front desk have the kitchen send up.

Polished off his final box of Arrowroots, after.

Placed telephone call to a friend.

A call which, no doubt to their surprise, he begged off from shortly.

Though he hadn't explicitly been instructed not to leave the Room Service tray in the corridor for retrieval, he decided it best to not bother.

Kept putting eye to peephole.

Half hour.

Hour passing.
Every conceivable anxiety pelted him.
Most of all, that some officer might be stationed in one of the rooms along the corridor toward the stairwell he needed to access.
Alert to any sound of doors opening.
Closing.
Their own eye ready to zip to peephole.
Squint.
Discover the fish-eye form of Glenn Gould slinking past.
Jot down when.
The absurdity of the entire affair made his mood, for a moment, almost jolly despite his unease.
Wondered should he crawl the twenty meters which needed to be traversed.
Except how the devil would he explain himself were he observed on all fours?
Not that he should have to explain or excuse *any* behavior.
'Preposterous ...' he absently chuckled.
When time came, he crept into the stairwell.
Upright.
Met by nobody.
Padded stealthily down several flights to ground floor.
Reciting silently the directions he'd memorized. From the sheets he'd stuffed down pockets before Dziurzynski's recent appearance.
The sheets he'd shredded.
Soaked.
Wrapped in a hand towel.
Stuffed into his bag alongside coat and other garments.
Soggy remnants he'd rid himself of out the window as he drove.
Head down, shivering, made his way through the hotel's alley to the lit streets it terrified him to venture.

While attempting to keep his strides and manner inconspicuous, he caught himself stiffening, wincing or scuffing shoe to pavement as considerations, second guesses pounded in his head.

Chastised himself, especially, for being so careless with the Von Hochmeister envelope and the *Maude Harbor* writing he'd discovered.

Should've obliterated both with the same overkill he'd visited upon other evidences. Not merely littered the shambles into the room trash for housekeeping to collect.

No matter how he tried to tell himself such was of little consequence, the action, or lack thereof, seemed a fatal oversight.

Especially with Dziurzynski now having seen the writing in the typewriter. Or, having seen it before, been able to leave it there, herself.

At least he was in control enough to've allowed that present page to remain.

Exactly there.

To clearly be present next time the detective-inspector visited. Defused of all possible oddity or indication he'd been unnerved.

His breathing grew unmannerly as he approached the final cross-street.

A left hand turn would arrive him to the waiting vehicle.

Alarmed how exposed the area was.

Had expected the transport to be tucked someplace dank and unlit.

But there it glared.

Green as an apple skin.

Parked in front of a tailor shop, a vacuum repair, a caged-tight pawnbroker, and a take-away restaurant which had closed down hours ago, the bunch.

Late night revelers turned the corner ahead.

Caroused in Gould's direction.

As they approached, he set down his carry bag. Acted out an

inspection of the contents of his wallet. Facing sooty glass of whichever establishment.

In glancing up, it was pleasing to honestly hardly know himself.

Hair slicked back.

Suit prim and closed.

Comforting to see the reflection of one of the young men who passed behind him regarding its own features through eyes obviously dim with the beer their passage reeked of. Eyes not even flitting to meet his own reflected before belching, bumbling onward.

Away.

Swallowed pill.

Swallowed pill.

Swallowed pill.

Pills which were loose in his suitcoat's inside pocket.

Having learnt.

Wouldn't be caught without meds, again.

So much as he could prevent it.

More in the carry bag. In the coat pockets, too.

Unbottled.

In the event something were to happen.

Carry bag absconded with.

The memory of that morning in the motel itched under his scalp like lice.

In his notebook, left at the hotel, he'd made coded indication of how many pills he'd brought with. Asterisks beside penciled markings. Set down in heavy graphite.

If some intruding party tampered with the notebook their trickery would be apparent. The only way to get rid of the markings to tear the pages out.

Pages he'd numbered.

So even if razor-bladed out carefully their absence couldn't be missed.

Yes.

Taking every precaution.

To know what he'd done.

What he'd not.

Decided to allow himself another twenty minutes. Sat in the chill. Arms bundled around himself. Car engine not yet turned over.

Twenty minutes, half hour.

Then would quickly step from the car.

Slip into his usual attire.

Back in.

Start the engine.

Let it idle while he thawed.

Plenty of time yet to arrive to the motel.

Meantime, teeth chattering, he poked around the car's interior.

Glovebox empty.

Nothing beneath either seat.

Nor in the seatback pouches.

Would pop the trunk when he changed.

Didn't imagine there'd be anything there to discover.

The car was a rental. Easily identifiably as such from the plates and various window decals.

Wondered was it rented in Von Hochmeister's name?

In his own?

Such queries shunted his mind to the paragraphs left in the typewriter.

To Dziurzynski's claim about having learnt the name Von Hochmeister through some connection of it to the Lang crime scene.

Was that how events had *honestly* transpired?

Could she have discovered the name by tracking down the Cashier's Check's origin?

Or perhaps the multiple suites had all been rented under the name to begin with. Her claim of different names assigned to each a purposeful obfuscation.

'When had ...' he wondered in a mumble, jaw clattering from cold while he pulled on coat, hat, gloves, scarf '... the Lang affair *actually* been discovered?'

He ought cease taking *anything* Dziurzynski uttered at face value.

For all he knew, the discovery of Lang *pre-dated* the housekeeper.

Dziurzynski could've already known the name Von Hochmeister from then.

Have already looked over the bundle of correspondence in the front desk cubby before he'd arrived.

Perhaps opened it.

Removed its contents.

Swapped out a different envelope, left empty.

Might well have been clocking Gould, suspecting him full stop, from the moment they'd met.

The engine grumbled to life.

Freezing post-midnight air blew from its vents while he waited for the heater to gain dominance.

Shouldn't be letting his thoughts get away from him.

'You're sitting in a *rental car* at the behest of a *disembodied voice* you've every reason to suspect belongs to a *psychopath*, Glenn ...' he had the mouth in the rearview mirror point out '... if ever there was a time to invest in sensible cautions, this present moment wouldn't be fair description of it.'

He concurred.

Sensibility.

That ship had sailed.

But no need to deny himself a moment to ponder why he hadn't thought these things, before. To commiserate with himself rather than pepper his mind with *tsk-tsks*.

'*You're* in this car *with* me, after all …' he grinned toward his reflection, feeling the tight of the smirk while meeting sarcastic eyes in the glass '… so let's not be too *uppity*, shall we?'

———

It'd begun to drizzle.

Windshield wipers beastly out-of-time with bubblegum pop from the speakers. Seemed to *thwap* on only the most incongruous beats. Soon warbled a repellent squawk on their return-arcs.

Gould opted to operate their mechanism manually.

Waiting until the glass became too sloppy to see through before allowing the blades motion.

One swipe.

Left-right.

Hardly mattered.

Road pitch dark.

Desolate.

Any emptier, he'd not believe *it*, or *he*, or *anything* in this night existed.

In his mind's eye crept the detective-inspector.

Through his unprotected hotel suite.

After knocking. Telephoning. Preparing some speech or incident to relate which might excuse her intrusion.

Or perhaps she'd legitimately sleuthed out whichever sinister machination he was gliding toward, at present.

Desperate to warn him safe from his fate.

No.

Dziurzynski was composed of nothing but schemes dreamt up

as pretext. Impulses heroic, even civic, wouldn't motivate her. Any notion she'd act in his best interests was elided from Gould's fantasy.

He pictured her hunched over. In examination of the notations regarding his pills. Re-reading the paragraphs left in typewriter.

Snuffling through his garbage.

Trying on his shirts.

Laying on his mattress.

Awaiting his return.

Wiper blades juddered.

Wailed banshee overtop advertisement for antiseptic wash.

With their wretched screech spiked an image of hatchet.

Gripped in two hands tight with leather.

Memory of laughter and music.

Around a corner.

Distant. But not.

The rain's pitter-pat of freckles grew to warped slather down the glass.

Was leisurely shoved clear.

View of the vacant road returning.

As Gould's thoughts wound back to Dziurzynski.

Perhaps already at the clapboard motel he was wending toward. Maybe laid upon that dingy, cracker-rough mattress.

As though all it'd taken was closing her eyes in his suite …

… opening them …

Presto!

She'd lay in wait for the scratch of his key to the room lock.

Would shackle him.

But not before tousling his hair.

Calling him a scamp.

Gould's hand griped and lifted upward the wiper-lever.

Percussive shiver of the blades side-to-side.

Sour squeal.

His hands in leather tight around leather hatchet grip.

Portly man's toad-bulb gullet hemorrhaging *glug glug glug*.

The radio crooned of love in some adolescent way while headlights approached from behind.

Caused Gould to grow tense.

Set wipers on full automatic as he drifted to the slow lane. Hoping this unwelcome motorist would hurry ahead.

Seethed when they didn't.

Averting eyes downward as he came to a halt at the road shoulder while the vehicle lazily leered past.

An over-articulated sound of tire *slursh*.

Feeling of suspicious eyes on him.

Wipers swung. Shook. Whined.

Swung.

Shook.

Whined.

Thwap ... thwap at the wide of either extreme.

These wet smacks summoned images of play money.

Floating atop cinema grade scarlet.

Puddle deepening.

His own face reflected in the sanguine mess.

Liquid so red it turned nearly brown.

Slop so brown it became nearly black.

Wiper blades swung.

Shook.

Shrieked.

Thunk.

Shrieked.

Thunk.

Gould shut them off.

Let the simmer of rainfall ensconce him.

Listened to the radio.

Lively teen dance tunes. Melodies oddly baroque.

He'd almost forgotten where he was, where he was going, when another car whooshed past.
Slowed.
Curved to the roadside ahead.
Taillights indicating it intent on backing up.
Toward him.
To investigate.
Feeling accosted, anxious, Gould pulled back onto the road.
Calmed, before long.
Knew in the dark and through the wet no particulars of his vehicle could've been made out.
Not that it mattered.
The car not his own.
Nothing to do with him.
Nothing to do with Glenn Gould.
Gripped lever for wipers.
Swung. Shook. Screamed.
Thunk.

Gould bypassed the motel. If for no other reason than it proved to himself he wasn't purely a creature of mechanical wind-up.

As precaution, intended to park the vehicle someplace whoever had summoned him wouldn't know about.

Couldn't guess.

No concrete idea what advantage, if any, this was meant to provide. But the fixation was entire.

Emblematic.

He was operating on his own steam.

Choosing out steps himself.

Of course, he couldn't keep an increasingly galling voice from running concurrent to any reassurance. Calling his every positive notion rubbish. A pestilent tally of the fallacies on which they depended.

Nor could he keep quarantined the bickering of another track. Detailing multiple defenses and safeguards he ought've previously employed.

Mockery.

Needling Gould gibbonish as he sought out an appropriate parking space.

'*Precaution*, indeed' this voice sniggered.

Whispered 'It's okay to admit you're scared, Glenn' in intonations of playground bully.

'But... to call this a *precaution*? *Really*? How can you *delude* yourself?'

Why not have left behind some record of *where* he was going and with which *intent*?

Mailed a sealed letter inside of separate envelope to a trusted friend or associate—the closed document only to be opened in the event he failed to contact them to issue a *Disregard*?

Why not have written out, better-or-worse, his personal, candid version of the events of these days, complete with admission of his secretiveness, false disclosures, and rationale for every action or failure to act?

More creative: still there remained time to place a call for a scheduled taxicar pick-up. Instructing the driver to please knock on the door to his motel room.

Worst come of worse, were some terrible happenstance transpiring, it might be interrupted.

Or the perpetrator *identified*, at least.

It cleanly on record how Glenn Gould had worked it out to have this driver summoned as witness.

His current search for hidey-hole to stash the rental car smacked more of *squirming panic* than *ingenuity*.

'Why not keep driving? Now. Do any and all of those things you've mentioned. From three hundred miles away.'

Dziurzynski would understand.

'You might even telephone her from an anonymous roadside. Fess to everything so far as you understand it. Your disquiet over your own self, included. *For the safety of all, I'm in hiding*. Tell her that.'

Barring a spate of insane butcherings cropping up wheresoever he landed, such would clear him of blame in any further horrors which might transpire *locally*.

'Since you're *innocent*, the detective-inspector will solve the case. No doubt thanking you for this cowardly help you'd been, scampering off.'

He snorted at this.

Had had his chance to *flee* at the tee-off to this nightmare.

Chosen to stake his claim.

Here.

Since he hadn't fled, he shouldn't flee.

After nothing but bland, empty road was discovered for fifteen minutes' drive, was forced to turn around.

Re-pass the motel going opposite direction.

Settled on a shuttered-for-the-night gas station.

Perhaps two mile walk from motel.

'You do know, Glenn, this is the *first* place anyone looking will look when they discover this car not parked in the motel lot.'

Not, he remembered to insist to himself, that it was certain he'd be kept from leaving the motel freely.

Could be that after whatever meeting with whichever party concluded he'd be left to his own devices.

Might, through a blush, explain how he'd a bit of a walk in store.

Pathetic.

Absurd to the point of piteousness.

'You don't even sound staunchly *convinced* of your innocence, to be blunt … ' he muttered, tightening his coat.

'Of course I am' he had his reflection insist.

As he cut the engine.

Car tucked tight near a dumpster behind the establishment.

Out of sight from the road.

Then said to the rearview 'You can't fault me for not wanting to believe the world will only recognize as much posthumously.'

The moon, starkly visible despite clouds and a now more insistent deluge of rain, made Gould feel somewhat poetic. Unlike himself.

Not himself.

At least not the *himself* he ought be.

Soaked to the skin, he trudged. Suborning whichever illness saw fit to pounce.

A wraith.

Drifting with cryptic purpose.

Smeared haze from motel's road-sign *No Vacancy* light and the simmering fluorescent from the closed shops across the way from it seemed to crackle. Visual equivalent to static behind the strains of old time radio.

Gould felt he was haunting the road. Almost chagrined no cars passed him by during his slog. Had been unable to extend arm, thumb. Play the part of some ghostly hitchhiker folklore had taught the sensible motorist to avoid even while they daydreamed fondly of what horrible fate would be theirs if they hadn't.

Crossed the perimeter of the motel lot in order to avoid the Office. Windows of which he couldn't see through. Shades drawn.

Redundant *No Vacancy* lit outside them in oily pea-green.

On the pocked concrete below it, a bundle of newspapers, uncut, reduced to worthless, pulpy cartilage by the elements.

He'd not been for sure on his first pass, at that time more concerned with a severe bout of sneezing, but now could confirm there was no vehicle parked outside the room he'd awakened in.

It seemed the several rooms around it were vacant, as well.

No car, van, truck sentry outside any.

Wondered, if as with Lang, an entire portion of the dismal block of lodgings had been paid for to ensure grim privacy.

Beneath the awning outside the room fronts, clatter of the downpour intensified.

Echoed.

A sound like several rainstorms intersecting.

Jockeying to be the forefront.

Most audible. Most pertinent.

The grit underneath his footfalls, though, seemed equally pronounced. As though each individual fleck of rough could be distinguished as his soggy footwear sloshed mop-like overtop.

Gould paced the dark, silent fronts of several rooms.

Stared at the first visible car.

Five units distant from the curb he'd first stepped up.

Partway illuminated by the dour, yellow-almost-brown glow of a vending machine.

Stood just at the limit of the arc of light produced by the device.

Grinned at the unit's filthy top.

Its weak buzz.

Disused spider webs.

Remnant insect carcasses vibrating as though the corpses still struggled for release, weakling strands yet straining to keep them strangled.

Shy of two in the morning, Gould returned to the end of the row. Snuggled tight against the very corner of the last room's brick façade.

Hadn't noticed any indication of life as he'd re-passed the window to his suite.

Curtains drawn, yes ... but with the same holes in them he recalled the sunlight slipping through.
These apertures betraying no lamplight.
All he'd seen was his own voyeuristic gaze reflected.
Ear pressed to unwashed glass simply clogging it.
Allowing the rain the other one pointed toward over his shoulder to swell in cacophony.
Might be his final opportunity.
To get the drop.
Secure an upper hand.
Could enter.
Wait in the dark.
Ashtray or lamp unplugged serving as bludgeon.
Might be he was being observed, even now.
That it hadn't been himself he'd regarded in the glass.
But another face.
Inside. Looking out.
Obscured enough by his reflection he'd mistaken himself for it.
Or else whoever had summoned him might be lurking.
Closed in a car.
Standing at a distance.
Under cloak of the rain.
Waiting to see.
Would he do as he'd been told.
Waiting as he was, himself, he supposed.

INTERMEZZO

INTERMEZZO

GOLDBERG VARIATIONS.
    Johannes Sebastian Bach.
    Variatio 15. Canone Alla Quinta. a 1 Clav. Andante.
    The performance easily recognizable as Gould's.
    All two minutes, sixteen seconds.
    All sounds of breath and humming along.
    Sixteenth selection on the record.
    Record which spun on the player.
    At arm's reach of the other man in the room.
    The man talking. Seated in a chair.
    The man Gould had hardly glanced at. Whose voice seemed screwed into the corner.
    A voice speaking in articulate purr. As much to itself as to imagined audience as to Gould.
    This voice, just then, commenting 'It's the most severe and rigorous and beautiful canon … the most severe and beautiful that I know, the canon in inversion at the fifth.'
    Gould kept his eyes fixed to the television screen.
    Device set mute.
    Whatever programme it showed a painful blur.
    His eyes unfocused.
    Forcefully unfocused.
    Unable to so much as blink.
    'It's a piece so moving, so anguished …' the man continued '…

and so uplifting at the same time ...' coughed, excused himself, ahemed playfully '... that it would not be in any way out of place in the *St. Matthew's Passion*.'

Gould's eyes watered. Stung as he finally shut them.

Stung worse as they sprung open again. Their closure having assailed him all the more violently with flashbulb stabs of what they'd seen when ushered into the room.

Before he'd staggered.

Desperately fastened his gaze to the screen.

Blood spots. Smears. Hand prints.

Chair overturned.

Contents of purse along carpet.

Coil of bedclothes.

A bare foot. Frail. Feminine. Toenails green polished.

Broken at the ankle entire.

Seemingly twined around twice.

Three times. Four.

Skin strained tight. Impossibly untorn.

'Matter of fact ...' the voice proceeded casually as the selection came to its close '... I've always thought of *Variation Fifteen* as the perfect Good Friday spell.'

No ... no.

Gould had turned his eyes toward the television too abruptly, too violently, to trust he'd seen *anything* in the room. Let alone properly.

Wouldn't allow himself to drift gaze from the blurry daub of the cathode-ray screen set atop the bureau.

There was a scent of recently percolated coffee.

A spill of which being perhaps what had made the last footstep he'd taken seem as though into a blemish of soggy carpet.

Even now the sensation of pulpy dampness underneath his rain soaked shoe, frozen toes inside what he knew was a sodden grey sock, stayed front and center.

Carpet.
Wet with coffee.
That was *all*.
'Don't you agree, Mister Gould?' the man asked exactly in tandem with the perky bang of *Variation Sixteen, Overture*, tinkling throughout the dismal suite.
But Gould could neither agree nor disagree.
Nor hear the music.
Nor see a thing.
Face twisting in anguish.
Fists pressing to eyelids.
Closed so tightly his forearms burned.
He collapsed to his knees on the stiff tile of the bathroom he'd scrambled toward.
Heat and scent of sour bile splashing the chill toilet water which speckled his face in a sneeze of viscous freckles from the impact.
Gould hugged the toilet bowl's porcelain.
Vomiting.
Fairly screaming.

'Here we are. You and I. Such as it is, eh?'
Gould allowed his body to be manipulated.
Gently.
Torso set this way then that.
Wet washcloth dabbed to his lips. Tapped along forehead. Touched soothingly to shoulders, presently bare.
Watched his shirt being examined.
Obvious splotch of discoloration. From his regurgitation. Couldn't be cleansed with the cheap soap, tap water, rough application of the towels on hand.
Garment promptly bunched up.
Discarded with a chuckle.

Striking to shower curtain.

Brief rattle of metallic circles holding the thing to the bar.

'Giving you the shirt off my back ...' Gould heard the man wryly quip as he gingerly undid the buttons of his own '... can't have you making so poor a presentation of yourself should you chance to be observed returning, after all.'

In fact, the voice supposed a proper swap, full outfit, was called for.

Why was Gould so *wet*?

'You didn't *walk* here, did you? Very, *very* silly. With your constitution you'll wind up bed-ridden! Not to mention the stuffy nose and all around *dismal* state your voice will be left.'

But this chastising almost immediately morphed to giggles.

The man unbuttoning, unzipping pants.

Removing them.

Setting the folded things on top of the television.

Stepping away briefly.

Gould chanced a glance at his own nude body in reflection.

But refused to look at the man.

Averting eyes as the voice teased over to him.

'We could play another round of *doctor*, while we're at it. Thoroughly catalogue ... what was it we called it that night? ... our *rather striking resemblance*?'

Gould closed his eyes.

Listened as the man removed underpants.

Socks.

Could almost feel the wink in the puerile quip 'We never *did* settle whether our endowments matched as lock-key as our shoe sizes, eh?'

Tensed from cold, shaky due to his recent purging, Gould shivered. Despite being stood directly beneath an overhead vent which spilled dust scented heat.

Wanted to say something.

Mention the holes in the curtains.

Someone might see in.

Wanted to turn. Rush across. Flap the wall switch to make the room dark. Ascertain for himself the security of the door, latched and chained.

But couldn't bear the thought of glimpsing whatever atrocity was splayed on the bed.

Heard his breathing intensify.

So horrendously, completely exposed.

Felt abdomen bullfrogging out, deflating, bullfrogging out, deflating.

Steeled himself.

Prepping to shut his eyes, charge blindly until he impacted the door.

Or the wall near it.

Or to crawl.

Pad his way across the carpet.

Anything.

To cover himself, cover everything with the dark.

His shoulders were jostled harshly.

Face held to place.

'Look at me' the voice demanded in a gravelly hiss. 'Hey!' A pressure of hands over his ears, fingertips tangled in his wet hair. 'Look at me.'

But he wouldn't.

'*Look* at me.'

Under any condition.

'Look at me, Mister Gould.'

Do that.

'You *need*.'

No.

'To calm *down*.'

Never.

'*Right now.*'
He felt himself slapped.
Hard.
Ears ringing razorblade.
'We have a lot to discuss … and I need to know you aren't as *entirely* round the bend as I so glumly must inform you you sure seem to be.'

'Do you see what *I've* had to do …' Gould was now being asked '… in addition to what I've *already* done? This plan of ours simply will not work advantageously for either of us without *trust*. Trusting each other to do as had been mutually decided. There is no room for … *spontaneity.*'

From where Gould was positioned at the restroom area sink, the man's address played out like abstract theater.

Dressed in Gould's discarded clothes, stood at the room's center, the man gestured emphatically in what Gould understood was the direction of the twin bed.

The design of the room, placement of wall and toilet alcove, kept Gould from actually *seeing* anything apart from the mounted hair drier if he looked in the direction the man had indicated.

Which he did.

While absently pulling on the dry underpants tossed to him gently the moment before.

Along with shirt. Pants. Socks.

Saw a dry coat, identical to the sullied one he'd arrived in.

Dry scarf, hat, gloves—also replica of his usual.

These across the room.

Draped over and resting on the seat of the chair in the corner.

His clothes.

But *not* his clothes.

The man wearing *those*, somewhat chagrined it seemed, noticing Gould's attention had fixated on the garments.

'Do you need the lot, now?' the man laughed.

Took a step as though to retrieve the coat.

Stopped short.

Retook the step then advanced two more in Gould's direction.

'Do you ...' he asked, face a mixture of bewildered and enchanted '... *really* think you're me?'

Absently put hands down soaking pant pockets, about to say something further when his attention seemed caught.

Look of giddy curiosity flashed Gould's direction as he pulled from both pockets several capsules and tablets of medication.

Three in one hand.

Two in the other.

For a moment, the man just stared at the colored pills in his palms.

'Are you ...' closed his fists '... *taking* these?'

Turned his gaze upward. Laughed toward the ceiling.

'Good God ... is *that* why ..?'

Gould merely stared, blank faced, as the man paced a circle.

Another.

Another.

Pills re-stuffed to pant pockets.

Hands swaying through the air as he seemed to be getting his thoughts in order.

'Is that why you've been ..?' he stomped his foot.

Squishy percussive.

From wet carpet.

Wet shoes.

Wet socks.

'You've ... *honestly* forgotten what you've done, haven't you?'

Gould blinked.

'What ... *we've* done.'

Blinked.
Nothing more.
'You've no idea ... what we're *doing* ...'
Wondered vaguely if he should brace for violence.
'... do you?'
Was alarmed to discover he couldn't picture himself in an altercation. Yet ... had thoughts what he would do. Where, how he would strike.
If this man attacked him.
If he ... attacked ... this man ...
If he ... *attacked* ...
... if he ... attacked ... *someone* ...
The man clapped his hands to get Gould's attention.
'Tell me who you think you are.'
'I'm Glenn Gould ...' Gould responded.
Not a beat between question and rote reply.
'*You're* Glenn Gould?'
'Yes.'
The man's eyes narrowed.
'Do you see *me* standing here?'
Gould felt his eyes narrow, too.
Focus blurring, sharpening, blurring worse.
'The subject has *squinted* his response ...' the man rolled his eyes sarcastically. 'What piece of music is playing?'
'What piece ..?' Gould mumbled after an awkward swallow
'... of *music* is playing?' the man picked up the faltering sentence. 'Right *now*. On the *record player*.'
Gould blinked.
'*The Goldberg Variations*.'
The man's expression shifted.
Amused?
Concerned?
Both?

Gould watched him stride to the corner.
Noting the holes in the curtains.
The music's volume grew violent, quite abruptly.
'This Variation ...' the man called across, affably but excruciatingly loud '... is Variation *which*?'
Gould shrank back.
Panic in his features.
Fanned his hands, a harried plea for silence.
Volume decreasing.
Music a dull crumple.
Something he wasn't certain he was hearing at all, any more.
'*Variatio Twenty-One. Canone alla Settima*' he eventually whispered.
As the man dragged the chair from the corner to the room center.
Over a swampy patch of carpet.
Took a seat.
Crossed his legs.

Signs it was increasingly distasteful to be draped in the damp garments, an almost nauseous grimace set to his mouth such that Gould wondered if he intended to strip down again, the man placidly asked 'Who do you think *I* am?'
A rhetorical lilt to the words
An unresponsive few minutes passed.
The man hadn't averted patient gaze from Gould.
Hardly seemed to've blinked.
To've done anything but sit.
An object.
Microphone waiting for input.
'Who ...' Gould swallowed '... do I think *you* are?'
No motion of response to the echoed query.

Gould's eyes tick-tocking.
Left-right.
Up-down.
Struggling to find words which would be at all appropriate.
Settled on the man's appearance.

'If I had to spitball ...' he finally ventured, hoarse, near to inaudible '... based on all available *evidence* ...' cleared throat, painfully, voice becoming more even '... I can't help but surmise you're someone who fancies themself me.'

'Fancy myself *you*?'

'Fancy yourself *Glenn Gould*.'

'You don't ... think *I'm* Glenn Gould?'

'I think ...' Gould sniffled, trying to relax to the countertop as though it were a proper perch '... you *think* you're Glenn Gould.'

'But ... *you're* Glenn Gould. You *think*.'

'I *think* ...' Gould almost grinned, enjoying this little volley despite all '... you think you're *me*. Glenn Gould.'

'But not ...' the man wetted lips, smirking '... *you think you're me* ... comma ... *Glenn Gould*.'

'Not at all ...' Gould purred '... exclamation point.'

The man laughed.

'You're being *hotly* nonspecific, aren't you?' Touched his knee tip-tap-tip-tap. 'Think of the poor soul who'd have make heads or tails of this were it *transcript*.'

'I think ...' Gould retorted, now conscious of some vehemence simmering '... you're the man who killed Paul Henry Lang.'

'Aha ...' the man nodded, switching which leg was crossed and which side of the chair he leaned to.

'I think ...' Gould continued, hands close together, almost touching lips, palms and fingertips of one lightly tapping to those of the other '... you're the man who killed a housekeeper at my hotel.'

The man let his head tilt back.

Quite far.

Slowly nodded it forward.

'And I think ...' Gould's eyes briefly ticked in the direction of the area of the room where the bed would be visible if not for the construction of the wall '... you're the one who ...' could feel nausea writhing, cheeks going flush, bowels squirming as though to leak soupy stool '... did *that*.'

'I *told* you I'm the one who did *that*' the voice mockingly playacted *pishaw*, hand flapped limp at the wrist. 'Right you are concerning our housekeeper, however. But you ...' squinted '... Mister ...' cocked eyes interrogatively '... *Gould*?' Shrugged, sniffled, rolled his eyes. 'Well *you* are the—shall we say *maniac*? *Madman*? How've you been phrasing it with your bedfellow Dziurzynski?'

Gould blinked.

Shifted in preparation to respond.

Lips parting.

Closing.

Wilted where he sat, saying nothing.

The man seemed hardly to be paying him any attention, now. Scratching at nose tip as he kept right on talking.

'I suppose epithets don't much matter.'

Cleared his throat.

'Point of order: *You* ...' thumbed in Gould's direction, paused, nodded as though to be certain all present knew who was being referred to '... are the fella who croaked Paul Henry Lang. Not as *elegantly* as you might've. But credit where credit's due.'

Gould felt his hands tighten to grip the counter.

'Were *also*, I hasten to add—without grudge, I promise—*supposed* to've been the one who did ...' titled head in the direction of the bed, tongue protruding cheek as though a finger pointing to the side.

Paused.

Shrugged.

'But seeing as you've gone a tad fuzzy round the edges, I've had to bat clean-up on the matter.'

Gave an ironic look around at floor, walls, fixtures, ceiling.

Then grinned, adding 'So to speak.'

Not to get bogged down in specifics, as such might derail the happy progress the man hoped yet to achieve by way of this meet-and-greet, he explained how it didn't much matter if Gould was presently a little cross-wired.

'It'll wind up the same, eventually, so no bother the path has grown thornier than need be.'

The two of them, it was explained as though casual recap, were engaged in a bit of business. Gould's existence—the man gestured an open palm in his direction—as *Gould* always a *transactional* arrangement.

Fifty-fifty.

'Meaning, in our present circumstance ...' he pressed on, saving Gould having to ask what he'd been preparing to '... you were to've tended to *two* ...' held up index and middle finger illustratively '... leaving *two* ...' closed fingers into the rest of limp fist '... for me.'

The man gathered from Gould's baffled, if not alarmed, expression that 'this is all news to you. Yet ...' sighed, lower lip turning out a beat '... here you are. As *requested*. Leading me to think *somewhere* in that noodle of yours lives a lizard understanding of our situation, at least.'

A silence stood.

Grew thick.

Whichever unnatural calm had slipped over Gould beginning to wither.

Yes.

Here he was.

Come of his own volition.

At the macabre beckoning of this ... lunatic?

He focused as directly as he could manage on the figure sitting all but close enough to reach out and touch.

The man claiming to be Glenn Gould.

In that moment, dressed as he was, room lit bleakly, Gould's perceptions as though a tangle of seaweed, it struck him they *could* pass for one another.

Perhaps ....

Given *situational* specifics ...

Especially cloaked in the trademark garments ...

Yes, it seemed admissible the chap could've infiltrated his life. Moved in his circles.

But ... under *scrutiny*?

No.

Conversed with acquaintances?

No one the wiser of being played a dupe hand ..?

As though hitting on Gould's precise train of thought, the man leaned forward. Folded his hands together. Legs uncrossing. Knees brought tight. Elbows positioned to rest on the shelf of his thighs.

'That's how *I* looked at *you* when we first met, I imagine.'

'I've never seen you before in all my life.'

Tut-tut-tut, the man grinned. No call to be dismissive of their history.

'You'd seen me for *years*, by then, of course. Such a fan, you'd explained. But seeing *you*—in the flesh? Could scarce believe my eyes any more than you seem able to, now. Same scene, reverse angle, eh? Me with the advantage, this go round. You'd been afforded the luxury of knowing I existed before introducing yourself, unsolicited—I, it seems, now get the honor of playing your role.'

Gould's ears began ringing.

Throat constricted.

Vision returning to absolute blur.

'You seem to remember *Maude Harbor*, certainly. Can recite the *company line* about that.'

Gould felt his hands had gone clammy.

Rubbed them over his shirt sides.

One.

The other.

Both.

'Everything alright, stranger?' the man paused his address to inquire.

Gould's lips parted.

Audibly.

Saliva thick.

Brow feverish.

Unable to utter a sound.

'You recall, you recall …' the man now batted his eyes, hamming it up, all but flirtatious '… Peggy and I. Zoltan Mostanyi, that uncouth fellow from Budapest with his blowhard monograph …' let lips stiffen predatory '… and the girl, of course. The girl and her mother. Surely you recollect … the girl?'

Gould heard, as though from beneath burial dirt, saw, as though from the throat of a cavern, the man taking theatrical pause.

Sitting bolt upright.

Whipping head in the direction of the bed Gould dared not allow himself view of.

Whipping eyes back to face him, square on.

Fingers snapping like a plucky detective.

'Say …' the man let his jaw hang as though processing a new revelation, nudging an elbow in the direction of the unseen bed '… they … do look *kinda* alike, don't they?'

Gould limply turned, bent a bit, teetering when he found position over the sink basin. Both hands, fingers spread, flattened to the counter at its either side.

Veins protruded overtop the bones leading to knuckles of his second, third, fourth fingers, these stiff but flimsy, trembling beneath his spongy skin.

Veins rounded his forearms, ropey as sumac.

Flesh colorless.

Mouth agape.

Waiting for vomit to fall.

But nothing came.

Even when fingers probed down his gurgling throat, only blunt quacks of air issued, sound of them rubbery, like flatulence let under pond water.

Eventually he'd produced a string of meaty saliva which was cleansed by filling cupped palms with water, splashing his face a half-dozen times.

Still bent over, he used wet hands to slick back his hair.

Then roughed it.

Slicked it.

Tugged a fist of it harshly as he spun, demanding 'I've no idea who you are or what you want!'

To which the man sighed.

Slouched.

His belly protruding cartoonish.

'Let me ask you, Mister Gould: why are you still *standing* here? Why are you *speaking* to me? Gracious, if you had the view I have ...' dragged lower lip along upper teeth—*pop* '... and truly believed you were who you say you believe you are ...' flared nostril, then snorted '... truly believe who-you-think-you-are had nothing to do with ...' tapped teeth together one-two-three '... *this* ...' ran tongue along gums, rubbed chin with the back of his wrist '... a *conversation galante* such as we're enjoying hardly seems the *sensible* course of action. Why not call out ...' he suddenly bellowed '... *Halp!! Halp!!*'

At the exclamation, Gould sprung from the counter. Almost moved to swing fist to silence the man.

Stopping short.

Gripping the wall corner.

Turning his head harshly to keep himself from accidentally catching so much as a glimpse of the bed mattress.

'You see!' the man gave a giddy clap.

Then, tittering, making *shh-shh* motions, hands up in apology, continued at stage whisper 'Calling for aid is the *furthest* thing from your mind.'

Stood.

Returned to normal vocal volume.

'I'll even do you one better ...' moved toward the door '... will make it easy for you, since this mess seems too beastly for your refined sensibilities ...' flapped the wall switch, the room all at once cast into darkness, only the minty light of the two bulbs above the mirror behind Gould yet shining '... go ahead, call the *authorities*. I'll wait right here.'

The toes of Gould's left foot, his left calf, began to spasm.

Forced his weight down.

Gritting teeth.

Tinnitus clearing up but ears clogging from the effort.

The man, shadowy, gestured in the direction Gould knew the telephone would be found.

'I'm certifiably atwitter over what you're going to do, here' the man cooed from the dark, volume of the record player raising so the plucks of *Variatio Eleven* could be heard but didn't drown out a single word spoken. 'Here *we* are. There is *she*. Such a shame. Tell me, Mister Gould, are you going to run to Dziurzynski? Tell the good detective *what*? *Everything*? Not a very sound idea, I wouldn't think. Seeing as, at the moment, you don't seem to ... *know* ... everything.'

Gould backpedaled.

Bumped the countertop.

Cradled himself against the wall.

The man's voice lowered as he made approach. Was revealed by the lights above the mirror.

Gould's head straining away.

Eyes only seeing himself in the glass.

Cowering.

'How would it go if—regardless who you think I *may be*, regardless who she thinks I *am*—I were to tell Dziurzynski everything, *myself*. Because *everything*, Mister Gould, is something I *do* know. And could relate to her. Wholesale.'

Gould closed his eyes.

Wanted to close his ears.

To sleep.

To vanish.

'You're here without having told anyone you were coming ...' the man's lips moved to Gould's ear, nearly brushing it '... because all this while you *know* you've been getting away with *something* ...'

Gould squirmed, but only enough to present his other ear to the man who now pressed against him.

'... even though you seem to have no idea *what*.'

The room now in total darkness, Gould pulled on his coat. Wrapped scarf around throat. Adjusted the fit of his cap. Hands slipped into fingerless, woolen gloves.

He staggered a few awkward paces, catching himself against the wall.

Where he remained.

Limply breathing.
Until he lowered himself to floor.
Jammed to the room corner.
The man turned the television on. Glow snapping stop-motion stabs of angular grey-blue watercolor while he busied himself with various tasks.
Gould closed his eyes.
Searching pockets for pills.
Any pills.
Something to swallow.
Something to unbecome himself with.
Found nothing in the coat.
Checked pants.
Felt his pulse racing.
Wondered how far he was from arterial fibrillation.
'Can I ...' he attempted to say, the words issuing as a crackling wheeze, voice the tip of a pencil breaking.
Two fingers at carotid, he continued to monitor his pulse.
Counted.
Beat. Beat.
Beat.
Was to nearly three hundred, no idea how much time had elapsed, before his hand began to tremble and he attempted once more to speak.
'Can I have my *pills*?' he managed with interminable effort.
Knew the words weren't loud enough to've been overheard.
In misery, he got to all fours.
Began crawling in the direction of the bathroom where he recalled the man had left the mound of his actual coat.
Could hear the man making efforts.
Thud of what must've been the body dragged from mattress to carpeted floor. Perhaps swathed in bedsheets.
Must've been.

A slow, cold hiss had preceded the dull sound of impact.
Further hiss as the man moved in the direction of the door.
Breathing labored.

A grin wound round the words as he asked Gould where on Earth he thought he was going.

Odd relief at hearing the voice ... *his* voice ... another voice, *like* his ... Gould welled with emotion.

An uncanny sensation passing over him.

It felt like he'd not been thinking for ... how long?

No recollection of any recent inner monologue.

Felt he may've been a husk, emptied of language, of idea.

Could've wept when he heard himself asking again for his pills, as articulately as could be accomplished.

Tone of parental exasperation, the man called across 'My God, is that what you're scheming for like a little mole, over there?'

Laughter.

Sneeze.

Sound of agitation at having to wipe at his nose.

Laughter again, though this time *sotto voce*.

'For a moment, I thought you were after the *hatchet*! After all my work rebuilding our quaint rapport, wouldn't that be the *shabbiest* manners?'

Only then Gould saw ... yes ... the hatchet was there.

In easy reach.

Thick with what must've been scalp.

Hair which he knew would be blonde matted and twisting outward from a portion of flesh.

Would be blonde if not drained alternately to blue, to grey, to briefly almost-orange, to blue, grey, orange, blue, grey, blue by flickers of the television's picture play.

Hand muffling through soggy tweed of coat to get any tablet he could find down his throat, Gould realized he'd not for a moment considered attacking the man.

Wouldn't have made any effort to even had he *known* the hatchet were in reach.

Wouldn't now.

Not because he feared the man would be braced. Ready to counter.

Not because anything.

He. Simply.

Wouldn't.

'Not, in fairness, that I'm in a position to cast stones with any semblance of good conscience …' the man said as he flapped on the room lights, Gould wincing, turning his back where he was braced at the sink '… but you *really* oughtn't be raiding my medicine cabinet. Though …' he mused '… I suppose I can't ding you for lack of commitment to your role.'

Gould listened to the chair being dragged back to the corner by the record player.

To the player's needle being reset to the *Aria*.

'For heaven's sake, though …' the man groaned in chummy tone '… you *can* turn around. Everything's squared away. Ship shape, bristle fashion.'

Sound of hands being dusted to emphasize this point.

'How in the *world* did you manage such sordid acts as rendering Lang to bitty pieces if this is how many pieces *you* go to over a spot of after-the-fact wet-work?'

To this Gould wheeled around, affronted to the point of growling. Was about to, for what seemed the millionth time, declare he'd done nothing to Lang when he noticed the man was caressing a hand over his left-side ribs.

There was genuine concern in the man's face which stopped Gould up utterly.

His own hand drifting to pat the outside of his coat where it covered his bruise.

Dropped the hand harshly.

Angry at himself for this self-inspection.

For recalling the wound.

Hip to armpit.

Almost banana yellow with streaks of moss green and smeared plum last he'd examined it.

'I'd guess that ruckus is what got your brains addled about ... except you comported yourself handily enough the following day.'

What exactly *was* going on in 'Mister Gould's poor old walnut' the man asked, tap-tap-tap to his own temple.

'It's more than a touch *disconcerting*' he admitted. 'Not ... that it's much use asking you. Seems you're in zero condition to play *credible narrator* on any point, you poor mutt.'

After a beat, Gould watched in the mirror the man saw hand through the air Shakespearian while declaring '*In quick determination I have thus set it down ...*' and settling himself to the chair he'd just tucked to its spot '... since you've already returned to the hotel, when you ought've done literally anything but ... and since you have—for reasons my apprehension faileth to grasp—gotten cozy with your darling detective-inspector, we shall from here on in simply keep our roles swapped, as they are. Frankly ...' he *tsk-tsk* gestured '... at this point *I'd* be crazier than *you* to trust you're up to the task of anything but. *The interim is mine* ...' he returned to his overdone tone of Hamletesque pomp '... *and a man's life's no more than to say one.*'

Gould's eyes held the man's until the man, as though certain of Gould's full attention, slowly drifted his gaze to the bedclothes which had been lugged near the door.

The powder-blue of the fabric was thickly fouled with the brown-black of settled coagulant.

Gould had already seen the state of the walls and glimpsed the dank slop which had absorbed into the bed-bugged bare mattress.

Had already watched the man set the despicable hatchet on the bed-stand beside the television control, as though a cute decorative accent.

'I take it I shall have to chauffeur you back wherever you've stowed the car …' the man opined, holding arms up scarecrow to denote the shabby state of his sopping wet, vomit-stained outfit '… but before then I'll ask for a hand stowing our charming young friend in my own.'

Snapped his fingers, gesturing Gould should fetch over the disused jacket, scarf, gloves, hat, still there at his feet.

It went without saying, the man supposed, how 'the two of us ought hardly be expected to *trust* one another, by this point.'

If, he added, ever they had.

'But there exists now an ingénue, dead as a doornail and snug as a bug, in the trunk of this car we sit chatting so enjoyably within.'

So unless Mister Gould felt like calling *olly-olly-oxen-free* and letting the chips fall where they might '… it's best we get of a mind concerning the extent to which we *require* each other.'

Gould had both hands, gloveless, positioned in front of the heater. Awaiting any actual warmth.

Quite anxious over the fact the car yet idled outside the vacated motel room.

Deciding it best to hold his tongue, however, and unable to discern whether the milky thick of his current thoughtscape was the result of psychic trauma over what he'd just witnessed or else of the medications he'd not twenty minutes prior two-fisted and might presently be overdosing on, he nodded in a fashion meant to be taken for concurrence.

As if this were the awaited cue, the man put the car in drive and made slow progress out of the lot.

Gould peered through the window as it passed by the few other vehicles currently parked.

Squinted intently at the ruined newspapers outside the shuttered motel Office. Glanced from the gloomy *No Vacancy* in the window to the only somewhat brighter version of the words on the roadside signage.

Eyes then settling on the rearview.

Disoriented when the face reflected turned its head first to regard the road for coming traffic, then in his direction, raising eyebrows in query.

Nothing to say, he averted eyes numbly to the gloves in his lap.

'I assure you ...' the voice said gently '... there's no reason we need see each other or communicate again until the appointed time. Indeed, it's for the best you pretend I don't even exist ...' sneezed, brought up phlegm he seemed to regret, glumly swallowing it down again '... which you seem a dab hand at *already*, eh?'

Gould returned his focus to the rearview.

Found the eyes of the man awaiting his.

Still quizzical.

Wrinkling from what must've been a smile the angle of the reflection kept hidden.

'*Appointed time?*'

Now came a struggling chuckle. The man sniffling. Angrily wiping his nose then roughing the hand over the dashboard.

'To make it the simpler, considering your present handicap ...' the voice set itself ominous as it added '... which in good faith I shall *assume* isn't mere *posturing* on your part but rather the result of *genuine* ...'

Gould waited for another word which didn't come.

Rather, the voice, tone chipper to the extent it was off putting, returned to the words '... the simpler, we'll leave it at this: once I've finished things out, I'll *contact* you.'

Gould again nodded.

Mind a cotton swab dipped in alcohol.

Briefly wondered was he being led to slaughter.

Or else already dead.

'Ridiculous ...' he mumbled.

Clearing his throat at catching the word being uttered partly aloud.

'You *are* still needed' the man said reassuringly.

Gould's eyes now closed.

'All you need *do* ... is nothing. We'll get through this. Together.'

Like before Gould wasn't sure if he heard ... thought ... dreamt.

Or if the words were ones which never existed.

Gould wasn't at all eager to leave the warmth of the vehicle's cabin. Nor certain it was the wisest idea to chance the roads in his present condition. Especially with the rainfall having metamorphosed to a steady downpour of snow.

Looked over at the car he'd parked by the dumpster.

Then at the dumpster itself.

Both, as well as the pavement surrounding, already covered as though by lace doily.

'Does not seeing each other, not *communicating*, include an end to your intrusions?' he asked.

The man was presently tensing against what seemed to Gould a monstrously uncomfortable spasm of chills so failed to answer.

Had fists balled and thumping to chest.

Jaw clenched.

Feet likely pressing down firmly to the vehicle floor at either side of gas and brake pedals.

'Your phone calls ... your tip-toeing to my typewriter all hours.'

Still unable to verbally respond, the man moved fist from chest.

Spread fingers wide.

Shook them side-to-side.

Scrunch of face clearly meant to express he'd no idea what Gould was referring to.

'If we are ...' Gould seethed through unparted teeth '... *comrades* in whichever *debauch*, I'd think it best you not pepper my days with unexpected agitations.'

The man coughed.

Seemed through the worst of his spell.

But rather than allow him to respond, Gould continued his spiel.

'I've no idea what this business of *Maude Harbor* means to you. You obviously think it should mean similar to me. It does not. So these repeated *prompts* had better be left by the wayside, let's agree.'

'Your *typewriter* ...' the man began, but cut off as he coughed viciously.

Thumping one hand hard to thigh, other to inside of driver's window.

Coughed to the point he threw open the driver's door to hack out a revolting amount of phlegm, a venous string of which still lined his chin like scar tissue upon his shutting the car and turning back to Gould

'... I've no idea what you mean. What *about* your typewriter?'

Gould snarled.

Sneezed into his own elbow due to the recent trespass of frigid air.

Tried to open his door.

Discovering it locked.

As he pulled the tab to remedy this, the man grabbed his thigh.

Contact Gould batted at, instinctively.

The man raising both arms, apologetic.

Slowly drifting the one hand to Gould's shoulder.

'You're to return the car to *precisely* where you found it ...' he began '... and then are to make your way back to your suite. *Unobserved.*'

After that?

Return to daily life.

Show up at the studio.

Humor Dziurzynski while she spun whichever wheels.

'It's a mug's game, at this point, to have you do anything outside the norm. All that remains is to *stay the course*. I'm the one, if either of us is, with reason to be perturbed over your curveballs.'

Gould held the man's gaze.

Lips still turned up.

Face only relaxing with the hand being withdrawn from his shoulder top.

'I'll finish this. You continue the life you were promised.'

The expression on the man's face was entirely sincere.

Though the statement was meaningless.

Which Gould could tell showed in his own face.

A fact which brought equal sincerity to the glimmer of fear the man quickly hid with a nod of his head toward Gould's waiting car.

'You be me. That's all you have to do, now. I'll be you. You be me.'

'Be ... *you*?'

The man issued a final, put upon, chuckle.

'Yes yes, Mister Gould ... I keep forgetting who you think you already are.'

ART OF THE FUGUE

GLENN GOULD WASN'T AWAKE.
   Sound asleep.
   Dreaming.
   In this dream, thought he'd awoke.
   Recalled, in this dream, having writhed to wake from nightmares. Images he, awake inside this dream, lay, eyes closed, unable to recall.
   Images of people.
   There. In his suite.
   Moving outside the bedroom.
   Trying their hands at the door.
   Discovering it locked.
   Then on the other side of it.
   His side.
   Inside.
   Locking the room behind them.
   Watching him.
   Faceless. Colorless. Featureless.
   Outlines which seemed one moment translucent, next moment opaque. Voids flickering. Blocking light and image of what was behind them.
   Approaching him slowly.
   While he lay.
   Watching them approach.
   Unable to draw sound from his throat. Which seemed stitched

shut, top and bottom. Sutures straining. Welling pressure of a scream growing as the closed passage heated and its flavor bent sour.

As the blank figures drew down on him. Automaton.

Missing pieces. Or pieces hanging wrong.

Where the figures had been hacked.

Where they'd been severed.

Awake in his dream, Gould next dreamt he'd felt a change to the mattress.

Someone sitting.

Light body. Scarcely enough to them their presence could alter the bed top so much as to cause a spring to creak.

Shush drawn from the sheets as they slowly leaned toward him. Not quite laying.

Gould dreamt he knew them from their scent.

Inhaled soft young hands rested over his eyes.

Eyes he opened to stare into the dark of their palms.

Felt sweet fingers shift over the bridge of his nose.

Two hands covering his face almost fully.

Base of each palm at his chin.

Tip of each longest finger cheekily smoothing the brow he kept furrowed.

Could breathe their fragrance.

Residual sweet of bubblegum pushed slowly to fingertips' pinch through lips plush and parted.

Knew he'd not taste the artificial strawberry were he to slip out his tongue. Tap it in pecks. Waggle a tickling caress.

Would taste nothing.

At most a sting of salt.

Were she perspiring.

As he was.

Parted lips. Slaked his broad tongue forward with force. Shy wet of it to unadorned skin. Exquisite.

Tasting blood.
Hands over his face stiffening tense.
Squeezing him so that his mouth couldn't close.
Fingers jamming over his teeth.
Writhing as they lengthened to probe down his throat.
Losing solidity. Turning gummy.
Decaying to clotted ichor which leaked down him.
Filling his belly plump.
Stifling under spasms his weakling attempt to scream.
To scream.
Scream.
Screamed the sound of telephone, braying from over the bedside.
Screamed the sound of giggling.
Raindrops of chuckled kisses to the tip of his nose.
Girlish whispers. Flirty.
Words spelled in Ss and Ps.
Words he couldn't make out.
Until they said 'He's right here ... he's right here ... just a minute ...'
Groaned brattish while telephone receiver was fit to his ear.
While young fingers tip-tapped a trail over sternum, down to his belly button, back up to his nose.
'I *know* you're awake ...' he heard the phone say.
Mumbled '... I'm not ...'
From the phone heard his own voice '... I *know* you're awake ...'
Not his own voice but his own.
'... Mister Gould, are you *awake* ..?'
Dreamt himself kicking legs to clear the girl from the bed as she batted them kittenish.
Dreamt he cramped himself sideways, as though his body could envelope the phone. Smother it.

Receiver bulb squirmed like an earwig into auditory canal. Melting to drainage tasted in the passage of his nostril.

'We need to talk …'

'You weren't supposed to call me, again …'

'I'm not … certain I *understand* …'

'You said I'd never have to hear from you …'

'When …' Dziurzynski was asking, confused '… did I say that, Mister Gould ..?'

'… *awake*?'

Dziurzynski. Her voice.

Was he awake, he heard Dziurzynski asking.

'Are you … *alright*, Mister Gould?'

Found himself sitting.

Legs draped over bedside.

Telephone limp at his ear.

Shivered. Startled. Stood.

Catching himself before he'd ventured far enough the telephone cord would strain.

Bedroom lacquered in daylight.

His eyes lacerated each time he attempted to open them fully. Even peeking a tentative sliver caused pain.

Viced them shut.

Under lids could see a carbonation of greenish-grey caused by the effort. Was certain his pupils would refuse to adjust without further sleep.

'To whom … am I speaking?' he coughed. Then, immediately and more aggressively, demanded '*Who* is this?'

Throat tasted of fever.

Tongue, cheeks, tonsils prickly as the tweed of his coat.

'It's detective-inspector Dziurzynski. Is something the matter?'

'*The matter*?'

A pause followed Gould's query.
Static pooled in his ear.
She'd tried ringing him at the studio.
Been told he'd not arrived.
Rang his suite several times.
'Had some poor porter pound upon your door' she said, allowing an affable musicality to the alliterative address but not keeping it entirely clean of disquiet.
He'd been asleep?
'Yes.'
Was awake now?
'Obviously I'm awake, detective-inspector ...' *what a ridiculous thing to ask* he wanted to add in a snarl but didn't '... we're speaking on the phone, aren't we?'
'*Are* we?' she replied, puff of joke crackling the connection.
'Is there some *reason* you've disturbed me, for once!?'
His temper alarmed him.
Immediately swung to apology.
'No. In fact, I'm not alright.' Or—no, no—he was *alright*. 'Of course I'm *alright*. I'm simply not *well*. Not altogether well. At this precise moment.'
Her manner of speech, as though he'd neither seemed flustered nor made his recent outburst, indicated quite clearly to Gould how, unless he abrasively demanded she hang up, the conversation was queued to continue.
So he'd acquiesce.
Spectacle to be avoided at all cost.
'Could you be brief, though?' he asked, even as he did realizing the question was based on his own train of thought rather than on Dziurzynski having said anything to justify the phrase.
No need to speak, at all—not just at the moment, the detective-inspector assured him.
Provided he was alright.

'If not altogether *well*.'
She'd merely hoped to arrange an appointment.
Could he make himself available?
Come round to her suite?
'Number *four four four*.'
Once she'd returned from her current business.

'I'd not've made such a ruckus had you seemed to be anywhere you ought to've been' she briskly added, voice in generic levity. 'You know the breed of mother-hen I am. Murder going on left, right, center? You supposed to be under lock-and-key? Suddenly neither hide nor hair of you anywhere there ought to be both …'

Composure fraying, Gould felt on the verge of lashing out.

Disguised a hiss as staving off a cough.

Was about to curtly insist immediate explanation as to just what the devil she was on about … when he noticed the time.

Two o'clock.

Past two o'clock.

Shifting toward three.

Coughed. First performative then genuinely then once more as affect. Before chuckling.

'We're always coming at such semantic loggerheads, you and I. From my vantage, I'm the exact place I *ought* be. In bed. Fuzzy slippers. Thermometer. Soup and oyster crackers. Just as the doctor ordered.'

'*Doctor*?' she asked.

Pregnant tone to the word.

Or perhaps not.

Gould simply regretted having said it.

Sighed.

'Merely an *expression*.'

'Do you *need* a doctor?'

'Not so acutely as the forty-winks even the laity know are the first step toward recuperating vigor and vim.'

Would it better if she met him there, then?

'In my dreams?'

'I was going to say in your *bedroom* …' he could picture her grin, maybe her tongue darting out '… but, trust me, have already gone crimson at how importunate I'd have come across.'

But: in his suite. If it pleased him.

Was this something which might wait until his skin was no longer scurvy?

'It is …' she clucked her tongue '… something, alas, which *cannot*.'

'I'll lurch by your abode, then …' he grumbled, unconsciously snorting up a rattle of phlegm.

Wonderful.

She'd leave him to the plop-plop fizz-fizz until then.

'Let's call it an hour. Time to tidy up. Clear the scent of stogies. Your precious lungs and all'

―――――――――

Pill. Pill. Pill.
   Pills pills pills.
   Gould shook his head after gulping each one.
   Rote.
   Counting.
   One.
   One. One. One.
   Two. Two
   Three. Four.
   Five. Five. Five.
   Meaningless.
   Tossed the notebook, not even unwrapped of its rubber band, to the side.
   Heard it impact the shower curtain.

But not hit the floor.

There it was.

Nestled in curtain bend. Suspended. Two-thirds over the arm of the tub.

'*Ta-da*!' he announced with a flourish.

Hand drifting to wipe his nose. Then to meet his other in genial applause.

'You need to pull yourself together, Glenn' he chided. Voice prim with condescension.

Turned his head toward the mirror as though it'd been the reflection there goading him with the snark.

Watched himself cross his arms petulantly.

Pouted his lip in reproach.

'Considering you've not proffered advice, to date, which even the most generous assessor would label *sagacity* you'll understand if I don't laud your shopworn bromides nor shift them to the forefront of my agenda.'

Rubbed his face. Ears. Roughed his hair.

Somewhere in the ruckus of doing so a voice cutting in with reminder 'It'd been me who'd suggested *Flee*.'

With hindsight, Gould would have to admit the word adopted a kind of prescience, yes?

Set to retort how *flee* hadn't been a suggestion so much as a bit of uneducated guesswork regarding 'what *the plan had been*' Gould instead sighed how there was no need to rake up old graves.

Explained to the empty air how 'Time might be better spent in deciding which antic disposition we might think it meet to wear.'

Watched the reflection wince.

At the Hamlet quotation.

'Yes yes yes ...' he knew who he sounded like '... just let me clean my teeth, will you? Before your nitpicking leaves me reeling and entirely hapless.'

'*Distilled almost to jelly with active fear*' he couldn't help making the reflected-him wink.

To which he flicked whatever speckle of water was left to his palsied fingers against the mirror glass.

What pills had he just swallowed, he wondered.

While tending to teeth.

Scrubbing hands.

Warm washcloth then draped over bare neck.

Shirtfront left open.

Moving hunchbacked to start the shower.

Abandoning course.

Sitting to toilet. Lid down.

He did, of course, need to get himself together.

Though he might refuse to admit the events of the previous night were anything but a kind of ringworm left over from a horrid spot of slumber, there nevertheless was no percentage in appearing rattled.

In a begrudging way supposed he was thankful for his dismal physical health, at present.

Muscle weakness.

Medicine head to the Nth.

Errant chills.

The lividity over his ribs seeming, to him, to've spread like spilt ink. Venous spider-webbing to his flesh.

'A shipwrecked sailor. Or at least a drunken one.'

He giggled.

Lost to time.

Discovered himself softly singing '*Put him in the cabin with the captain's daughter ... put him in the cabin with the captain's daughter ... put him in the cabin with the captain's daughter ... early in the morning*' while his fingers tinkled on his thighs as though they were a child's toy clavier.

What pills ... *had* he just swallowed?

Closed eyes.
Pretended to be looking down.
Straight out his bottom.
Through the uncomfortable lid he perched on.
Considered forcing himself into upchuck.
But all that would mean was he'd have to swallow something else.

'What do you care what you'd swallowed, anyway?'
At this point, why have concern with the specifics of anything?

He'd been in the suite. All night. Proof positive.
The inverse of a locked-room mystery.
Made full-circuit of the environs, regardless.
Even looked under the bed.
Would've stuck hat pins through the mattress were any at hand.
Satisfied himself the windows had remained unmolested. Inspected the locks themselves and the hidden bits of invisible tape he'd affixed to the sill and the frame.
An overabundance of certainty, certainly.
After all, not only was the desk chair yet secure beneath the suite door's handle but the armchair was snuggly abutted to it.
As he returned this furnishing to its proper station, fit precisely to the divots its feet had left indented to the carpet, he tensed.
Regarded the darker path of carpet fibres pushed out of place from his dragging the chair.
Dziurzynski said she'd sent some errand boy to knock at the door, hadn't she?
'Pestered the poor *porter*...' he whispered pedantic '... though it amounts to the same.'
Had this porter, after reporting Gould's lack of response, been instructed to intrude on the room by way of skeleton key?

'*Master* key' he clucked in correction. Though supposed *skeleton key* as a phrase more befit his paranoia.
Could picture the scenario.
Dziurzynski granting allowance.
Police Emergency or some such excuse.
Paced about in consideration.
Something had put a spur to the detective-inspector. Whatever it was might've justified heroic measures, in her eyes. Perhaps a flashback to that drowned man from her case-gone-amok.
'If such man even *existed* ...' he muttered, then muttered in counterpoint '... her manner on the phone clearly suggested anxiety, *regardless* ...'
Strode to suite door.
Went to knees.
To belly.
Tried to make out any evidence the legs of the desk chair had been jostled. From someone unsuccessful trying the door. Someone who'd have deduced it was reinforced. Thudded shoulders against it.
But it didn't seem so.
When he personally gave the doorknob a tug, an honest-to-God jostle, the chair legs only entrenched themselves sturdier.
Did that mean the door hadn't been attempted?
Or did it make it all the more likely it had been?
Had report been relayed to Dziurzynski?
'The kook's *barricaded himself in*, I think!'
For all Gould knew, this very exchange might've happened moments before the detective-inspector's call had finally stirred him.
If he hadn't picked up the line, her next move might well've been the fire brigade!
Felt his pulse turning surly.
It beat at his temples like shots from a blunderbuss.

Not wanting to release the tension with a yelp, he instead crossed to the desk and pounded palm to the blotter *kabang kabang kabang*.

In a rush of anger he snatched the sheet of paper from the typewriter. Breathed heavily enough a bubble of mucus formed under nostril. Popped. Chunky dollop of the muck striking down to the keys with an audible plop.

The writing.

Yet again the same writing.

'Impossible' he grunted.

Then with a whimper he crumpled the page.

Wheeled from the area of the room.

Wanted to hurl something against the wall.

Find a person to grip by the lapel. Slap them until they explained to him what the meaning of this writing was.

'Do you think *I* wrote it?' he mock-shouted, lashing arms as though accosting an accuser. 'Sat down before collapsing to bed?'

Wasn't the only other explanation that someone else had entered the suite?

Entered, barred the door, so therefore yet remained?

A latch in the ceiling?

One of the pictures on the wall disguising a tunnel?

'Turn a candlestick and *voila*!?' he honestly did exclaim.

Before doubling over in laughter.

Laughing until his ribs, which already ached sinister, positively scowled with cramp.

'The *other* explanation being …' he now more placidly said, as though to someone he was admitting a terrible misunderstanding to '… that it's *obviously* the exact same paper I, quite on purpose, left in the device. Precisely so it wouldn't be missing the next time Dziurzynski came by.'

The paper, now crumpled, near the closed bathroom door.

Covered with words he still didn't know who had typed.
Now words he would have to retype, again.

'The detect-tet-ive ...' stammered the hotel ambassador '... had been quite ... *concerned* about you, Mister Gould.'

Relaying this concern, the man seemed hardly relieved by the sight of Gould, leaned to front counter, quite vital.

'*Worry* is the species of *wart* our tax dollars have incentivized her to be is all' Gould sniffled.

Glanced about for a tissue. The younger desk clerk on hand quick to proffer one. Whisked the thing over, quite perky. As though a light to some fatale's cigarette.

'I was to have a closed door session with her, about now—could you tell me if she's yet returned?'

Hotel ambassador hadn't seen her, at any rate.

Touched base with the clerk. Who shrugged. Grudgingly apologetic over his lack of observational prowess.

It'd been a busy day.

Hadn't really kept track of ancillary comings and goings.

Satisfied he'd seen no incriminating ticks to anyone's expressions, Gould gave vague perusal to the few pieces of correspondence he'd been handed.

Returned the bunch to the clerk.

Explained he'd retrieve it all later.

Stepped away in the direction of the elevators.

Yes ... His illness would be of great benefit.

Kept his narrative simple. Contained.

The hypochondriac who, like the proverbial stopped clock, couldn't help but be proved right, once in awhile.

Felt confident in the clever precaution he'd taken before leaving his suite.

A call to the studio.

Explaining he may not be in the next several days.

Wished he'd had time enough to've called some friend with whom he typically commiserated about constitutional frailty.

Or at least a business acquaintance.

Discussion of updates to the documentary's timetable.

But he'd get to things like that, later.

Was pleased he wasn't much thinking about …

'… that *dream* I had last night …' he whispered as descriptor. Hissed. 'Other than my thinking about *not* thinking about it now …' added afterward as though such hyperconscious quip would take the curse off the matter.

Neutralize it.

First step toward banishing the events to unreality.

A few days of self-imposed quarantine, out of medical necessity, would afford him ample opportunity to edit events around to his liking.

Nevermind the ominous undercurrents.

The unease over how the man-in-the-dream's assurance that whichever matters yet needed tending to were being sorted without need for Gould's input or presence honestly relaxed him.

Nevermind how some unspoken part of himself *trusted* the-voice-in-the-nightmare.

Its promise the horror of the past week was coming to a close—Gould's hand no longer required.

Nevermind his tacit acceptance that, at some point, his hand had been not only required but *utilized*.

Nodded pleasantly at two members of housekeeping staff as the parting elevator door revealed them.

Only one nodded back.

One he vaguely recognized.

As someone who'd wormed her way out of conversing with him while she'd tidied his suite.

Closed his coat as he crept the corridor toward suite *four four four*.
Crept.
Yes. Knew he was.
Had better knock it off.
Now figured the housekeepers had been planted there on purpose.
To report on his demeanor.
Whether he'd stopped short at the sight of them.
Shown some sign of ... something ...
Figured at least one, if not every, door he passed on the way toward Dziurzynski's concealed an underling Peeping Tom.
Notepads out.
Jotting astute assessments of his approach.
'I'm ill!' he wanted to announce. Turning a circle so anyone watching would hear him as he did. 'That explains everything which might strike you peculiar!'
Added to which, he might under cross-examination further expound, he was under the impression Dziurzynski might not even be in her suite.
'Therefore ...' he had to restrain himself from subvocalizing with aggression '... any awkwardness observed might well be considered representative of my considerations for tact and propriety!'
Second guessing himself.
Ought he to've telephoned first?
So forth. So on.
Stopped in front of the door to Dziurzynski's suite.
Faced it.
Stared at its peephole.
Counted down thirty.
Let out a long breath.
Knocked.

However he'd envisioned the detective-inspector's suite, this was far from it. Though, point of fact: Gould couldn't recall whether he'd ever given a moment's consideration to what the interior of *four four four* would resemble.

Resemble?

Well, not so different than his own suite.

In principle.

Or any other guest room in the building.

What was striking was how Dziurzynski had taken pains to make the place seem quite empty.

Writing desk pushed into the far corner. Against the wall.

Next to it the sofa. This tipped to its side, legs facing outward toward the entry door.

Oval coffee table was also on its side.

Stacked atop sofa.

Its legs pressing to the wall, one resting snuggly against the base of a window pane, half-inch above the sill.

In a neat row beside this lay a collection of dumbbells.

Squinting, Gould couldn't quite tell if any two were of the same size, weight.

Multiple colors.

Several grey.

Most black.

One green with a medicinal yellow gauze wrapped around the grip.

The armchair was flush against the closed door to the bedroom. Faced in the direction of the windows. Bed pillow, bedcovers arranged on it. Clearly rumpled from use.

The short lamp table, like in his own suite's library nook, was set in front of the armchair at exactly such distance he could picture whoever sat in the one resting feet, perhaps crossed at the ankles, atop the other.

Where Dziurzynski *slept*, he was certain.
As to the bookshelf, the thing was entirely empty.
Where the books had been relocated wasn't immediately clear.
None stacked on the floor.
Nor anywhere visible.
Might be in the bedroom.
Or the bathroom, he supposed.
The pedestal which in his room would've held the record player, before it'd been spirited to the suite where the housekeeper's body had been discovered, was also absent.
Maybe no record player had ever been present in Dziurzynski's suite, of course.
At approximate center of the floor stood a metal chin-up bar. Collapsible. Which Gould was testing the stability of when he heard the toilet's flush.
Held a dubious expression on his face until, a moment later, the detective-inspector exited the privy to rejoin him.
Cocked his eyebrow while giving the bar a light shake. Its flimsiness more than apparent.
'Is this department issue?' he teased.
Couldn't imagine the contraption would be good for anything besides coming loose at every screw, winding up in pieces along the carpet, if someone of even his own slight heft were to utilize it in earnest.
'I just like walking under it' Dziurzynski shrugged. 'Plus, it was gifted to me by somebody *noteworthy*. Who also mailed me a jump-rope—but I chucked that right in the bin.'
She scoffed.
Could Gould picture her jumping rope?
'You're an imaginative, artistic sort, after all. Who knows what all images *you* can conjure. But even if you can, I can't. Jumping *rope*? No, sir. Don't even like lifting my feet when I walk if it can be circumvented.'

Gould sneezed.

Excused himself.

Then assured her he could well understand.

Focused now on the paper bags lining the far wall.

Labeled for days of the week ... and times of day.

Wondered if Dziurzynski kept her garments in those. Would be cumbersome to move the armchair to get into the bedroom every time she needed to change.

Now, for example, she was adorned in yet another intricate outfit he'd not seen a single item of before.

Was about to remark 'You're quite the clothes horse ...' when she, perhaps noticing the look of curiosity on him and understandably thinking it referenced their previous chatter, pointed to the chin-up apparatus, remarking 'You can try it if you'd like. The maid who set it up for me could do *fifty*. In-a-row. And you've seen her, eh?'

Big wink.

'*Trust* me ... it'll hold.'

From the floor near the overturned sofa, Dziurzynski took up a cup of what Gould presumed to be coffee. Gave it a sniff.

Judging from how extremely she'd tilted the container in order to attain her sip, he reckoned it must've been dregs in the thing, only. Barely enough liquid to cover the circular base.

So after taking what ... must've been ... a second entirely *imaginary* sip ... she asked him 'Do you know anything about *fugues*?'

Seemed it took her a moment to notice the bemused, somewhat wary, squint he was purposefully aiming her direction.

Through glaze of his watering eyes.

Which itched.

Distracting.

Felt as though he could pluck the bloodshot straggles from them as though errant eyelashes.

When she did pick up on his expression, ticked her head a tock. Smiling.

Gould supposed the cutsie expression was meant to match whatever he looked like to her.

After a long moment of this chipper staring contest, Dziurzynski asked, with seemingly no hint of guile '... have I said something *strange*?'

She must forgive him. Not only his appearance and general malaise, which he thanked her for being demur enough not to remark on, but also for his present caginess.

'Your *question* ... might be a nimble wind up of sorts, no?'

Now it was she who must beg pardon.

'For nothing fancier, however, than having no idea what you mean.'

Tilted her cup.

Not as far as before.

Flicked its handle three times, after.

Holding its rounded side toward her, palm curled around.

'I'm known for being somewhat of an *expert* ...' he dragged toe of one shoe, affecting aw-shucks.

'Expert ...' flicked cup '... on ...' *ding ding ding* '... what?'

'*Fugues,* detective-inspector. Though ...' gestured deprecatingly '... perhaps *smarty-pants* is how it'd be denoted in my case. Depending on to whom the inquiry was addressed.'

'Oh that's a type of *music*!' she exclaimed. Both arms swung out grandly, despite cup. 'Like the *Phantom of the Opera.*' Wiggled fingers of one hand to mimic dramatic organ play, other hand wobbling unevenly, cup in it turning, at times, all the way over. 'He was kooky for those, right?'

'He did ...' Gould chuckled as though in on the joke, his job to draw attention to it so that it might be spoiled and moved on from '... yes, take a shine to *one* of them, at least. Lugged it to the top of the Pops on sheer cult of personality.'

'But did the Phantom of the Opera *kill* people?'

She'd never read the book.

'Or *any* books. Especially *old* ones.'

Someone told her he'd killed people, though.

'Is that true?'

'Is ...' he felt his pulse attempting to quicken through blood sludged to cake batter '... *what* true?'

Knew his face must've appeared utterly at a loss. Bumpkin like. Couldn't sort out whether Dziurzynski was being purposefully *non sequitur* or if he was lagging in uptake of stimuli.

'It doesn't matter ...' she waved her free hand while returning cup to the floor where she'd lifted it '... I'm being a fatuous priss.'

Clapped her hands.

Wiggled her hips.

Clapped her hands, again, pointing them at Gould and said 'You're an *expert* on fugues, you were telling me?'

Broke off from her odd dance.

Paced broadly as she continued.

'What are they, exactly? Little *songs*, right? But much more complicated, no doubt.'

Snapped her fingers, tone suddenly like a pal asking to borrow a sport coat to impress a date 'Hey—gimme a smart soundin' tidbit I can pawn off as my own to make some crook think I know all kinda things.'

Gould swallowed.

Coughed.

Excused himself to turn his back and sneezed.

Groaning afterward as though repulsed.

Waved away Dziurzynski's offer of tissue box while he instead took one of the many he'd filched from the front desk and wadded down his coat pocket.

Blew his nose.

Gritting teeth afterward at feeling the nasal cavity immediately re-clog. To the point of strain. Ready to freely leak.

Once he was composed, he discovered Dziurzynski hadn't moved or changed her demeanor.

Stared at him, eagerly.

Tongue pinched in teeth.

'Something nifty to rattle off about *fugues* ...' she prompted.

Hem-hawing he'd no idea where to begin, eventually said to her 'The idea to which the fugue is most conspicuously the servant is a concept of unceasing motion.'

She set one finger to chin.

Posture of keen fascination.

After silence for another moment, Gould widened eyes at her.

Did she want ... *more*?

Puffed cheeks, rolled hands and continued by saying 'Within the forward movement ... each phrase ... each musical sentence will ... inaugurate its own special problem ... its own ...' he coughed, dead certain she was about to finish his thought for him, would have had he held the pause an instant longer '... unique cause for anxiety.'

Bowed head to indicate he'd finished.

Emphasized this by making pantomime of pauper with pockets turned out.

Dziurzynski crossed her arms.

Nodding.

'You really oughta write a thing like that down, bravo.'

Here she was being a liar, again.

Confessed it, outright.

'It's getting to be a shabby habit between you and I' she laughed, whipping arm in the air, stopping it short as though she'd have thumped him on the shoulder if not considerate how unwelcomed the physicality would be.

Then, as though unable to help herself, did a motion like she'd have tickled him in the ribs. Index and center finger of each hand curled to pincers.

By *liar* she'd meant 'Of course I knew you were the Big Man On Campus about fugues.'

They'd told her downstairs.

'*Mister Gould is quite sensitive* the hotel folks intimated. Over and over. All the while fully aware I was tending to the corpse on the premises. Everyone so worried my longshoreman manners might've ruffled your genteel feathers so fierce I'd never get a word out you.'

What she'd figured they'd all meant by the heads-up was to tacitly affirm how nastiness such as cleaving ladies' faces in half would never be anything to do with Glenn Gould.

'Wanted me to understand you needed to keep your too-cool-for-school *aloofness*. The *artiste* and all. Mustn't be *rattled*.'

Or maybe they just didn't want him to scamper off to a room down the street, she winked.

'Piano players are good money, I'd imagine.'

Gould had been nodding along in good humor but felt his smile becoming increasingly tight. Kept eyes held wide hoping it would hasten her toward some concrete point.

An expression she presently acknowledged.

'It's what got this pesky idea in my head …' she said as though corralling her rambunctiousness '… sometimes just a *word* can do that to me. A glut of *actual* clues can gum me up and get me glum. Nice to vacation in the esoteric, awhile.'

'And I'd sure be honored to join you there ...' he said, looking around for someplace to actually seat himself '... provided you might deign to clue me into precisely *which* esoteric climes you've taken holiday in.'

'*Fugues*. Which are also a thing to do with the human psychology.'

Did he know that?

Well, they were.

'A kind of believe-it-or-not some people get the wrong end of. We've all heard of *sleep* and we've all heard of *walking* ...' she said, meeting the plea in his eyes for a perch but only shrugging to indicate she didn't see any place, either '... but to the majority of us the concept of *sleepwalking* is quite theoretical. *Fictional*, even. We know the *one* thing, know the *other*, thus lazily reckon the third must be ... *kinda both*.'

'I've heard tell of fugues' Gould patted hands to thighs, giving up the hunt for a chair. Lowered himself, crisscross applesauce, to the carpet. 'Even once I'd dreamt I was eating a giant marshmallow and when I woke up ... well, I won't bore you with the rest.'

Gould's new position seemed to delight Dziurzynski.

She adopted an exaggerated posture of school-marm, touching nose like to straighten glasses, before continuing her address in the style of lecturing a kindergarten class.

Gould grinned along.

Lacings fingers.

Pressing hands to lap.

Leaning forward, eager beaver.

'You see, Mister Gould, most people say things just like your little joke and think they have the gist. But every one of them's way wrong. Not wrong enough you'd want to break their hearts correcting them, of course—because ten-out-of-ten times, what could it matter?'

She abruptly dropped to the floor.
Joined him at eye level.
Legs crossed. Leaning back.
Arms behind her. Palms pressed to the carpet in support.
'But sometimes ... you *want* to set them straight. At least enough to point out how repeating things you don't *really* know can come quite close to *lying*.'

Gould, of course, had simply been cracking wise about gobbling up his poor pillow—but Dziurzynski promised him, so far as fugues went, he wasn't far off the mark.

There were blokes, for example, who might raid the fridge past bedtime. Really chow down. For love nor money not be able to explain their migrating waistlines.

'The sight of a bin full of chicken bones or the heads bit off their kiddos chocolate bunnies doesn't give them pause. They just go buy another chicken, another bunny, nothing's nothing.'

Even when their bank book doesn't tally they'll not raise a whisker in suspicion.

'*The mind ...*' she wanted to impress upon him '... doesn't register anything about their consumption. Before or afterward. Much like how everyone has a physical blind-spot the wrinkles of their grey matter work to fill in with composite details, these poor wretch's noodles caulk in *events*.'

Another guy, to give Gould wider context, might up and leave his apartment house. Middle of the night. Stroll to some pub, twelve blocks away. Drink a brand of bourbon on recommendation from a barkeep.

Next day?

Recall nothing at all.

'Might throw darts or try to scam billiards. Oh some people do all manner of things they'd, no pun intended, never *dream* of doing otherwise. Make a pass at some lonely loose lady, bum cigarettes by the half-pack, or get into fisticuffs with someone they thought was eyeing them queer.'

There was a word for it.

The phenomena documented, here and there.

Pills could be prescribed to combat it.

Or else more shocking therapies employed to get the weirdos back running at factory specifications.

'Only in extreme cases, that last bit. Like once-upon-a-time this certain fella would cut himself up and down the wrist. No idea he was up to it. Only when he was *asleep*, Mister Gould, did he understand how much he loathed himself. How sorely he hoped *his own quietus to make with a bare bodkin.*'

'Yes yes ...' Gould waved off these more salacious details '... sleep-walking. Sleep-talking. Sleep ... *mutilation*—why not?'

'But that isn't the half of it' Dziurzynski whispered, scootching closer. 'Other people, wide wide *awake*, go about their exact lives—home, hearth, promotions at work—but will, when you ask 'em, relate *radically* alternate narratives of their days. Different cast of characters. Have a different name, themselves. None of their remembrances *true*. Nutty thing is, all the stuff they *say* is happening to them doesn't interfere with their going right along with the events everyone else who actually knows them tells them they're living and breathing. These loons don't know they're *forgetting* what they've *actually* experienced ... because ... they never *knew*.'

Except, once in awhile, they discover schisms.

Did he follow her?

'Some kook will chance to drift into full awareness of their daughter's piano recital, for example—know who their daughter is, who they are in *relation* to their daughter, why they're in the audience *et cetera*.'

During these clarities, such people will possess the memories everyone would expect them to ... but would get befuddled to the point of mania when they chance to recall some event from their *fantasy*.

Some *conversation* they can quote verbatim.

Some *place* they can draw out a map to.

Some *event* they feel happened maybe the day before, maybe long ago—but which they are at a loss to square with their life.

'Mister Gould ...' Dziurzynski said, hands in front of her like stoking shadows from out of a campfire set between them '... in one zany happenstance I read about there was a lady who kept two households. Paid the bills for a family of four and another set for a family of two and a dog. Meanwhile, she lived in a cold water squat all on her lonesome. Jockeyed the till at some Launderette—no idea she'd have the means to do anything but!'

Why didn't her families think something was fishy? Gould might wonder.

'Because she had *zero* families! Paid for two empty townhouses. Cities apart. The jobs she thought she worked in each narrative pure poppycock.'

It wasn't real.

It never happened.

'The mind's a jerk' was her conclusion so far as that situation. 'Even when they told the woman the truth, Mister Gould, presented her the War Bonds grandmother had willed her and which she'd cashed to finance the daydreams it didn't make a lick of difference. Woman wouldn't trade her Launderette for the world.'

Now standing—'Pardon my old lady joints'—Dziurzynski wanted to float him a *What-if?*

Would she mind terribly if he lay down for it?

'Not at all.'

She had a sofa, same as him, by the way.

'Somewhere around here.'

If he wanted it badly enough, she could play the better hostess and lug it upright.

No need to make the extra trip on his account.

Laying prone helped with the sinus congestion.

'I don't taste pleasant going down, by any means, but do prefer it over having to spit like a common camel.'

What-if: somebody knocked on his door.

'This is you, plain old Glenn Gould, doodling your records and avoiding everyone and all that, keep in mind.'

What-if: this somebody announced they'd been looking for him. For ages.

Turns out, they explain, he was an experimenter of great repute who'd gone missing.

Via his experiments 'the cure for what ailed certain people' had been on the brink of actualization.

But his notes were incomplete.

At the crucial juncture.

His insight required to polish things off.

What-if: somebody could prove it.

Witnesses, photos, collegiate adoration up the wazoo.

'To *you* they'd sound daffy. If they didn't? If you *believed* them? Tough luck! You may've once *been* who they say you were ... but you're merely you, now.'

What-if: another knock on the door.

This time an officer is so sorry to say he'd been a Nazi or some other outrageous sort of person.

A tribunal demanded his presence.

Luckily deemed it inhumane to proceed against him due to the provable amnesia he'd been afflicted with.

Then a third knock.

'I promise you, I'm almost done. This time some lady. Says she's your sister. You'd vanished. Brave gal never lost hope about finding you. Having done so, wants you to return with her to the workaday drudge of small town wheresoever.'

Did Gould get the idea?

'I'm none of those people.'

'Precisely ... ' she clapped '... they have zero rights to you.'

Unless ...

What-if: a final knock.

From the Big Brain of some cutting age laboratory.

Able to literally reinstate Gould's *actual self*.

'This is what *they* call it ... but here's the rub ... they can only reinstate *one* of your actual *selves*.'

Dziurzynski clapped, again. Stamped her foot and made balking sounds as though such a puzzle were quite the corker.

Looked down at Gould who, after realizing she'd lapsed into silence, opened his eyes, hand held up as though to shield himself from light.

'Who ... would I choose to have myself *reinstated* as? Is this the *quandary*?'

Didn't he agree, were it possible, each claimant had a solid case?

'It's never nice to be a runaway Nazi' he sighingly supposed.

'And think of the poor kids with clubfoot you might make life on Earth gentler for!'

He laughed at this.

Regretting it, immediately.

Coughed while trying to say 'Not to mention ... who would help ... my sister at the Launderette ..?'

Didn't bother about repeating it cleanly once he'd recovered from the garish, indiscernible mottle of language his hacking fit had made of the words.

Dziurzynski not so much as suggesting he try.

'If you stay *you*—plain cake Glenn Gould—all the world would lack for is another record, eh? Of music you didn't even *write*. Music a billion others have *performed*. Zillion others will *keep* performing. Some maybe to *spite* you. What else? Some liner notes about fugues? Moot arguments concerning the prospects of recording which their own thesis make instantly obsolete? You've no lover to abandon, as you lack a head for the dames. Have curated a fanbase who're custom built to dig you even better once you've kicked the bucket, regardless. *The more posthumous the better* is the motto of you classical wonks! Glenn Gould *vanishes*? Nothing lost to the ages save the stubs of tickets to a few concerts you never wanted to give!'

'Except I don't play concerts, anymore. As you know.'

Supposed she did.

'Even there, though ...' she held up her finger like a know-it-all '... with you still here ... *why* you don't has never been revealed ... not to anyone's satisfaction, at least.'

'Maybe I became not me' he sarcastically let drift from his lips in mock dreaminess.

She'd been going to say maybe he'd never been him.

'Just a silly rhetorical, in any event.'

Still, if her career in murderer catching veered south she'd make a decent hack playwright, wouldn't he say?

'Heaven forfend this comes off curtly ...' Gould groaned as he propped to elbows, too depleted to move further to his feet '... but I'd like to verify that all this discussion, stimulating though it may be, is *apropos of the wet snow*, as they say?'

That's not how he'd earned himself the sniffles, was it?

'How's that?'

'Did you get caught out of doors? The air has been biting shrewdly, since last night.'

'No no no. Safely stowed. Windows barred and locked. The cuddliest flake couldn't have found its wayward way to me for trying.'

What he'd meant was he found it difficult to believe someone as busy as the detective-inspector would've summoned him from his sickbed to 'shoot the existential breeze.'

Aha. She understood.

Clicked feet together. Gave a military salute.

'Down to business, then. Bit of a nasty business it was, at that. *Again*. Last night. You think *you've* got it bad with your rhinovirus, Mister Gould—well this other sad soul caught the acute end of yet another hatchet. An ab—'

Gould blanched.

Strained to hold down a rise of nausea.

The crawl of sickness incidental to what had been imparted, nevertheless something he chose to milk the moment with.

Get himself centered.

Gestured Dziurzynski to pause before going on.

She having already cut off mid-word.

Picking up on the precise syllable she'd halted with once he'd laid back down flat, motioned she ought feel free to proceed.

'... solute house of horrors' she was sorry to say.

This time, the slaying seemed to be something trenchantly personal.

'An almost palpable ... vindictiveness ... to the savagery' she explained, pronouncing *vindictiveness* to come off as cruel, as morbid as it might be made to.

Head severed. Completely.

'Or not exactly *severed*.'

Hacked. Pried.

'Crowbarred off, almost. Not quite all the way. Attached, yet

... simply ... *dangling* ... like a sack full of skull.'

Not that it was necessary to bore or burden Gould with the gnarliness.

Except to mention how 'Peculiarly enough, a finger had been removed. Chopped digit left by the record player. From all appearances, this done to remove an heirloom ring the victim wore.'

Shrugged.

Tidbit about the ring was 'according to the old biddy living next door who, shock of her long life, discovered the body' Dziurzynski added, offhand.

'When ...' Gould asked to illustrate he was earnestly following along '... was *this*?'

Last night, this morning.

Another woman.

'Big fan of *yours*, it so happens.'

By which Dziurzynski didn't mean merely the presence of record player spinning 'your trademark tune.'

Nope.

Victim was 'a *bona fide* enthusiast.'

Also interesting was how the fine gal had it in her head 'this per the old biddy living next door' she might soon have occasion to *meet* Glenn Gould

'Face to face.'

He opened his eyes.

Saw Dziurzynski flashing him a silent-film pantomime of *don't look at me* concerning when, where, how, or why the victim got herself possessed of such a notion.

'Story goes it was something her *daughter* might've been able to broker.'

'Her ...' Gould struggled his way to elbows '... *daughter*?'

Took in a measured breath.

Steeled to attempt lifting himself.

Promptly wilted with a pitiful chuckle.

'The ... dead woman's *daughter* ... was orchestrating a pow-wow with me ..?'

'So the old biddy living next door alleges' Dziurzynski nodded. Extending a hand to help Gould to his feet.

'The dead woman's daughter ...' she added while straining him upright '... who has gone missing.'

The face. Her face. A Polaroid face. Flat and eternally glossy.

A girl. Young.

Young girl's blonde hair to shoulders, not quite.

A smile. Meant for someone. Beyond the camera.

Noncommittal pleasantness.

Flashbulb in her eyes.

A mother perhaps telling her 'Hold still' or telling her 'Really, please *smile*, now.'

Because ... this smile.

Wasn't real.

Wasn't quite ... anything.

Gould had the square of this image in his fingers.

Giving inspection at Dziurzynski's request.

He regarded the face.

Watched it.

As it became the only object apparent.

Cheeks beginning slowly to breathe.

Jaw in tension.

Seesaw. Tip tap.

It chewed.

Smile growing.

A bubble blown.

Pink sugared globe.

Pop.

Hair a gentle rustle. As from a breeze.

Which seemed to carry on it the scent of brine.
A scent he put down to the growing clog of his mucus.
The thick needing to be cleared.
Photo handed back while Gould's head turned. Embarrassed.
'Excuse me.'
Tissue fished from pocket.
A long, pulpy honk.
Three sniffles.
Apologies, again.
'This girl is …' he began.
Paused.
Dziurzynski finished for him '… the *daughter*. Of the *dead woman*.'
Did he know her?
Forgive Dziurzynski for saying so, but it sure seemed he did.
'Yes.'
He knew her.
'I *think*.'
She resembled, very much, a waitress he'd recently met.
'A … *waitress*?'
The detective-inspector became quite direct.
'*This* girl—you're certain?'
' … no …'
No. He'd stop short of *certain*.
'… no …'
But he was *fairly* certain.
'It's very good you've said so' Dziurzynski said like a sigh. 'Oh no, nothing like *that* …' she added, waving a dismissive hand as though in response to an expression of affront over some accusation, though Gould couldn't imagine what expression or posture he'd taken to warrant such action '… it simply cements some other information I've been given. Regarding the disappeared girl. Right now, we've very little to go on. But that you

knew … her … the missing girl, anyway, is a waitress, yes—a *waitress* you're exactly correct.'

If the detective-inspector didn't think it too shabby him asking it, might he have a seat?

'In your *bedroom*' he gestured a polite sweep of hand toward the chair with undone bedsheets slung from it.

No need to've asked, but permission kindly granted.

Could put his feet up on the pedestal there, too.

Perhaps it was a tad personal to tell him so, but as far as she was concerned 'Beds are for the birds.'

Ever since her girlish days working security overnights, the most restful slumbers she'd experienced were those atop chairs.

'Preferably laid across three cheapo, collapsible ones. That's just how I slept. When I ought to've been more responsible.'

But it was only a feed mill she'd guarded, she explained with a blush.

'Streets around it overrun with cockroaches you could build bridges with. Real fists, the grimy vermin.'

She'd sleep with head on one chair, second used to support her ample bottom, and third for her jackbooted feet, legs crossed at the ankles.

'Add plump, company issue-coat overtop me? Place could've burnt to the ground with me in it, I'd never have known.'

Gould found this anecdote charming enough.

But wouldn't lay.

Needed nothing more exotic than 'a seat with an armrest to look rakish with Victorian pallor upon.'

Dziurzynski gamely flashed thumbs up.

Now that he mentioned it, she saw what he meant.

'You look dismal. Like there's a portrait of you someplace getting spiffier by the minute.'

Only that ought to happen the other way round, right?

'I'm forever bumbling Dorian Gray matters such as that. But at least the canvas will fetch handsomely at the estate sale. I'll be remembered for a beauty not my own. Some kittens will live well off the proceeds after I've ...' he rolled his hands, keeping himself from adding *shuffled off this mortal coil.*

But he'd looked robust enough when last they'd spoke, hadn't he?

'Though the weather *has* turned flip and chill' she winked. 'Sorry ... you've been snug inside. Must've caught an *indoor bug*, you told me.' Then, a bit stricken, she motioned like she'd touch his shoulder were they friends before adding 'It's not something I've *said*, is it?'

He blinked.

Again.

The question not processing.

'Some remark maybe that made you feel yucky?' she explained.

'No no no' Gould finally muttered.

He'd just had difficulty ...

... picturing the girl dead.

But let's not get ahead of himself, Dziurzynski implored.

'Right now, she's only just *missing*.'

Did he remember which day it'd been he'd met the waitress, exactly?

One morning since he'd been in town, these weeks.

Supposed that much was obvious, though.

'As well as quite vague.'

Let him think.

One day, recently.

Please understand and forgive how 'even with these intrusive, altogether unnerving, happenings set to one side' he'd much *else* on his mind.

Work taking intense concentration.

Sleep irregular.

'The days blend, detective-inspector. One atop the other. Flatten down into a mush. *Before* seems to happen after *After* and *After* before *Before*, in retrospect.'

Had it been only the once?

Twice?

A time or two. Yes.

'Only ... *once* in conversation.'

'At *your* prompting?'

At neither his own nor at hers, exactly.

Gould further explicated, for context and clarification, how he drove at night. As a habit. Plus harbored 'an affinity for the fine dining only a greasy spoon can offer. Add in how I can be loquacious, if given half an excuse, and the recipe for eventually chatting with a waitress is complete.'

Night working types were always quite welcoming.

'Especially those paid to be.'

He imagined this girl's interest was simply in passing the time.

'Though I tip well, too. Her motives may've been multiple' he chuckled.

Not exactly certain why he was saying what he was saying.

Nor certain where to cut off without the cessation seeming conspicuous.

'You hadn't had any occasion to meet her *socially*?'

'The girl was no more than minutes old' he bristled.

Posture stiffened.

A *tsk* of tongue to teeth he regretted having made.

Blushing as though only right then picking up on what might've been implied by her question, Dziurzynski whisked hands behind her.

Bow of remorse.

Explaining she'd meant 'the girl's mother.'

Not satisfied by this excuse, Gould demanded that if Dziurzynski had thoughts in any degree tawdry she ought spit them out, there and then, so he could, in no uncertain terms, put an end to their little conference.

'You didn't lure me up here in order to tell me some other person, nothing whatsoever to do with me, has been killed, after all. Aghast though I am to learn of it, let's not continue playing pat-a-cake, you and I. I'm here because you have something to ask me, so *ask*.'

Waitaminute.

She admitted her folly.

'My thinking gets ahead of itself, Mister Gould. That segue was the pits, I'll allow.'

But she'd offered to meet him outside of his own suite in the spirit of *camaraderie*.

To solicit his help, in fact.

'It's getting a touch difficult to keep certain facts from the Press and, therefore, tricky to ensure your privacy.'

A photograph of an empty corridor outside her hotel room wouldn't move a lot of evening editions. While had they met in his room—'Which I offered to do'—an officer would need to've been posted at the door.

'Which would make for a terrific image to caption, eh?'

As it so happened, the girl had been witnessed by many parties as recently as yesterday.

'I'd hardly accuse you of kidnap when, meantime, I've been imping your every step, eh?'

While on such subject, let her add, in earnest, how she hadn't a thought in her wily little head about accusing him of the mother's *murder*, either.

'Seeing as time of death, so best as it can be figured by those versed in the proper forensics, has you chatting with front desk and signing for scrambled eggs and ...' she trailed off, shrugging palms.

Gould's ears, meantime, had begun ringing.

Exactly when she'd uttered the word *kidnap*.

Now cleared his throat. Tilting brow in apology.

She was quite correct.

Had made it clear, multiple times, he was under no cloud of suspicion.

His reaction must've seemed markedly odd, he realized.

... based as it was on the image blurry in his mind's eye ...

... on the dead certain understanding the body in the sheet he and a man like him had lugged to a car trunk had been tiny ...

... about the weight of a dead waitress, sure ...

It made perfect sense. Gould quite took her point.

'Occasion to see the woman, the missing girl's *mother*, socially.'

A visit to this woman, at home.

As the old biddy living next door had hinted at.

The dead woman speaking to the old biddy of such visit because of what had been taken as an assurance such meeting might be arranged.

Or because the missing girl had promised to extend an *invitation*, at least.

Yes.

Certain things Gould had imparted to the missing girl 'more or less in passing' could've been reported to her mother.

Elaborated on.

Wishful thinking inserted.

Dziurzynski's question had made sense.

'The missing girl ...' Gould took pains to use this phrase, now, though took greater pains to not come off as taking pains, full stop '... had enthused to me how her mother was quite a fan. Of my piano music.'

So the missing girl had known him, on sight?

'Not hardly, no no. The fact she'd no idea who I was partly the reason the matter of who I was had come up. While being affable during my repast, incidental comments brought us round to my making mention, rather obliquely, to my previous profession. Some question of whether I were a ... man of ... *note* ... or ...' he slowed his pace, affecting expression meant to suggest the specifics were hazy due to their lack of having seemed of any consequence at the time '... some one of those ... *odd* ways conversations go.'

He rolled his eyes to Dziurzynski grinning wide.

'The missing girl ...' Gould re-began after a deprecating ahem '... told me she'd brought up our conversation to her mother ...' tensed his jaw, his ears popping a moment, rush of air in immediately clogging them '... who was ... it seemed ... an *aficionado*.'

Dziurzynski assured him this was so.

Had items with his autograph on them and all.

'Positively *avid*, she seemed.'

But if the detective-inspector may flag a point for clarification: had the girl telephoned her mother, there and then?

'Between refilling your water ... or what?'

Gould felt exposed.

Found he was unbuttoning his coat just to button it back as though doing so made it buttoned twice over.

Secluded him.

Worked the length of the middle finger of one hand beneath the wool of the glove over the other.

Scratching at his moist palm.

In thinking it over 'No … Yes …' no, he'd chatted with her *twice*.

Again used hesitation and fraught facial expression to denote how little impression such chats had made, thus how dubious their linear composition.

Meanwhile, his mind whirring to sort out where he'd claim these two meetings fell on a timeline.

Dziurzynski, however, seemed entirely disinterested in probing further. Instead asked him what he'd said that might've been interpreted as possible opportunity to meet the parent.

Keep in mind he was saying this speculatively, felt it was a stretch, but 'We'd made a deal that were she to remember my order, fetch it to me unprompted when next I dined in, I'd let her in on select, juicy confidences she might use to curry favor with the old lady.'

'Curry favor?'

Gould shrugged as though suddenly his entire notion seemed lame brained.

'I'm overthinking it, now. At the time it was off the cuff, gregarious chatter … I just meant, maybe the import of that *deal* had, through the Game of Telephone, me-to-girl-to-girl's-mother, got lost in translation.'

Dziurzynski understood.

But motioned him to elaborate about '… currying *which* favor?'

'A bigger allowance …' Gould puffed breath out cheeks, face a cartoon of *who-knows?* '… a later curfew … whatever a *child* thinks is of value these days, you see?'

She saw.

It made sense.

'So either …' Dziurzynski took over the idea '… the girl had outright *introduced* the idea to her mother, after seeing the effect delivering whichever tidbit you'd gifted her had on the woman

... or else the girl's mother had, with no outside prompting, begun a *daydream* of her own. Got caught up in it. Spun it as a certainty in order to put on airs with the old biddy.'

Yes.

That made sense.

'What sensitive morsel had you promised to divulge ...' Dziurzynski perked nose, chipmunk '... if I may make bold to inquire without having earned it through couriering your ketchup and eggs?'

Their eyes held.

Gould unable to hide the batting of his at her inclusion of this interrogatory detail.

Caught himself.

Chuckled how 'the lass had been given quite the healthy carrot to dangle. Told her I'd whisper in her ear ...' lowered his voice to grandiose hush '... the *real* reason I left the concert stage.'

Dziurzynski whistled as though impressed.

Shook her head as though heartbroken at the bad luck of it all.

'So *still* nobody knows, for *real*, why you did it, eh?'

Matching her tone of good humor, Gould darted eyes cheekily, rubbing hands like mustachioed villain.

Broke the caricature.

Sighed.

Wondered, at this point, if anyone would believe him were he to tell.

Then, performing an overplay of being crestfallen, explained his theory might be falling apart in front of them.

'I never did see her *after* the challenge was given. There was no ... next time.'

Even as he said this, felt confusion growing inside.

Was he honestly misremembering?
Confused?
Was he ... *lying*?

Wiped at nose with back of glove, a slip of mucus having slimed from nostril to top lip quite suddenly.

Was rather glad for the abrupt necessity which allowed him to alter track.

'Or rather say: there hasn't *yet* been a next time. We mustn't think the worst, after all.'

'Hear-hear' Dziurzynski concurred with a bolstering nod.

Even still, it didn't sully the idea of Big Time Stuff getting into the dead woman's lonely narrative, did it?

'Her daughter likely mentioned the challenge. Either was hatching some scheme in cahoots with her mom or else the lonely old gal just wiled her hours away in fantasy. As so many do.'

Gould imagined either possibility still existed, yes.

Reason she'd asked, Dziurzynski explained, quite spryly hopping over to her line-up of dumbbells, changing the arrangement of a few while she spoke '... is because there'd been no sign of any funny business at the home. The crime scene. No windows broke. Doors jimmied.'

Other than the slaughter and some very specific burglary, no one would ever suspect anyone but the residents had been there.

'So I was thinking someone might've been *invited* in ...' she whipped around, urgently gesturing Gould calm, at a rush assuring him '... I didn't mean y*ou*, Mister Gould ...' though, again, he'd not given any reaction he was conscious of in response to her preamble '... or else: say you *had* been there, for example, I'd thought *someone else* might've seen you *depart*, waited a quick minute, knocked on the door, themselves. The mother, thinking the delightful Mister Gould had forgotten his hat and scarf or some such, quite giddily undoing the double latch ... then ...'

Dziurzynski made a harsh cutting gesture with the edge of one palm impacting the flat of the other.

'Because the victim had *certainly* known her killer. Or, at any rate, been quite at ease with them. Savagery of her dismemberment notwithstanding, there was none of the pomp and circumstance evidenced in either the Lang or the housekeeper slayings. Mommy was hacked up in one spot. Probably hadn't even struggled. Seated happy as a lark until the moment of crisis, judging by the tea laid out so accommodatingly. Arrowroot cookies. Program from a certain concert she'd either attended or had bought memorabilia from secondhand on the coffee table with pen at the ready.'

Quite nonchalantly, Gould interjected to inquire what had been meant by *very specific burglary*.

'No one would guess it from seeing her at the green grocer, but the dearly departed owned a small fortune in various jewelry. Heirlooms, no doubt. Or if not a fortune, *per se*, enough the word *boodle* could be used in the dictionary correct sense.'

Gould was correct, she supposed, despite Gould had proffered no comment of any kind '... that whoever did her in sure knew all about it. Made off with the treasure. Including the ring on her finger. A bauble, alone, the old biddy kept saying was worth more than the eyeteeth of everyone down at the Bingo Hall.'

Gesturing now, with a casual emphasis, how the point was likely quite trivial, Gould told her he'd simply wondered.

'Seeing as robbery played no part, so far as I've been told, in the earlier crimes.'

'Good point ...' Dziurzynski blinked.

Reaching to back pocket.

For the first time since Gould's arrival jotting something in her yellow notepad.

'I need to remember to think of things like that.'

Removing her peppermint pink blazer, patches of plaid at the elbows, whisking it carelessly toward the pile of coffee table and sofa, Dziurzynski tapped out what seemed a specific beat on her thighs then attempted, unsuccessfully, to make a *Pop* with palm to loosely puckered lips.

She explained with zest how she felt the time was apt to confide in Gould what she personally suspected was afoot.

All these tiddlywink theories were fine and dandy, so far as they went, but each one petered out.

She knew that.

Was a Big Picture kinda dame.

Always had been.

'We start from what I presume to be the correct profile, Mister Gould. That the murderer is a homicidal paranoid. Some … *schizo*.'

Snapped at him three times, finger wag afterward almost admonishing, as though he, or whoever her imagined audience was, had raised immediate and strenuous objection.

'Anyone who kills with such frenzy *surely* does so in a state of temporary insanity.'

Gould mugged to illustrate, sure, he supposed.

'In everyday life, this person could appear quite normal. Like you or I.'

'Or, even better, like anyone *except* for us two' Gould attempted levity which Dziurzynski acknowledged cursorily by rolling her eyes.

'*When he kills* …' she pressed on '… I'll betcha he needs to recreate some specific conditions which trigger the release of all his madness. A particular time and day of the week. Even clothing. Something which replicates for him the same images framing the context which provoked trauma in the past.'

Let her explain, before getting ahead of herself, that when she says *insanity* she doesn't mean *idiocy*. That when she says *temporary* it might just as well be *ongoing*.

How much of anyone's life do they really remember, after all?

'Think of the trillions of inputs coming in, all the doo-dah day.'

Aural.

Olfactory.

Et cetera.

'The brain takes it all in ... but most of it? Gone for good.'

The events one might've, at any given time, focused on quite intently slough off like skin cells, eventually.

'Physically, intellectually, down to the very *memory*, you might not be the same person this year to that.'

Unconsciously, everyone edits themselves to smithereens.

'Why not? Obviously we can get along with our business in life only *actively* retaining perhaps one-percent-of-one-percent of what actually *happens to us*.'

What's the big rush to learn you'd have cared more about fifty things your mind chucked overboard like bilge?

'Not even events. But thoughts. Ideas. Apprehensions. Passions. You're the *you* you are, after all, and it'd be torment to be told otherwise.'

Here she paused.

Was he catching her drift?

Yes. He supposed so.

'Except ...' she barreled on again '... if, simultaneously, all the things you *do* consider you *disappeared* and were *replaced* by things—events, memories, desires—which had *previously* been *ditched*, you'd never know it, would you? Blink and you're someone else! Who, from their perspective, was never anyone else! Tracks running overtop each other. One silenced. Another given prominence.'

She paused until he nodded.

Yes, yes.

Oh, he followed her, bang on the money.

He promised.

Let her continue, then. It was about to get good.

'Say those things that used-to-be-you weren't really gone ... or else consider how there are things so close to them that no one could tell there'd been any switcheroo.'

'Alternate takes, so to speak' Gould offered with an impatient air.

He put it exquisitely!

'You, before, had a memory of *these five seconds* of a walk down the street—that memory of those seconds is flushed, but now a memory of *the subsequent five seconds* or the *previous* replaces it. What's the difference?'

Gould nodded.

'Then: the part that'd jostled you from who-you-used-to-be is jostled out, itself, by something else, just as similar.'

Gould nodded.

'Say that could happen over and over and over. Quite often. Harmoniously. *Zip* ...' she gestured left '... *zip* ...' she gestured right '... *zip* ... ' she gestured left '... *zip* ...' she gestured right.

'A fascinating philosophical and psychological thing to consid—'

She clapped to silence him while overtop saying emphatically 'But what if only when you were over *here* ...' gestured left '... *zip* ...' closed her fist, shook it with vigor '... were you out of your *zipping* mind?'

Wonderfully amusing, wasn't it?

The detective-inspector laughed right along with Gould.

'Such a raucous hoot' she guffawed while he blew his nose.

So very relieved an intellect of his caliber, a gent of quiet refinement, was on the same page as her.

'But but but ...' she false-started, attempting to catch her breath '... it gets better and better.'

Imagine one of the two people this theoretical person *is* happened to be afflicted not only with homicidal schizophrenia but was one of those wretched sleepwalking *fugue-heads* they'd only so recently agreed must walk among the common throng.

'Not the mimbly-bimbly sort, but the full blow nut-bags! Living one life whilst entirely unaware of it despite having home, friends, children, and the stresses of the everyman.'

In their mind, concurrent with punching the clock every day, they're under the delusion they have a professorship, a different family, set of vices, desires, habits, ideals.

'In *real life* their brain compensates. They are, to themselves, giving an important address before the Hague but, to us watching, they're saying all the correct things to successfully purchase a cuckoo-clock from Gimbals.'

Now ... say their Other Self was a sleepwalker, too.

The forgotten parts of themselves fantasizing an entirely *different* deviant life.

'Here we see them: buying an artichoke. In their mind: dismembering a prostitute in the London fog. Meanwhile: here's them dismembering a prostitute in the London fog ... but in their mind they're deciding *Naw, not an artichoke—how about a cumquat, instead*?

A complete, seamless, inverse split, is what she meant.

'Each *Self* dreaming the events of the other. Events which, to the *Other*, are real.'

Could Gould comprehend how clicking this-minute to one life, this-minute to another would lead to *exponential* complications?

'More and more versions ...' he ventured, hesitantly '... unable to sort the *real* from the *imagined* ... from *the imagined-which-is-real* ... but ... which happened not at the time ... the imaginer was imagining it ... right?'

'Eventually ...' she gave an OK gesture with a wink '... there will be a *fritz*. A short circuit.'

Gould, though still giggling, had to admit he was losing the thread.

'Would it be so hard to conceive ...' Dziurzynski looked ceilingward, almost religious cast to her eyes '... that while a murderer strangled some dumb slob to death they were thinking about strangling some entirely other slob to death and then when they *really did* strangle that other slob they did so under the impression they were strangling the first slob they'd strangled?'

Realizing she'd paused, needing a direct answer to proceed, Gould numbly nodded his head.

'No ... it's easy enough to *conceive* of such situation, I suppose. You've, after all, just this moment done so.'

Another wink.

'Now say, both times, they're *acting out* some *initial* killing. Some *third slob* who'd been strangled maybe *ages ago*. Purging the trauma both versions of them recall snippets of. Committing a deep seeded, proto-act again and again by way of countless new ones—each forgotten by the *original version* of themself because this version, in fact, might not have any idea such trauma ever transpired! Any of these killings, original and subsequent, edited out of their inner narrative.'

Another pause.

Gould nodded.

Pinching absently at his lower lip.

Face a baffled tangle.

'But sometimes ...' Dziurzynski slowly started up again '... when all the switching around happens, Version B remembers some bit of what Version C did. Or remembers, oddly, thinking about strangling Slob A while strangling Slob B—all the while compulsively doing so based on the strangling of the Proto Slob they don't actually recall! All the twisting around upsets each version's orderly concept of themselves. Until, at one point, for one version, Slob B *becomes* the Proto Slob being repeatedly unconsciously replicated.'

And so forth.

'But all the time ...' Gould honestly had caught on, felt a rush of pride '... because the changes from the *original not-nuts* self into whichever *totally-nuts* selves are only moments long ... *all* the nuts *always* see themselves at the grocery store or at home with the kiddos making funny voices at bath time—despite whatever horrors they're enacting.'

'So no matter where they are, what they're doing, they'll say all the right things, remember the same lives ...' she nodded '...the same *original life*. Never aware of missing time or having hurt so much as a fly.'

Maybe, over the years, the most vicious, brutal version of *Them* becomes *aware* of their general affliction and so compensates.

'In its moments-at-the-wheel, so to speak, purposefully plans its clever butcherings, then uses the other mixed-up versions as instruments.'

Say the *original* was the most vicious.

'Learned how to consciously hit the switch. Turn into deviant versions who share his life and think they aren't doing the things they do while those things happen.'

'A *contrapuntal madman*' Gould did her the favor of coining.

Well, she sure was gonna pawn *that* off as her own!

'But yes. Exactly.'

Part of them aware of it all.

Composing.

Orchestrating.

'But, for all intents and purposes, never really existing.'

———————

Dziurzynski was talking about Lang, of course.

'Paul …' Gould's face screwed into an expression almost like a child making grimace at something stinky served at supper time '… *Henry Lang*?'

Nod nod nod.

Here, he'd have to part ways with the detective-inspector's suppositions.

Certainly he understood she'd insist her theory tidily covered the bases of any offered reason it'd be absurd to think such ugliness of the man, but nevertheless 'It's utterly impossible.'

Not to mention, Gould had until now understood the going theory to be *Lang had been killed*.

Admittedly he couldn't, at this moment, recall precisely whether Dziurzynski had out-and-out said so …

'… but that hardly matters. How in the name of God could Lang be alive, considering the offal you'd described?'

'The *Controller*-part of Lang …' she began explaining, quite matter-of-fact '… was concocting whichever elaborate schemes. Always. No matter how it looked from the outside. Selecting victims assiduously. Inventing scenarios in which to perpetrate the kills. Eventually, to ensure he gets away with it forever, he lands on the most obvious gambit: make it appear he was a victim, *himself*. To such an extent there'd be no second thought about it *despite* no corpse ever surfacing.'

Gould, again, directed her attention to the carnage she'd described. 'The blood …'

So he'd bled himself, a little bit here a little there—so what?

'Not even painful as, in his mind, he'd be thinking he's down at the park feeding pigeons, eh?'

Over enough time, he'd amass jars of the stuff.

Gould sighed. Shaking his head.

Dziurzynski continued, unabated.

'Tells people he's gotta travel to meet Glenn Gould. Meantime has *previously* secured a whole block of suites. Leaves for the trip, full-on believing the two of you have talked about it. Arranged whichever interview. An entirely plausible scenario to anyone he knows. You're in town, after all. Living your weird little hermit life ...'

He chuckled. Granted her he was doing so. But nevertheless began to object, overall.

Dziurzynski acted as though she'd not noticed.

'Gets to his room. Takes his sweet time bashing it up. Arranging that horrendous spectacle. Even smashes his own face against the mantle! Though, it'd be better to say: *has* himself smash his face against the mantle.'

No.

Gould was entirely finished with this.

In fact, was alarmed he'd listened as long as he had.

What exactly *had* he been listening to?

Became irate.

Though ... didn't understand why he was engaging in so unhinged a display ...

... or what he was objecting to ...

... considering what he actually *knew* ...

Felt discombobulated.

Absolutely certain he'd been led into a wilderness, become turned around, was presently in great danger.

Flailing without compass.

Any of his words seemed capable of securing him march to the gallows pole.

'Why hasn't he killed *me*, then?' he blurted.

'You ... would be specifically who he *couldn't* kill' Dziurzynski slowly explained.

As though the fact were so obvious she was appalled at having to verbalize it.

Barked a laugh.

Then fixed her attention on him.

An expression of abject confusion.

She didn't believe the killings had to do with Gould, personally. Not a wiff. Absolutely no scenario in which she included Gould as driving factor made a single lick of sense.

'Which is why so much trouble has been undertaken to make the murders appear *operatically* about you. To have every madcap thread *insist* it has *Glenn Gould* written all over it.'

No idea why Gould had been chosen instead of someone else.

But she wasn't a lunatic, now was she?

'If not *you*, someone *else*—but that just means if not someone else … *you*.'

Consider this most recent victim.

The missing girl's mother.

Who is she?

'A member of the *Glenn Gould Fan Club*, local chapter.'

But what *else*?

'She's … *fodder*. The Controller part of Lang isn't stupid. Takes its time. Gathers in the perfect raw material. Then lets the beast out to do its hog wildness.'

The real question is: What does the woman *represent* to Lang, so far as trauma being re-enacted?

'What do I represent?' Gould, suddenly heavy with fatigue, interjected.

That was her point, though.

'You might only be Glenn Gould, *incidentally*.'

'*Glenn Gould incidentally*?'

Roughed his hair.

Slumped.

'So humor me with who I am, *specifically*.'

Dziurzynski's seemed disappointed he failed to see it.

In no way keeping this disappointment hidden from him.

'You're …' her posture deflated as she for the first time seemed reluctant to try for eye contact '... the one he's going to frame for it all.'

If the detective-inspector was quite through with this ugly 'whatever this is' Gould would bid her good day and return to his suite.

'Of course.'

Sweet as can be, entirely self-deprecating, Dziurzynski requested he kindly not repeat any of what she'd discussed with him.

'Ongoing inquiry and all.'

Then gestured him on his way adding 'You've been so courteous and accommodating in not obstructing my methods, to date— just think of it as *undeserved* extension of that grace.'

He'd oblige, rest assured.

Quite merrily.

She'd gotten away from herself. Knew she had.

'But all on account of the things I've seen. In the course of my storied career.'

Did he understand her, she hoped?

'I'm meticulous about not leaving stones under-turned.'

'Fully aware of the Latin, yes yes' Gould bowed.

'So fearful I import stones from exotic climes just to have a peek beneath.'

Profuse apologies for her distasteful meanderings.

'Though ...' she scuffed the carpet '... remember at *some points* you were laughing along ...'

'Nothing in the world to apologize for. You are the pink of charming company.'

Dziurzynski scuffed toe, again, in wordless Thank you.

'The real reason I brought you up here was to let you know,'

Lang or otherwise, there's someone in this town taking great pains to pass themselves off as Glenn Gould.'

Just to his feet, these words drained him, utterly.

Limply sank back to the cushioned armchair.

Head lolled to allow mucus free passage, nose raw to the point of pain and every tissue he'd brought already squandered and squirreled soggy down coat.

'What the devil do you mean by that?'

Almost wanted to take a swing at her as tension over where this new song and dance was leading crept in.

Dziurzynski's tone remained placid. Absurdly nonchalant as she explained 'An individual, very much *like you*, has been reported at times and in places you couldn't have *possibly* been.'

This was more of her nonsense, though.

He steeled to remember that.

No time to take any of her chicanery at face value.

Best let her get it out of her system.

Inject as little of his own commentary as possible.

This was her *talking*.

Not him talking *to* her.

Nothing she said meant a thing.

'Very much like you *superficially* …' she hastened to clarify '… in the sense of decked out in your usual finery.'

No one had seen the individual's face 'without hat and glasses' but when she'd displayed a photograph of Gould in typical apparel 'no mention who you were, of course' an assortment of folks could swear they'd met him.

'At least two of these citizens did a decent impersonation, too. Meaning whoever is trick-or-treating appears to be doing so to a purpose.'

'To … *which* purpose?'

Was she allowed to guess?

'Just this once …' he'd begrudgingly allow it.

'To make certain you *can't* be suspected.'

'Why ...' he pinched the bridge of his nose '... would such a tactic benefit a killer if their endgame is to present me as *culprit*?'

As though reluctant over having to say so, Dziurzynski let out a long breath.

'Number one: it allows for the possibility you may've had an agent acting on your *behalf* ...'

Gould waited for her to continue.

Certain her shy trailing off was mere playact.

'Number *two* ..?' he finally prompted when she'd remained silent to the point it grew awkward.

'The man is clearly insane.'

'... *whoever he is*' Gould added, as though helpfully.

A bit piqued when she failed to perform her usual gee-golly repetition in praise of the aptness of his insight.

Though Dziurzynski didn't make it easy, Gould wanted her to be aware 'I *do* trust you.'

It bolstered her flagging esteem to know it.

'I'm not always so happy-go-lucky as I present. A real wind-up device I feel, sometimes. Imposture syndrome ...' she winked '... and when you throw on the dyslexia I often can't help fearing I've had elbow for backside ever since the academy.'

Wanting to leave on as cordial a chord as could be struck, Gould pressed her on the remark.

'If it isn't prying: your speech had the air to it of playing the straight man and I, admittedly, fail to see where the punch was to land.'

'You'd make a terrific vaudevillian' she smiled, bashfully.

Her reference had been very personal.

Reservations about her style of detecting.

'I've lived by the motto: once you've eliminated the *improbable*, whatever remains, however *impossible* ... well, that's gonna be neat when it turns out to be the thing.'

Stuck out her tongue and made motion like she was smacking herself for the lame joke.

In response to her comically taking on an expression meaning could they, pretty please, move swiftly past her ham-handed wisecracking, Gould, quite humbly, stated his hope that she understood he'd not been cross with her, however his behavior might've indicated otherwise.

'Not a bit of it. You're under the weather. I can tell a hawk from a handsaw. Frankly, I'd be more perturbed if you seemed like you, at this point.'

Which he oughtn't take wrong.

The quip meant all as a bit of good fun.

'Think nothing of it' he said.

Had certainly done zilch to make the remark unwarranted in the short time they'd kept acquaintance.

'I am a smidgen concerned about your remarks concerning the Press, however. Shutterbugs. Paparazzi.'

How much information about him had been released for public consumption?

Absolutely *none*.

She ran a tight ship.

'Those people are like louse, though. Lurk about. Draw whatever lurid conclusions to earn their daily bread.'

Trying briefly to concoct a toothless quip along the lines of 'I think by *louse* you means *birds-of-a-feather*' but coming up dunce, Gould mumbled something indistinct.

Waited a beat.

Then flatly asked if his name was mentioned in any of the daily rags.

'Not even a line to announce you were occupant of the same

hotel as the victim. So far as the world is concerned, Glenn Gould's not here.'

This pleased him.

Or at least he said he supposed it did.

Dziurzynski had meant to inquire: had he spoken to any of his colleagues or acquaintances about this grisly affair?

'Just so I know who's holding out on me if I'm grilling them and push comes of shove.'

Gould chuckled.

'No.'

He was keeping more to himself than usual.

Was stricken with a sharp bout of coughing.

'Do you think the girl will turn up alive?'

Got himself under control.

Snorted phlegm.

Swallowed.

Not certain he'd quite overheard what'd been said.

Turned to find Dziurzynski's back to him.

Not quite certain she'd … said … anything.

Awkwardly ventured 'Isn't that … something I ought be asking you?'

Now facing him, she blinked.

Nose a scrunch.

Blinked twice more.

Then slowly said 'You … can ask me that, yes of course. And, *yes*. Yes, I think so. But I'm kinda paid to. Do … *you*?'

Gould noted her face hadn't relaxed.

Still fixed in a confused wrinkle.

Scratched behind his ear, self-consciously.

'Do …' he gaped, shut mouth, cleared throat '… I *what*?'

'Think the girl will turn up alive?'

His heart beat harder, faster, stirring another sizzle of irritability which he made certain to damper.

'Which *girl* are we talking about, so I'm certain?'
'Is there more than one?' Dziurzynski returned the chuckle.
Golly, she hoped not.
'No.'
No, not that he knew of.
'Sorry.'
He'd lost track of who it was had spoken first.
'Funny …' the detective-inspector replied as she opened the door for him '… so have I.'

GOULD VOMITED. OR RATHER HE DIDN'T.
   Acrid. Fetid.
   Mostly air.
   Strings, perhaps only whiskers, of bile-orange saliva.
   Mucus peppered with speckles of beige or blood-brown.
   He clung to the curve of the porcelain bowl.
   Fully dressed.
   Bleats of anguish.
   Cramps at both sets of ribs like kicks from the toes of boots or switch blades driven home, leaned on.
   Felt suspended. Upside-down.
   Held by ankles.
   Shook shook shook.
   As though to have coins drop from his pockets.
   Nothing rising from his bowels. After each gasp, tight peristalsis machined a gummy substance, one-third solid, down through him.
   Mind blank.
   Listened to the hollow echo of each breath.
   Rustle from the circle of water, clean from its most recent flush, at the bowl base.
   Sight of this obstructed by the blunt of his own head and hunched shoulders.

Unconscious of the act, he extended his tongue as though to probe his blind surroundings.

Straining.

Tip inches from surface of water but seeming to him millimeters.

He might lap a balming trickle of cold down the crisp of his razor-wire gullet.

Eventually, such ridiculous effort caused him to spasm.

Percussive gagging.

A flash in his mind:

Dank, turgid waters.

An open, screaming mouth.

Fistfuls of worms, leeches, dead minnows scrambling out of the throat beneath it.

Mound of something which had felt egg-shaped as he regurgitated it splashed water and residue of itself back onto him.

Throat kept glugging.

Struggling to empty more.

So intense he couldn't catch his breath.

When this exorcism passed, Gould recoiled from the bowl.

Eyes clamped shut.

Soon climbed into the bathtub.

Pulled curtain closed.

Tugged as though to bring it down, shower bar as well.

The effort so weakling he abandoned it.

Slapped the drape like a tired kitten.

Over and over.

Until it was parted enough he could make out the counter.

The mirror.

The closed bathroom door.

Chair from the main room wedged to bar entry.

Pill bottles.

He let sight of them slip in and out of focus.

... pills ...
Should he be taking those pills?
Could they be responsible?
'For what?' he mumbled.
Or rather issued vague burbles. So depleted he couldn't even mouth his lips up-down like a cartoon of speaking.
Had already forgotten the question by the time he pretended to be asking himself 'Why would you even *ask* that, Glenn?'
'Quite the stodgy state we find ourselves in ...' he imagined someone sat nearby telling him.
Care in their voice.
Though tone not free of irony.
'What *state*?'
Yours he thought.
While answering himself, at least in the sound of a groan '*Ours*.'
'Yes yes...' he chuckled '... I speak for us both, these days.'
Tried to stick out his tongue, but peeking tip through what felt like serrated lips brought instinctive recall of his violent voiding just moments before.
Limbs pushing tense to the tile wall and tub sides.
Wave of nausea cascading.
Eventually settled.
He may or may not have fallen asleep.
May have been telling himself those very words.
'May or may not have.'
Either after having done so or else just before.
Now certainly mumbling them, again.
Saddest thing of all, he supposed when able to keep thoughts cogent enough to engage with, was he'd no way of determining the root cause of his present condition.
The pills?
Whichever illness he'd genuinely acquired?

Stress of his latest joust with Dziurzynski?

Anger at himself for considering, either honestly or defensively, the notions she'd poisoned the air with?

Or was he simply terrified?

Generically terrified.

To the point his body bent as incoherent as his mind.

After managing a genuine shower, Gould's ability to reason, conduct his movements, had returned.

For the time being, even his sinuses were clear.

A reality which prompted him to yet remain in the barricaded washroom. Snuggled in steam.

Laid to the slick floor.

Coat overtop him.

Knees bent so the garment covered him all the way to his ankles.

Remainder of clothing bundled into pillow.

Folded towel under buttocks because the weight of himself direct against tile caused pain at his hips, especially.

What had Dziurzynski even been *talking* about?

Pack of lies, whatever it'd been.

Not even lies.

Nonsense. Genuine *lunacy*.

Not an idiot, Gould understood the woman was an investigator. Method to her madness.

Though knowing so didn't disallow how the ratio might be off.

Two-parts-madness for every one-part-method.

Like her backward *Baskervilles* quote.

'Madness to her method, then ...' he muttered.

Which might be worse.

All that rubbish concerning Lang. Suspecting him.

In no world would Dziurzynski be permitted to conduct a legitimate investigation on the strength of such outlandish, even scandalous, suppositions.

Imagine the detective-inspector moving to requisition departmental resources based on the funny book theory Paul Henry Lang, respected critic and musicologist, was some hybrid orchid of insanity and murder.

Without a scrap of physical evidence ...

... unless she *had* such evidence ...

... but suddenly Gould wanted to be thinking of anything apart from Lang.

That preposterous scenario had been injected into him.

For the purpose of running his mind ragged in profitless circles.

A premeditated snare.

Set by Dziurzynski.

Meant to muddy his senses even more than they were.

Exhaust him mentally with his own obsessive-compulsive considerations of the pseudo-scientific philosophies she'd gibbered ... when really he ought be thinking about ...

... what?

'Thinking about *what*?' he demanded aloud.

Opened his eyes.

Regretting it when the overhead light, fogged in lessening wisps of shower steam, sliced at his vision.

The first words which crept into the foreground after his wince—headache, possible earache, nipping at their heels—were *Physical evidence*.

'Which ... physical evidence?'

Dziurzynski had pointed out herself how Gould couldn't have been present at the time this most recent woman was killed.

Added to which: he knew he'd not been.

'What about the *motel*, Glenn. You'd been *there*. Do you trust that man to clear away every one of your—'

Lashed head left-to-right to knock clear the intrusive thought.
He'd not seen any *man*.
'Do you trust *yourself*, then?'
Trust himself to what?
Those events hadn't *happened*.
He'd not *been* there.
Nobody had.
So he couldn't possibly have left—
'Fingerprints …' the intrusive voice finished for him. The voice of the other-him he still pictured only as reflection in mirror glass, not stood in the room proper.
Where were the fingerprints?
Three crime scenes.
He hadn't been asked for his.
No legal reason he could've been.
Dziurzynski would know that.
Even if she persuaded him to give an official set of his own, she'd be obligated to explain to her superiors why.
Not to mention … weren't his already on file?
Not to mention running risk of tipping her hand if—
'… she suspects you.'
Palm to face.
Squeezed.
Clenched jaw until ears and sinus muffled, closed, clogged.
Needed to stop thinking this way.
'As though you're guilty.'
Of anything.
Otherwise, ran the risk of starting to believe he might be.
'Of everything.'

Dressed. Fully.
Shivering.

Pacing the suite.
Gould felt them inside of him.
Thoughts.
Tapeworms. Blood parasites.
Dziurzynski's thoughts.
Yes, he was *infested*. Ideas not his own.
Hatching. Scrambling. Feeding on his own thoughts.
Growing plump into themselves by devouring him.
His psyche replaced with their desired version of it.
Trouble was, he couldn't quite hear them. *Know* them.
What she'd said only seemed to exist as a tickle left behind after limb being amputated. A partition in his mind refused him specifics to interrogate.
Dissect.
Dismiss.
At the same time, he was cordoned off from his *own* mindscape. Couldn't, for example, recall had he swallowed more pills before existing the washroom.
Didn't dare take any more, now.
He was pure agitation.
Dwelt in the space between a thought and a thought.
A string of those spaces.
Nothingness.
Which, yes, Dziurzynski had droned on about.
Those ghastly spook stories of Lang she'd pelted him with.
Lang existing as someone inside someone inside someone else … with no idea that he was.
Gould couldn't tether himself enough to recall how she'd suggested such aberrant mechanism would function.
Of course he *couldn't*.
It was lunatic ramblings.
Hers.
Now *his*.

Or had she outlined a perfectly sensible theory and his own mind had contorted it?

'If you can't remember, you can't *know*, can you?' he said.

Kicking at the side of the writing desk, limply.

Realizing he'd become calm.

When had that happened?

Was it actually happening?

'Oh for goodness sake, *woe is me*, eh?'

Here. Again. This incessant *Hamlet*!

As though he couldn't start down any avenue of idea without bumping into some reference.

That script in his head.

On account of …

Wanted to laugh.

To howl and hurl something across the room.

Wondered if he had.

Wondered, if he did, would *he* have.

Wondered was he cracking up or just thinking about cracking up.

How would it go?

How would he behave?

Looked around the suite.

See?

Nothing thrown.

Still calm.

Still unnerved by the fact that he was.

Understood he was failing to take the easiest escape.

If he wanted to be shut of this, he ought go to sleep.

Desired *sleep*.

With every fiber of his being.

But *wasn't* sleeping.

Therefore some fiber must *not* desire it.

Enough to overpower all others.

That fiber in *control*.
Despite being minority.
Or was it minority?
Perhaps the dominant part of him was serenely watching whichever part this was, *he* was, calmly pacing while inwardly tearing itself asunder.
Watching with not one care in the world.
Waiting.
To have control of his limbs and intellect.
This distress never to be recollected.
All this anguish and assail queued to disappear.
These moments were merely his being conscious of what it felt like to *forget*.
Just like he'd wanted thoughts of that motel from last night to vanish. Those events he'd insisted wouldn't exist come today.
He'd proclaimed right to the face of some man he'd promised not to remember how he'd not remember.
Only to find himself here.
Remembering.
Remembering, *barely*.
Gould hated how he found what was happening to him fascinating.
Stimulating.
Yes—he didn't want the tension to end.
This interior *warring*.
If his mind suddenly went clear he'd be disappointed.
Feel cheated.
Or at least so he felt in this moment
What he hated was how he *loved* every moment of this.
Observing. Not knowing.
Utterly in the dark as he watched himself edited down.
Excesses thinned out.
All which was unnecessary cleaved off.

Creating the record out the many rough takes of what would from then on be considered the only.
The genuine.
Him.

Foot touched down on crumpled paper.
Quickly whipped eyes around to typewriter.
Expecting a sheet pinned to the roller.
Nothing.
Blinked.
Drifted eyes back down to what he stood on.

> I had scarcely begun the first supper show of my gala season …

Read no further.
But behind his eyes felt himself reciting.
As though these phrases perpetually writhed circular in him.
Record on a loop.
Endless. The same.
Endless sameness.
It'd been so important to him that the writing remain present. Because Dziurzynski had seen it. He'd needed it to be there, yet, if she returned.
As though unmolested.
Recalled, also, how before he'd left for the detective-inspector's suite the sight of it had infuriated him.
Enough so he'd thought to destroy it.
Had regretted the crumpling.
Deciding he'd need to retype it.
As he held the misshapen sheet, he fancied what was written on it an organism. Alive.

Trying to preserve itself.
Procreate.
Hadn't the words found their way back from the dead, in a sense?
Shredded once before, he'd found them on the typewriter.
Discarded them.
About to be typed, again.
As though by invisible hand.
His invisible hand.
The same words had wound up on that mysterious reel.
Spoken in his own voice.
Or the voice of some unseen party in mimic of his.
In this moment, he wondered ...
Stared at the sheet.
A bauble of light. Unfocused.
Wondered ...
Shook his head.
Set the paper to the desk blotter.
Not only was it *immaterial* whether the words remained in the typewriter in the event Dziurzynski stopped in, it was utterly *irrelevant* whether he recopy them.
Despite this, he eyed the typewriter.
Rubbing fingertips together.
Wetting lips.
Keen for the *tick-tick-tick-snap* of setting a new sheet to roller.
Eager for clacks from the keys.
Dings as the mechanism demanded reset for another line of text.
Fingers waggled. Phantom typing.
Until he noticed. Closed his fists.
No more drifting from thought to thought, like this.
Each state of mind undefined.
None of them a thing to do with each other.

Until they were.
Where was his *panic*?
His *terror*?
Even a general *unease*?
How could he stand in place, tranquil, as though neither nothing about his life had changed nor everything?
Still wanted to type the words.
Full through.
To the end.
Grinned.
Catching the clever game being played with him.
'Now, naturally, I have to question that, do I not? I've never seen the entire document, so far as I know. Therefore, it's faulty to believe it means so much to me to write it ... or ever meant anything to have.'
This couldn't be argued with.
Waited for himself to attempt.
Nothing?
'Good ...' he sniffed '... so we can proceed to the next matter on the docket.'
Cleared throat.
'I claim I could write this, start-to-end ...' re-crumpled the paper, tossed it in the direction of the window '... because I claim to *know* the end. To know the start, the end, everything in between.'
But did he?
Why didn't it occur to him?
Right now, when he desired to know, once and for all, what this present nightmare was all about. Why he should care if he created it or had destroyed it.
'If you even *do*' he teased at himself.
Nodding.
'If you ever *did*.'

But again: a trap.
If someone else had written it then there *was* someone else.
'And if there *is* someone else …'
His nose began leaking.
Despite him tensing against it doing so.
Keeping tensed against the sensation of needing to snort the mucus up before it dribbled over lips.
Over chin.
But he did snort.
Exhaled afterward.
Forced butts of palms in rotating pressures against his closed eyes.
Hissing 'I don't know that I know how it ends.'

Tack. Tack. Tack. Tack. Tack.
… Tack … Tack … Tack …
… tack … tack …
… tack …
Dressed like him.
Gould was staring off toward the bookshelf.
Across from where he sat at the typewriter.
Whatever he'd been thinking receding. Growing silent.
This other idea raising in volume.
Mingling with the one prior to it.
Overpowering it. Gaining focus.
That's what the detective-inspector had said.
There'd been a man *dressing like him*. For reasons as yet unknown.
To which Gould had replied … what?
What *had* Gould replied?
Shifted where he sat.
Bookshelf blurring.

Eyes drifting to the spot where the armchair would normally be.

Finding nothing.

Drifting further to see it titled to buffer the suite door against being opened.

Drifted back to its blank, vacated spot.

Imagined he saw Dziurzynski.

Saw her speaking. Volumeless.

Tried to sort out how their conversation had gone.

Hacked up phlegm. Which he realized, with a touch of displeasure, he'd presently expectorated to the carpet.

'Had that been Lang?'

Gould hadn't asked that.

Hadn't asked *anything*.

Not that he could recall.

Would the question have struck the detective-inspector peculiar?

'Do you believe it'd been *Lang* … dressing as me?' he said toward the empty wall.

The idea got foothold.

An idea of a man, like him, adorned like him.

Being Lang.

Make-believe Dziurzynski fading out.

Blank spot of carpet.

Blurry bookshelf.

Leave off all the insanity about Lang being some schizoid man—could it've simply been Lang, stone sober, in full control of his faculties, set to grim purpose, disguising himself up as Glenn Gould?

Shook his face.

'Preposterous.'

Soon was staring blank at the bookshelf, again.

Watching it lose cohesion.

Eyes unblinking. Watering.
Until he blinked tears from them and ran gloved hand over face, against nose.
Hocked. Spit.
Could it've been Lang ... last night ... in that *motel* ..?
'Sweet Lord in Heaven, Glenn. Whoever that man was had stood naked in front of you! You and Paul Henry Lang couldn't be less alike!'
'Think of the state I'd been in ...' he argued, barely audible, lips not quite moving '... the tension of the day. That telephone call. Dziurzynski's intrusion. Enacting my escape, per instructions. Sneaking free of my guard. Roaming in ill weather. Driving. Trotting through rain. The dark of the room. The music. The shock of the scene ...'
Could he truly conjure memory of *walking into* that room?
How had it *precisely* happened?
He'd waited freezing outside ... *then* what?
Music. Blood.
Television flicker.
Knowing the presence of someone behind him.
'Are you legitimately entertaining this B-movie tripe, Glenn? *Rationally* is this a consideration you're giving voice to?'
He'd scrutinized the man.
Hadn't he?
His spitting image.
Not Lang.
Him. Himself.
Or ... had the man only expressed his deranged *opinion* of a resemblance to Gould?
Surely, seeing the man, at first fully dressed, hearing him insist they were *doppelganger*, could've left harrowing impression ...
... Lord only knew which medications had been contraindicating all through his bloodstream at the time ...

... how numb the brief sight of the corpse and surrounding violence had made his mind ...

Could he have witnessed Lang, flat on, stripping off garments, and somehow managed to replace the occult madness of such sight with something ...

... something ...

'Something *what*?'

No answer to offer himself, Gould settled on the word *Else*.

Something *else*.

... mind recoiling from shock, fearing its own slaughter, the entire world it moved within incomprehensible ...

... blind desperation that whatever was happening not be happening ...

That *nothing* be happening.

Anything.

Anything *else*.

Why not have been Lang?

Hadn't he, even yet today, been willing to convince himself there'd been *nothing at all*?

The events which had transpired in the motel room *nonexistent*?

If he was capable of believe it *nothing* ... why so resistant to believing it *Lang*?

Blinked. Blinked.

Blinked.

... blinked ...

No.

Impossible.

'Though once you discard the *improbable*, whatever remains, however *impossible*—'

Worked finger down ear with rough violence.

Stood to twist his body side-to-side.

Giving face gentle smacks to return his focus.

This pointless examination was robbing his attention.
Diverting him.
From writing.
Drifted eyes back to the page, reciting interior '*I had scarcely begun the first supper show ...*'
... abruptly startled.
Looked at the words on the page.
Blood stopping.
Breath stopping.
Everything.
Stopping.
On the page discovering only

    gg: What happened in Maude Harbor, Glenn?
    _____

Or since such subject seems unpalatable, perhaps Mister Gould would care to expound on other matters?

Though, if it would be forgiven him pointing it out, the events of *Maude Harbor* never seem but a hop skip from Mister Gould's mind.

'Not, perhaps, with focus on what *happened* there, but rather decidedly on what never did.'

What else then?

Perhaps *l'esprit de jenusse, et de corps, et d'art*?

Did Gould have any thoughts from such prompt?

What did he think would be said if he ever had occasion to cross paths with '... an honest musician willing to recount his most memorable experiences of musical performance?'

Does Mister Gould feel, as the venerable Doctor Herbert Von Hochmeister might, that '... let me recall the quotation ... yes ...' one might be assured such musician will cite among them when some green kid, still swaddled in conservatory blazer, stripped the clichés from a worn out warhorse of the concert repertoire and revealed, as for the first times, its charms *au natural*?

> gg: Being human as well as being honest, our professional will most likely feel compelled to hedge his admiration by allowing that when the junior turned to other staples the affinity seemed somehow less pronounced, yes?

> GG: Forgive me, but not being familiar with the alleged thoughts of the alleged Von Hochmeister, I am shy to venture into either debate or agreement.

> gg: Commendable—if a tad wimpy, let's not be remiss by failing to say. Perhaps a subject you are more well acquainted with could be plumbed. Someone in our studio audience has called out 'What happened in Maude Harbor?'—would you care to expound along those lines?

Removing fingers from typewriter keys, Gould huffed.
Pinched top of paper as though to remove it.
But halted.
As though being reminded 'No need to be hasty, tut tut.'

> gg: Is there a subject you'd particularly like to discuss?

> GG: I hadn't given it much thought, really—but, just off the top, what about the political situation in Labrador?

> gg: Well, I certainly don't want to bypass any headline grabbing areas of that sort, Mister Gould, but we should, I think, at least begin our discussion in the area of unrepentant murder in cold blood.

The page was hastily zipped from the machine.
A rather high pitched whine as roller spun and Gould's hand raised above head.

Leaf containing what had been set down the moment before discarded blindly behind him.

A sweet shush as it settled to carpet.

Gould's mind perturbed by the memory of the sound of the *plonk* of Dziurzynski's ill-formed paper airplanes.

Paper airplanes he … did not … exactly recall … having cleaned up.

'Then who had?'

'Housekeeping' he answered.

Raised brow in objection.

'*Housekeeping*? Who you've had such authoritative word with the front desk regarding? Your edict known. None ought enter your sanctum under penalty of—'

'Very witty, yes' Gould hissed.

Having had about enough of the freewheeling wit of whatever fever dream this was.

'While having murder on the mind is more than *excusable*, considering the environment into which I've found myself thrust, I must insist it is *you* who sure seem to have murder on the mind. So far as trying to tinker with retro-continuity enough it will have taken place here, there, and *Maude Harbor*-where.'

Surely Mister Gould wasn't suggesting *Maude Harbor* to be the sole destination on Earth blessed with only having graveyards for those who'd reached expiration on nature's inscrutable schedule!

'You're not suggesting no one was ever *murdered* there, are you?'

Sat.

Fingers to typewriter keys.

'I'm suggesting no such thing. I'm a realist. Not a fantasist.'

Tack. Tack. Tack. Tack.

> gg: So what then, really, happened in Maude Harbor? Just between you and I.

'Perhaps piano sonatas by Scriabin and Prokofiev would be a more palatable subject matter? Or are you going to tantrum if I bring up that business, as well?'

Gould shrugged. Brattish.

'Dandy. Shall I begin? Or do you have thoughts on the matter?'

Gould crossed his arms.

Settled harrumph into the chair.

'Very well. The … Third Sonata, perhaps? Let's say … second movement? A scherzo with an angular barline—defying primary motive in the left hand and with a Vincent d'Indy-like series of harmonic twists in both. In the third movement, Scriabin turns his unnerving harmonic sense to the task of undercutting the expected cadential climaxes. Whenever the gelatinous, post-Wagnerian chromatic texture seems to augur some emphatic Heldenlebenish climax, Scriabin demurely steps aside, reiterates the just concluded phrase with elaborations, only to step aside again.'

Long pause.

Gould pursed his lips.

Narrowed eyes.

A stab it was impossible to not notice the *So what?* lurking within.

'A little like yourself, Mister Gould, eh? At least somebody might rhetorically posit so. You, teasing the clueless detective-inspector with what seems the cliché conclusion to her *giallo* only to keep her from satisfactory resolution with the appearance of what, for all intents and purposes, is an entirely new case. It's childish, even mean of you, to leave the record player on, each time. Not to mention, wouldn't it be more polite to diversify the method of dispatch, one corpse to the next? Why *hatchet* the bunch? Maybe try *candlestick*—or piano wire as *garrote*!'

Gould wheeled to his feet.

Lost balance.

Caught himself against the wall.

Sucked on the thumb such catch had jammed painfully then shook the hand in the air as though clearing dust from it.

'To begin with ...' he seethed '... such comparison is not only clumsy and *inaccurate* but abjectly fails to be *cute* in the way I assume you had puckishly hoped. As penalty, the subject of Scriabin is off limits, full stop.'

'Perhaps for the best. After all, the *Dodecacophonist's Dilemma* is much more fruitful soil for gentlemanly discourse.'

'You're claiming to be a *gentleman* now, as well?'

'It only seems polite, seeing as how I'm you' Gould had himself retort.

Charmed by his smugness.

'Returning to our new subject, now: One can surely engage in no more disenchanting an occupation than the perusal of a forgotten thesis in which one confidently reinforced an argument with a prediction. As was evidenced for you, if memory serves, upon rereading the manuscript of a commemorative lecture which you'd delivered at the Royal Conservatory of Music of Toronto in observance of the death of Arnold Schoenberg. This paper was primarily eulogistic in content and for most of its length apotheosized the deceased despot of dodecacophony. Toward the close, however, you fell victim to that age-old curse of orators— the search for an effective ending.'

Gould bristled with understanding the puerile implication found in this.

Also, he seemed to *understand* he understood this and so allowed no objection before doubling down, veering from the perfectly banal and innocent memory under scrutiny to present day concerns.

'You hadn't, in these grim undertakings of yours, expected so ... shall we say *unique?* ... an investigator as this Dziurzynski. The bulbous accents you've given these crimes, meant precisely to draw attention *to* you in order such attentions might be swiftly directed cleanly *away*, have backfired. In Dziurzynski's mind, if you'll pardon a layman's observation, such efforts seem to've made her all the more certain you're the chap *dunnit*.'

'She knows, as *you* know …' Gould patiently offered as rejoinder '… that I've done no such doing. Had been under her personally ordered observation at the time of this most recent crime, for example.'

'So … all is going according to *plan* …' he couldn't help needle, growing sheepish afterward before adding '… or so it might seem … if there *was* a plan.'

Gould turned his head. Petulant.

'The trouble …' the interrogatory voice forged ahead '… being much what you'd encountered with regard to Schoenberg. By which I mean you *confided your trust to an unspecified adherent into whose loyal hands it gave you great pleasure to delegate the future*. But this partner of yours, Mister Gould, doesn't seem to have any more reason to trust you than you her. Nor to keep loyal to your aims, as you so inelegantly, at least according to the man in the motel, seem to have abandoned course, yourself.'

Gould turned his head in the other direction. Unblinking.

'Perhaps, since this subject is also toxic, we might return to our discussion of *Maude Harbor*?'

Gould gave a final squint to the handwritten note he'd opened the piece of correspondence to address.

Read it over, in full.

Reflected on it, preparing to respond.

Drummed fingertips against his chin after setting the letter down.

Removed the current sheet from the typewriter, very offhand.

Either set it down or let it fall to the floor at his side.

Hardly mattered.
Fresh sheet from the dwindling stack was set to roller.
Advanced.
Pinned to place.
Another few adjustments of it.
Tick-tick-tick-tick.
Ding of typewriter when he moved the trolly to starting point.
Yawned.
Tack. Tack. Tack. Tack.

>Dear Miss Taitt-Werenfeld:
>
>I am afraid your signature was just a bit on the illegible side, so if I have misspelled your name, do please forgive me.

Cleared his throat.
Took another swallow from his bottled water.
Teeth tapping out imitation of the typewriter's metal slapping each letter to place as he composed.

>The probability of a recital in Montreal is, I am afraid, rather remote. I haven't given recitals for several years now – found that whole way of life rather distasteful – and would be most reluctant to go back to it.

Munched a cookie placidly.
Squirming toes around in his socks.
Little snap-crackles from them.
Reminded him to also crack his knuckles.
Which presently he paused to enact.
Mangle of *pop-pop-pop-pop-pop-pop* all at once feeling quite pleasant.
Then returned to his reply.

> Your question about 'gesticulations' is a rather difficult one …

Eyes drifted closed.
Met first with blank dark.
Then the sound of his breath like the lapping of lake water.

> … I have never been able to play the piano without gesturing semiphorically toward an imaginary horde of sidemen …

Blade of a hatchet.
Face reflected in cabinet glass.
Not quite a mirror.
As though he, himself, weren't quite there.

> … I suspect it has to do with a desire … an impulse … which becomes irresistible … the only answer to the fury which tortures me. It's why I committed my first act of murder, in any event.

Lips plipped.
Lips plopped.
Lips plip-plopped.
As he walked the way walking was walked in a dream.
More as if it were floating.

> I had broken the most deep rooted taboo and found not guilt, not anxiety or fear, but freedom.

Heavy breath soundtracked what ought've been screams.
Screams soundtracked what ought've been laughter.
Laughter and a record on the player across the room.
Tip tap of *Monopoly* tokens ticking their way square-to-square were overdubbed with sounds blunt and wet and dull—of hatchet

driven down to the bone, severing vein, opening throat, burying in the very heart the beat of which seemed to be replaced with the heavy huffs of breath from his own mouth hanging brutishly open.

> Every humiliation which stood in my way could be swept aside by this simple act of annihilation: Murder.

Opened his eyes.
Tack. Tack. Tack. Tack.

> That sounds rather strange, I know, but I have thought a good deal about this question and, as of the moment, it is the only relevant answer I can arrive at.

Gould scratched at his chest through his shirt front.
Worked his fingers into the space between one button's clasp and another's so his fingernails might give the skin an honest, thorough scour.
No doubt red lines from the rakes of this motion would be, for a moment, apparent were anyone able to look.

> Again many thanks for your note. With all best wishes.
>
> Sincerely,

Whisked paper from machine.
Set it in front of him.
Reached for already uncapped pen.
Testing it, per usual, on the scratch paper before signing.

> *Glenn Gould.*

'There are only so many pieces of fan mail you can answer, Glenn. Only so many quaint diversion you can find. I'm not going anywhere. *Nothing* is. Nothing *ever* does. It's the pesky thing about life. About …'

Gould ran tongue over envelope adhesive.

Sealed it.

Glanced to desk to discover the pile of correspondence, in fact, was gone.

'By all means, grant yourself another several minutes of respite. Quaff the fine nepenthe of rummaging out a handful of promotional five-by-eight portraits. Dash to the drugstore for a tube of lipstick. Press loving kisses above your signatures. Might as well make your *Goodbyes* as memorable as possible.'

Balled his fists.

Relaxed them.

Balled them.

Pressed one over each ear.

White noise of their pressure doing nothing to shut out or shut up the voice. The one which required neither mouth nor tongue.

'Paradise is too perfect for humanity. You've *always* hated them, Glenn. Since you were a kiddo. Don't you recall it? Your desire to have them all *disappear*? When you were twelve, you began to sketch the libretto for that opera, did you not? About the self-destruction of the human race. The takeover of the planet by species of morally enlightened frogs, fish, and associated reptiles. What you had in mind, I think, was a sort of aquatic *Tod und Verklärung*. Though there was, of course, to be one human character on stage, wasn't there? The part conceived for a boy soprano. Well … I'll give you one guess as to who was to perform it.'

Leaned forward.

Now pressing sides of his knees over ears.

Hands dangling.

Knuckles lightly caressing the carpet.
'You can't stomach these *people*—and why should you? Nor can they understand an iota of you. Relish in morphing you. Shaping you. Even their *admiration* is counterfeit. Or, at best, exists dependent on individual delusions. Can you accept the lauds of such ... *people*? The same ones you've always thought the face of the world reflect better without? Don't the bovine in any field show you as much appreciation when you sing to them? Isn't their response the more honest? The only way you can bear people is if they might be gone at your *whim*. Like thoughts. Be ignored. Like reconsiderations. Be dependent on your grace.'
Sat upright.
Elbows digging to thighs.
Hands clasped.
One rolling over the other over the other over the other.
'But they can't *vanish*, Glenn. They are *permanent*. With aims to control you while all the time designating you *aberrant*—touched in the head for your own desire to control. They treat you as a carnival curiosity. Only accepted by *their* definition but meanwhile never never never letting you alone. If you won't tell them what you *mean* or who you *are* ... Glenn, they're more than content to do so in your stead. If they outlive you, it'll be *their* definition, *their* desire, which'll be taken for *you*. You'll become their *performance* of you. Their insights will replace your own. You'll be mere effigy. A carcass dressed up, sat to the table, still served dinner to or in honor of.'
Lolled head back.
Eyes empty and blinking at the ceiling.
Mouth open.
Seeming to dangle, in full, to the lap of his pants with the line of thin drool issuing from it.
'*Let's ban applause*, you'd exclaimed! But, I promise you Glenn, they are legion who are applauding that! Ready to hoist

you to shoulders—*hip-hip-hurrah*!—while flowers are strewn at your feet and the hands of those in audience thunder and bury your sentiments in their appreciations. Swine. Villains. Product of the vulgar artistic hostility of those sun-baked societies who have built an operatic tradition in which their primal instinct for gladiatorial combat has found a more gracious but thinly disguised sublimation.'

Found his hands on the typewriter.

Eyes set with determination.

Found mouth moving.

Voice evenly, pleasantly drifting from it.

'Yet there is a way, after all, to ignore them ignoring your wishes, isn't there? A method by which you might banish their applause, in perpetuity ...'

Finished typing, Gould snorted.

Worked at a pain in his shoulder.

Weathered a surge of dizziness.

Titled water bottle, empty, to his mouth.

Set it inside empty cookie box.

Both moved over to the extreme edge of the desk.

Turned the latest, four page document over to read through from the start.

> I had scarcely begun the first supper show of my gala season at the Maude Harbor festival when, as was my habit, I glanced toward the boxes. And there, seated on one marked LIVE BAIT—DO NOT REFRIGERATE was a vision of such loveliness that it instantly erased ...

'These are words. Always will be. Words which can change nothing, Glenn. Nor take the place of events. Words aren't time-machines. Your regrets, quite frankly, at this point are unseemly.

You've done what you've done. Cannot control the posterity of your actions.'

Told himself he wasn't listening.

Just read.

Contentedly.

The concert.

The girl.

The reception.

Swimming.

The picnic.

The skiff.

The night of games.

Why was he writing any of this, at all?

That question was the one the voice truly wanted an honest answer to.

Little matter if eventually a version of this document found itself in front of eyes other than his own. The events it described all a disguise. Pure fantasy.

He could present it as a story or as an article written in mimic of the memoirs of Rubenstein. Could claim it to be whatever he might desire.

Perhaps the truth underneath would go unrecognized.

Perhaps this would please him.

'By why *chance* it?'

Why mix the desire to conceal with an act of semi-revelation?

No one had knocked on his door.

About what he'd done.

Not until now.

Those knocks nothing to do with *Maude Harbor*.

He shook the pages as he finished the last of them.

Set them aside.

Attention drifted to the final paragraphs which remained set to the typewriter.

But his eyes refused focus.

'Or is it *braggadocio*—is that what this is? A *taunt*? A letter to cover up your own little Whitechapel? *Dear Boss*, eh? *They say I'm a doctor now haha*. Is this your desire to showcase *virtuosity*? Watch, when the questions come, half the world clamor in your defense while the other half is certain you're capable of exactly what you'll be accused of! These words cultishly fawned over. Your secret confession. Which pulp stories will be writ in speculation of this yarn once the whole truth comes ugly to light? Are you as *childish* as that? Isn't getting away with it enough? Having gotten away with it, must you get away with it, again?'

The voice merely wanted to know whether what he was doing was on purpose or an actual, uncanny failing of his faculties.

'They say the reason criminals eventually confess, Glenn, is that, in the end, a man cannot bear to not be known for who he is. Such is unbearable to the soul's constitution. What worse anonymity, then, than a killer who goes uncaught? Than dirt over a grave without your signature fingered in it—is that what you're doing, here?'

'You sound like *Dziurzynski* ...' he snarled, dismissive '... but to answer your question: No. I'm doing nothing more nor less than answering your question: *What happened in Maude Harbor*?'

This.

Which he'd written.

Which ended exactly as he now read back.

> I could no longer be content to abandon myself to vain and idle pursuits; I could no longer rely upon the surpassing agility and spontaneity of my art and abuse these unquestioned virtues while I followed a life of frolicsome indulgence. Henceforth, the superficial gesture, the hedonistic pursuit would be forever exiled from my nature. I would dedicate my life and my art to my beloved.

I would forsake all others, work my fingers to the bone, and create for myself a place of pride in the great world which I would lay before my consort's feet as a token of my love. I was a new man, and she alone, with the redeeming power of innocence, had brought about this transformation. I resolved that when next we met, I would ask her for her hand and, indeed, for her name, which I had neglected to elicit.

Only having read it realizing the *Tack Tack Tack Tack* which had continued to sound while his eyes were occupied.

Further words revealing themselves to the page.

Words which seemed borne of someone else.

And to which his eyes didn't turn.

Gould rolled to his side on the mattress.

Coughed.

Mouth muffled by pillow which his arms wrapped tightly around.

Knew from the chill he'd sweated through his clothes.

Likely through the sheets as well, though these were no longer round him.

Heat from the vent above the bed drifted down. Though after traveling such distance might as well have been air conditioning. The slight touch of it resulted in small shivers he curled himself tighter in defense against.

Lips sticky, gummy as they parted.

Eyes not wanting to open.

Dreamt imagery still coiled his thoughts.

Himself seen from overhead.

Glenn Gould at the typewriter.

Floor covered in a sea of haphazard papers.

Each sheet matted thick with typeface.

All floating on a pool of scarlet which the carpet seemed unable to absorb.

Fingers tapping away.

Each one dinging a note.

Some piece of music.

Melody hodgepodge.

All out of order.

Rolled to his back.

Stared at the leaking vent directly above.

Opened his mouth as though to catch a trickle of rainwater.

Soon was sitting upright.

Feet over bed lip.

Toes curled to grip at the discarded coat they pressed down on.

Limbs limp.

But rejuvenated.

Like from the passing of an ailment.

Bleary, he padded his way to the washroom.

Splash from faucet to face.

Another.

Pill bottles popped.

Swallow swallow swallow.

Glanced to his notebook, but decided he'd fill it in later.

Recited to himself what he'd swallowed.

A few times.

Until the repetition lost cohesion.

And he found he hardly felt it mattered.

Had second thoughts as he put hand to doorknob to enter the darkness of the suite, proper.

Sat to the toilet.

Unwound the green rubber band.

Uncapped the pen.

For a moment his concentration broken by a sneeze which seemed to go a long way toward entirely clearing his head.

Absently flipping the notebook pages, he discovered his watch wasn't on his wrist.

No recollection of whether he'd glanced to the clock upon waking.

Would fill in the timestamps, momentarily.

Repeated the names of the recently gulped medications while focusing on the newest page.

Confused to find the log filled in.

Up to the present day.

No gaps.

Cleanly notated were a set of pills allegedly swallowed in the afternoon.

His usual batch.

Along with pulse.

Blood pressure.

Stared at this.

Not confused. Not not.

Verified also how no page had been torn.

No entry mislabeled.

Found himself squinting at the tile of the floor near the tub.

At the closed shower curtain.

The two towels, bone dry and neatly draped over the rack.

Made a sharp swivel of his head toward the cabinet area where additional towels were stacked.

Full set. Prim and proper.

As were the hand towels along the sink basin.

Stood.

Flapping the toilet lid open with too much force.

It struck the cistern. Banged closed.

Raised it more cautiously.

Small, crisp circle of clean water at bowl base.

No indication of sully on the curves down toward it.

No speckle along the rim.

None under the seat.

Wastebin was entirely empty.

Not so much as a tear of toilet tissue he might've used to blow his nose.

Gould's suite was immaculate.

Both the desk chair and armchair set as barricade to the door.

The dimness to the room, lamps not lit, was indicative of an overcast morning rather than the falling of dusk.

As he closed the door to washroom to move to the desk he was disquieted by the sight of the stacked correspondence.

The empty typewriter.

Water bottle.

Box of Arrowroot cookies, half full.

His foot touched down on paper.

Lifting it with grip of his toes high enough to take it with fingers, he uncrumpled the sheet to read the remarks about it being the first night of his gala season …

Lost his balance as he reached to pull chair from behind typewriter.

Chair which wasn't there.

Caught himself on window sill, quickly pivoting to sit on the desktop facing the suite's rear wall.

Gathered his breath.

His bearings.

As best he could.

Patted curled palm to forehead.

No fever.

No sense of over-cold to the skin of his hand.

Nor much sign of perspiration.

While it was clear from a tangy odor and slight tinge of pain when he breathed in that he'd recently been congested, for the moment air entered and exited more or less unimpeded.

Full stack of unblemished writing paper, seemingly as much as ... yesterday? ... was in place beside the typewriter.

Flitted through the envelopes on the desk.

Both piles.

Discovered all of them sealed.

No indication of tampering whatsoever.

All the same correspondence as had been there for days.

Many pieces hand addressed.

Impossible to believe duplicates might've been left.

Not to mention the dates from postage ink on this one or that.

Dug the last crust free from his left eye, afterward wiping his hands on his pants.

Again reached for the chair.

Again tottered slightly.

Using the misstep to start himself in the direction of the bedroom.

Immediately wheeled around.

Checked the security of the windows. While reminding himself of the distance of his room from street level and the lack of anything but sheer drop to the pavement.

Wouldn't accept he'd dreamt ...

... had dreamt ...

... what would he call it?

The last things he recalled?

The past several hours of his life?

Called it neither.

Didn't want to commit.

Nevertheless ... understood whatever he'd *thought* had happened ... *dreamt* had happened ...

... hadn't.

Or someone had been able to remove any evidence it had.

Though that was no mere matter of mysterious individual having discovered a means of ingress and egress to the suite despite the single entryway being secured against them.

There was the matter of the envelopes.

The paper.

The presence of the water.

The cookies.

The …

… Room Service tray was set on the small table near the sofa.

He took quick strides to it, almost giddy.

Discovered the carbon version of a receipt slip he'd signed.

Or the receipt … *someone* had signed … in exactly his hand.

Creep of unease set in.

Despite there being no evidence of letters he'd *opened*, he might still have *drafted* one. Sealed it.

Tendered it to hotel staff to post.

Then what?

Cleaned up?

Asked for new towels?

A fresh ream of paper?

Water?

Cookies?

Dropped to the sofa.

First sitting.

Then laying.

Feet over the armrest. Hands to chest. Fingers interlaced.

Blinking rapidly.

As though attempting to get an engine to turn over.

Mind churning fruitlessly.

No specific question locking in.

Not even one which might panic him.

But he wanted one.

Any question.
Anything but this halfway state without narrative.

Was there correspondence for him?
'Nothing's come in today, Mister Gould.'
Anything of his left to go out?
The desk attendant looked three times through the items piled in a section designated for outgoing mail while inquiring whether Gould would only have dropped whichever item off yesterday evening.
'That's correct' Gould said just to keep matters moving.
'Then it *would* be here ... anything small would be. I see nothing of yours. Had it been ... a more *substantive* parcel?'
Chuckling at how absurd it was to reply 'It *may've* been' Gould nonetheless said exactly those words.
Attendant's face failing to conceal a bit of good-natured befuddlement while moving to another area where such items would be stowed. Again wanted to be certain 'This had been in the *evening*?' Then added generally, how 'Well, obviously it must've been, seeing as I was on duty all day and would recall a larger package. Or *anything* left by you, for that matter.'
Gould almost, by way of excusing himself for so odd an inquiry, adlibbed how a friend had visited him. Left his suite with materials of their own as well as various items Gould had written. Gould uncertain whether said friend had decided to post them from this hotel, directly, or from elsewhere.
For a moment grew queasy.
Thinking of the debacle which would certainly have ensued had he uttered something so idiotic.
Felt he was risking enough by asking about letters which would turn out not to exist.

Dziurzynski was more than crafty enough to find some coy way of obtaining transcript of this present conversation.

One Gould was doing his best to keep low volume.

His back turned to lobby.

Surveying the public space in reflection of mirror behind the attendant.

Absolutely certain at least one of the men reading newspapers or mass market paperbacks was with the police.

Would mark down the time and duration of this chitchat.

'Do you know whether detective-inspector Dziurzynski is in?'

The attendant explained how, unfortunately, she didn't make a habit of announcing her comings and goings.

'In and out. All hours. I don't think she sleeps. Except how one of the other officers mentioned to me she has a subordinate drive her everywhere—catnaps with her head against the window.'

Attendant chuckled.

Confidentially added that it seemed 'She has a penchant for *drooling*.'

Offered to ring her suite.

'One of the *other* officers ..?' Gould asked slowly, ignoring the offer, turning his body as though hoping the attendant would glean from such motion his curiosity over whether such officer was on site, at present.

No luck.

The attendant did volunteer, however, how nobody involved with the investigation, other than Dziurzynski, kept a room at the hotel.

'That seems to bug a few of them. Complain they're a limo service. Their time could be better spent.'

With a shrug, the attendant then editorialized how he didn't see why they had much call for bother, on that count.

'Not as though the *police force* is paying for her room—she's hardly grifting a swank vacation on the public dime.'

'She ... pays to stay here with her own monies?'
Attendant gave a big nod. 'It's kinda weird.'
Gould concurred.

'But then *she's* kinda weird ...' the attendant smiled '... from what everyone *says*, anyway.'

Gould responded how he'd never noticed.

'Do you still want me to ring her room?'

Put on a face of preoccupation while considering this.

Briefly curious whether he'd even had a conversation with the woman, yesterday.

'No ...' he finally answered '... it's nothing worth troubling her.'

Thanked the man kindly.

But raised finger suddenly to inquire 'Members of the *Press* ... they haven't ... been lurking about, have they? Snooping for details about my staying here?'

Rather emphatic shake of the attendant's head.

So far as he knew, there was a strictly enforced off-limits policy.

'Per the *police*.'

For the entire building.

'We're asked to keep eye out for any *loiterers*, too.'

Gould nodded his thanks, once again.

As the elevator door closed on Gould and some random woman, he began reconsidering what he was doing.

Were he honestly entertaining the notion the entire previous day hadn't happened, what good would come of poking the detective-inspector?

What reason for an *impromptu* visit if it turned out she were in her suite, just now?

'Not ...' he assured himself, the voice edging in from another track, barely able to keep from vocalizing the sentiment '… that I'm *remotely* willing to believe I'd lost *another* day.'

Semi-lost a day?

His mind was becoming too clear.

Moment by moment memories solidifying.

The details of his conversation with Dziurzynski.

No dream could be lucid enough it'd hang on him so distinct.

Except … obviously everything he recollected from returning to his own suite onward … which he was beginning to recall with *equal* precision … never *happened* …

Felt the woman in the cabin with him tense over his presence.

Closing herself, protectively.

Remaining mutely focused on the lit indicators as the floor pushed up beneath them.

Expending terrific energies to keep herself from stealing glances at him.

This current of unease compelled Gould to flit his eyes her direction again and again.

To the extent he might as well have been *staring*.

She exited on the level of his own suite.

The moment the door closed him alone, he began pacing a tight circle.

Drifted his hands about.

Clasped them behind him.

Again moved them through the air.

Numbly urging himself to turn back.

He briefly fantasized confessing to being the perpetrator. Without any allowances made to mitigate his guilt by way of insanity or whatever olive branch might be extended.

This make-believe bleed into another.

Perhaps he might fabricate a compelling turn of events. Inform Dziurzynski he'd been contacted, exactly as *prophesized*.

Claim a man had telephoned.

Requesting they meet.

At that motel.

Why it was only *now* that the full weight of the crisis he'd been all but slumbering through landed square upon him, Gould had no idea.

For days, he'd desired nothing more than to treat all the escalating horrors around him as insubstantial.

Bad weather.

Some trifle he could take or leave, all the same.

Vagrant occurrence in his life which would sink into irrelevance the same as might the tiny pangs of guilt associated with canceling an appointment last minute.

Nor could he account for why he felt near to serenity as soon as the elevator opened on *Four*.

As he stepped into the blank, silent corridor.

Not just *serene* …

If not for the fact he'd no understanding of his own intentions, he'd swear himself *confident*.

In control.

Proceeding according to plan.

'After all …' he whispered, purposefully heading down the corridor in the incorrect direction '… it isn't as though you've done anything …'

… *which could be proved*, he continued, entirely interior.

Next moment, he turned in the proper direction.

But as he took the first step toward *four four four* his legs went gelatinous.

Any self-assurance drained away that same instant.

Hit the call button for the elevator.

Stepped inside.

Hit indicator for his own floor.

Breathing becoming labored as he waited for the metallic doors to shutter him inside.

Finger went to carotid.
Pulse jackhammered.
Headache bombarded him, nearly migraine.
When the floor jostled and began lowering, he could hardly stave himself from sicking up.
Knees buckled.
Retched.
Horrendous sound.
Chorus of toads croaking all at once.
Felt as though one side of his throat was grinding against the other to strangle him.
Into his corridor.
Hobbling almost.
Certain a housekeeper moved her cart in front of the open door to a vacated room she was prepping to tidy.
Frozen at the sight of him.
Gripping the keys she held.
Knuckles draining white.
Gould felt this woman's eyes on him.
Pictured her neck craning.
Head poking around corner.
To be assured that he'd actually gone.

Had almost expected the room to be in the turmoil he'd dreamt. But as suite door drifted closed behind him, all was exactly as he'd left it.
'So to speak …' he chuckled, unable to help himself.
With back pressed against door, he glanced around.
Slowly.
Not focusing on any detail, exactly.
Breathing *out* the count of twenty.

In the count of twenty.
Pausing ten.
Out.
In.
Pause.
Heel of left foot tapped in time with heartbeat.
At first enough he bobbed in place.
Then more relaxedly.
Until coming entirely to rest.
It remained a possibility he'd left the room again overnight, yes?
Even from last he could readily recall, more time had elapsed than during his jaunt into the cold and wet the ... night previous?
Conversation with Dziurzynski.
Sick spell at the toilet.
All the typing he recollected but hadn't actually done.
Yes ... even *after* all those occurrences ... more time existed between them and waking this morning than ... the night previous?
Shook his face.
Timeline in shambles.
Night previous not sounding correct despite being so.
Night before last.
Yes. That was the motel. Was the man in the motel.
Or ... *wasn't* the motel ... *wasn't* the man in the motel ...
But *last night*?
He'd no idea.
Found it comical how the *night before last* was the one he'd insisted would be expunged from the record while, instead, it was the night just awoken from which was found *absentee*.
Would this be repeat of ... 'However many nights ago ..?'
He sighed pathetically.
A replay of *waking in the motel room*?

Following crumbs to learn his whereabouts leading up to that moment?

Only to remain ever in doubt.

Would he again take some sheet of paper handed to him by the detective-inspector as proof of his movements—sign off on it, commit to its fiction?

His life might be like that, from now on.

This part his, this other-part anyone else's best guess.

'Or *this part* my best guess, too' he corrected.

Pushing tongue into lip over upper teeth.

Bringing lower teeth into it until the pain caused him to involuntarily grab at his jaw.

Resolving to take absolutely no further action, to remain locked in his suite to the bitter end, Gould crossed to retrieve the desk chair from the typewriter.

Squinting on approach.

Mistrustful of the crumpled paper on the desk.

Of the empty device.

A part of his mind wasn't certain *why* this distrust.

A part of his mind understanding *entirely*.

Neither one able to articulate itself.

Were it true he was involved in something …

'Or true …' he held up hands as though the previous statement were casting things irresponsibly too far '… that I am a …' what was the word Dziurzynski had used … *Link* ..? *Conduit* ..? *Totem* ..? '… for some lunatic …'

Could it not also be true his best bet was to trust whoever the lunatic was?

Let whichever machination they'd begun run its course?

Do whatever it took to allow it to do so, in fact?

'Even if it means more deaths, Glenn?'

He hissed.

No desire to admit even *peripheral* responsibility in anything.

There was an entire police force actively engaged in curtailing any further violence and to lawfully revenging whichever had to date been allowed to transpire.

What difference would one more hand on deck make?

'Other than it would be *you*, specifically, allowing it to go on by recusing yourself?'

What was his head these days, moot court?

Let him put it this way—*yes*.

'Yes.'

Even if there were further deaths.

Was it Glenn Gould's *duty* to risk dying so that some anonymous party might not—any more than it was *beholden* on this nobody to accept their fate to spare him his?

Dragged the chair behind him toward the door.

Having had quite enough of himself.

Valium in an amount just shy of overdose ought be plenty guarantee he'd sleep through to the end of this trial, eh?

Place a few phone calls so no one expected him any place.

Word to hotel and Dziurzynski he was alive.

Barricaded.

Intended to remain so.

Not to be rousted until all was resolved.

Wedged chair to place.

Tested the fit.

Growled.

Turned his back.

In that exact moment a knock sounding to the door.

———

No effort made to conceal the alarm on her face, the detective-inspector glanced from the desk chair to Gould.

Was everything *alright*?

Peered around.

Squinting behind him, toward the bedroom.
Hands at the ready to cinematically unholster a sidearm.
Which she didn't seem to be wearing.
Though considering the length of the light paisley coat draped down her to well below the knee, who could tell?
As Gould assured her everything was perfectly fine, she cautiously ventured past him.
More than apparent how she absolutely expected trouble.
'Is everything going well with *you* today, detective-inspector?'
This casual query earned him a wink, out of place among her nervous motions of progress toward bedroom door.
He figured her eyes were darting between it and the ajar entrance to washroom.
Perhaps an extra tick to the crumpled sheet of paper, now back on the floor.
'Are you alone?' she asked, half-whisper.
'*Alone?*'
'*The only one here*' she translated without inflection of any kind.
'*You're* here …' he replied, adopting an entirely breezy demeanor '… I *think*.'
Dziurzynski responded simply with 'Mmn …'
Had stopped moving.
After a moment of silence explaining to him she'd meant the question in earnest.
'You see me …' she whispered, still faced toward the door '… on my mark, get set … yet I'm guessing have hands idly in your pockets or else are blithely tapping a snuff box … which one might consider *peculiar* … all things considered.'
Unwitnessed by her, Gould made croupier gesture, hands clean.
Focusing past her.
Fixating on the bedroom door, himself.
In a detached way.

Waiting for some maniac to burst out.

Gunned down without quarter.

Leaving Gould with Dziurzynski to thank for not waking with his throat slit.

But as she crept nearer, reaching hand for knob, he told her he was on his lonesome.

'If the precaution with the door upset you, rest assured it was done on account of I'd digested your sound advice, taken it firmly to heart, and have made such security measures a fervent bedtime habit.'

'It's nine in the morning.'

'*Touche* and all.'

But now she was *worrying* him.

'Ought you be worrying me, detective-inspector?'

'Who can say?'

Regardless, she informed him she intended to have a peek in the *boudoir*.

'Feel free.'

He supposed she'd feel better if he left the suite door open, too?

'If you'd do me the courtesy, please and thank you.'

Like a feature film, Gould observed Dziurzynski acting out all the motions which, in reality, seemed quite silly despite their sensibility on silver screen.

Everything short of drawing a gun.

That missing element convincing him this was a put on.

Per usual.

While Dziurzynski satisfied herself as to their isolation, Gould took a seat in the armchair.

Wasn't enjoying this vignette one little bit.

At a loss how to insist she knock it off, however.

The last thing he wanted to seem like was *like* anything.

Bristled with affront, already, how his *not* seeming like something seemed to seem to her exactly like he did.

Exiting the washroom, she shrugged.

Gould about to quip how she no doubt had deep seeded caution baked into her due to some venomous clown she'd once found under her bed or the alligator which'd spawned in the septic tank of the house where she'd grown up and once nibbled her great-aunt's bottom mid-void—but he resisted the urge.

In fact, grew anxious when she crouched to take up the crumple of paper.

'To what ...' he started, more imperatively than he would've preferred, watching her reading the typewritten words '... do I owe this *latest* unsolicited intrusion?'

Taking her time to finish with the paper, pausing a good while afterward, Dziurzynski said nothing.

Then, casually, told him he should close the door.

———

Been *looking* for her?

'They'd said.'

Said?

'At the desk. Just now.'

At the desk, just now?

'That you'd been asking after me, Mister Gould.'

Dziurzynski just wondered if there'd been any reason *in particular*.

As it happened, she'd been making her way to check whether he was up and about.

'You know my distrust of *coincidence*.'

Gould explained he'd been at the front desk.

Incidentally.

Wondered whether she was in.

Nothing specific had prompted the curiosity.

'Then you went up to my *suite*, did you?'

'*Did* I?' he mugged confusion.

'You *didn't*?'

Had someone fibbed otherwise?

'At least one person certainly seems to have. Add in these tedious rumors circulating how more than one of you might be lurking about and you'll forgive a mother for fretting.'

'I'd been at the desk ...' Gould kept his voice dulcet '... for reasons *unrelated* to you ...' trying to reckon if his calm was making matters better or worse '... asked after you and then scampered back here.'

Now, as though the insinuation of falsehood in her previous utterance had never existed, Dziurzynski moved toward the desk, setting the crumpled sheet down and helping herself to a cookie.

'I thought you might've had something to ask me. Since I'm here, now, only natural to've petitioned the horse's mouth, directly. Spare me having to wait until next time I see you. Inquiring then. *That'd* sure seem cuckoo, eh?'

Not altogether on the same page, Gould shrugged.

Shifted conversational line to explanation how it'd been on his mind 'not now, but recently' to apologize for his lack of helpfulness, yesterday.

'In fact, though I know we spoke, my head is pure pudding about what. Tossing and turning, I kept imagining we were talking *still*. Would wake to find myself in the dark. Alone. The process would repeat. Come this morning, I can't for the life of me recall anything with clarity.'

Such as?

'Such ... *as*?'

'Such as *what can you not recall with clarity*?'

'The trick there, of course, is once I've remembered I'll have remembered. Eliminating you from the equation.'

'Wittiness aside, though ... *such as*?'

What was happening here, precisely?

Was she goading him?

Didn't matter.

As his mind was unable to find a method of asking her whether she was without it seeming he was specifically affronted and therefore inviting ever more probative lines of inquiry, there was no value in broaching the subject.

'I must not've seemed entirely *attentive*, is the long and the short of it' Gould said with a bow and a bit of a blush. 'Truth be told, when I mentally venture back to the interview, I've a mutt's time sorting which of what you'd said had been in jest from the things you'd meant in earnest ... from things I may've merely dreamt.'

'*Jest*?'

Gould cleared his throat.

Bluntly asked 'Detective-inspector, why were *you* on *your* way to see *me*?'

Dziurzynski put on a hurt face.

Like she'd been turned down for a date to the prom.

Obvious playact.

All the more purposeful in that she slowly returned face to chummy, nothing-was-nothing, ignoring Gould's query with remark about how he seemed to be feeling better.

'Pink bismuth, like the miracle of asbestos, was gifted from a kindly genie. All it'd been was dyspepsia run rampant. Often my whole body stuffs up when my tummy isn't fond of the wider world.'

Taking a bite from the one she presently held, Dziurzynski hoped it hadn't been the cookies to blame.

'Eggs were more likely the culprit ...' Gould ticked his head toward the Room Service tray. 'It's hard to distrust chickens, but I might have to start.'

'You don't much want to talk to me right now, do you?'

To the contrary, he was doing his college best. But like with the jazz music he wasn't famous for playing couldn't quite cotton to what she *was* talking about *between* what she was actually *saying.*

Dziurzynski nodded.

Pointed to the desk chair.

'Mind if I sit on your doorstopper?'

'*To visit you, my lord, no other occasion*' Dziurzynski grandly orated.

Gould watched her eyes narrow.

Widen when he gave no reply.

'*Pepto* cured you of the Bard too, eh?' she winked.

Certain he'd no idea what she meant, Gould would nevertheless be more than happy to explain not only about the chair but why he'd asked was she in the hotel, at present.

'So there *was* a reason?'

Not much of one. But yes.

His current plan, which she was one of several he intended to keep abreast of, was to sleep until her brave work was completed.

It was true how he'd told her barring the door was a recently adopted habit.

Nothing to feel uneasy over.

Had wanted to make the front desk aware that he was to receive no calls.

Wouldn't be requesting business from the kitchen.

That no visitor, if there should arrive such person, ought be given *any* information concerning his present whereabouts.

He'd be explaining to those at the studio where he worked he was taking a respite. They shouldn't be alarmed or seek him out.

Likewise, he'd make certain friends and representatives privy to his temporary monasticism.

'By these methods ensuring I am present and accounted for, at all times. The world given permission to spin without my presence.'

Dziurzynski's expression had grown more concerned by the moment. Not enough he'd altered the stern of his stentorian address, but enough he'd nearly wanted to.

Excuse her for having to admit herself even more alarmed than previously. Indeed, his preceding announcement might, to a certain ear, have somewhat an ominous ring.

Would she care to elaborate?

'You once told me you *weren't* being threatened.'

'And grateful I am for the good breeding shown in your taking me at my word.'

'You *still* aren't?'

Being threatened?

No.

'Other than *existentially*. My nervous system in a state of fray. That's all.'

'Not frayed to the extent it'd cross your mind to … *your own quietus make*?'

'For heaven's sake, detective-inspector. It's hardly as desperate as that.'

He laughed.

Hoped it sounded healthy.

Nodding nodding nodding, Dziurzynski suddenly seemed embarrassed.

'Frankly, I can't help blaming myself. For everything you're going through. It's a decadent pathology with me. Feeling *guilty*. Guy goes around with some hatchet, playing your records—every day I don't catch the brute I can't imagine the earaches you get. Then I go on about parasomnias and fugue states, no doubt agitating waters further. Foisting such putzy and lame brained notions onto you when you're clearly under strain …'

He laughed, again.
But now as though to indicate gratitude.
'It'd take more than a few stories of haunted houses to get me to join such an attraction.'
'*Phew* ...' she now laughed, herself '... because not catching the killer *and* killing the guy who didn't do it would look really bad on a plaque.'
Gould was simply relieved to hear himself so described.
'So ... described?'
'As the *guy who didn't do it*, detective-inspector.'
Of course of course.
Well, as long as he *hadn't* done it that was the quickest way to describe him.
'You'll inform me if you change your mind and *did* do it, right?'
Gould frowned.
But when Dziurzynski made cartoon mimic of the expression back at him, hers slowly shifting to wide grin, he smiled as well.
'As soon as I land someplace averse to extradition, you'll be the first to know.'
Promise?
He did.

As was unfortunately becoming too often the case, Dziurzynski regretted to confess *her* reason for darkening Gould's doorstep was far from delivering baked goods.
Was on her way to 'yet another crime scene' and, in this case, had been rather hoping he'd feel up to tagging along.
'A bedbug motel. Far cry from either the classiness of our present environs or those where whatever had happened to Lang had

happened to Lang. Not even on par with the quaint homestead wherein our missing waitress's mother, until quite recently, hung her hat.'

About an hour's drive.

During which she was keen to collect Gould's insights into another matter.

Was his presence strictly *necessary*?

'You think your tummy isn't up for the trip?'

'*Who* ... has been killed?' Gould meekly inquired, three times clearing his throat, two times apologizing for doing so between the first word of the question and the second through fourth.

'Somebody, it seems. Or it sure looks like it. I'm eternally fingers-crossed it was *nobody*. Prefer great big misunderstandings to corpses, if you'd like the truth.'

At present, she'd merely been told it was 'one of mine.'

An expression she rolled her eyes while relating.

Air of honest annoyance at whatever this current matter was having been dubbed so.

Even if Gould wasn't keen for a fieldtrip, she'd have to *insist*.

If it was a matter of indigestion, she'd bring along a bag for him to empty in.

'I imagine car sickness is one of your many crosses to bear. The motel is bound to have bathrooms, once we're there.'

Gould let his lack of enthusiasm for the errand show plainly.

Suggested it might be leaning a tad *much* into unorthodoxy.

Was there some *compelling* reason she required a sidekick drawn from the laity?

Rather than answering, beginning to speak before he'd quite finished and as though distracted with roughly scratching herself up an armpit, the detective-inspector explained the motel was near the diner where the waitress had worked.

House of her dead mother about halfway between the two points of interest.

'Not a whole lot else out there' she shrugged. 'Some clusters of shops. A gas station. Those sort of things.'

There was a *specific* hand he could lend, though?

If it was all the same, he'd prefer to wait for the recap he'd no doubt have the pleasure of being delivered.

'No doubt' she winked, puffed down nose, grinning only after both those acts were complete.

As she'd mentioned, there were a few things 'I don't *think* are related but *maybe*' she'd been meaning to look him up to bend an ear about right before the call about the motel had come in.

'Lots of whatnot happening upside-down-all-at-once, today.'

Normally she slept in the car.

But would make an exception since he was being a sport.

'My cleats are more than a little worn out from all the previous gridiron, detective-inspector. If it won't be held against me, I'd rather—'

Aw geez, does she really *have* to insist?

After *all* they'd been through, lately?

'It's a car ride. Compulsory, I'm afraid. Need you for *official* reasons.'

Believe her, she was quite put out to have to throw her weight around like this.

'It's distasteful, really. Though I *am*, I don't *like to be* the boss of you.'

She stared at him.

Wet her lips.

Held hands out like asking for seconds to be slopped into her porridge bowl.

Then sighed.

Turned toward the door.

'Chilly out there, by the way. I'd say grab your coat if you weren't already always in it.'

At Dziurzynski's heels down the corridor, resolved to absolutely not step foot inside the elevator despite whichever action against him she'd brandish, Gould insisted she explain herself.

'I'm under the impression it's my legal right to remind you you're *required* to do so.'

She swatted in his direction, flirtatiously.

'Lookit—you're *already* out the door.'

Sorry for the schoolyard thuggishness, but it'd seemed the shortest path to breaking a stalemate.

'Nobody likes a crime scene, I know. But I shouldn't have been so spooky about it. If you wanna make things a federal case, yeah yeah yeah, the world has written allowances for citizens to be as mulish as they fancy—but I was only joshing ya about the doom and gloom.'

Was there any advantage in pressing his argument here?

Held his face indignantly, just in case.

Meantime Dziurzynski tap-tap-tapped the summons button and retied her left shoe.

'Do you want her to—what, Glenn? Arrest you?'

He'd almost vocalized the question.

Worded just that way.

Mind rolodexing through what confrontations his holding firm might lead to.

Mind-reading act, spoken with almost obsequious affability, Dziurzynski said 'It's not like you can *go* anywhere. Even if you *weren't* already blockading your door.'

Made a dismissive *tsk* as she stood upright.

'How much *sleep* are you gonna manage in the meantime? You'll be pins and needles—so don't be a stick-in-the-mud.'

What's it all about, then?

Tell him that.

Elevator door opened and Gould, mostly due to how hippity-hop Dziurzynski had done so, broke his vow from moments earlier.

Watched the doors close.

Pressed the button for *Lobby* when she tapped her nose toward the console.

'The usual ...' she began once the elevator dipped into motion '... bloodshed and Johannes Sebastian. That's *really* all they've told me, thus far.'

It was getting to be a bit much, by this point, was her honest opinion.

'Plus you're running my underlings *ragged*! Why on Earth did you have to cut such a swell record, Mister Gould? Any idea how many of those hot cakes you've sold? It's not like we can track the specific ones from the death-traps to exact stores or anything ... but we have to *try*.'

In this case, there'd been a spot of good fortune in that they knew the *present* record had belonged to the dead woman.

'By which I mean the mother of the *waitress*.'

A custom made *Property Of* label affixed to the reverse side of the jacket.

'Not that, with all the *coincidences* flying around, I put much stock in incidentals like that. Still have my goons scouring Yard Sales in the area. Just in case she'd gifted it to someone and the killer had picked it up that way.'

Her lackeys despised her for having such bright ideas.

'But as you're probably sarcastically quipping to yourself even now: I *surely* have my reasons.'

Which she did.

But no need to bore him with shop talk.

Meantime they'd crossed the lobby.

Were through the carousel doors.

Gould breathless.

Wondering had Dziurzynski kept the pace as intense as she had to purposefully wind him.

Make slipping into the seat of the idling car, held open by the officer who'd be driving, seem his own idea.

Despite her every word making it anything but.

Closed inside.

Hand at wrist to take pulse.

Pulled on seatbelt with awkward immediacy at seeing Dziurzynski getting her own buckled up.

Then, not bothering to backtrack through her mile-a-minute chatter *en route*, Gould fumbled out the question 'What *else* was it you needed to *discuss* with me, in the meantime?'

She blinked.

Gould half expecting her to behave as though she didn't comprehend the question. No further need to lead him by the nose since the vehicle was in motion.

But she snapped her fingers merrily at the query.

Thanking him for the reminder.

'Wondered could I ask you about a place called *Maude Harbor*. You played some Scarlatti there, once upon a time, I believe.'

'IT'D HAPPENED BEFORE. QUITE LIKE THIS. Imagine the look on my face, learning that.'

Dziurzynski had said those words to Glenn Gould.
In the car.
Her mouth moving, now.
In the motel room.
Finger pointing.
To the record player in the corner.
Record left spinning round upon it.
Gould wasn't taking in any present sound.
Neither music nor Dziurzynski's voice.
The words he was hearing were the ones from the car.
Lack of sync to lips and words.
Spaghetti Western *doppiagio*.
Only select background sounds to make the memory embed, hyperreal.
As now, when the detective-inspector tapped one-two-three toward an object set atop the television.
Turned to regard Gould's reaction.
His nodding.
Her smile.
Both out of joint.
'This was several years back, mind you. You, in fact, were *there*. Though, it seems to me, must've never heard tell of it. There was a woman. You knew her, I believe. Peggy Mulhheim.

Sad little fate for her. Butchered on a *Monopoly* board. Shoved down her gullet they found the deeds to *Connecticut Avenue* and every one of the railroads.'

Dziurzynski pointed now in an arc.

Finger extended in trace of a pronounced spatter of blood.

Wall stained like with notes from sheet music leaking through lines of the staff.

Gestured from this to the bed mattress, stripped bare.

Obviously once soaked in a dank, morbid brown.

Color now dry.

Stiff seeming.

Sour.

There'd be a crunch to it as with a tissue left in the bin after clotting off a bleeding nose.

'A man. Zoltan Mostanyi. From Budapest. Known for a monograph. *Hayden and Serfdom: The Tyranny of the Minuet*. He'd gone missing. But left behind signs of desperate struggle. Enough bodily fluid one would think he'd been trussed up and bled like a pig.'

Dziurzynski stood with back to him, now.

But he met the eyes of her overdubbed face in the reflection.

Mirror cracked. Her mouth cracked in it.

Many towels in stale disrepair on the sink counter underneath.

Some tinted heavily of gore.

Others not.

From the splintered glass watched her pluck a blonde hair.

Lodged in the fissures were many others.

Watched as she pointed to it. Had difficulty getting it to fall from her moist fingertips when she waggled them, hand bobbing rubbery at wrist.

'Then a woman. Older woman. Not found until later. Zero direct connection to Peggy or Zoltan. Who only had vague connection to each other, themselves. Two connections, to be precise.

One: they happened to know each other. *Two:* they happened to be acquainted with you.'

Dziurzynski politely stepped past him.

Doing her best to respect his necessary distance.

Difficult, as he didn't make way for her.

As though he weren't present.

Watching from in front of a screen. Elsewhere.

She seemed to be on about some aspect of the room door.

Its handle.

Whatever she was explicating ending in a shrug.

'This poor woman, though, wasn't so random as she seemed at first blush. *Had she a daughter?* you might ask. She *had*. One daughter. Who vanished from the face of this Earth. As had the monograph scribbler from Budapest, you'll recall my just having said. Before going *poof*, though, she was a girl who'd left a room quite like this.'

Dziurzynski clapped.

No sound inserted for it from Gould's point-of-view.

Though he did wince at the sight, touched at his ear.

Dziurzynski appearing to giggle.

Before clapping, again.

Slowly.

On purpose.

Quiet clap.

From her posture it was apparent how whatever she was saying now was spoken in whisper.

'All very curious, this room she'd left behind. Only trace of her personally some teeth. Same, by the way, as it'd been for poor Peggy. Chompers battered out. Found upon coffee table. Some of the fella's found in the corner of his room. Even the old woman had had some knocked out. Though it'd been tough to tell it due to her head having been nearly removed.'

Dziurzynski had fastened her gaze intently to Gould.

Gesturing off behind her.

The room corner.

Head again turning so Gould couldn't see her mouth.

'You might ask *Was there music? The* music. *Your* music. At the murder scenes, back then. See—that's an intriguing bit. There *wasn't*. Not in the house rented by Zoltan. Nor the mother's quaint abode. Not in the shabby motel the young girl's absence was discovered in …'

Dziurzynski turned back to face him.

Mouth entirely still.

Overtop of this Gould heard, as though soundtrack at a delay to the image '… but there was … at Peggy Muhlheim's crime scene. The first of the four. *The* music was there. *Your* music was there.'

Gould blinked as Dziurzynski tilted her head.

To again indicate the record playing behind her.

The sound of which now bled into the present moment.

The words 'This *exact* record, in fact' coming from Dziurzynski in real time, too.

Gould had never been to this motel.

So he'd said.

But Dziurzynski needed him to consider the question.

Carefully.

'Maybe not in this room, *specifically*. But I want you to tell me, one thousand percent to the best of your most accurate recollection: have you ever been here, *at all*?'

Driven past?

Walked the grounds?

'Even some visit as offhand as using the lot to turn around in. Perhaps on your habitual, late night excursions?'

Gould assured her he'd 'selected the word *Never* from all the umpteen other numbers he might have' because it was 'even more precise than saying *zero times*.'

He would drive, if she'd care to know, on roads quite in the other direction.

Couldn't name them all. Couldn't name any.

'But most gladly I'll play automotive *gondolier* if you'd care for a spot of nocturnal road touring, yourself.'

With him for happy company, she was certain such jaunt would be quite stimulating.

For the moment though, she did have to remind him the reason behind her asking.

The *several* reasons.

'Namely, there's this trouble of the proprietor being clean positive he'd interacted with you. On several occasions. One quite memorable, wherein you'd behaved ... *curiously*.'

'Not half so curious as his behavior of claiming so comes across to me' Gould calmly responded.

Drunk, was what the proprietor had thought.

'Demanding to be rented a room despite you already had. Which he'd struggled to explain to you against rather seething consternation.'

In fact, what'd struck the man so oddball was the fact Gould had rented *several* cabins.

Paying out many many days in advance.

In exchange for assurances no cabin would be perturbed.

For *any reason*.

Gould not only suggested politely the proprietor was sorely mistaken, but offered polite reminder of the detective-inspector's own mention of reports claiming a man bent on seeming his duplicate was known for haunting various locales.

'True, true ...' Dziurzynski seemed to give a solid think before continuing '... though in this case there were no Groucho Marx glasses, flat caps of the working class, or mufflers to muffle behind.'

Point of fact: Gould was *distinctly* remembered to've been put out over not having such items on hand.

'Insisted a taxicar driver give his backseat the fine-toothed comb.'

She shrugged.

'This cabbie saying there was nothing doing about your apparel. Guy also double quick to make the photo ident. *That's the doctor*. A *music* doctor, he was dead convinced you'd explained.'

'Then I've little doubt whoever he's *mistaken me for* had told him that very thing.'

Could be.

Though for her money the cabbie wasn't very good at being mistaken.

Date.

Time.

Typewriter case.

'*Honk honk honk* he'd blared the horn at your request.'

'At *his passenger's* request, he may've even gone *honk honk honk … honk*' Gould made rejoinder, allowing combativeness to seep into the words.

Well Dziurzynski thought Gould was doing himself dirty, there.

'A strikingly pretty man like yourself is tough to mistake.' And if he didn't mind her stating so 'There's not a lot of penny's your polish merely laying around for good luck, do you think?'

'I've never been to this motel, detective-inspector' Gould said, gesturing this was his final word on the matter. '*Somebody* has. If they prove I'm not so much the diamond in the rough you flatter me to be, that's a pity. But, as you've pointed out, I'm not tough to mockingbird. Whoever this *somebody* was might've made efforts beyond parlor caricature.'

'Whoever they were?'
Dziurzynski blinked and appeared confused.
'They ... were *Doctor Herbert Von Hochmeister*. Hadn't I *said*?'
If not, she felt she'd put elbow grease into implying it.

Dziurzynski apologized.
It must be a bum time for Gould to sit there.
Enduring her prattle.
But what was interesting in all this convoluted business was how, in *Maude Harbor*, he'd been present while a murderer ran cleverly riot '... but present in a capacity it seemed *impossible* you'd have had anything to do with it. Despite, like now, your having *relationship* to some of the deceased.'
Leaving the door to the room they'd just exited ajar, the detective-inspector apologized for the cigarette she presently lit.
'We're outside, after all.'
She shrugged.
Paused through three casual drags.
Looking around.
Gesturing grandly *'This most excellent canopy, the air—look you*—has enough carcinogens to choke a horse. I once heard an old codger make that witty retort when a hoity-toit objected to them lighting a cigar on a restaurant terrace.'
Gould nonetheless took a few steps back.
Widening the space between them she'd made certain to leave.
Pulled his face in, unconsciously. As though the fictional millimeter such discomfort awarded him was the difference between elder care and early grave.
'What I was driving at, since you hadn't asked ...' she made a point to turn around with each exhalation, a full circle every time

instead of the mere twist required to distance the smoke '... is that, in *Maude Harbor*, a handful of folks recalled the girl who'd gone missing being in the presence of the man who'd gone missing. Quite often. One time ...' she held cigarette behind her back after abortive motion for another drag '... it was reported the wee lass had gone out on a *skiff* with the guy. Intent on meeting up with Peggy and yourself. Who were out for a picnic swim.'

Not yet acclimated to the abrasion of cold sunlight, now relentless due to the dissolve of the day's earlier overcast, Gould made no reply.

Arms wrapped round himself, tense.

Jaw clenched against unwelcome chattering.

'Or maybe *not*. You'd know the reality better than I. Far too many gossips in that neck of the woods to get a story exactly *straight*.'

Gould didn't *recall* the girl, did he?

Hanging off Zoltan ... on his skiff?

'Nothing in your *memoirs* about that, is there?'

Shook his head with deep breath and fists firmer down pockets.

To which Dziurzynski nodded.

Asking him to promise he wasn't getting the wrong idea of her going on about this ancient history.

'I stress: there's *absolutely* no chance of your being mixed up in any bad recipe ...' gave rabbit punches to the air with hand holding cigarette '... as your movements during the debacle are *conspicuously* known. From your performances to the receptions to the day you boarded the *Siddhartha* and set sail.'

From what she'd learned, he'd been spared any questioning.

It'd taken until the day following his departure for the full extent of the nastiness to be revealed.

'If you say so, detective-inspector. I, after all, wouldn't know.'

'Never wondered why Peggy stopped sending letters?'

This was asked in a tone of sisterly concern.

Enough of a change from the pronounced cattiness of her previous interrogations Gould couldn't quite keep up his antagonism.

'We'd parted in good humor on fine terms, Peggy and I. I'm not one to ... *dwell*.'

'On matters of the *heart*?'

He'd said no such thing.

Hoped his putting up with her official lines of inquiry wasn't expected to extend to allowing her to pry unfettered into subjects he held private.

'Not much of a lothario ...' she nodded, appreciative '... or not one to kiss and tell, anyway' she winked with the flick of her cigarette away.

Gould followed Dziurzynski into the motel room next door to the stale crime scene.

Watched her turn off the television which'd been left playing mutely atop the bureau.

Watched her move to the mirror.

Make adjustments to her coat.

Test her breath in cupped palm.

Fish a tin of breath mints from rear pant pocket.

Gingerly select three, replacing one with an alternate before popping the bunch into her mouth.

Crunching down.

Tin left to countertop in place of the yellow leather pad she retrieved. Scratching beneath her chin with its rounded top as she turned but not flapping it open.

Gould adopted a brisk air.

Wondered aloud was Dziurzynski's theory that Lang had been present in *Maude Harbor* during that fateful season.

'I seem to *not* think so ...' he added with affect of genuinely straining to recall '… as his presence would've been brought to my attention, no doubt.'

'*Lang*?' She raised an eyebrow. 'That'd sure be neat. But …' she waffled her voice '… as a theory is kinda gimcrack.'

Oh, Lang.

She'd thought *bunches* about Lang.

But on that subject, admitted she'd been barking up the wrong tree.

'Until recently, I'd been cobbling up sensational notions I now can't help going crimson over. It's a lucky break I never aired a word of my suspicions to anyone but *you*.'

'Notions …' Gould rolled hand entreatingly '… *such as*?'

In one scenario, she'd envisioned the entire spate of killings an elaborately sinister creation on Lang's part.

When the waitress went missing, most especially.

'Could've been they'd been a *scandalous* couple, some lascivious bond the Hep Community would never approve of between them.'

Lang maybe had grown bored of the buttoned down life.

Wanted to reinvent himself *a la* Humbert Humbert.

'Then he'd learnt of his young doe's dowry …' by which she meant the missing heirloom jewelry, the priceless ring loped from the fourth finger of the girl's mother '… and thought *Gee whiz, that's the key to it all*!'

Man couldn't die and hope to still have access to his bankbook. It'd smell ripe were his accounts drained, funds horded in cash before making himself scarce.

'Wasn't like if he did a runner there wouldn't be all manner of well-meaning sorts beating bushes about him. Making his story less like *Lolita*, more like hounded by a pesky private dick in the Highsmith novel old Nabokov had lifted inspiration from. Being hunted to the ends of the Earth—that's no way for a dirty old coot to show his yearling a good time, is it?'

Money from the purloined items could be fenced cleverly, though.

While a life was propped up in some foreign clime.

Did Gould see why it'd at least be worth a dime to flip through such a novel idea?

'More than that. You're selling your *detec-tet-ing* short, I daresay.'

Theory made as much sense as any.

Seemed to vindicate her personal philosophies, into the bargain.

'No *common* thuggery. A crime custom tailored to go on the books unsolved until wilting to cold case.'

Grinning, nodding girlish jackrabbit, Dziurzynski beamed.

'It's even *impossible*!' she exclaimed.

Knew there was a reason she'd always liked the cut of Gould's jib.

'It's your attentiveness, most of all. Your ear and keen eye for detail. Makes even an out-to-pasture old mare like me weak kneed, such considerateness. We women, you know, are loopy to feel we've been *heard*.'

'*Why* impossible?'

'Mainly on account of Lang's not a *nut* …' she pouted with a clown frown '… not even the sleep-walking sort. Which leaves only the theory he's calculating. Cold blooded. If he were, I'd be a dunderhead to suppose he'd chop up bystanders, take on infinity risks, when he coulda simply asked his young beloved to *yoink* the jewels from their safe box while he fixed it to look he'd been lost at sea. Or …' she shrugged '… even do all this head bashing in his *hometown*. Why try to frame *Glenn Gould*? Who'd *howl* his innocence, dawn till dusk?'

She shook her head, definitively.

It'd be counterproductive for Lang to've killed anyone.

'Positively tasteless.'

Gould nodded with a chuckle.

Reminded Dziurzynski it was Paul Henry Lang she was speaking of.

'So there's no accounting for *taste*.'

It was Gould she had to thank for steering her head right.

'A *coincidence* ...' she snapped fingers merrily, pointing at him with the pop '... but for once one I could get behind.'

That Gould had chosen to be at work on his *Maude Harbor* article was serendipitous.

'Now of all times. Here of all places. Just when I was chasing my tail—a *miracle*.'

She'd happened to've been captivated by her sneak peek at the rough draft.

Did he remember?

'The one you'd taken a disliking to. Shredded up something fierce.'

She'd no idea why he'd done so.

Having read it, even those opening few paragraphs made her sure it woulda been a success.

'Whatever it was you'd *planned* to do with it.'

Tightening cautious, Gould moved hand in a limp arc as though doffing his cap in gratitude.

Claimed, however, he didn't quite follow her thread as to how this connected with her investigation.

'*Maude Harbor*' she replied, as though it were obvious. 'Sounded a lovely place. Figured to look into vacationing there. First thing that stuck out to me was reports of murder murder murder. Just like *my* murders. Place was too good to be true! I intend to spend a fortnight there, this spring.'

Opened her yellow pad.

Withdrew from it a folded photograph.

Held it up as though for Gould to see but didn't move it near enough he could.

'*This* girl. Remember *her*?'

Gould craned forward without moving feet from where they were planted.

The detective-inspector leaning forward, as well.

Feet also unmoving.

Arm extended so the picture wound up not hand's length from Gould's nose.

Same photo Dziurzynski had shown him in her suite.

'The ... *waitress*?' he puzzled, three quick little breaths after which he tried to disguise by standing swiftly upright and making a *tsk* of displeasure, working imaginary kink from his hip.

'They do look quite *similar* ...' Dziurzynski admitted, regarding the photo, herself '... although I wouldn't call the resemblance *uncanny*. Still ...' she coughed into elbow, excused herself '... one might've thought they'd seen a ghost had one seen the second girl after having first seen the first.'

'Your ...' Gould swallowed roughly, hiccoughed, cleared throat, apologized under his breath '... mathematics seem sound but your calculus eludes me.'

The photograph was of the young woman who'd vanished from *Maude Harbor*.

Long pause.

As though Dziurzynski was waiting for Gould to be dazzled.

'Not the waitress *at all* ...' she continued, a nudge-nudge to the words, eyes widening like a bar flirt.

Gould nodded.

But claimed not to follow, even considering that distinction.

Meantime, Dziurzynski had taken to giving the photograph deep inspection, herself.

'After all ...' she slowly drawled out, tone like granting Gould the benefit of some doubt '... you'd only seen her once or twice.'

'*Seen?*'

'The *waitress*, obviously …' she tucked the snapshot back to leather pad, leather pad tossed onto the smooth of the motel bed's comforter '… as you'd *never* seen the other girl before. Not enough she'd made any *impression*. Or had you seen her? Just not enough you'd *noticed*?'

'Never.'

Dziurzynski nodded. 'Meaning *even more precise than zero times.*'

These words a statement.

No hint of inquisition to the flat she kept her inflection.

'Meaning precisely less times than even *that*' Gould answered, regardless.

The detective-inspector took a seat at the bedside.

Stared at him.

Let herself drift back.

Laying.

Arm spread.

Finally asked aloud, generally '*Where* … was I going with this?'

'*Truthful?*'

Gould claimed he'd been *truthful*?

With *her*?

'Quite a funny epithet to lob at yourself. It'd be akin to my claiming to never have cut down a cherry tree, Mister Gould. Well, no one would ever mistake me for *truthful*. I flatter myself, in fact, to be somewhat a *weasel*. You might not've noticed how untrustworthy I am in the midst of all this lunacy.'

What hadn't passed unnoticed, let him assure her, was her propensity to treat him with baseless and self-confessed *mistrust*.

From the moment they'd met it seemed she derived tawdry pleasure in tweaking his nose and flagrantly calling into question his veracity when '... in good faith I've taken your advices to heart, humored your dithering postulates, and let you impinge on my time and privacy—all in aid of your investigation.'

Meanwhile, it'd been *she* who'd gone out of her way to behave without scruple. Numerous offenses he'd turned the other cheek concerning.

'Or have you forgotten a certain telephone call placed to me in the guise of a *threatening madman*?'

Forgotten?

No.

But she didn't know he knew she'd *lied* to him about that.

'When did you deduce this?'

Clumsily got herself sat up from where she'd been prone to the mattress.

Seemed earnestly curious.

'Or *had* you deduced it?'

Gould squinted. 'You *told* me so.'

'I *told* you so?'

'Told me you'd placed the call ...' he said, breaking eye contact with put upon face of he-couldn't-believe-this '... or had your *underling* do.'

She stared.

Mouth partway open.

Head seeming to nod slightly while also seeming not quite to move.

Eyes drifted upward as though working a riddle out.

Then, slap to her thigh, announced she saw where the confusion was coming from.

'You didn't know I was lying about *that*.'

'About ...' Gould scrutinized her as she twiddled thumbs a few times then got standing '... *what*, exactly?'

'*Calling* you …' seemed confused to find her pad on the mattress beside her '… having my underling do …' looked from it to the tin of mints she'd left at the sink. 'That call sure didn't originate from *me*, Mister Gould. I only *told* you it did. Police ladies are permitted to employ such lowdown deceits so long as we write the word *Induction* in the report. My preferred poison, so far as methods of *reasoning* go.'

Not to worry, not to worry. The call had been *investigated*, lickity-split.

Much legwork over it.

'We take threatening telephone calls under advisement, *always*. With utmost regard for the safety of whichever party is under threat.'

In this case, had taken care on account of Gould's sensitive artistic constitution.

'It'd be cruel to cause you fuss—have you believing some fiend meant you mischief.'

The way matters had played out was the best of both worlds.

Gould had made her aware of the content of the call.

She could verify the call had actually taken place.

Then, at her leisure, could ponder these clues.

'*Clues* …' Gould held up a finger in pause '… I only … count *clue*, detective-inspector.'

'What the call might mean, *in itself*. What your *telling me about it at a delay* could be indicative of. *Plus*, I could scratch my head over your *behavior*—if I went from the assumption I'd told you a lie you knew to be phooey. From all that make *deductions*. Not as much *fun* as inductions. But if I want my paycheck drawn every week they insist I try both.'

It was customary to treat utter strangers as suspects from the moment she laid eyes on them, was it?

Was … that a real question … or was he being ironic?

'An unexpected query, coming from you, I must say, Mister

Gould. Frankly, I'm starting to need a flowchart to figure out who's fooling whom.'

The detective-inspector was in need of a further cigarette.

'Gonna stand right outside. You can join me or else hide under the covers where the air will stay fresh.'

Gould kept expressionless while she winked and lit up.

First mouthful of smoke dribbling over face, uninhaled, Dziurzynski asked 'How did we meet, you and I?'

Humor her with his re-telling of the fabled event.

'I collect first impressions. Most people *loathe* me, at tee off. After awhile, many come around. Always fess up how I'd rubbed them wrong, initially. Can't help but eventually spill their beans.'

'You were *there*' Gould replied flatly.

Pretend she wasn't.

'Or that I'm not me. *We first met when* ...' she made scooting motions he ought get on with it.

After a pause, Gould snorted.

Positive blat of derisiveness.

Dziurzynski seemed nonplussed.

Or to simply not have noticed.

Working to get a stray lash free of her left eye.

Was rubbing closed eyelid with thumb knuckle while Gould told her 'You asked me if I play the *harpsicord*.'

Smiling, the detective-inspector flashed a thumbs-up.

'But *where* was this?'

Paint her a picture.

'In the *corridor* outside my *suite*' Gould answered. 'Pardon so minimalist a rendering. I've not brought anything but crayons.'

No matter.

Dziurzynski rubbed her hands as she explained she'd never have thought a thing odd about that corridor encounter, itself.

He'd been *anxious* having learned of the housekeeper's murder.

Mind *elsewhere*.

Occupied on his documentary.

'Which had sounded so *fascinating*.'

Even when Gould hadn't greeted her by name she'd have put it off to 'the darn thing being so funny sounding. Figured you were looking for a cute way to not let on you'd lost the sound of it.'

But when she'd recited verbatim the entire bit about having just there and then made up the harpsicord question '... and your being so *pretty* ... well, that got me a bit glum. I'd thought you'd found my part of our previous conversation more memorable.'

C'est la vie, she shrugged.

Her ego had endured worse.

Now shifted shoulder to rest against the other side of the open door portal.

Leaning quite sloppily.

Speaking without removing cigarette from her lips.

An articulate mumble.

'I still think about your wonderful arguments concerning *studio techniques*. How keen you'd seemed to school me when told I didn't much care for musical records. Didn't *trust* them. For all I knew, five different performers played on every Nocturne I'd heard in my life. Performances jigsawed together. A real conjob.'

Gould had moved the chair from the small table over toward the center of the room.

Perched himself on it.

Crossing his legs.

Refusing to meet her gaze.

Dziurzynski supposed their chat wouldn't have been *as* memorable for him. But she'd had it scrambling around like a roach in her forebrain, ever since. Just aching to think up some astute observation which might force him around to her point-of-view.

'Turns out it's your ideas swaying *me*! I admit it. All your passion about the tape splice. So gung-ho to let me know ...' she touched her pockets as though in need of some reference, eventually spotting her notepad on the bed top, gesturing at it like she might ask him to fetch it to her '... but I think I recall it exactly. How ...' paused, nodded as though certain '... *the great majority of present-day recordings consist of a collection of tape segments varying in duration upward from one twentieth of a second.*'

That was alarming to her.

She repeated this, chaining a second cigarette from the very dregs of her current.

'*Alarming*!'

Hadn't been able to stop thinking about it, in fact.

Flicking spent cigarette away, she addressed him dead on.

Said her main point in bringing this conversation up was how it 'Had been outside your studio. Morning after Lang's death. Before I'd got called to your hotel. Having learned why he'd been in town. *To meet Glenn Gould.* Wanted to put a face to a name and, gosh, hadn't you been accommodating.'

Gould remained seated.

Implacable.

Mind unruffled.

Hardly a thought in it, in fact.

Simply listening.

As though at work in the studio.

Reviewing raw takes.

Something to the words he heard.

But not yet settled on a way to shave them to fit a specific need.

Behind Dziurzynski, the day had re-darkened.

Scuttle of debris from the dumpster Gould knew was across the way suggesting wind.

Coming rainfall.
More snow.

'Then there was the jolt of that envelope I'd left in your post …' Dziurzynski suddenly began again, making no remark concerning Gould's long silence '… the *empty* grey one. Addressed from *Von Hochmeister*. Which seemed to catch your eye right before, just like that, you got hot-to-trot to tour the crime scene.'

Boy howdy, it'd taken effort to play it cool when she'd watched him notice who it was addressed from.

Yes, she was a bit of a snoop, it was well documented.

'Bit of an *eavesdropper*, too.'

Later loitering outside his door.

'Figured I'd not hear anything, what with you being so tuckered out … but instead overhead such curio! You pacing about. Muttering. Jibber jabbering this and that.'

What a man does in private is their own business, of course. She wouldn't want to have to explain her every quirk under oath.

Doors give such an illusion of *isolation*, don't they?

'But when it sounded like something being torn to smithereens? I simply *needed* to know. Laid myself down on the hall carpet, no matter how daffy it'd look.'

Sure sounded like he'd gone full into panic mode.

'Shadows shadows. Scuff scuff of scooping remnants from the carpet. What *could* it have been?'

That envelope was the *only thing* missing from the room when next she visited.

'Geez o Pete, it sure seemed to mean *something*!'

Gould shifted to one side.

Switched which leg was crossed.

Wriggled shoulders beneath coat, briefly touching at the lapels while he did.

Of course, she'd no way of getting him to turn out his pockets. Figured 'Oh well' when he'd left the scraps in the room trash.

'I was disconsolate. Must not've been anything you'd mind anyone finding. Figured papers you didn't want there to be a snowball's chance someone would stumble upon you'd have lit to flame. Flushed to toilet.'

Gould unfolded his hands long enough to cough into one limply curled fist.

Returned them to the exact position they'd previously occupied.

Didn't seem aware he'd not blinked a single time during the past several minutes.

Though ought to've been.

From the blur.

His eyes quite noticeably glazed.

'The pieces were right the *garbage*. Which makes them public property, is how I understand the statues.'

The maids, at any rate, didn't mind her borrowing the contents of the basket.

Envelope.

And a whole *bunch* of torn up papers.

'Had a subordinate piece every single sheet back together. As nothing had been in the trash, one minute ... the bin by your writing desk ... the bin not there and neither the envelope, next ... now these five other sheets of narrative, too.'

That had to mean *something*, right?

Gould closed his eyes entirely.

Held them that way.

Lips fused together.

Strained against letting them part.

Fearful doing so would allow some response he didn't know the content of to escape him.

What a puzzler it all had been.

She'd likely not have latched on so tight, let her add, if not for Gould, of his own volition, bringing up a *sinister* telephone call.

Which she'd been able to confirm had originated from a booth across the street.

'Add in how you played along with my balderdash about arranging the call myself. Admitted outright you'd received not only an *envelope* from Von Hochmeister but one containing an invitation you *fabricated* the details of … and then, later, hardly batted an eye at the paragraphs of your writing I'd retyped on your machine … listened to me read from them just as calm as you please … only to crumple them up …'

She fanned herself as though faint from foreplay.

Finished her cigarette.

Flicked it away.

Watched Gould keep his eyes shut.

Stiff.

Silent.

'*Trifluoperazine* is an antipsychotic. You're not *psychotic* are you, Mister Gould?'

His eyes opened.

Blink.

Blink blink.

Dziurzynski's voice was behind him.

As was the *tink* of her tin of breath mints being opened.

The titter of finger pushing them around while making a selection.

'I'd noticed your medicine collection. One time when over for a visit. Then again before coming here. While checking your restroom was vacant.'

Anyway, she supposed such trifles were what he'd consider *no business of hers.*

'You've been taking the candies though, yes? Bottles seemed emptier when I'd given them this most recent wiggle.'

Gould rose to his feet.
Turned slowly to face the detective-inspector.
Smiled primly.
Would gladly forgive her such intrusion if she'd come to her point.
'No point.'
Was on several meds herself, if he could believe it.
'Which is something I suppose you can.'
But, as long as she was asking things, could he finally let her know just exactly where he'd been.
'... *been*?' he asked.
Cordial.
Eyes widening.
Clueless to her meaning.
The detective-inspector was facing the mirror glass.
Directing her reflection's questions Gould's way.
Or, in that moment, rather was watching him.
Awaiting response to 'The afternoon and evening of the *housekeeper's* slaying.'
'What *is* this?' he groaned.
She'd had her cohorts truffle those details up.
Had furnished him a document detailing every spot their snouts had sniffed him.
'Which you *verified* ...'
She smiled.
'... *precisely* ...'
Went blank faced.
Rolled her eyes.
'... oh come come, Mister Gould ...'
Was she suggesting she'd made all of that up, to boot?
'Not *suggesting*.'
Up until he'd inspected his correspondence was confirmed.
The rest?

Pure hogwash.

'You left the hotel. On foot. Never to any bookstore. Never ordered a bite of Room Service. Seen exiting hotel garage. But not one living soul saw you until you pulled back in, one in the morning. Spent next day at the studio. Returned to hotel. Whereupon, so you seem to think, we first met.'

So: *where* had Glenn Gould been between walking out the carousel doors and parking his car?

'Detective-inspector, this is beyond tedious ...'

Tell her about it.

No ...

... he meant he was at the end of his patience.

Would countenance her nothing further about *this* nonsense question or *any*.

Which should hardly matter.

From what he could glean, the detective-inspector was more interested in linking fancy unto fancy, conflating ludicrous *suppositions* with verifiable *facts*, using *coincidence* to excuse no-doubt illegal *falsehoods*, and treating him like ...

Dziurzynski waited for him to continue.

Didn't prompt him along when he failed to.

'Everything's coming out in the wash ...' she whispered, after a moment had passed '... so what could those few hours matter? You must've been *somewhere* ... doing *something* ... possibly with ... *someone* ..?'

Gould turned his back.

Gently tapped the leg of the chair he'd arranged with his toe.

'I know you were at that roadside diner. Know you left your car there. Hopped a cab. Had a tiff with the keeper of this very motel. Know you left this motel in that same cab ... know you ...'

Dziurzynski abruptly stopped speaking.

As though flabbergasted.

Held up a finger to indicate Gould ought give her a moment.
Dotted the air randomly.
Over here over there over here over there.
Off to one side, shoulder height.
Above head.
At navel level.
To the other side, arm crossing over her chest.
Dotted more precisely.
Tapping the air several inches from her nose.
As though intently following segments on a timeline.
Then pointed her finger at him.
One eye closed.
Dot dot dot dot dot went her fingertip.
As though painting Gould standing there by means of pointillism.

'Waitaminute …' she mumbled '… that … can't be right, can it?'

Someone was *mistaken*.
Or *many* folks were.
Namely, as well as first and foremost: *her*.
As Gould had made plain to enunciate since their arrival: 'I've never been to this motel. Rode in no taxicar to it. Left my car at no diner. Had no meal at that diner—not on the night in question, at least.'
Blunderbuss of laughter, Dziurzynski gave her forehead a whap with the butt of her palm.
'Yes—you had said so, hadn't you?'
Plus, it was correct of him to assert himself.
He'd no need 'and obviously no inclination' to let her in on the nitty gritty of his personal affairs.

'Because, anyway, you *must've* spent the night at the hotel. You left in the morning, plain as a pea.'

So '… okay … okay …' Gould was in the right.

She seemed to always be having to apologize.

Asked him once more not to tattle on her.

'The whole ghastly saga is turning my head to soup' she shrugged.

Plopped herself back to the mattress.

'I feel I'm in five places, at once.'

The toothache was mainly on account of those reports of a person a whole bunch *like* Gould running amok.

'Take the guy seen arriving through the side door of your hotel, yesterday morning, eh?'

Gould had been down for the count.

Secured behind a bastille no revolution could storm.

'I'd first thought…' Dziurzynski sighed, laying back '… you'd taken a bit of exercise. After you'd knocked on my door for a chat. Night-walking does the physique and the digestive tract wonders. Except … it'd been raining cats and cats and cats—and then the snow to top it off! Anyone out in such weather woulda been a sorry sight and nevermind the distress to their clothing! But your usual duds seem none the worse for wear.'

So who could the mysterious figure have been?

'Whoever it was *whoever-else* has seen, detective-inspector …' Gould patted himself up and down '… wasn't only *not me* but I hardly think much *existed*. Neither did the *witness*, I'd say. I wonder if you need to draw yourself a diagram, frankly, seeing as I'd not visited your suite that *night*, had I, but only *next day*? Or isn't that supposed to make any difference?'

Perhaps what she was driving at was culled from her freewheeling adventures into the world of pure fantasy?

'You reckoned Lang was a murderous sleepwalker, after all, thus I imagine you'll now ascribe the trait to me?'

Good Lord, he'd neither the heads nor the tails of what this interview was meant to achieve and was sick to the teeth, in addition!

'I don't think Lang is a *sleepwalker*, Mister Gould. I think Lang is stone *dead*.'

Swallowing hard, automatic, Gould felt himself shiver.

Took a moment to compose himself.

Concentrating to keep any glint of rage from his eyes.

'You're quite a weather-cock in your estimations of people. Now he's an ephebophile, now he's a sleepwalker, now he's a corpse, now he's a killer.'

No doubt she was gamely swapping between the same identities concerning himself.

'Which I've been polite in entertaining, seeing as you've shanghaied me under feint of authority, once more subjecting me to the trauma of a lunatic's carnage—but enough is enough, even you must think so.'

'I don't think you're an *ephebophile*.'

Charmed, he was sure.

'I don't think you're a *sleepwalker*.'

Her flattery was growing too much.

'I can see for myself ...' swayed hand through the air between them '... how you're far from a *corpse*.'

'I'd be *meticulous* about your next pronouncement, detective-inspector. My gallantness has *dwindled*. Boards of Inquiry can be summoned up, *abracadabra*.'

Dziurzynski screwed up her mouth.

Tilted head.

Popping sounds with her lips.

Then snapped fingers, nodding how she understood what he was driving at.

'You think I'm gonna spout out something shocking like *I guess that leaves you're a killer*.'

'I've always been quick with declensions.'

'You're way wrong, Mister Gould …' she winked '… there's no such stuff in my thoughts …' dragged teeth over lower lip '… I don't think you're a killer, at all.'

Gould swallowed, again.

Holding head staunchly.

Shrugged with his hands.

'Do you know something *else* I don't think?'

He watched the quiver of her mouth fighting off a grin.

'What's something else …' he asked placidly '… you *don't* think?'

'That *you* … are Glenn Gould.'

Think about it, Dziurzynski clapped.

A guy like him looking like a guy like him.

'That first *him* meaning *you,* that second *him* meaning *Gould* …' she paused, flitted fingers between he and an empty space, waggle-waggle '… or *vice versa.*' Chuckled. '*These hands are not more like* …' she proclaimed with performative bombast '… you two could quote that line to each other, eh?'

Shook her head, apologetic, not wanting to get off track.

'You've been such a chum playing sounding board, I can't help but trouble you this once more around.'

Honestly, she didn't think her theory was *extraordinarily* outlandish.

Physically it'd be a marvel, in its way—of course it would.

Though personally she felt it was silly to envision people being entirely gobsmacked over it.

'Any old wive will tell ya, we've all got a *doppelganger* lurking out there.'

Dziurzynski would lay awake in bed dreaming about meeting hers. Fantasizing what hijinks they'd get up to.

'Though perhaps I ought not turn the conversation to such *salacious* subject matter.'

'Not at all ...' Gould chuckled at the detective-inspector's little joke '... who could blame you? Do go on. At this point, the more unprofessional the comments the better.'

'What with your sudden *litigious* bent ...' Dziurzynski heartily concurred '... this newest concept will be fodder enough for you to drum me right out of town!'

'Here's hoping.'

Gould had taken to pacing.

Hands clasped behind him.

Head drifting as though along to a melody he was working out the intricacies of.

But as Dziurzynski piped up, again, he briefly let his face illustrate how his patience was honestly thin.

'Could be the two of you bumped into each other, out of the clear blue. Gawked. Whole cliché of *it's like I'm lookin' in a mirror*.'

But to her thinking—'Just a feeling'—she bet he—'being *nobody*, really'— had known *all about* Gould, prior to whichever initial liaison.

'Made a study of the guy. Found him *worldly. Accomplished.* An *Iconoclast*, even. Nobody like him on Earth. Nobody except ...' mouthed what might've been the word *you*.

What a story it'd be.

'*Once upon a time* ... Gould was someone you'd pinned pictures of above you bed. Used your peculiar resemblance to get dates. Impersonations of the guy your party trick. His *persona* a fun part of your *personality*.'

Took some piano lessons.

Taught those little fingers to play.

'Slouched low in the chair while you hummed like your hero.'

But then ...

… some night …
… some stupid liquor ridden night …
… someone rubbed cold reality in his face.

'*You're no Glenn Gould!* they must've belched at you. I can't imagine the lambasting. The unique cruelty which could only be derived from this one-in-a-billion confluence of physical features on a man possessed of genius matching those of a man possessed of dandruff and putting on airs. The most you could ever hope to achieve, at your day job or through your hobbies, was to be *humdrum*. Something your idol wouldn't even remark as he scraped it from his boot heel. Oh it must've anguished you to know they were *correct*! Your ham-fisted mediocrity on the keyboard and your regurgitation of dandy philosophies robbed of all its charm. Every time you thought of Glenn Gould, you knew you *weren't* him. But more and more, oh, how you'd *longed* to be.'

Gould applauded softly.

Now leaning where Dziurzynski had in the open frame of the door.

'Spellbinding tale, detective-inspector. I enjoyed it even more profoundly than your previous efforts in the field of pulp fiction.'

The Lookalike he whispered expansively.

Holding hands up as though in awe of a Broadway marquee.

The one thing he wasn't quite cottoning to, though, was 'If *I'm* not Glenn Gould … where exactly *is* Glenn Gould, in all this?'

She'd only met Glenn Gould the once.

Quite briefly.

'You'd remember … except you don't …' she jibed with a strum of fingers on top of her head.

Her guess, going from the impression the man had made on her, was the entire arrangement was the sort of jape he'd be giddy for.

Approached by his very image.

A *devotee*, to boot.

'Would've welcomed you with open arms—I'd bet your bottom dollar if you'd lend it to me.'

It'd amused her immensely to think of what a frolic it must've been for Gould.

'As for you—must've seemed a dream come true when he'd offered to time-share his life.'

'Oh ...' Gould put fingers to lips as though intrigued '... is *that* the way it'd worked?'

'*Probably* ...' she chirped, sitting in the chair Gould had sat in, previously, crossing her legs as he had crossed his '... it's what I'd have done if I were him.'

Make rules.

Do test runs.

'Say there was some social function. Gould would mingle a bit. Arrange to step out. Have you step in. Dressed up identical. Down to the hanky in your pockets. You'd have your good time, awhile. Arrange to slip out and same time he slips back in.'

Wouldn't take long for a *system* to be perfected.

A method of existing as a merged personality.

How to *act*.

What to say.

Glenn Gould's life, from what she'd gathered, was custom designed for such an *avant garde* endeavor.

Especially *these* days.

Having retreated from the bright light of the public eye.

'Did he ever let you play on any record? Splice in your hitting a final note or doing a trill, even?'

'You'd have to tell me, detective-inspector. *Did* he?'

She imagined so.

Imagined he must've been over the moon when Gould'd got him trained up like his well-heeled terrier.

'If he desired to vanish into the anonymous expanses for ages, he could leave you with the keys to the castle. Trust you to behave. Fill in his bank ledgers. Type up his articles. Did you ever get to write any words all your *own*?'

'You'd have to tell me.'

She'd guess it was share-and-share-alike.

It'd have to be, right?

'To keep matters from growing *volatile*. Same as any friendship. Any *partnership*. All parties would have to know their place. Toe the line. Gould would have to be *Gould*. You …' she put a cigarette to her lips '… would have to *appreciate* …' fished matches from pocket '… being anything he *told* you to be.'

End of ciggie dipped into flame with a crackle.

Match blown out.

Poof.

That *second condition* was what troubled her.

How Gould would hold all the cards.

'Gould being *Gould*, after all. You being …' long drag, spoke with breath held in '… *nobody*.'

The genuine Gould could prove himself Gould in any way chance might require.

Gould had Gould's fingerprints.

Gould's memories.

Gould's multiple talents.

'But what would *you* say? If the two of you came at loggerheads? If he got *bored*? Outright *disowned* you? You were a *renter*, nothing more, therefore beholden to the *homeowner*. Your only claim to fame that you *looked like* someone. Easy to make you seem a *liar*. Deluded about being some classier figure's partner-in-life.'

Dziurzynski blew a drag of smoke ceilingward.

'In other words …' Gould grinned '… how could these two people *trust* each other?'

She stared at him.

Tapped ash to the carpet.

'How *could* they?'

'Unfortunately, detective-inspector, this being your tall-tale ... you'd have to tell me.'

'I don't imagine they *could*, Mister Gould.'

'I'd have to agree ... but likely for more basic a reason than you mean.'

'A more basic ..? Oh! His not *existing*, you mean? Or *you* not existing?'

'There only being *one* Glenn Gould, in any event.'

Yes.

She took his point.

Liked his wit well.

Always had.

It did his confidence wonders to know it.

'But you didn't *understand* my question, I don't think' he sniped.

Dziurzynski let smoke seep from lips.

Thick as milk.

Snake up her nostrils.

Cycle back out thin, translucent, through lips flirtatiously puckered.

'Which question?'

'Where is Glenn Gould ... in all *this*?'

Gestured around the motel room as though it were the one caked in stale blood.

'*You'd* have to tell *me* ...' she sighed, moving to the sink to douse her cigarette.

'I'd tell you I'm standing right here.'

'Well ...' she opened her tin of mints '... *touche*, I suppose ...' poked through them '... though as I said ...' popped only one '... it was just an *idea*.'

Gould wholeheartedly hoped the detective-inspector would accept it in the spirit of constructive criticism intended when he pointed out 'You sound as though you're out of your ever-lovin' mind.'

Dziurzynski balked in faux-affront.

If so, Gould was the guilty one.

From her perspective.

Humoring her every zany tangent.

Listening to her in a way which made her feel there were things he wanted to say, himself.

Listening in a way, all the moreso, which made it seem he desired to hear every morsel of what was going on with her investigation.

Suss out what she was thinking.

'Were *that* my goal, I humbly accept *failure*' he said, still stood out of doors, fanning the air in front of him. 'I promise you, capital P, I've no clue how your gerbil wheel spins.'

To speak to her point, though, and begging pardon for being so blunt 'Have you accomplished any *actual* investigative labor? Made a *single* advance toward determining who is responsible for this mayhem?'

All he'd heard had been suspicions that dead men were alive.

Out there making other dead men.

Or dead women.

That is, until he'd heard, suddenly, the dead men had been dead, all along.

'That and much esoteric incoherence about psychological Case Studies. Though, I confess, the bulk of those sounded too much like your own whimsical theories and make-believe anecdotes to put much stock in. Top it all off with this new Theory of Everything you've trotted out. *There is not one but two of Glenn Gould.* In a way, quite appealing. Except even were it true, it'd shed no light on pesky subjects like *means*, *opportunity* and some third word I hear is splendidly important to present before the magistrates. Not to mention it might be nice to have a carcass. Missing *two* of an alleged *four-set* ... what crime are you even investigating, next door?'

Sheesh.

She got the point.

'I need all the help I can get, Mister Gould! But now when I come to you, hat in hand, you're dead set against telling me where you were during a handful of crucial hours.'

Allow her to be honest—

'No.'

He'd allow no such thing.

But if she'd permit him the floor another moment, there remained several matters he'd like to have his say over. Because this present outburst from her demonstrated the reason for his frustrations, quite aptly.

'Dance about however you want but, by your own admission, of the two *confirmed* murders you are investigating I am *confirmed* to have had no hand in them. Therefore, I don't in any way feel compelled to make myself a *resource* for you. My whereabouts *at the time the crimes were committed* aren't in question. Thus my whereabouts *when people weren't being killed* are immaterial. That you, for whatever reason, have fabricated the idea of *another Glenn Gould* isn't of interest to me. Nor to any responsible, rational person. You cannot *invent* a guilty party and utilize such invention to compel or coerce cooperation.'

'Have you forgotten *Maude Harbor*?'

'*Forgotten* ..?'

Gould threw up his hands.

'I've forgotten nothing of *Maude Harbor*. I played concerts there. Notably Scarlatti. As you're well aware. There is nothing *to* forget. What the devil is the fascination with *Maude Harbor*?'

She'd only just told him.
On the drive over.

'You're one to beat the band, detective-inspector!'

Gould rubbed his eye roughly a moment.

Shook both his hands after, aggressively.

'Yes, you told me. How, unable to solve these two-to-four *present* murders, out of whole cloth you've prestidigitated two-to-four *more*.'

Did she have any idea what it'd sound like were he to *actually* lodge a complaint against her?

'Now now, Mister Gould ... I hope you'll not feel so compelled.'

She rolled her neck over shoulders with audible pops.

'That'd only serve to turn our relationship ... *adversarial*.'

'Everything in your own narrative to me, detective-inspector, proves one overarching point: you've traded in nothing but *deceit* while I've been *honest* with you at every turn. When one deception fails to please you, the solution you find is to pile on another. Reverse this one for that. You become suspicious of an envelope because it has a name written on it connected to your investigation. Ask after it. I'm forthcoming. This doesn't satisfy you. *Why hadn't I told you sooner?* I explain. You flatly say you mistrust me. Yet unsatisfied, you prevaricate how you yourself *planted* the envelope. Claim nothing was inside it. Who knows what you'll suddenly reveal as the truth when this present nonsense leads nowhere.'

Or how about suggesting the two of them had met before the two of them had met—conveniently in the witness of no other soul?

'Though first presenting yourself to a work colleague of mine. Not introducing yourself or your business.'

How about choosing this same fiction to reveal, if he'd heard her correctly, how she'd known of Lang's murder the *same day as* the housekeeper's rather than learning of it after having him tour the scene of the poor woman's slaughter?

'Perhaps *you're* the sleepwalker. Not *Lang*. Not *myself*. Dreaming up incidents which would serve you marvelously if not for the bad luck *they don't exist*.'

How were any of her techniques, so-called, meant to catch a murderer?

'Do you like a single suspect in the case, other than me?'

Curtly smecked his lips to sarcastically add '*Another me* doesn't count.'

Dziurzynski picked up her mints from the counter.

Slipped them to coat pocket.

Looked at him blankly.

Shook her head.

'Would it be alright if I told you *No*?'

Gould bristled.

Slumped in the doorframe.

'Will this be much longer? I do have a life. I'd quite like to return to it.'

Let her address that.

As well as this question of *honesty*.

'You seem perturbed, but are being irascible.'

Never once had she accused him of anything.

Quite the contrary.

'As to *honesty*: I've explicated my concerns for your safety. Numerous times. Every investigative step I've taken has been with said concerns placed first and foremost. No course of action has been initiated without aim toward preserving your peace and your privacy.'

'It's as though you believe a word you say' he snorted.

How comes it, then, that the few hours of *privacy*, the scant moments in these past nightmarish days he'd managed to carve for himself, to keep *unmolested*, she is, once again, Hell bent for leather to probe her grimy fingers into?

'You profess I'm in *danger*. Suggest I behave as under threat of a *horrific* fate. Then insinuate I've *declined* to avail myself of any assistance. Yet here I stand. Alone. With you. Full spate of police protection. Means of egress from whichever clutches you fancy I'm in. I am *here*. Entertaining, as many times previous, your preposterous philosophical tangents and potboiler plotlines. Always with it in mind you are the *police*. Corpses to be revenged. So on.'

Only to be informed, other than fairy tales, the investigation had come up dunce.

To have it suggested that a few hours not *excruciatingly* accounted for are of paramount importance to … to … *what*?

'No …' he made a violent cut of his hand, diagonal '… no, detective-inspector, it's *finished*. As of *now*.'

Dziurzynski had perked up during Gould's discourse.

Rocking ball-of-foot-to-heel and back.

'… *what* is?' she asked.

'What is *what*?'

'*Finished*.'

'This.'

'This?'

'*This*.'

Gould flapped pointed fingers through the air between the two of them.

'Gotcha' she nodded.

Limply gave thumbs-up with both hands.

Was sorry.

Had been a terrible police lady.

He was right.

'I take your point.'

She took his point.
Yes.
'This is all finished.'
For a moment, Gould felt on the verge of hurling invectives at her. Of demanding she, immediately, explain what *she* meant by *that*.
But her posture, demeanor, entire nature seemed so abruptly piteous he merely sighed.
Hands stuffed down coat pockets.
Waited a moment through silence.
Before reminding her she was his ride.
That he'd like to leave.
'*Now*.'

Closed into the motel room toilet.
    Overhead fan a chug-a-chug of lackluster white nose.
    Gould rubbed his face.
    Unable to get words right in his mind.
    Dziurzynski.
    Her whirligig chatter.
    Meant to get him turned around sidewise.
    No doubt everything she'd said played to a purpose.
    Leading him in a dressage.
    Wanting him to step foot in something unintentionally.
    Moved fingers from carotid to wrist.
    Pulse bip-bopped while he counted.
    But hadn't kept track of numbers.
    No idea what they'd mean if he had.
    Nothing made *sense*.
    Least of all why he bothered to care.

Hands dug through coat.
Probing for a pill to sort out his head.
Checked pants.
Left pocket, right pocket, rear.
Coat, again.
Thup thup thup against thighs from the motion of his hand slapping through fabric.
Hadn't he loaded his pockets, just in case?
Had he already swallowed those pills?
When?
… remembered soaking wet garments …
… stripping them off …
'No no no …' he muttered through teeth squeaking from clenching so hard.
What about this morning?
He'd taken his doses.
Before departing with Dziurzynski.
Was … *half*-certain he had.
If he'd been going without, wouldn't his hands be palsy with tremors by now?
Look there: Steady.
Enough he could conduct a surgery.
Attempting to focus on this little mystery only shunted his thoughts back to Dziurzynski.
Continued his attempt at indexing the subjects they'd discussed.
Had he let slip some piece of information, carelessly?
In all her merry-wheeling of true-and-false, might he accidentally have shown himself possessed of insights on matters he ought be ignorant of?
'What do you mean, Glenn? What could you've said?'
Slapped himself.
Again.

With more force, a third time.
Then abruptly froze up.
Dziurzynski might be eavesdropping.
Have the room wired.
'Or you're a funny one, aren't you?' he had himself sigh at himself. 'Either you're *innocent* or you're *not*. If you *are*, what could you've said?'
He *was* innocent.
Promised himself he thought so.
Yet couldn't shake the notion she'd set a snare.
Tripped him up.
He'd spoken of the victim in the room next door as though aware it was the waitress.
The dead woman's daughter.
Ought he know that?
Had Dziurzynski told him?
'She had. If not, it'd be only natural you'd assume.'
Sat to the toilet bowl.
Only partway agreeing with this assessment.
Or what about ... when she'd claimed the Von Hochmeister envelope had been a plant ..?
She'd *known* it was empty.
Had he *agreed*, knowing the same for himself?
Shut his eyes.
Hard.
Yes ... No ... Yes ...
'*No*, Glenn. You'd insisted it contained the invitation to a conference.'
Was that even *worse*?
Since she more than likely *had* planted the envelope?
'So what ...' he growled '... *so what!*?'
He'd say he'd misremembered.
Confused due to the stress of that evening.

Or she'd misremembered his seeming to agree.
'Even if she'd planted an envelope ... what does that *matter*?'
Hands were still steady.
Eerily so.
Enough looking at them troubled him.
Did his best to concentrate.
Tick-by-tick combed over his memory of the recent interrogation.
He'd become livid over some accusation ...
Over some revelation ...
... but *which*?
When she'd admitted the timeline of his whereabouts the day of the housekeeper's murder were of her own invention ...
'... you'd gone along with that, Glenn.'
Yes ...
Literally *confirmed* he'd misled her ...
Lost his composure concerning that point.
Gone on and on and on about it.
Insisted it was *emblematic* he keep the truth to himself.
To *spite* her.
Which was the sort of behavior Dziurzynski was bred to *induce*.
Read into.
Deduce from.
She'd surmise he'd reacted *honestly*.
To her telling the *truth*.
Because, knowing the truth, it was only natural he'd have reacted as he had.
No doubt such was the entire, buried purpose of this ghastly show-and-tell.
'Fallen for her bluff, Glenn ... *tsk tsk*.'
Knew this should panic him.
But his hands remained steady.

Perfectly.
Paper flat, almost.
Head beginning to clear.
Breath calming.
Calming ...
... calming ...
Calm.

Paced the room.
    End to end and back.
    Door was locked.
    Security chain set.
    Though he hardly remembered doing that.
    For a moment wondered ... had he?
    Took longer than it should've to reason he must have.
    Impossible for Dziurzynski to've entered, ear to bathroom door, locked up on her sneaky way out.
    This idiocy in his head.
    This doubt.
    Doubt.
    The room had been rented in tandem with the room next door, however.
    Interior doors connecting them.
    Anyone could've come in from the room adjacent while he'd been in the toilet.
    Toyed with things like latches and security chains.
    Exited the way they'd arrived.
    Shook his face.
    Flapped his arms around.
    Absolutely needed to stop thinking this way.

What was he supposed to do, after all?

Challenge Dziurzynski about the grey envelope?

Double down on treating her version as incorrect, despite knowing full well otherwise?

Ask her why she was lying?

Furthermore, ought he behave likewise concerning her assertion the two of them had met the day *before* the housekeeper's murder?

Move ahead as though the detective-inspector's statement was another inductive play-pretend, a tool to clock his reactions with?

'Think about it, Glenn. Lang was killed *first*, but Dziurzynski hadn't been told until *after* the housekeeper.'

She'd told him this.

Now wanted him to ask about that very discrepancy.

Was egging him toward it.

To what end?

'Say you did, Glenn? She *confirms* she knew of Lang's death, first. *Lied* about the fact after having already told you about it when, in her version, the two of you first met? What would you *do* with that information?'

Doubt it.

Like he was doubting it *now*.

Had she actually stated she'd *told* him about Lang being dead … or missing ..?

Or only she'd stopped by to see him, never explaining her business, exactly?

This was what Dziurzynski wanted!

Him to coil his mind around every possible version of what *could be* until he blurted out something fishy about what *actually was*.

Not what he *said* was.

What he *knew* was.

Trust.

Trust was paramount.

Gould thought these things as he verified the bed in this room, like the other, had no space underneath it.

That the windows behind the shabby curtain were shut securely.

Dziurzynski *had* been bluffing.

Trying to unfoot him through a tangle of contradictions.

She must've been.

Because Gould knew he'd done nothing.

To *anybody*.

Trust in that.

Proceed.

Worst came of worse, doing so served as a method of resetting the game board.

The detective-inspector had manipulated him into reversing himself, so he'd reverse himself, back.

Take a page from her own playbook.

Provided he *trusted* himself.

Trusted there was nothing *to* discover.

That whatever Dziurzynski *had* discovered, about the *crimes*, about his *movements*, about the *past*, was all there was to be discovered.

All of it nothing to do with him, still.

The trap she'd concocted was these very thoughts he was allowing countenance to.

Getting him, however shakily, however mootly, to consider the possibility he might've done ... anything.

Such thoughts only existed on account of the poison she'd poured in his ear.

Her wild suppositions had clogged up in him.

Due to stress, fatigue.

Due to being commingled with the chemicals he'd been ingesting by the handful.

Fill a man's mind with enough confusion and he'll uncouple.

Shake someone around, they'll eventually profess their own opposite-views—even if just to prove to themselves the originals.

Instead of berating himself, regretting, thinking he the one responsible to *disprove* someone else's *version of him* or else live *beholden to it*, he needed to enact a *choice*.

Trust his gut.

Control of the narrative.

Gould peered at the vents.

Imagining recorders hidden behind them.

Shook his face.

Slapped himself harder than the three times, before.

Was Dziurzynski going to throw shackles on him?

Parade him around like a freak at the station house?

Sweat him under the hot lights?

Slapped himself.

No.

She'd no right.

Knew what she'd done to him, in fact.

So desperate he be guilty had tried to corral him into admitting it even a *possibility*.

Opening a door to wielding legitimate authority.

Leaning on him, further.

The moment he entertained her beliefs, all was lost.

He knew what was possible.

Knew what was *impossible*.

Impossible he was a killer.

'And what is *impossible* …' he mumbled, breaking off into a chuckle.

A snort.

Full laughter.

Knew *exactly* how Dziurzynski would've ended that statement.

How she'd end it twisted reverse and all wrong.

The detective-inspector was a length off from the car they'd arrived in. Arms out to either side. Keeping balance as she put one foot's heel to the toe of the other, maintaining the straight line of a painted stripe on the pavement as though negotiating a balance beam.

One hand became a friendly wave as she watched Gould approach.

Determined to rebuild at least the superficial aspects of their rapport, Gould laughed while giving a gregarious wave in return.

'Full of hidden talents' he called across, wanting to seem in no hurry.

'Alternate on the Olympic Team' she laughed back, matching his attitude exactly.

Added, as she returned to normal standing, how she'd have something to fall back on when the force gave her the heave-ho.

'Let's not hear *any* such talk, detective-inspector.'

He hoped she'd be around a good long while.

She batted the air kittenish while making a curtsy.

Then, bowing himself, hand rolling amiably round and around while he straightened, he told her he felt it his turn to apologize. If she'd permit him to play the penitent.

No, no. She wouldn't have a word of it.

But he *insisted*.

Had been *wrong*.

Would tell her *why*.

'In the heat of our recent conversation, I'd divorced from my better angels. There's no avoiding how I lashed out, most inappropriately. Hermetic by nature, these constant strains, of late, and being surrounded by company, however pleasant, has my nerves worked rawer than I'm comfortable knowing they can become. There exist zero excuses for not only my discourtesy but my petulant antics.'

He had the unmannerly tendency to make all the world about himself, did she see?

Subject to such vainglory, allowed his own feelings of *victimization* precedence over the fact that there were actual *victims*.

'Victims you're working diligently to secure closure for the relatives of and, indeed, for the greater ease of society, at large.'

Dziurzynski nodded.

Seemed appreciative of this commentary.

Even moved.

'Some things I'd said ...' Gould continued '... had been uttered with nihilism and vitriol. So I want to explain myself in hopes of preventing my pettiness from robbing away one moment of your creative attentions which, no doubt, will corner our actual culprit.'

Chuckled.

Excuse him.

'Humility isn't my strong suite.'

Long story short, it'd been unforgiveable of him to muddy the waters by bringing into doubt the fine work of her subordinates.

'My whereabouts, as documented and presented to me, were accurate to a T crossed and a dotted I.'

He'd gladly reaffirm as much by way of affidavit.

Would avail himself to her humor, however he may.

Again, Dziurzynski thanked him.

Would accept his apology in the spirt offered.

Provided he accept how she personally deemed it unwarranted.

'I'm a bit of an odd duck in my field, Mister Gould. Prone to get away from more sociable and sensible displays of reason and tact. If anyone of us did the other dirty unduly back there, it was I.'

Of *course* she knew the researches she'd presented him were *accurate*. Had known in her heart, as he'd so righteously defended himself, she'd taken her shenanigans too far.

Extended her hand.
Which he accepted.
Without hesitation.
Giving three hearty pumps.
The both of them laughing during the exchange.
'You're terrific company, Mister Gould. You might not believe it, but even my closest colleagues have, on occasion, got fed up with me. I think crossing paths with someone who doesn't begrudge me my mind was more of a treat than I knew what to do with.'
Extended her hand, again.
Which he accepted.
Without hesitation.
Giving three hearty pumps.
The both of them laughing during the exchange.
Then she gave his shoulder a girlfriend shove.
Thumbed behind her toward the car.
Opened the door.
Holding it for him.
Closed him inside.

Ten minutes into the drive, four-and-a-half songs from the radio having played through at abrasive volume, Dziurzynski asked the officer at the wheel to please turn it down.

The officer complied and Dziurzynski gave Gould's knee an offhand pat while turning her head to cough.

After this, she positioned herself to face him.

Gould scooting to adopt similar position.

Resisting the urge to unbuckle his seatbelt in mimic of Dziurzynski unbuckling hers.

'Von Hochmesiter ...' the detective-inspector said, puffing long breath out afterward '... the man we're *after* ... the man who *did* these things ...' gestured around as though the vehicle were haunted with the victims she referenced '... I believe to be psychologically *unstable*.'

'Was the *second* body your *first* clue ...' Gould grinned, flitting eyes a moment to glimpse the rearview, noting the driving officer's reflection had clicked a smile at the jocular tone of the remark '... or did you hold off judgement on a sensitive thing like that until the *third*?'

Gould was glad the driver was present.

A witness.

To him acting unruffled.

Offering assistance, cordially.

A united front with the detective-inspector showcased.

'What I'd meant ...' Dziurzynski explained, chuckling the words while rolling her eyes '... is that the business at the motel was *well out of character*.'

Not this ghastliness they'd just inspected the aftermath of.

She wanted to make clear.

But rather the interaction with the motel's proprietor.

'I wonder if he can *trust* himself ...' she mumbled, somewhat inwardly.

Eyes drifting out the window past Gould a moment.

Drifting back over him then out her own window.

Without meeting his gaze even a flicker.

Perhaps she hadn't explicitly said, but prior to the odd scene witnessed by taxicar driver, Von Hochmeister had put in no appearance at the motel.

Rather, as with Lang, the arrangement for the rental of the block of cabins had been tended to, remote control.

Telephonic communication. Monies sent via postal mail.

Keys for all the rooms left inside of just one.

An agreement how that room would remain unlocked.

Renter able to enter to retrieve all the keys, sight unseen.

'On the night of the interaction in question, and the further interaction the morning afterward, this Von Hochmeister had clearly gone to great lengths concerning his physical appearance. Matching it to yours.'

Perhaps the man had background which had versed him in the craft of *disguise*.

Rubber skin.

Prosthesis.

'Considering the degree of aberrant behavior he's displayed, I wouldn't put it past the monster having *surgically* altered himself. Such things are certainly *possible*. Especially if there were natural resemblance as basecoat. If the fiend honestly *believes* himself to be Glenn Gould, there's no telling what lengths he'll go to in order to avoid such conceit being challenged, even unconsciously.'

Therefore, the gaudy, obvious way he'd behaved on those occasions, the attention seeking nature of his activates, not to mention having also left garments behind at the restaurant where'd he'd been witnessed, was markedly out of step with any other behavior displayed.

'The man might as well be a *ghost*, Mister Gould. Not to mention a *virtuoso*. The deadly machinery he'd set into motion without a glimpse ever made of him is almost mindboggling. Not a fleck of forensics left behind, no matter how occult the horrors he'd arranged to be discovered.'

Did he see what she meant?

'Why would such a calculating, meticulous personality so abruptly act in the outlandish and undisciplined manner described by taxi driver and motel man? What could it add to the overall dimension of whichever insane song and dance being played out?'

'It might be ...' Gould cautiously ventured, uncertain if it was his turn to actually respond to a prompt '... *to frame me*?'

Dziurzynski had once suggested so, hadn't she?

He was on target, there.

That had been the adhesive holding together her entire theory of the crime, to be honest.

'But then ... why act out in so *identifiable* a manner at a time when it'd be dead certain to cause nothing but *paradox*?'

'Paradox?'

Von Hochmeister must've known where Gould was, after all.

Knowing where Gould was, it was a cinch he'd know Gould could be easily verified to have been exactly there.

At the *hotel*.

At the *studio*.

Not the diner.

Not the motel.

'Yet he'd picked a time and a place where and when Glenn Gould *couldn't have been* to paint as though that's where Glenn Gould *was*. Done so with an abundance of vigor. Suggestive of unmistakable *purposefulness*.'

The only thing Dziurzynski could reckon, bringing things around to her primary point, was that the man had experienced '... a ... a *mental fracture* of some nature. Mind come off its track. Maybe unwittingly. Without realizing what he'd done. Post-incident, after all, he's returned to being an utter spectre. So either he'd *briefly* come *unglued* ... or else had meant to *make plain* the possibility there might be *more than one* Glenn Gould roaming around ... or else ...'

Gould nodded.

Waited.

Eventually prompted '... *or else*?'

'Or else he'd made a *mistake*.'

Which just didn't strike Dziurzynski as the sort of thing, with wits intact, a fiend like him would allow himself to do.

Gould requested to be left off at the studio, were it not too inconvenient or out of the way for Dziurzynski and the officer.

'Understand how grateful I am we are of a mind, detective-inspector, and how sincerely I appreciate the thoughtful concerns you've exhibited for me at every turn ... but being penned in like a factory animal, no agency, waiting for fates outside my control to strike or be stayed ... it's all made me ... *weary*.'

Surely she could understand.

To be made captive for just one more day, even were the conclusion to his troubles *guaranteed*, the solution entirely *satisfactory*, was untenable.

If he allowed one more beat of his heart to be made per the dictates of entities outside of himself and unseen, he'd have shown himself no more than a tune which could be called.

'Such a state is loathe to me, detective-inspector. To be at the command of some *audience*. Letting their whimsies decide me. No. I've lost days of work on a project near to my soul and couldn't allow my passions to be further delayed by the perverse fascinations of this ... *subhuman*.'

Gould made his voice tranquil as he explained how he could not see the harm in returning to his pursuits.

A child wheeling-and-dealing with mother.

Wanted his doing his own bidding to seem *Dziurzynski's* idea.

A choice she'd *counseled* him to.

Were he to strong-arm, insist on his basic rights, she'd have cause to think he'd swindled her through this shift to kindness.

If she thought he was swindling her, presently, but found his method too clever to allow her any recourse besides going along with the gambit, she'd have less ground to protest.

Or, at any rate, would have to taste for herself what it was like to second guess her own motivations.

In front of the witness of her fellow officer.

So it was odd how it didn't feel pleasurable, Dziurzynski raising no honest alarm.

Even when he explained his intention was to pull an all-nighter so some hours of purloined existence might be reclaimed.

'You're amenable to *protection*, however?' was all the detective-inspector responded.

'Certainly.'

'*Overnight*' she'd meant.

'Still certainly.'

Though he'd appreciate being humored with the specifics of said security detail.

Let her stay inside with him, Dziurzynski suggested.

'I'll be quiet as a titmouse. Find a seat in the corner. You'll never know I'm there.'

This wouldn't do.

Nothing after that fashion.

His work required deep concentration.

A sense of having himself to himself.

'The building is more than secure. Especially after hours. The area where I toil is locked to the outside world, three times over.'

Gould assured her he wasn't one to idle by the vending machines or step out for the fresh air of a cigarette. No. If he had things his way, he'd spend two-hundred-fifty days of the year snug inside a recording studio. The world could pass him by.

'In only one sense is it a shame I'm an innocent man, detective-inspector—that being I've always fancied I'd make an excellent prisoner. Provided, of course, my cell could be painted battleship grey.'

Dziurzynski took these remarks in apparent good humor.

Even the hesitation on her face had a cordial tang of inevitable allowance to it.

'I'm worried what'll happen if I let you out of my sight' she told him after another minute of silence. 'But I can't go supposing you'd let me share a bed with you, eh?'

Would it help if he promised her, were he murdered, his last words would be *Told ya so*?

Spoken on her behalf, obviously.

Dziurzynski explained to the other officer he was to request a car come retrieve him.

'They should stop by my room for two changes of clothes, first. Then grab a bag of bacon cheeseburgers from that gas station I like. *Three*. But say *one* is for Mister Gould.'

Pushed her knee into his.

He tapping his back against hers.

Then, abruptly, she opened her door.

Gould following suite.

Bracing against the briskness and wind of late afternoon.

To set Dziurzynski at ease, he mapped it all out.

Would progress through the main doors.

Up two stories via elevator.

Down corridor, through locked door to reception.

From there, a secure area where a technician worked sound booth controls for several more hours.

Locked on both sides.

The rear door another he'd pass through.

Into corridor.

Into triple locked, private work area.

'You recall the place, I think?'

'No doubt you'll be cozy as a clam' Dziurzynski replied, making quick business of changing the subject to whether it'd be alright with him were she to order surveillance of his hotel phone.

'I'm startled to learn such hasn't *already* been done.'

'Oh you ...' she batted her eyes '... I only *seem* despicably unscrupulous.'

Beyond requiring the hotel furnish her logs of numbers incoming and outgoing, she'd lacked grounds to play full-fledged wiretapper.

'When you eventually return, I'd not want you put off from chatting with buddies over knowing I'll hang on your every word.'

'Fair enough' he said with a bow. 'Though regarding the present: be forewarned, I'm apt to stay on through the day, tomorrow, perhaps into the next night, as well.'

Should he come check on her periodically, during the wee hours, in case she needed to potty?

'I'd say *Yes* ... but then remember I don't trust you. So oughtn't leave myself at your mercy.'

Adopting a sober tone, Dziurzynski now made a series of gestures.

Pointing at the building in what seemed an entirely random way.

Such pantomime hardly necessary to illustrate her explaining she'd not budge from her car.

Which would remain parked exactly where it presently idled.

It was growing irksome to Gould how the detective-inspector kept turning up one more line to add to the transcript.

Extending their conversation despite the chill and his politic body language meant to suggest unambiguously his aim to get cracking.

Kept his composure by reckoning she thought it an unspoken agreement he'd remain until the other officer's vehicle arrived.

Though once ten minutes further had elapsed, began to wonder if, in fact, it was *his* lingering coming across peculiar to Dziurzynski.

Her mind at work concerning why he was indulging increasingly insipid topics of small talk.

Before the terminus of the five minutes Gould silently assured himself would be the final he'd loiter, a car arrived to ferry the officer off.

Brown bag of what Gould assumed were takeaway burgers left on the humming hood of the car the detective-inspector would dwell in.

Along with two of the labeled bags he'd seen arranged in her suite.

Dziurzynski introduced him to the two officers who'd vacated the newly arrived vehicle.

Handshakes he could do nothing to slip the obligation of.

Finally, Gould managed to break off.

Many awkward head nods, half-waves, and general pleasantries.

As he approached the building, could make out in the door's reflection how Dziurzynski and the trio remained engaged in whichever banter.

In order giving.

Order taking.

The sight stirring nausea.

Anxiety palpable.

Made him feel hunted.

Feel cornered.

Trapped.

AFTER FOUR HOURS, GLENN GOULD would hardly know himself.

Or rather, he knew himself, precisely.

Locked in.

Flanked by his equipment.

Documentary transcript before him.

Had swallowed medications from the bottles kept in the locked cabinet, lowest drawer.

Valium.

Aldomet.

Clonidine.

Jotted notations on scrap paper.

Would fill in his notebook upon return to the hotel.

Yes.

Secure in the muffle of his mind.

Working against the resistance of the chemicals.

Like listening to piano music through the whir of a vacuum cleaner elsewhere in the house. Able to pick out notes plucked even buffered by walls from rooms away. Perfect pitch aided by hands clamped over ears.

No idea how he'd been able to function without the meds.

If *functioning* was the appropriate word for what he'd been doing.

The encounters with Dziurzynski, the intrusions of earlier had slipped away.

Faded.
Seemed nothing more than ideas he'd once idly contemplated.
Events which'd been related to him, secondhand.
Anecdotes from another life.
A life nothing to do with Glenn Gould.
The transcript he worked from appeared final.
Refined to its perfect state.
Listening to the whittled down raw recordings of each participant voice, he found nothing to reduce further nor a word to add back.
Dutifully spent the hours splicing.
Per protocols previously determined.
Stitching the cut fabrics of language into a garment of pristine expression.
Lost in a womb of words.
Spoken.
Rewound.
Repeated.
Narrowing in on the perfect mix.
When and where each voice would obscure the other.
Overpower.
Could be finished the project this very night.
One more round of jointing the polished pieces which now couldn't be altered for his trying.
Everything nailed down such that an attempt at altering a syllable was tantamount to self-violence.
Gould's thoughts drifted from the task at hand to the simultaneous relaxation and sorrow of *completion*.
From there to the safety of *isolation*.
Very few efforts remained before he'd be sequestered behind finality.
He'd become the still center of the roulette wheel.
The only thing the world might have for him were questions.

Questions were things he could answer or not.
Answers were things he could affirm or turn against.
He was *authority*.
The world's lot simply to listen.
To embrace.
Or not.
He, in effect, was anonymous.
Cloaked in what he'd fashioned with the words of others' strains toward self-expression.
What they'd said reduced to what it meant to him.
What would be remembered of them only what he'd decided.
What would be understood of those decisions understood by him alone.
'Or not ...' he chuckled '... or not.'
Took a wrong swallow of water.
Giggled.
'Is that monumental enough an event for the memoirs?' he asked aloud, with a yawn.
Or, like a billion-million other things, was it mere *occurrence* he'd never recall?
An action the recollection of would be meaningless.
Unless he forced onto it some pithy attribute.
How silly that, in the course of his life, he'd probably mis-swallowed water enough times the total count of the seconds, minutes, hours such experiences added up to would, if he felt it reasonable or worthwhile to give each equal consideration, take up a full day.
Twenty-four hours of incorrect swallows.
Were he to recall the five seconds leading up to and away from each instance, practically a week of his life could be spent remembering the inconsequential failures.
Giving individual reflection or a single remark to each would bloat that to a month.
A year.

Years.

If he exclusively thought about what he'd thought about thinking about those miniscule accidents, only allowed new thoughts to reference those thoughts, remembering choking on water and giggling about it would eat up a lifetime.

Same as anything might.

If he *allowed* it.

―――――――

Soon enough, however, Gould had to ask himself who he was fooling.

Dziurzynski sat outside.

Listening to her car radio, he supposed.

Mind plump with delusions.

Fixated on him.

Glenn Gould.

The man who sat there.

Wanting nothing more than to sit there.

Linking his whimsies along until supper.

Until bed, the next night.

Wanting that.

Forever.

Each day not a mere repeat but a perfectly duplicated Start Again.

He'd walk out of the studio.

Whenever he would.

Hours from now.

Days.

Eventually.

When he did, she'd be waiting.

Never forgetting the task she'd been assigned.

Living in these murders until their purpose, their perpetrator, was brought to light.

Some manner of *justice* with it.

No amount of time would relegate these events to the file room for her.

Gould wasn't stupid enough to think that.

Dziurzynski would delve.

Invent.

Hang on until she expired.

Imp Gould for all of his days.

No matter which remedies he might seek legally.

Anything built of lawyers or complaints would only entrench her.

Get those creative juices *flowing*.

So long as she had these bodies left unrevenged as excuse, no one was right likely to take Gould's side in things.

Every moment of his every day would be poked at.

Turned over.

Listened to.

Looked at.

From every direction.

The more time elapsed, the more even *reasonable* people would, if only *idly*, give consideration to her most outrageous confabulations.

Supposing he had means and energy to keep the detective-inspector from mutating his life into a carnival, he couldn't keep her from reducing his existence to a fishbowl.

Her fishbowl.

Not *his*.

Dziurzynski's grubby nose pressed right up to the glass of it.

While goldfish Gould swam a moment.

Noticed her.

Startled.

Forgot her, as a goldfish is wont to do.

Swimming a moment.

Seeing her.

Startling.

Or else she'd tap the glass enough that despite his learning to avoid taking note of her looming presence he'd be rattled out of his seclusion.

Perpetually.

'What hope?' he muttered.

In response to his mind meekly inquiring 'Wouldn't it take only as long as until the killer is *caught*?'

Shouldn't he rally round Dziurzynski until then?

Pray for her success every night before tucking in?

What *hope* could he have?

He was correct to ask himself.

With all that had transpired, at least so far as he could discern, she wasn't a footstep nearer apprehending any villain.

Suppose he were to believe she'd *stopped* suspecting him, as her paly behavior in response to his affected camaraderie in the car made all but certain she *hadn't*—still she'd given no indication there existed someone *else* she'd move on to harass.

Here she was.

Had crept her way back into his head.

Causing his sitting here, in the quiet triumph of artistic completion, to be focused solely on her.

Fearing the next clue she might ferret out.

The next visit she'd have him make to her or else the next she'd suddenly visit on him.

Revisit and revisit.

Until she was satisfied.

Until she deduced he'd thought these very thoughts.

Until every crumb of him had been tasted.

Swallowed.

Until he was digested.

Gould understood she'd walk him back in time.

Pollute him with talk of deaths died ages ago.
Corpses living forever some place where he'd been.
She'd virus herself into every day of his past.
Sniffing for other things.
Until, like the slick of a fever, he'd discover her present in his every memory.
Pursuing her fantasy of him.
Backward and forward and sideways.
Piling versions of his life onto his life.
All of them entombed under her.

'In the future ...' he dreamt Dziurzynski was saying to him '... I've no doubt I'll browse in some bookshop until in some pages I find you, dead to rights. Biography. Postmortem. Yes, even if you were to die, bone thin, content as a Saint in a bed among the Eskimos surrounded by stray cats, I'll never cease investigating you. Immortality only dooms you to me. I'll prove what you've done. In volumes I'll buy, in paperback, likely at discount, I'll pursue you. *Peruse* you, perhaps better say.'

While other dilettantes would take Gould at his word, or at least the gist of his word, she threatened to forever read deeper.

While scholars searched for the *Why* of Glenn Gould she'd take satisfaction in the *What* and the *How*.

'Which terrifies you, Mister Gould. Because those things *can* be proved. You cannot escape into theory or semantics. I won't allow your life to be *alterable*. Open for *interpretation*. I'll hang these four corpses, these eight, however many others, on you until the *Where, When, How, What* of *Who* you are makes irrelevant the mystery of *Why*. I'll rob you of posterity by turning you specific. Commonplace. Another mad dog from the latest dime story. Fodder for a movie-of-the-week.'

Gould dreamt Dziurzynski saying all this to him.

As though they both sat.
Relaxed.
Somewhere out of time.
She with the book she'd referred to propped open across the knee of her crossed legs.
Dreamt her outfit.
One he'd never yet seen.
As it'd been every time they'd crossed paths.
This time a Kermit green pair of rough linen trousers.
Socks unmatching, one of them seeming meant for a man.
Suspenders visible under calico blazer a size-and-a-half too large, its fabric bending peculiarly atop the overtight fit of a tee-shirt the writing on which was cracked, faded, and indecipherable.
She wore a hat like his own.
And only when he noticed it did he touch his head.
Feel his hair through the fit of lemon yellow gloves he didn't recall donning.
'Listen here, for example …' his dreamt Dziurzynski wriggled a bit, chirped her enthusiasm over some passage she wished to single out '… I think this is a fine example of what I mean … from this book about you …'
Dreamt a brief flash of the cover, but couldn't glimpse any details, mind *zip-zip-zip* slapping fifty possibilities onto the dust-jacket before it was tilted down to allow the detective-inspector to continue.
'… it doesn't seem the author is really attempting a biographical study—indeed, the author writes, at one point, how your private life is *austere and unremarkable* and that *a book on your life and times would be brief and boring* …'
She paused here, worried he'd taken offense.
In his dream, he hadn't at all.
'… but from time-to-time the author pays his respects to the

psycho-biographical process and, on one such occasion, seeks support from Anthony Storr, referencing how Storr had said ...'
Cleared her throat before reciting.

'... *Since most creative activity is solitary, choosing such an occupation means that the schizoid person can avoid the problems of direct relationships with others. If he writes, paints, or composes, he is, of course, communicating. But it is a communication entirely on his own terms ... He cannot be betrayed into confidences which he might later regret ... He can choose, or so he often believes, how much of himself to reveal and how much to keep secret.* Now ...' Dziurzynski whispered after a silence to allow appropriate reflection to take place '... the citation seems indicative of the biographer's own attitude in regard to his subject and adroitly summarizes your abhorrence of city life, your distaste for public appearances, your predilection for telephonic communication, and your belief that solitude nourishes creativity while collegial fraternity tends to dissipate it.'

Then, as though Dziurzynski no longer sat in a chair before him, no longer held a book, no longer spoke in a tone of chumminess, but instead had her lips pressed right to his ear, Gould heard her intone 'What do you think someone like *me* would think, reading *that*?'

Gould found himself mumbling.
Slowly waking.
Forehead on crossed arms rested on desktop.
Sleeve of thick coat wet with drool.
Eyelids opened and closed some number of times.
Slow brushings along the rough of the garment's heavy fabric.
For several minutes, mumbling ceased, he remained in that position.

In that state.
But the rising sizzle of needing to urinate eventually compelled him upright.
Still another few minutes he didn't stand.
Numbly, bleary, glanced around his workroom.
Took a sip of water.
Saw from the mounted wall clock he'd slumbered at least an hour.
No.
Closer to two.
Perhaps longer.
Imagined it possible he'd been asleep for twelve, thirteen, fourteen hours.
Fifteen.
Or else add another twelve to that.
Another twenty-four.
Thirty-six. Forty-eight.
No way to tell from the white face, black hands, red whiskers of ticked off seconds whether it was morning, night, today, tomorrow, or weeks from whenever it'd been.
Except, of course, it wasn't possible Dziurzynski would've let swaths of time so immense pass without busting down the door.
If he hadn't popped head from gopher hole for so long a stretch, she'd have dragged him from it by the scruff.
'It's been *two* hours, Glenn, no need to be fatuous' he grinned.
Working a kink from his back.
Absently scooped up the complete reel of the documentary.
Snuggled it into his armpit.
Drained the remaining water from the bottle.
Almost went for his pills but a half-hearted squint toward the scrap paper reminded him it was a touch early for such.
'Even for you.'
Rubbed eyes.

Looked to desk.
Cluttered.
Various canisters of audiotape stacked.
Others arranged without thought for organization.
But he could tidy up, later.
Wanted to listen through the finished product in the studio booth.
Drift without headphones.
Take it all in amidst the perfect acoustics of soundproofing.
Absolutely certain there'd not be a spec to add or elide.
Not another splice to make.
No.
None.
Everything was finished.
The corridor was pitch dark save for the orange-red of *Exit* signs.

A buzz from ... something ... he'd never figured out what in all his time working on site.

Sniffled and smecked lips as he slouched along toward the restroom near the cafeteria.

Shoulders hushing against the wall.

Eyes not seeming much to adjust to the darkness by the time he'd bumped his way through the door and flapped the light switch.

The mirror revealed evidence of his sleep.

Rash-like coloration of coat sleeve indented his cheek.

The skin to the left of his mouth was reddened pink, somewhat pruned from the soak of saliva.

Sensitive to the touch.

Opened mouth to seek evidence of cankersores when, despite slurping three draughts of tap water from cupped palms, the sensation of cottonmouth wouldn't vanish.

His lips seemed crisp.

Produced pricks of pain as though lined with papercuts whenever he ran his wheat-dry tongue along them.

Though he'd just voided himself, a growl of needing to do so again afflicted his groin.

As before, nothing much emptied when he stood at the urinal.

Sensation of needing relief corkscrewed through him as soon as he moved to rewash his hands at the sink.

Fretted some infection of urinary tract.

Face showing no signs of returning to standard complexion.

Dehydration sallowing his flesh.

Drank from the faucet.

Giggling as he lapped the water bowled in his palms like a sickly, domestic Tabby.

En route to the technician's room, Gould stopped short.

Hesitated turning the handle to proceed to the booth.

Overcome with a desire to verify whether Dziurzynski was, in fact, still sitting sentry.

To ascertain whether, in this witching hour, there might be evidence of additional out-of-place vehicles.

Other officers summoned to man all the exits.

Couldn't put such maneuvers past her, after all.

She'd pulled a neat disappearing trick on her previous visit.

Which meant she might either think he'd do the same or else could've found alternate means of entry, herself.

Be present.

Lurking.

There was a sensation of someone else about.

An instinctive tingle Gould couldn't rid himself of.

Not wanting to inadvertently suggest an invite or some reason Dziurzynski might feel compelled to, at the very least, attempt telephoning him, Gould moved to the interior elevator, round the cafeteria corner at the extreme of another corridor.

Would ascend two levels.

Stealth his way into one of the unlocked conference rooms.

Peek out the blinds.

Satisfy himself.

Dziurzynski, despite the mild snowfall, was outside her car.

Leaned to its rear passenger door.

Chaining, in that moment, a new cigarette from the remnants of the one she exhaled a final drag from.

Exhaust hacked from the vehicle's tailpipe.

The beige of the parking lot lamps cast syrup thick shadows which doubled in this smog.

No other cars. Vans. Trucks.

Not anyplace Gould could see.

Made his way to rooms at the other side of the building.

Verified the rear lots and delivery areas were unpeopled, as well.

It'd be ridiculous to assume Dziurzynski had ordered whichever helpers to park elsewhere.

Hike over.

Spend hours upon end exposed to the freeze in the off chance Gould tried to be sneaky.

Even more absurd to think she'd summoned agents to infiltrate the building.

Keep hidden.

While she acted as decoy.

Also pointed out to himself how absurd it was to be spending a single minute thinking this way.

Snorted phlegm.

Found no tissues to gently squish the mess into so swallowed it bitterly.

Though ... didn't Dziurzynski have a *job* to do?

How could she justify wasting all this time playing nanny goat? 'Glenn, *you* need to get back to work ...' he had a voice sigh.

Then had it further explain '... your darling's *justification* would be that it's two in the morning and she'd be *asleep*, otherwise. No duties shirked.'

True.

He allowed himself this was true.

Plus, likely, she'd nap in the car.

'There's nothing left for her to do but *think*, anyway ...' he added aloud, hitting the elevator summons button '... and one can think from anywhere. Might as well be where she feels satisfied she has *you* under wraps.'

As he descended, the full bloom of this intrusive mindset got him fuming.

In one moment, wanted to lash his arms in frustration.

All but forgetting he had the recording pinned to his side.

Had to catch it from falling.

Twisted an ankle slightly in doing so.

Limped back all the corridors he'd come.

Feeling quite the goblin.

Tapping teeth.

Then clenching them.

Hoping some physical gesture would magic-wand him back his focus.

Spooling the complete reel and preparing to pipe it through to the booth, he sank back into himself.

The rote gestures, tender administrations of fingers in flicks to apparatus controls *clack click thunk tick-tick-tick* putting him at ease.

It was only *him* here.

Or only *he* and *Dziurzynski*.

Only the two of them.

A thought which relaxed him into a grin.

A grin only broken by the winces from each slight pain his limp snapped up him as he made his way to the booth.

Ecstasy.
Ecstasy.
Gould floated in the playback.
Arms out as though a kid playing aeroplane or winged creature.
Angelic.
Drifting left arm down ... up as right arm lowered.
Turning unconscious circles.
Hands at the ends of each wrist seesawing in mimic of arms but at different tempo.
Knees bending.
Body leaning forward, back, side-to-side.
Brushing fingertips to one wall, along it until corner, then across another.
The third time through, he'd still found nothing to alter.
Not a word.
No—not a *sound*.
His mind no longer processing *words* or taking in *ideas*, differentiating one from another, digesting content or nuance.
Sound. Melodious.
Sound. Only he could hear.
Floated as though on the very tip of the Dead Sea's surface.
Breathing in air which seemed to whisper across his face from another world.
Into his open mouth.
Down lungs expanding in gratitude.
Not wanting to exhale a single molecule out.
After the piece came to an end, a fourth time, Gould hop-skipped to the booth console.
Tapped this button.

That.
Recuing the experience.
Spreading arms.
Waiting for the voices to begin.
Woman's first.
Man's creeping over.
Woman's again.

> … frightened me a little, because it just seemed endless …

Such sublime evenness to the tones.
Voices out-of-time. Out-of-place.
Never to find time. Place.
Completion.

> … we seemed to be going into nowhere, and the further north we went …

Gould's own voice, hardly there, perhaps no more than a thought, seemed to say to him '*Trust* … trust is so very *important* … to *trust* … one's *self* …'
He pressed gloved hands together.
Tenderly.
Brought then to his cheek while the recording continued.
While his aimless, repetitive dance followed along.

> … I know about these people who do claim that they want to go farther and farther …

Gould's own voice, like a whisper '… to give one's self *over* … over to one's *self* … such as it is … *trust*, Mister Gould, is all the more the *necessity* …'

> … but I see it as a game …

Gould now roughing his ear.
Digging finger deep in.
Concentration broken.
Standing stock still.
While the playback bounced around him.
Innocent.
Irrelevant.
Intrusion of his own voice now silent.
Perhaps never there.
The playback continued.
But its spell had broken.
Gould now hearing himself, but in control of such hearing.
What he asked himself.
Had himself reply.
No voice of his unbidden.
The memory of the voice from moments before overran all other focus.
He strained to listen through the recording in the air around him for some imperfection.
Which couldn't have been there.
He hadn't heard himself during any previous review.
Not the slightest glitch.
No ghost of anything he'd once recorded mixed in through oversight.
'Mister Gould, may I have your attention?'
Plain as day, the voice filled the booth.
Still keeping a subdued tone.
Gould's eyes whipped to the speakers.
This one.
This other.
Mounted near the booth ceiling at each corner.
His recording breathing down over him while he stared.
'Far be it from me to interrupt, Mister Gould, but this is getting

a touch self-indulgent. I think even you would admit to as much. Not that I poo-pooh your enthusiasm. Knowing, myself, how it's *perfect*. Being the fellow who conceived and composed.'

Gould smacked the console control.

Playback halted.

Nothing emanating from the speakers.

Silence like the womb or the dead of deep space.

Just him.

His breathing.

His staring.

Which seemed to have a sound to it akin to the creak of the boards of a ship's floating deck.

With a chuckle, a voice, like his, came from the speaker.

'Are you not coming *out*?'

Another chuckle.

'That's just as well. Since I can't see you from out here, however, and my amateur lip reading skills would hardly suffice for meaningful interaction even if I could, might you be a darling and press the button, lean to your microphone, let me know I'm not talking to myself.'

After a single clap of panic, Gould's body took over entirely.

As though automatic, he moved to the seat at the booth console.

Depressed the button to communicate with whichever party occupied the technician's room.

'Who is speaking?'

A hearty bit of gentle laughter emanated from the speaker.

Then a voice filled the booth with the words 'This is Glenn Gould. And this program is called *The Idea of North*.'

'Trust trust trust, Mister Gould. A quality I'd thought had developed between us. You, like me, a piano man. Or, rather, you're far from me in such respect, but proficient enough in the basics

I'd felt you'd understand. One hand needs trust the other knows what it is required to do. What it is *doing*. Is proceeding with its own ministrations without need its partner hand should *worry*. Should have to *look*. Have to ... *correct*, shall we say?'

How was the voice to have taken it, then, witnessing on several non-consecutive occasions such principle trust being cast aside?

How ought it react when, having gone so far along, secure in the belief there'd be no underhand dealings, it'd discovered, increasingly it seemed, the deck Gould was playing from had no top but only a perpetual bottom from which cards kept being drawn?

Gould depressed the console button as though to interject.

But after ten seconds silence found he'd nothing to say.

Finger lifting.

He sinking back in his chair.

Eyes drifting between the several speakers before his chin bobbed down and they closed.

'Yes ...' the voice returned, presently '... I *concur* with your silence. Better you *listen* before going off half-cocked. There'd be no percentage, at this point in our little venture, in becoming argumentative, you and I.'

The present situation had amply revealed how they stood at cross purposes.

'Or so it can't help but seem.'

While there was little use in such queries, the voice admitted it felt obligated to explore the dubious proposition of *Why*.

'*Why did you veer off script?* I mean. You'd never shown yourself to be in praise of improvisation. Knew *knowing your place*, it might be said, is what had *earned you your place*. Me, in time, being so kindly as to make our places *equal*. Reciprocal.'

Hadn't the voice kept to every part of their bargain?

'That's rhetorical, Mister Gould—I insist you remain obedient with your muteness until I reach my point. I'm miffed at you. A vexation which warrants preamble, I daresay. To keep you being confused where we stand.'

As to the bargain: it'd worked to Gould's favor, he could admit, couldn't he?

'Didn't I allow you the driving seat, plenty of times? Even as it, Big Picture, benefitted neither of us—indeed caused me consternation, image wise, now and again. I'd allowed you to be my walking, talking pseudonym. Or, rather, let you be me while I tended to my own affairs under guise of *nemo*.'

The voice explained it'd jumped to no conclusions.

Had done due diligence to explore any *plausible* excuse.

Had desired to happily discover Gould had 'for the benefit of us both, pivoted with aplomb at some *unexpected* occurrence we both always knew might crop up ...'

But, again, stated such times would be where *trust* came into play.

'You scarce could expect to be me, I think you'll agree, were I to keep you ignorant of *crucial* aspects of myself—cut you out of the loop concerning important *developments* ... and in this connection I can hardly think to, with any sense of ease or comfort, be myself when you refuse to share-and-share-alike some aspect unique to *your* personhood and experience.'

The voice didn't *want* to think ill of Gould.

Far from it.

'For goodness sake, you know I'd bend over backwards—partway for my own selfish purposes perhaps, I admit as much—to keep from holding you in poor regard ... but with what has happened ... with what *appears* to be going on ...'

Well ...

Did Gould have something to say for himself?

Now was the time.

'Please. Set my mind at ease.'

'Who is this?'

'Who am *I*, you're asking?'

'Who *are* you?'

The speakers above Gould sighed.

'This is you off to exactly the *terrible* start I'd dreaded but yet held out hope you'd *avoid*.'

'Who is this—who are you?' Gould repeated, jab to the console button.

Now on his feet.

'We've never had a falling out before, Mister Gould. This seems the silliest time to start.'

Gould, holding a fist out to one side as though brandishing telephone, hissed that he'd call the police.

'They're right outside.'

Ah yes.

His lover girl.

His *plucky betrothed*.

'I didn't know what to make of your ... *infatuation* with her. Your constant *assignations*. Despite it becoming clearer and clearer. Mister Gould, have the hands on our clock come to this? You aren't at the advantage, so let's use our words before matters grow ... *complicated*.'

Gould demanded the speaker identify himself.

Would go no further until this condition was satisfied.

The voice, seeming unperturbed by the outburst, changed tone to a general address. Moving ahead as though Gould were in tandem, understood its referents and subtext, despite all evidence otherwise.

'*Why had you left the motel?* I couldn't sort it, Mister Gould. Things had gone swimmingly to that point. Or had gone to plan, at least. You'd had your scuffle while dispatching Lang, of course. Black and blue, but not come out too much the worse for wear. So I couldn't imagine it'd knocked the sense from you. So dexterously you'd managed to behead him, sprinkle his offal about, portion and package his body. Wits about you enough to lug heavy luggage off site. Bearded and outfitted adequately, it seemed. A grisly business, you'd described. But all in time we'd managed our switch-o-change-o to maintain appearances while I'd dispatched our prissy housekeeper. Some *suspense*, of course, but hardly a *hitch* to be found.'

But when the call hadn't come in confirming Gould had been successful with the waitress?

'That truly gave me the *creeps*, Mister Gould. Not a peep from you *all night*. I'd departed the hotel for the studio come morning in such a tizzy I'd left my medicine log behind, even. Then had to vacate the studio in a terrible state of *nervosa*. But ... there you were. Motel, as arranged. Snoring away. A spot of work on our Beethoven article, to boot. All seemingly right with the world. Figured the ... *task* ... had depleted you.'

The voice explained it'd been happy to return to studio.

Plug away a bit more on the documentary mix.

Except that *Dziurzynski* had shown up ... earlier than expected ... not something they'd been *entirely* unprepared for, of course ...

... but still no call ...

... well into the morning ...

... no call ... early afternoon ...

'You can imagine my shock when, on top of this, I'd discovered the waitress was still vital!'

The voice laughed.

Claimed it'd nearly swallowed its stomach when the kindly old supervisor at the diner said the girl had arrived to her shift, happy as a lark, same as always.

'I thought the worst of you, Mister Gould. Saw the writing on the wall, well enough. Thus, determined to have stern words with you, I *again* left the studio. Only to find your room vacated. Typewriter and all.'

Never one to shirk a duty, the voice had thought to itself to hup double-quick in order to take up the next pre-arranged position.

At the hotel.

'So what was I to make of it when I witnessed *you* strolling in like a lost pup!?'

Could Gould conceive how things would've gone had the voice arrived ten minutes sooner?

Gould bumbling on in while it was in conference with the police, as planned.

'Fate had our back on that one—enough to stave off fiasco, at least. But I'd something of a conniption fit. We'd not even had chance to speak about my chat with Dziurzynski. Her stopping by could only have meant Lang's room had been discovered, prematurely. I was mortified at the thought of you winging it with the woman. After all, we know what tangled *weaves* we *web* when we try our first *ad lib*.'

No time to focus on it, though.

Some on-the-spot rearranging of *who* was to do *what* was baked into the recipe, after all.

'We'd reshuffle and soldier on once you'd debriefed me, I'd reckoned. Except, in this case, my mind got squirming trying to suss what your *purpose* might've been. Not making *any effort* to communicate with me. Going out of your way to *avoid it*, from all available evidence. When I telephoned, you hardly spoke! Even were you in the company of someone, I couldn't square that.'

The voice'd had half-a-mind to've burst on the scene, calling curtains to the entire affair simply to spite Gould.

'But considering to do so would leave equal blood on my hands as on yours ... well, I'd needed to play it by ear, hadn't I?'

That, by the way, was an *actual* question.

If there existed any mitigating circumstances Gould might care to relay ...

'... now would be the *propitious* time.'

Though what could it possibly matter?

How could the voice *trust* whatever words would utter from Gould's mouth would be anything apart from *deceptions*?

'Lies and desperate ploys.'

Dziurzynski waiting outside, even now, proved the entire matter. Yes, the cahoots the two of them were in had become increasingly apparent.

'Though what your endgame is I can only boggle over.'

There'd been ample opportunities for Gould to have reached out.

Never once had.

Meantime would meet the detective-inspector for lengthy tea-talks.

Seemingly lived at her beck-and-call.

His movements kept secured.

Like clockwork.

So the voice hadn't any means of finding time alone with him.

Or alone with her.

'Apart from those two instances I had no *choice*. My God, Mister Gould, can you comprehend how nerve wracking it was, venturing into her suite, blind? Navigating myself in tip-toe to sleuth what the two of you had spoken about. No idea if the information verified concerning my ... *your* ... *our* movements was something you hadn't already blundered some tap-dance about otherwise.'

But when, on the second visit, risked in order to make ironclad Gould's alibi for time spent *en route* to the motel, Dziurzynski had casually asked about *Maude Harbor* '... I understood, well enough, how I'd more to worry about than your perhaps having said you'd never gone to a bookstore.'

What could've compelled Gould to mention *Maude Harbor* in the detective-inspector's presence so *egregiously* ahead of schedule?

The very notion had dumbstruck the voice.

'The wildest suppositions shook me around. While meanwhile I'd been running myself ragged to finish out our work.'

A sigh turned chuckle turned sigh filled the air.

'When I summoned you to the motel, when it was apparent you hadn't attempted any snare, when you looked at me as though neck deep in an opiate daydream ... when you denied, to me, the two of us alone, knowing of *Maude Harbor* beyond the *official-story* so to speak ... when *you* asked *me* about the *Maude Harbor* document and the recording ...'

The voice broke off.

Tone abruptly altering to one of childlike curiosity when it began again after a beat.

'Was it possible you'd dispatched our patsy, *already*? Trusting me to tend to the remaining victims while Dziurzynski might be distracted looking into the past?'

No. That would be *insane*.

The entire, structural thesis of the endeavor required all victims accounted for, all evidences arranged.

'Only *then* could the suggestion of remembering the horrors of *Maude Harbor*, learnt secondhand, seem to serendipitously be offered by me ... *us* ... *you* ... Lang, alone, or even paired with the housekeeper, wouldn't have been *enough* to play the thing *naturalistic*.'

So many questions.

Ones the voice figured would be answered when it met with Gould to swap places.

'But then ... we never *did*. And by the motel, when our tasks were complete, it seemed we'd never be *able*. Next day, you'd no doubt be informed by Dziurzynski of the murder of the young girl's mother ...'

It only served to reason Gould couldn't have told Dziurzynski all that much, up till then.

'... not if she'd allowed me to go about the nasty business of executing old woman and child as well ...'

So perhaps there'd be time enough to regroup.

Feel the way forward.

'Arrange the poor patsy to hang for every crime.'

Except Gould, rather than freeing himself up, awaiting contact as planned, had, it seemed, tipped the detective-inspector to the motel.

'I've had to keep an increasingly queasy eye on you, haven't I? Discover you're driving out to crime scenes with her! Having a perfectly happy time of it, from what I could observe. But, if you can believe it, *still* I thought you might've been working in both our best interests. Confident in the fact your life was safe. Playing your part to throw Dziurzynski off scent.'

Perhaps, even yet, an accord might be reached.

The dials reset.

'Except ... you brought her *here*, Mister Gould. Brought her here, *tonight*. To me, it doesn't seem she's keen to be anywhere *else*! You seem well aware of this. Have been sitting in that box like a deaf-mute, not lifting a pinky to alleviate my obvious concerns.'

The arrangement only worked if the two of them shared all duties and privileges *equally*.

Most especially the power.

The *guilt*.

'We've done exactly the same as each other, from the get go. You've been given every chance to walk away.'

But Gould hadn't done so.

Not in *Maude Harbor*.

Not here.

'The devil's hand isn't one you can *unshake*.'

The only way Gould would be permitted to *continue being* Gould was if everything remained spread between the two of them.

Same as the voice couldn't call quits, cast Gould out without Gould being able to bring down wrath as like was thundered on Sodom.

'If *I* know that … *you* know that.'

Which meant, the voice stated with vindictiveness '… you cannot be surprised I've come to the same conclusion as you regarding how all this will be wrapped up, nice and tidy.'

Somewhat wistfully, the voice continued, as though to itself.

Lamenting, as though nostalgic, what a shame it was how tawdry a turn life had taken.

'I kept every ounce of my promise to you. Have since the day we met.'

It wasn't something for nothing, after all.

'In our case, it had to be *everything* for *everything*, in fact. If you wanted to be me, Mister Gould, you had to be *all* of me. Until now, that's just what you've been. Until now, you've been a pleasure to know.'

But the voice wouldn't sit idly by while being made culprit.

Villain entire.

'I feel to blame, I suppose, if this is a case of your growing overcome with remorse. Conscience catching up with you. But, all the same …' the voice seemed to be prompting Gould to say something, to beg for a last out, plead his case '… you could've confided in me you wanted to part ways. We'd have found a *compromise*. As you knew right well what had happened ... would happen ... again.'

Though Gould, perhaps, had decided the voice too dangerous.

Untrustworthy.

Apt to act selfishly.

Turn everything against *him*.

'Could that be it? You didn't trust me to trust you to go your merry way on whichever reasonable stipend or annuity we'd agree upon? Didn't consider it possible I'd let you strike out on your own with my blessing?'

Perhaps that was insightful of Gould.

The voice admitted it wouldn't have trusted him to do so, *easily*. Ever believe Gould would, no matter the guilt such identity required, be prepared to *cease* being Gould.

'Our present situation, it seems, being exemplary of how correct my distrust would've been.'

It was now evident to the voice why Gould had *Maude Harbor* dragged into the light, prematurely.

Presented to Dziurzynski the sanitized version they'd so long ago agreed would be their steady word on the matter.

'Raking up those old graves while I was a busy beaver digging fresh ones—abandoning *your* work, half-finished, to *me* in order to know I'd be occupied while you conned your safe passage, can only serve one purpose. *Your* purpose. To make *me* the patsy. Sole perpetrator of our joint endeavor.'

Such behavior simply couldn't be permitted to stand.

'As to *Maude Harbor* ...' the voice seemed to be holding back laughter '... I've left you a gift. In the workroom.'

Gould might like to give it a review.

Consider it carefully before the two met again, face-to-face.

'*Last chance for a last chance*, as I hope somebody was witty enough to once say.'

Gould sat in silence.
Blinking.
Finger hovering over the console button.
Eyes fixed on the speakers.
Then the booth door.
Then closing.
Finally, he depressed the button and meekly peeped '… hello?'
Silence.
'Are you still there?'
Eyes ticked to the door.
Expecting it to fling open.
But no.
Nothing happened.
Nothing at all.
Finger still on button, Gould repeated his previous query.
Several times.
Then realized he was no longer at the console.
Or seated.
Was, instead, walking tight circles.
A loop. A repeat. Or an echo.
'… are you still there ..?'

One desk lamp, only, gave off paltry illumination.
Light nearly grey.
The technician's area was empty.
Unchanged from how Gould had left it.
He'd swear to it that even the attitude of the chair he'd sat in while spooling the documentary hadn't been altered a degree.
He let this relieve him.
Despite how it didn't explain away what had happened.
If anything *had* happened.
Took himself to task over his own recollected behavior.

Or lack thereof.

The relief suggesting nothing but that he'd perhaps fallen asleep.

Again.

No.

He wouldn't entertain arguments from himself.

Those he felt welling.

Be they reassuring or mocking or matter-of-fact.

Clung fast to one line of reasoning and refused to budge an inch from it.

To wit: he'd dreamt of Dziurzynski reading to him from a book, only just before.

That was indisputable.

Provided all the credence needed to lump this recent episode in with it.

To excuse himself of both happenstances by simply terming himself *under strain*.

With all that had happened today?

With the intensity of his focus, the past nearly full-day's worth of work, on the documentary?

Not to mention evidence he'd promised to forget but would, for the moment, allow into consideration concerning other dreams of opening his mail at the hotel, responding to letters, only to discover no such things had transpired!

'Is *this* what you're sticking to, Glenn?' he spoke softly.

Not knowing he was, at first.

Regretting the lapse when it dawned on him.

But then answered himself 'If what had happened *had* happened ... *where is anyone*?'

He'd not accept the obvious conclusion: whoever it'd been had merely exited the room.

Waited close at hand.

Monitoring him.

'Why would they *do* that?'
Dziurzynski was within arm's reach, wasn't she?
The voice, had there been such a thing, had pointed out exactly as much.
'Why don't I go to her, then?'
A good question, yes.
'What's stopping you, Glenn?'
Nothing.
Nothing was.
Stopping him.
He wasn't beholden to any agency apart from his own to proceed down such road or not.
Plenty of reasons not to roust the detective-inspector.
'Plus ... roust her with *what*?'
If he was to mention this gibberingly insane narrative from the studio booth, why not mention his dream of her?
Exactly as much proof either event was real.
All he'd accomplish, at best, would be to gift Dziurzynski her desired rationale to insist he return to the hotel.
Exhaustion.
Psychological turmoil.
'For all I know, she'd suggest I'd suffered a *psychotic break*.'
At worst?
Gould didn't want to respond to this, but nonetheless went ahead.
'At worst, I'll literally have extended her personal invitation to investigate the case from the perspective of a psychopath claiming I'd killed Person A while they'd killed Person B—in the process directly affirming, whether it was a third party's mad scheme or not, how there was reason to poke her nose into *Maude Harbor*.'
But ... what did he care?
Let her.

Let her catch out this lunatic, shouldn't he?

Shook his head violently.

Disbelieving he'd let himself float such defeatist propositions.

For overlooking how easily somebody could've *implicated* him in any number of things.

For all the abundantly evident reasons he ought do anything *but* allow that.

'If I start the ball down that path and then this creature never rear's his ugly head again, all Dziurzynski would be certain of is that I'd *lied* to her. Wasn't where I said I'd been. Was where I'd said I *wasn't*.'

A worse perdition he couldn't conjure.

Matters left perpetually unresolved enough his entire life, forever more, would be contained in this madness.

Righteously picked over.

His life pickpocketed from him.

Relinquished to this madman who thought himself Glenn Gould.

Who'd promised if they both couldn't go on, neither would.

The *Maude Harbor* reel.

There it was.

In his locked workroom.

On the recently vacated desk.

All the more terrifying for not being left out alone.

Rather, as with the technician's room, Gould couldn't shake the feeling no item in the workshop had been altered since his departure.

Not even the air seemed to've been disturbed.

Heavy.

Thick.

Like the inside of an old burlap sack.

The same reels he'd been working from, some in stacks, others set about variously, remained out.

The *Maude Harbor* reel simply amongst them.

Perhaps he'd pulled it from the secured cabinet with the rest, inadvertently.

Or perhaps it'd been mingled in by a third party.

He'd been meant to discover it, earlier.

This second option seemed impossible.

Unless this mysterious Other had known he'd fallen asleep.

Which couldn't have been determined from outside the locks and the heavy door.

To imagine they'd ... taken a chance?

'Preposterous.'

Yes. *Preposterous*.

This all settled Gould, briefly.

The notion of nervous exhaustion becoming more plausible with each passing moment.

These recent dreams—he officially dubbed them such, *dreams* is all they'd been—were merely composites of abrasive information which'd been jammed into his mental space over the past week.

His unconscious trying to sort Up from Down.

No crime in being *overwhelmed*.

His constitution was world renown for being weakling, wasn't it?

Strains far less than these current had not only put him on the ropes, before, but down for the count, more than once.

The *Maude Harbor* reel would be blank.

He'd erased it himself.

All it'd contained, regardless, was his recitation of that text about the Festival ... which ...

... he didn't recall writing ...

... or why ...
... but ...

Shook his face with vicious aggression, as though to cause himself pain.

Perhaps he only didn't recall having written it, *now*.

'What does that mean?'

That he'd written it before all this business began.

The strain and trauma of the past days and of this criminal supposition attached to the thing blurring his proper recollection of having innocently typed the words for some innocuous purpose.

Which didn't matter.

Nothing mattered.

He was here.

Now.

Whoever had recorded the *Maude Harbor* reel, for whichever purpose, was immaterial.

He'd *erased* it.

'Begging pardon, but is the theory that you *hadn't* recorded it, someone *else* had? Or is the theory that there *isn't* someone else ... so you *had* recorded it ... then *forgotten*?'

His breathing became more labored.

Sharper. Shorter.

He stared at the canister.

Demanding explanation from himself for the myriad things he'd lost track of and his confusion over what he'd told himself to believe about them, whatever they were.

Felt himself about to speak.

So clamped the rough wool of his glove over his mouth.

Pressure building.

Words of response clawing from throat, from teeth and tongue.

Finding no way out, such words issued as a voice in his head.

Too loud to ignore.

Despite being expressed as fearful, accusatory whisper.

'The motel ... *how* ... did you wake up there? *Why* ... were you *ever there*?'

Knees buckled and he dropped to then.

Doubled over.

Slap slap of hands painful to tile floor.

Heaved barks of foul air but no solid or sloppy content urged up from his tremoring guts.

Growled.

Using one hand to strike at his abdomen as though vomiting would force whichever treacherous part of him squirmed within to be expelled.

Did this for some interminable length.

Before finding himself at the desk.

Cushioned speakers cupped over both ears.

'My name is Glenn Gould. This will be my confession. Everything I've done, I shall herein relate. I've no explanation to give, nor feel any warranted. One either understands or one fails to. But I will be far, far away from here by the time you hear this. Anyone. Whoever is listening. If anyone ... ever is.'

Unblinking, Gould let the words fill him.

Felt his flesh disappearing.

Replaced by *sound*.

Sound devoid of *meaning*.

Felt himself detaching from himself.

From any of what was being said.

Anything which may have been his doing.

Any coming thing which might yet be.

Listened.

Neither in horror nor with familiarity.

Just listened.

The way one might to music.

Having never been told what music was.

'I could no longer be content to abandon myself to vain and idle pursuits; I could no longer rely upon the surpassing agility and spontaneity of my art and abuse these unquestioned virtues while I followed a life of frolicsome indulgence. Henceforth, the superficial gesture, the hedonistic pursuit, would be forever exiled from my nature. I would dedicate my life and my art to my beloved. I would forsake all others, work my fingers to the bone, and create for myself a place of pride in the great world which I would lay before my consort's feet as a token of my love. I was a new man, and she alone, with the redeeming power of innocence, had brought about this transition. I resolved that when next we met, I would ask her for her hand and, indeed, for her name, which I had neglected to elicit.'

Shut his eyes.

Picturing, as the recording went on, the photograph Dziurzynski had held up for him in her suite.

Once again watched it animate.

Blow its pink sugared bubble.

In his vision observed his own hand reaching toward the face.

To caress the cheek.

Only to have it recoil.

The girl wheeling from him in disgust.

Flinging herself to the embrace of another man.

'Zoltan Mostanyi had found her, somehow. Had ... *taken her*. Or rather ... she'd *given* herself to him. And they, all of them, everyone had accepted how she had. How he *possessed* her. Was *his*. They ... mocked me ... had mocked me even before ... before I'd known the company she'd sold herself to ... Peggy had swam, singing, finding the very notion I might be desired or find coupling with the girl risible ...'

The recording continued.

Ugly. Putrid.

A fiction of filth.

Gould listening to every word.

How he'd slaughtered Zoltan.

Dismembered him.

Disposed of his remains down a well on an abandoned property.

Heaved stones in atop.

How he'd butchered Peggy.

Shoved the *Monopoly* cards she'd refused to let Gould rightfully play, simply to *spite* Gould, rob him of victory, barring him from so much as a childish bit of boastfulness, pride of victory over Zoltan in the eyes of the girl.

How he'd visited the girl's mother.

Made a proper fool of himself.

Beseeched her with promises that if arrangements could be made he'd worship her daughter.

Provide for them both.

The woman looking at him as though he were some song-and-dance nobody.

No man of the stature of Zoltan.

Who she already knew of.

Endorsed the affair between the bloated old man and her child.

Her daughter who Gould would have given his very soul to keep inviolate.

'The girl ... who I cut to pieces. Who I interred under worms and leeches and rocks ... before sinking her to the bottom of the black waters of *Maude Harbor*.'

Wresting the lunatic narrative from his head, Gould ripped the *Maude Harbor* reel from the device where it spun.

Hurled it against the wall.

Gnashed his teeth and cleared the desk violently of all properties.

Stomping on them.

Smashing whatever he rested eyes on for so much as a beat.

Strangling any stray paper he touched upon.

Screaming.

Wrapping arms around his head.

Before wilting to the floor.

But all at once stood.

Brushed at himself.

Rubbed at his face.

Made efforts to get control of his breathing.

Unlocked the drawer.

Poured pills into hand.

Indiscriminately.

Innumerable.

Was about to swallow all of them.

Blindly.

But stopped.

Stopped.

Nothing on the recording was true.

No.

Not a word.

And understanding this, the horrific plan he was victim to became clear as day before him.

That was it …

… weaken him down …

… drive him to abject desperation …

… close the walls in around him …

… leaving behind this evidence to show he'd taken the coward's way out …

The pills struck the wall.

Tittered about unseen across the floor.
The floor he now dropped to, with purpose.
Crawled along until he retrieved the tangle of the *Maude Harbor* reel.
Whatever was going to happen, he'd not allow such slanders to be left his legacy.
Those abominations accepted as spoken by his voice.
Simply because it sounded like him.
For a moment was overcome.
With shame at the notion that, were this *Maude Harbor* reel to be heard publically, it would be believed.
People *could* assume these ghoulish narratives true.
Enacted by him.
Force themselves to *accept* them.
Reconcile themselves to what they proclaimed being the reality of him.
Sobbed with self-pity.
Knowing such falsehoods might efface from existence any speck of his life else.
His soul would be defined by these acts attributed to him.
Forgiveness impossible by even those who held him most dear.
The thought of such opinion of his humanity being *possible* emptied him.
Made it seem reasonable to claim the entire narrative honest.
It would serve just as well.
This or that—who would care?
Why continue life in a world which would believe him his inverse just for having been told so?
Who did he think would listen to anything he had to say or express—the same people he thought capable of believing these falsehoods he'd heard?
Such were those who'd been and might yet be his audience.
Just as quickly, however, this battering of sophistry relented.

His hand around his own throat, attempting to stifle his bawling, drove home how he wasn't some abstraction, but an entity whose life contained a genuine truth.

One he'd demand to be the figure who defined.

Never some vessel into which this devil could pour their escape.

He'd done nothing.

Killed no one.

No matter how it might seem, this was not an adjustable property.

He'd march himself to Dziurzynski.

Tell her all.

Not break and blubber, pinned in the trap set by this vermin.

Would confess every last detail.

Allow himself to be put under lock-and-key.

At least he'd retain a voice.

Announce his innocence to those who sought to serve him up as scapegoat for unspeakable acts of barbarism.

Hand on the workroom door, Gould stopped up, yet again.

Behind his eyes rattled every variant of how, in fact, this present decision could well be the exact step his tormentor had hoped he might take.

Look, even now, how he'd not destroyed the *Maude Harbor* reel.

Ought he to?

Did its existence serve his defense more than its absence would?

Stared at the mess of the reel left on the otherwise emptied desk.

Stared.

But couldn't decide what to do.

Stared, as though waiting for some other party to leave him no choice.

Force his hand.
Compel him into doing what he might later discover had been his honest desire.

Before pushing open the door leading out of the studio building, Gould paused to close up his coat.
Adjust scarf.
Could see, still where it'd been, Dziurzynski's car.
Plumes of exhaust yet rising from the rear of it.
A final few seconds to assure himself of his composure, Gould exited. Accosted harsh by the shove and sound of the wind which had turned persistent and intense.
The snowfall tumbled heavily, now.
Coming sideways.
Almost enough it seemed it shouldn't rightly be able to grip to the ground.
Nearing the concrete steps, Gould took notice of multiple sets of tracks in the otherwise unmolested white covering the pavement.
Three sets.
Leading to or from the parked vehicle.
Squinting, crouched for closer inspection, Gould determined one set moved in the direction of the vehicle.
Two sets returned from it.
Under the awning he'd the moment before moved beyond the protection of were evidences of feet having been stomped.
A collection of mashed snow.
Moisture.
Hands tight down pockets, Gould made his way across the lot.
Eyes the whole while tracing the three pairs of footprints.
For much of the distance, knew he was creating a fourth.

But found himself, the back length of the venture, matching his steps to the prints already present.

Dziurzynski's car windows were fogged.

Windshield wipers active, yet even with their efforts he was unable to determine whether the car was occupied until his nose was direct to passenger-side glass.

Vacant.

Glanced around.

Expecting to discover the detective-inspector with cigarette.

But nothing.

His mind cobbled up some explanation.

Perhaps another party had been working late.

Before departing had noticed the lulling car.

Approached it.

Dziurzynski grateful.

This unknown person leading her inside.

To use the restroom facilities in the lobby.

As though to keep this from being jinxed untrue, Gould lingered in the bitter chill what might've been five minutes, might've been ten.

Growing increasingly anxious.

Still no other vehicles, around.

No tracks in the snow.

He'd seen nothing on his way out to indicate anyone had been in the general lobby.

If there'd been someone, perhaps waiting to be certain Dziurzynski had exited after tending to her needs, he'd have passed them on his way out.

If they'd been using the restroom, themselves, surely they'd have exited by now.

Shivered.

Nothing to do with the cold.

Squint solidifying as he focused down to sort things.

Could, by incredible chance, whoever the unknown party was have had access to the studios on the floor Gould had just come from?

Been taking one elevator up, with the detective-inspector as companion, as he'd been on his way down in the other?

Panic at the thought of Dziurzynski discovering the state he'd left his workroom in.

Without him present to explain it or brace her.

Gould took off at a rush.

Lost his footing.

Skidded.

Landed on his bottom.

Standing immediately to lurch ahead even as he realized she could've proceeded no further than the technician's room, the corridor at best, without his key.

Nevertheless, it wouldn't do to have her poking around.

Prey to whoever else might still be present.

Re-entered the lobby and noted, yes, evidence of wet shoes left a trail to the elevators.

Hit the call button of the unit the splotches of wet indicated two parties had utilized.

Nausea riddled him as the indicator above the doors lit up *Three*.

The floor of his studio.

Blinked *Two*.

Dinged *L*.

Doors opening on an empty cabin he trembled to enter.

Floor freckled with grungy droplets of melt and a clump or two of yet grit-grey snow.

The placement of one puddle suggested someone had leaned against the far wall.

The other pattern evidenced someone had paced to-and-fro.

Technician's room had been empty.

Dark except for, still, the single desk lamp.

Gould proceeded briskly through it to the dark corridor littered with specks of red-orange reflected off the dull tile.

Workroom locked tight, Gould hurried along, limp more pronounced with each step, to verify no one was in the cafeteria.

This accomplished, he returned to and unlocked the workroom.

Peeked in without entering.

Reviewed the aftermath of his fit.

The space vacant apart from the wreckage.

The certainty Dziurzynski would be discovered waiting inside the studio booth became irrepressible.

This notion horrifying him for reasons he neither could nor attempted to articulate.

Instead of making direct passage back to the technician's room, however, Gould rode the inner elevator back up to the conference rooms.

Hoped to make out Dziurzynski returning to her waiting car.

To spy her outside of it, smoking.

Or, at the other windows where he hadn't before, find evidence of any other vehicle.

Any other person.

Anywhere.

Descended to studio level.

His shivering rampant.

Teeth chattering.

Arms unable to relax.

Despite the idiocy of such act, he opened the door to the women's lavatory.

Meekly called in 'Detective-inspector?' despite the lights being out.

Flipped them on.

Room empty.

Tried men's lavatory, as well.

'Detective-inspector?' he asked, again into a cavity quiet and unlit.

No voice in his thoughts suggested *Flee* but the word, as though solid object, seemed to weigh headache behind his eyes.

He neither rejected the ungiven suggestion nor assented to it.

The word simply hung.

Heavier with each step.

At the bridge of his nose.

Threatening to break it.

Thinning.

To razor tight.

Threatening to saw his mind in half.

Called out 'Detective-inspector?' again upon re-entering the technician's station.

Flapped on the main light as though doing so might reveal Dziurzynski attempting to secret herself some ridiculous place.

Under desk.

Behind potted plant.

Clambered upon one of the cabinets.

Scrutinized every surface for a single dot of evidence there had been recent presence, other than his own.

Wanted finding nothing to spare him entering the studio.

At the technician's console, Gould depressed the button allowing him to address himself into the booth.

'Detective-inspector, are you there?'

Waited.

Tried button again.

This time explaining in detail which button she ought press to speak back, in case the lack of reply was on account of her being flummoxed by all the dials.

'Or if you don't see it ... could you meet me out here?'

Waited.

Waited.

A touch of unguarded anxiety cracking his voice, Gould called into the booth, once more.

Dziurzynski might be playing one of her illustrious tricks.

Bent on unnerving him before whichever confrontation.

'I think I'm in *danger* ...' he found himself almost whispering, a childish warble to the words '... so if you can hear me ...'

'She can't, Mister Gould.'

The voice.

His voice.

Over the reply speaker.

Gould's vision faded.

Remained black as the beat of his pulse ached his temples.

Then slowly fizzed back in.

'You and I should catch up, however. Would you grant the immense honor of joining me? In your own time, of course.'

The word *Flee* expanded.

Caked the inside of Gould.

Stiffening cement.

Throat constricting as he held the *Talk* button down.

Unable to utter anything beyond a crackle like car tires in slow progress over gravel.

'I didn't get that, I'm afraid ...' was chortled over the speaker '... but if you'd prefer, I can come out to *escort* you.'

It made no difference, the voice supposed.

As Gould would wind up back in there, regardless.

Glenn Gould saw himself.

A man like himself.

In every respect.

Clothing to facial feature to posture.

Glenn Gould saw Glenn Gould.

Grinning at him.

In that moment moving to sit rakish on studio booth's console counter, telling him to shut the door.

He complied.

Wordless.

Thoughtless.

Attempting to keep his eyes from the sight of detective-inspector Dziurzynski.

Crumpled.

One leg bent, positioned as though to render the number four by touching the bottom of its foot to the straight thigh of the opposite leg.

One arm seemed as though it'd turned round entirely incorrect, now pressed up in this bizarre contortion by the weight of her torso lumped into the wall.

Fingers of the hand spread.

Tensed to claws.

Blood in a pool beneath her.

Sanguine tar which seemed not to deepen due to being soaked into the fabric of her clothing.

Hatchet buried in her face.

Head chopped almost all the way through ...

The man now clapping with the question 'Are you listening?'

Gould's teeth chattered.

Left hand shaking so violently he wouldn't believe he wasn't making it do so on purpose.

Could taste vomit half-risen in his throat.

'Are you listening, Mister Gould? Because it doesn't *seem* like you're *listening*.'

Gould made glugging sounds.

Attempted to utter the words 'I am' only to finally sick up.

A brief, painful spasm.

Like a sneeze.

Spatter of the mess sullying the booth wall percussively.

This seemed to displease the man at the console, a moment.

Though in the next he sighed, ponderously.

'Did you really like her *that* much? While here I so innocently hoped for some signal this was part of your own sinister plan, too.'

Gould vomited, again.

Full force.

All down the front of himself.

Not moving from his stock straight posture.

Hardly seemed aware that he had.

The man shrugged.

Resigned.

'I suppose a bit of puke can be massaged to fit with the narrative. It would've been helpful had you also lost your lunch over Lang. But likely the mess will be forensically explainable. Even *maniacs* might get queasy when the adrenaline is up and events spin unexpectedly out of their control.'

Backpedaling, Gould pressed to the booth door.

Slid down it.

Legs entirely limp.

Spread out before him.

The man gave intense regard to Gould's positioning. Held fingers to lips as though considering it aesthetically in reference to the position of Dziurzynski's corpse.

Sniffled. Winked and *tsk-tsk*ed his fingers in admonition at Gould.

'You really aren't being the least smidgen helpful, are you? Mister Gould, I have to be able to *exit*, you know? Otherwise the overall effect is *spoiled*. I have someplace to be …'

The man trailed off.

Seeming puzzled.

Moved from the console top to squat to his haunches.
Inspecting Gould.
Head tilting to all angles.
Lips pursing.
Flattening.
A genuine expression of confusion mingled with exasperation in one blink giving way to an expression Gould, though not certain of anything he was seeing at all, could only term *Wonderment*.

'I'll admit ...' the man eventually said, standing straight, stretching legs with a shake of each afterward, awed curiosity on his face not diminishing but becoming, in fact, almost etched permanent '... I'd not considered you could possibly have wound up *this* far far far gone ...'

Puffed cheeks and let out a long breath.

Clucking tongue in cheek afterward in the manner of someone deeply rethinking a matter.

'... makes me a bit glum for going this route. Though, in my defense, your *taciturn* nature is more to blame than my *hatchet-urn* tendencies are ...' rolled his eyes in disappointment the little quip hadn't come off as cleanly as he'd thought it might, then pivoted to address Gould directly '... though your answer to the following will go a long way toward *how* rotten I ought feel in the *final* tabulation ...'

The man stared at Gould.

A long time.

Until Gould realized he was waiting for an indication of full attention.

' ... what ... *question* ..?' he managed.

'Do you—I ask in candor, now, so please reply in kind—*really* think ... *you* ... are *me*?'

'It's beyond remarkable.'

The man said so.

Again and again.

After each time he'd satisfied himself with a query Gould numbly gave guileless reply to.

Question after question after question.

'How had this happened?'

'*When* ... had this happened?'

'After *Lang* ..?'

But, no no no, the man couldn't believe any great change had come over Gould due to *that* violence.

'We'd met afterward. Taken the steps to vanish his packaged remains. Made all arrangements for our next maneuvers. You knew right well who you were, then ...'

The man laughed as he nearly set foot in Dziurzynski's blood, halting a step downward then regaining his balance quite awkwardly.

Now made indications of fingers in the air.

Tip-tap ...

... tip-tap ...

... tip ...

... tap ...

Eventually snapping them as though a puzzle piece had clicked to place after a long bit of bother.

Then waved the hand as though, no, he must *still* have it wrong.

Reminded himself aloud, as though making excuses to a general audience, that ' ... all had gone well enough ... you'd done Lang, I the housekeeper ... both of us agreed on next actions ...' turned attention directly to Gould '... so if you *still* knew you were *you* ... after *all* that ... what *else* had happened?'

Here, Gould saw the man's features widen.

Go somewhat stricken.

This eerie expression of discomfort only lasting a moment before being blinked away in a kind of giddy disbelief.

Whipping head to regard Gould straight on, the man went to his haunches, again.

Scooting close with awkward little hop-steps.

'Was it because of the *girl*? You hadn't killed her as arranged … and she sure seemed *happy* to see me before *I* did … she had, I daresay, *eagerly* acquiesced to a ride in my automobile …'

He took Gould's chin firmly, even violently, in his right hand, though Gould was too numbed to register any sensation but a cold tingle like a limb fallen asleep where their flesh met.

'Did something … *happen* … between you and that *waitress*?'

Gould felt his head being waggled around roughly, no idea for how long, before hearing himself blurt 'Nothing happened between me and *anyone*!'

The man removed his hand.

Brought both together.

Fingertips bouncing off lips made into the shape of a kiss.

'*Something* …' moved one hand to rough his hair, other now tapping his chin '… *must have*. Seeing as she was still *breathing* after you ought have arranged the *polar opposite* … and her mother had been practically *expecting* me.'

'*Why* …' Gould interjected, a cough of the word, brief bout of hyperventilation the man waited for him to subdue before motioning he ought continue with the thought '… did you kill them?'

'Why did *we* kill them' the man patiently corrected, standing to shake out his legs before squatting back down.

Meanwhile, Gould writhed his head side-to-side, croaking the words 'I have never … killed … *anyone* …'

'You *haven't*?'

'I … have … *never* …'

'What about *Lang*? What about *Zoltan*? Or *Peggy*?'

Gould's face twisted in disgust as he took peculiar breaths, attempting to shape his mouth appropriately to spit on the man.

The man, for his part, let this display go on until, as though bored it were taking so long, said 'Yes yes, I get the idea.'

Pressed finger in a hush to Gould's lips.

A finger Gould would've bitten off had he been able to do anything but hiccough, clenching eyes down against rising tears.

'As to your question, however ... that always unimaginative *Why?* the general populace seems so loopy for ... in this case I'll have to disappoint. Couldn't tell you if I wanted to.'

Pumped hands that Gould should remain still. Look of *give me a minute* crossing his features as Gould again writhed and gurgled with attempted speech.

'You listened to my own recorded memories of *Maude Harbor* just now, I imagine. In which I was very forthcoming about *my* rationale, *once upon a time* ...'

Gould could tell the man understood he'd listened to the reel, his harsh rabbit-breathing and eyes bulging apoplectic more than evidencing as much.

'... but this modern lot was all *your* idea. I understood, as *you* explained it, the *exercise*. The *composition* made exquisite sense. Lang and your newspaper ornaments, the records for purposes of theatrical linking. All in service of eventually pinning the deeds on some quote-endquote *psychotic sycophant* who believed themselves to be acting out some balderdash tribute to me before taking their own crazy life. You suggesting we model this on our *previous* endeavors was an *artful* touch. Allowing, were it to come to such, some verifiable credence be given the notion the fiend had acted back in *Maude Harbor*, as well. You'd even scouted out a lowly nobody who could, superficially, fit the part. Right times and places in both epochs. No alibis. Now ... I've zero doubt you must've had some *specific reason* for choosing *Lang* when you floated me the proposition. That mad gleam in your eye suggested something *private* at the heart of it all. My personal *assumption* was he'd hurt your feelings something awful when he'd given your inaugural performances such a drubbing. Held a grudge for years, during which you masterminded this artistic act of revenge. But I felt it indelicate to *ask*. And *irrelevant* toward the greater purpose. Being the good neighbor I've always striven to be, I didn't *question*. As *you* hadn't questioned me, back then. You'd merely done as I'd asked. Part of the deal. Being me meant *being me*, after all. It was well understood you were now telling me it was *your turn*. How else to *truly* be me but to *originate* and *execute* while I *acquiesce* and *follow along*. Fair was fair. If it's what you wanted, I'd do my part.'

Look of playful *hey, waitaminute* then tickled across the man's face.

'Though, in my case, I've done *more* than my share. *Three* for me ... *one* for you. Hardly in keeping with *tradition*.'

Gould watched the man drift gaze to Dziurzynski and chuckle.

'Well *four* for me, I suppose ... though I won't begrudge you *that*. Not really fair to count *her*, all things considered. We'll both take a Mulligan. Considering our friend's death, after all, saves the life of that unwitting lad we'd have had to stick the business end of a barrel beneath the chin of.'

Gould offered no resistance as the man dragged him across the floor to the opposite end of the booth.

As he felt himself shoved into the corner.

Mind on the fritz. Survival default apparently that of a baby fawn.

Even aided as the man unlaced his shoes.

Kept this leg then the other extended tight as the footwear was removed.

Made no effort to stand when the man moved off to the side of the room near the door, again.

Removing his own shoes.

Setting them carefully aside.

Nor did any plan of physically fighting the man cross Gould's mind.

No burst of adrenaline he needed make efforts to stifle.

Nothing.

He simply *watched*.

Even curious.

A set of eyes and a mental notepad.

Now the man lacing Gould's shoes onto his own feet.

Now pulling from his coat pocket a second set of latex gloves. Snapping them *pop pop* over those already covering left hand and right.

When the man recrossed the room and told Gould 'Would you be a darling and stand up' Gould, with embarrassing amounts of effort required, did so without resistance.

'You haven't wet yourself or lost control of your bowels already, have you? Olfactory, at present, doesn't suggest any advanced soiling, but there's a lot of stench about, so if you could tell me it'd be nice to know.'

Gould shook his head.

The man clucking how he'd only been joking.

Not only wouldn't it matter, but other explanations would soon present to satisfy those who might 'trace Alexander's noble dust until they find it stopping a bunghole, eh?'

'Where should I stand?' Gould heard himself asking.

Watched the man eyeball him as though searching out some hidden treachery.

Then let himself be patted up and down until, seemingly satisfied, the man stepped away.

'You're remarkably *compliant*, I'll award you all due gratitude, there. *Chivalry*, at least for another few minutes, it seems isn't dead.'

Now the man busied himself as though choosing where to stand to manipulate the carcass of Dziurzynski.

Looked from it to Gould to it.

Seemed disappointed, inwardly, at something he saw.

Announced with forced jocularity 'I honestly might've thought this through, better ...' trailing off with a flash of exasperation huffed down nose.

Features returning to placid, business-at-hand.

'I need to remember the order of events, here ... *raw material* is easy to compile ... but you know the pressures of preparing a *final cut* ...'

Moved Dziurzynski's coat from where it was bunched so he could observe her entire torso.

Made gestures of calculating some action.

Gould weakly taking notice the man's attention was fixated on her weapon holster.

At her right hip.

'That means she *shoots* with the right hand, yes no?'

'Unless she's a cross-draw' Gould chimed.

Hearing himself as though from the other side of the wall.

But heard the man laugh, clapping a squeaky thump of double latex, as though standing exactly where he did.

Sound of the hands smacking together seemed to bounce about the room despite the composition of the walls making such impossible.

The man settled on a remembrance of Dziurzynski being right handed.

'You'd know better than I, having become so tight knit with the dame. Not ...' the man added with a wink '... that she seemed the *trustworthy* sort. Probably ambidextrous and double jointed, to boot.'

'She was *dyslexic*, anyway' Gould again heard the muffle of himself saying.

No laughter following.

No clap.

The man busy removing what Gould assumed was the detective-inspector's firearm from his own left-side coat pocket.

While regarding her body.

Shaking his head as though still not pleased with himself over whatever had been his previous regret.

Awkwardly draped over the detective-inspector, fixing the fingers of her inert hand around the pistol's trigger, no way to keep his feet clear of the blood, though no longer seeming at all to attempt such, the man jabbered away.

'There are some benefits, in general and in this case quite in particular, to being Glenn Gould *legitimately*.'

Trained Dziurzynski's hand off to one side.

Depressed the trigger.

Gould tightening where he stood.

Legs juddering.

All his concentration required not to collapse.

Watched the pigtail of cordite smolder from the weapon's hot muzzle.

Ticked eyes to sort out where the bullet had struck.

But the room hand gone a blur and his ears rang to the point he felt submerged in bathwater.

'Some of my attributes are such that a quick study, like yourself, might acquire them with practice and time. Those in fine addition to the strikingly pretty features nature has blessed you with.'

The man removed pistol from Dziurzynski's hand. Trained it,

while slightly crouched, toward the wall Gould was fit to the corner of.

Fired once.

Again.

To Gould these reports almost soundless.

His eyes rolling back as though to slink into the shell of his skull.

'My *idiom* ...' the man meanwhile continued '... my *handwriting*, my weather-vein *philosophies*, and various anecdotal *memories*. Those, yes, can be learnt.'

Gould watched the man return the gun to Dziurzynski's fingers.

Raise her arm so the muzzle was trained ceilingward.

Heard the gun fired off.

The room blurring further to incoherence.

'But certain things ... well, no amount of studiousness could earn you. My *fingerprints*, most importantly. Being Glenn Gould, I come equipped with a set. Nature's handy way of getting me out of this pickle you've put me in, I'm happy to report.'

Some indistinct sounds of further efforts being made with Dziurzynski's carcass.

Then Gould felt his own arm being raised.

The man suddenly right up on him.

Manipulating Gould's fingers to grip around something.

Gently tugging the front of his shirt to have him move forward from the wall a half dozen paces.

'*You*, being whoever you are, alas only possess the commonplace mitts of whoever you are. The inimitable pattern of swirls which go with them. My *bona fide* prints being on official file various places, there seems to've been no occasion for the long arm of the law to've requested from you a fresh set. So when your touchy-feelers are inked, as they no doubt will be, what'll be discovered is *your* snail trails every place *mine* won't be found.'

The man cautiously moved his hand from around Gould's

which, Gould could discern from a teary glance downward, now held the gore caked hatchet.

The sight caused him to twist his head.

Heard himself blubber as he felt the presence of the man drifting away.

'They won't find *my* prints at all, in fact. Not at your suite. None on the keys of your typewriter. Oh they won't find a single one all kind of places, really.'

More sounds of Dziurzynski's body being manipulated.

A thick bubble of mucus leaving Gould's nose.

Squirming over chin.

His lips clamped as though horrified of getting a taste.

'Therefore, Mister Gould, when I eventually re-emerge, finally having managed to free myself from whichever *radiator* you'd so rudely left me *bound* to, they'll be one reason less to believe I had anything to do with these unmannerly murders of yours.'

Now the man issued a long, rather put upon sigh.

'I'm going to be pestered with so many questions. Especially with *Maude Harbor* brought into play. But will, understandably, have dunce to offer by way of explanation. Won't even know *how* I'd wound up where I'd been kept captive.'

With the hand holding the hatchet, Gould involuntarily wiped at his face.

Used the other hand to wipe further.

Working fingers over eyes to clear them.

Trying to focus on the man where he spoke.

Discovered him crouched beside Dziurzynski's body.

Pistol trained directly at him.

'Was there something you'd like me to tell folks you *said*? Some ... statement of *purpose*? Any words you'd like to be remembered by, if in utter infamy? I can just as well tell them you never spoke a sound to me. That I'd come to, already bound. That you remained mute whenever you'd stop in to feed me. But if you have a desire to be known for some sentiment, tell me now. I promise the words will live on. *Your* words. All your own. *Unblemished.*'

Gould swallowed.

Eyes tick-tocking as he braced.

As he wondered why he neither dropped the hatchet nor wielded it.

'I do have to be running along ...' the man chuckled, almost sweetly '... but it's the least I can do, if you'll hurry up and draft something. It'd be nice to give the audience a sense of *closure*. Everyone will wonder who you *are*, for example. Who it was could do such unspeakable things. So let's have it—who shall we *tell* them you are?'

'I'm ... Glenn Gould ...' Gould sputtered.

Felt ashamed for the pusillanimous oink of the words.

'... I'm ... Glenn Gould ... Glenn ... Gould ...'

Teeth chattering, Gould watched the man nod.

'Very well, Mister Gould ...' he squinted one eye, setting the gun's aim final '... I'll be certain to tell them you said so.'

NOTE

In addition to generally referencing aspects of Glenn Gould's life, works, and philosophies throughout the book, brief excerpts have been drawn, near verbatim, from Gould's writings and radio documentaries.

The Dodecacophonist's Dilemma: from *The Canadian Music Journal*, Fall 1956

Let's Ban Applause: from *Musical America*, February 1962

So You Want To Write A Fugue?: article accompanying a plastic disc bound into the April 1964 issue of *HiFi/Stereo Review*, containing the first issue of Gould's *So You Want To Write a Fugue?*, a seven minute composition recorded by the Julliard String Quartet and four vocalists, under the direction of Vladimir Golschmann

l'esprit de jenusse, et de corps, et d'art (one of three articles published under the pseudonym Dr. Herbert von Hochmeister: from *Musical America*, December 1965

The Prospects of Recording: from *High Fidelity*, April 1966

Letter to fan Judith Taitt-Werenfeld, April 12, 1967

The Search for Petula Clark: from *High Fidelity*, November 1967

The Idea of North: from the original transcript of Gould's radio play, 1967

Piano Sonatas by Scriabin and Prokofiev: Liner Notes from Columbia MS 7173, 1969

Glenn Gould Interviews Himself About Beethoven: from *Piano Quarterly*, Fall 1972

Glenn Gould Interviews Glenn Gould About Glenn Gould: from *High Fidelity*, February 1974

A Biography of Glenn Gould: from Gould's review of *Glenn Gould: Music and Mind* by Geoffrey Payzant (New York: Van Nostrand Reinhold, 1978); from *Piano Quarterly*, Fall 1978

Memories of Maude Harbour, or Variations on a Theme of Arthur Rubenstein: from *Piano Quarterly*, Summer 1980

Two other brief quotations are taken, near verbatim, from the following sources.

Glenn Gould's Toronto (documentary film, 1979). Written by Glenn Gould. Directed by John McGreevy. Part of the *Cities* series of films.

A State of Wonder (disc 3). Sony. Glenn Gould and Tim Page *(2002)*

Additionally, short excerpts have been utilized, near verbatim, from the following films of director Dario Argento: *Deep Red* (1975) and *Tenebrae (1982)*.

Also, a line of dialogue from director Ole Bornedal's film *Nightwatch* (1998) is used, verbatim.

A summary of plot elements from director Lucio Fulci's film *Murder To The Tune of the Seven Black Notes* (1977) is presented as a radio news report in a section of the novel.

A brief quotation from Paul Henry Lang's *New York Herald Times* review of Gould's performance of the Brahms's D minor Concerto (with the New York Philharmonic, conducted by Leonard Bernstein) also appears, verbatim.